SLEEPING WITH PARIS

City of Love Book 1

JULIETTE SOBANET

SLEEPING WITH PARIS
City of Love Book 1

Copyright @ 2020 Juliette Sobanet

All rights reserved. Except as permitted under the U.S. Copyright Act of 1976, no part of this publication may be reproduced, distributed, or transmitted in any form or by any means, or stored in a database or retrieval system, without express written permission of the publisher.

This book is a work of fiction. Names, characters, places and incidents are either the product of the author's imagination or are used fictitiously. Any resemblance to actual persons, living or dead, or to actual events or locales is entirely coincidental.

Juliette Sobanet asserts the moral right to be identified as the author of this work.

Print edition published by Saint Germain Press 2020.

ISBN-10: 1657371336
ISBN-13: 978-1657371330

Previously published by Amazon Publishing, Montlake Romance.

❀ Created with Vellum

Juliette Sobanet's Free Starter Library

Sign up for Juliette's newsletter and receive three of her bestselling books for *free*. Details can be found on Juliette's website at *www.juliettesobanet.com*.

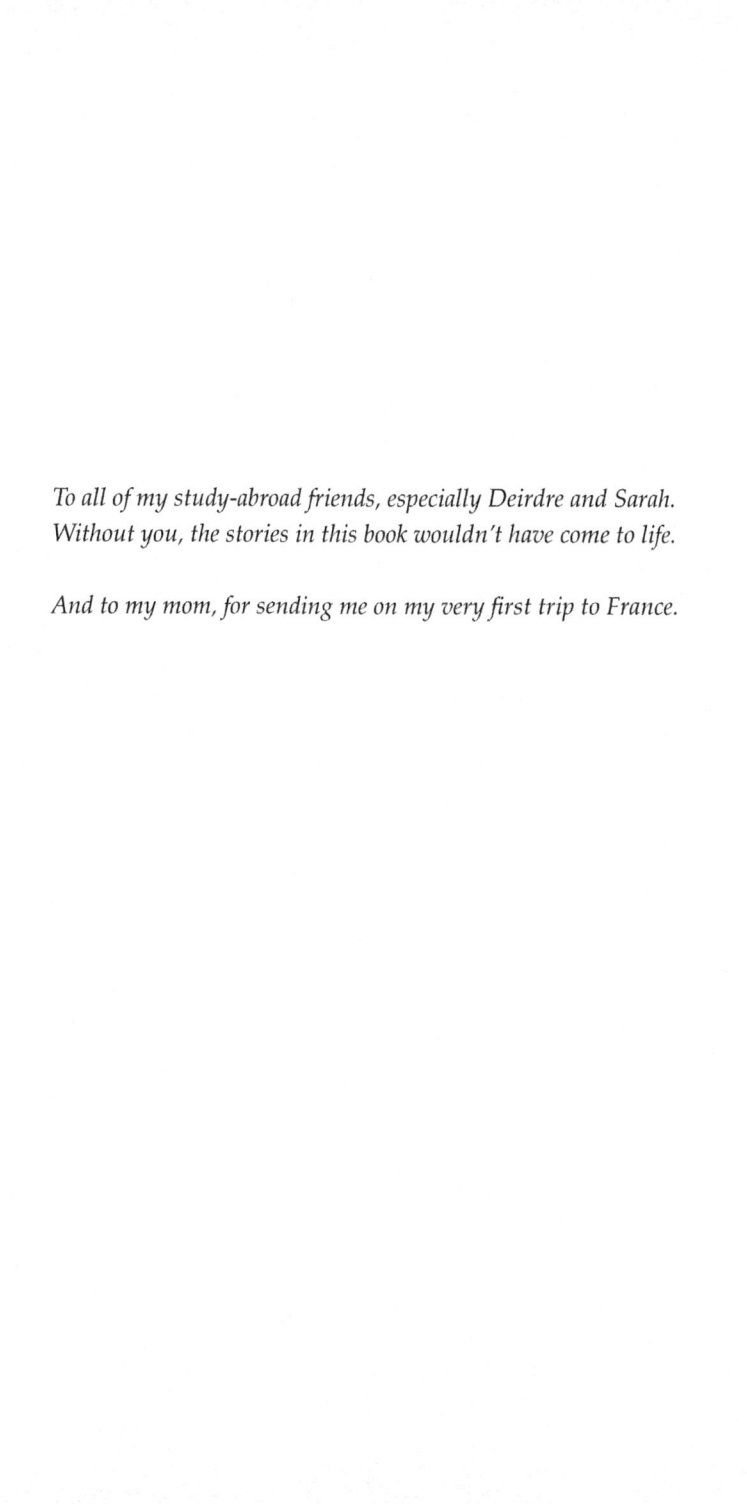

*To all of my study-abroad friends, especially Deirdre and Sarah.
Without you, the stories in this book wouldn't have come to life.*

And to my mom, for sending me on my very first trip to France.

ONE

vendredi, le 24 septembre

Never hire a lawyer who doesn't know how to tell a good lie, and definitely don't marry one who does.

"Keep in touch," I called, waving a not-so-tearful good-bye to my coworkers for the last time. I stepped out into the muggy DC heat and was so happy to be done with that hellhole that I felt like ripping off my little black suit and skipping down M Street in my underwear.

After seven years of practice, both as a student, then as a poor college graduate, I'd become quite the expert at strutting in heels down the brick sidewalks of Georgetown. Today, as I glided along in a state of total disbelief that this day had finally arrived, my normally uncomfortable heels effortlessly carried me away from my boring part-time translating job—make that my *ex*-translating job—down to Wisconsin Avenue, where my fiancé was wrapping up his last day at his Georgetown law firm.

Unable to hide the enormous grin spreading across my face, I reached into my purse and pulled out my flight itinerary just to make sure, for the hundredth time that day, that this was, in fact, my life. I scanned the piece of paper for our names.

Charlotte Summers and Jeff Dillon. One-way flight departing from Washington Dulles International en route to Paris Charles de Gaulle. In two days. *Two freaking days!*

After stopping at the liquor store and splurging on a fancy bottle of champagne, I bounced into Jeff's posh office. His bubbly administrative assistant, Tara—a former hometown beauty queen who would've made so much more sense in a place like Los Angeles—greeted me with her pearly-white smile.

"Hey, Charlotte," she said, her gum popping like miniature firecrackers in her mouth. "You getting excited for Paris?"

"Well, I just put in my last few hours at the office otherwise known as hell, so excited would be an understatement."

Her platinum-blonde ponytail bobbed as she giggled. "Jeff sent me the pics of your new apartment over there. Oh, my God, it's gorgeous!"

I beamed. "I know. Can you believe it? This firm doesn't mess around."

"Girl, you two are going to have so much fun. But don't forget about us back here. We're going to miss you so much."

"We're going to miss you too. But don't worry, we'll be back in the spring for our friend's wedding, and *technically* we'll be moving back in a year…unless I can convince Jeff to stay longer." I winked at her. "Hey, is Jeff in his office?"

"No, he just stepped out for a minute, but you can go on in and wait for him. He should be right back."

"Thanks, Tara."

"No prob, dear."

I walked down the long corridor, let myself into Jeff's secluded corner office, and ran my finger around his immaculate desk. Over my new ruby-colored bra and thong set, I was sporting a sexy black skirt coupled with a silky violet tank, in the hope that we could relive the steamy sex we'd had the last time I wore this hot little number to his office...which was also when I gained a new appreciation for his extra-cushy swiveling office chair.

I plopped the bottle of champagne onto a neat stack of papers on Jeff's desk as I took a seat in the swivel chair. After I jiggled the mouse to bring his computer out of sleep mode, I signed into my e-mail account and clicked on a message Jeff had sent me the week before so that I could, once again, gaze at the pictures of the charming Parisian apartment that awaited us. In his e-mail, Jeff had written:

Welcome home, babe. Can't wait.

xoxoxo,

Jeff

My heart melted all over again, just like it had the first time I opened his e-mail. God, I loved this man.

Just as I was opening the first picture, a message popped up on the bottom right-hand side of Jeff's computer. I wasn't a nosy fiancée; I trusted Jeff. I couldn't help but read the bubble on his computer screen, though. It read:

Brooke: You there?

Brooke who? Must be a colleague, I reasoned. But then another message popped up:

Brooke: Give me a call when you have a minute...

I racked my brain trying to remember if Jeff had ever mentioned anyone at work named Brooke. Nothing came to mind. I considered responding to her and pretending to be Jeff to see what she would say, but then I thought better of it. I had nothing to worry about. I had faith in Jeff and in our relationship—so much so that I'd decided to pack up my life in DC, quit my full-time French teaching position (which, by the way, I loved) *and* my summer translating job (didn't care for that one so much), and move to Paris with him. So, whoever this Brooke person was, she was probably harmless.

But then, another message popped up.

Brooke: I really want to talk to you…xxx.

A sickening feeling took hold in the pit of my stomach as I stared at the *xxx*. Who *was* this girl?

Closing my eyes, I took a deep breath and told myself to relax. She was probably just an old law school friend who was still hung up on Jeff. She obviously didn't know that he was engaged now, that we were moving to Paris together, and that he was in love with *me*.

But then I thought about my college boyfriend who'd been cheating on me for the entire last year of our three-year relationship. I remembered how blindsided I'd been. Wondering how I could've missed his infidelity when all along, it was right there under my nose.

Jeff wasn't like my college boyfriend, though. He'd fallen for me so quickly, so completely. He was sweet and honest. He wore his heart on his sleeve. He was different from all the rest. Which was why I'd fallen head-over-heels in love with him and why I hadn't hesitated to say yes when he'd proposed only six months after we met.

But when I opened my eyes and read Brooke's messages again, especially the *xxx* part, I couldn't ignore that nagging gut instinct telling me something wasn't right.

Hoping Jeff stayed out of the office longer than a few minutes, I launched into detective mode. With our impending move only days away, I figured a little investigation couldn't hurt. And besides, I was *sure* it would turn out to be nothing.

I pulled up the Internet history on Jeff's computer, scrolled through the most recent websites visited, and let out a sigh of relief. Nothing alarming.

But then, at the bottom of the list, my heart dropped.

Match.com popped out at me first. Then I saw OKCupid. And, last, but definitely not least, eHarmony. As my stomach began doing flip-flops—*not* the good kind—and the blood rose to my head, I clicked on the OKCupid link.

There I saw a picture of Jeff, a picture I had taken on our engagement night, posted next to a caption that read:

Successful lawyer looking for fun in the nation's capital.

My hand trembled over the mouse as I blinked my eyes to make sure what I was seeing was real. This had to be a joke. There was no way, no way in hell, that my fiancé, Jeff, the love of my life, would ever do something so deceitful. He wouldn't hurt me like this. He just wouldn't.

I desperately skimmed the page for some glimmer of hope.

Member since April.

It was now September.

My hands continued shaking as if I was holding a loaded gun and wasn't sure if I should pull the trigger or let it drop.

As I scrolled farther down the page though, I saw it. The clincher. The mother of all blows. A message from a redheaded, big-busted girl named...Brooke. It read:

I've had such a wonderful time with you this week, Jeff, I can't wait to come visit you in Paris...xoxoxo, Brooke.

Brooke. All I could see were her giant boobs bursting out of her porn-starish, shiny blue tube top. Red hair. Boobs. xoxoxo. Brooke.

My vision blurred, refusing to see what was staring me in the face. I shook my head in an attempt to regain composure. This could not actually be happening two days before we were moving to Paris together. And less than six months after Jeff had proposed.

It had to be a mistake.

I clicked on the instant message from Brooke, and without thinking, I responded.

Jeff: Hey.

Brooke: There you are, sexy. Busy day at the firm?

My hands quivered over the keyboard as I continued, not caring in the least that Jeff could be coming back at any second.

Jeff: Crazy busy. You?

Brooke: Feeling a little tired after last night...

What the hell happened last night? Who did she think she was?

Jeff: What happened last night?

Brooke: LOL. Like you don't remember.

Jeff: How could I forget? I love hearing you talk about it, though...

Brooke: You kept me up all night!

Stupid whore. I was going to kill her. Just as soon as I killed Jeff. Filthy, scum-of-the-earth bastard.

Jeff: Tell me more. I love it when you talk naughty.

Brooke: You really want me to give you the details?

Jeff: Work is really boring today...throw me a bone.

Brooke: Well, I remember your naked body on top of mine... Does that jog your memory?

I could feel my breakfast making its way back up through my stomach. But I had to get it straight. I couldn't lose Jeff without knowing for sure.

Jeff: Yes, but I want to hear you tell me the full story. All the details.

It took a few seconds. But then I got more clarification than I had ever wanted.

Brooke: LOL. Well, first there was the time in your office last night, and then all night long at your place, and oh yeah, this morning in the shower. And, that's right, one last time on the kitchen counter before you left for work.

A fiery-hot, uncontrollable rage boiled up inside of me as I remembered Jeff calling me the night before to cancel our dinner plans. He'd said he had to stay late at the firm. It had become the routine for the past few months. *Staying late. Lots of work to do. Can't make dinner. Sorry, babe, I love you.*

God, I was such a fool.

Just then, Jeff burst through the office door.

"Hey, babe, no more summer days in a cubicle! And you brought champagne, how sweet."

I stared up at Jeff in disbelief, at a complete loss for words. There he was—my six-foot-three, blond, blue-eyed, gorgeously built fiancé. The man I had trusted with all my heart, with every fiber of my body. The man I was going to build a life with. How could he have done this to me?

As my eyes darted from Jeff to the screen and back to Jeff, a stray tear fought its way down my cheek.

"Babe, what's the matter? What's going on?" he asked as he rounded his desk to comfort me.

I rose with more force than I knew I had in me at the time and glared at him. "*You* tell *me* what the hell is going on."

"Charlotte, what are you talking about?" he asked defensively as a hint of panic passed through his eyes. "Are you okay?"

"No, Jeff, I'm not okay." I wiped the tear from my face, determined not to let any more of them fall. "Tell me what's going on. Who's Brooke?" I demanded as I pointed a trembling finger at his computer screen.

He glanced at the screen long enough to see the nasty sex talk from Brooke, and then looked back at me with desperate, pleading eyes. "I can explain, it's not what it looks like—"

"Then what the hell is it?" I rounded the desk to get away from him and that revolting computer screen. "You're sick. How could you do this to me? To us?"

Jeff ran a shaky hand through his wavy blond hair and shook his head. He didn't have an excuse. Because there was no damn excuse.

"How long? How long have you been seeing her?"

"Charlotte, don't—"

"Stop lying to me. Just tell me how long it's been." My legs felt like they might give way, but I forced myself to stay standing.

"About a month," he mumbled as he locked eyes with the floor.

"And these dating sites? All of your online profiles? How long have you been doing that?"

Jeff shook his head in silence, his eyes darting frantically around the room as if he were desperate to escape. Desperate to jump out of his skin and be anywhere but here.

"Answer me."

"Charlotte, I love you. I didn't mean to hurt you, really," he pleaded as a couple of stray beads of sweat rolled down his forehead.

"You sure have a sick way of showing your love." I couldn't take any more. I had to get out of there. I pivoted on my wobbly legs and bolted for the door.

"Charlotte, don't go. We're leaving in two days. We can work this out. We can get through this!" Jeff grabbed hold of my arm, but I yanked it back and smacked the champagne bottle in the process. The tall bottle of Veuve Clicquot flew through the air in slow motion, then shattered all over the shiny hardwood floors. I stared at the shards of glass and fizzy bubbles that circled our feet, my heart aching for what should've been a celebration of our love, but what had now become the aftermath of Jeff's deception.

I lifted my eyes to his, knowing that this was it. No matter how much I loved Jeff, I couldn't stay. "*We* are not leaving in two days. I'm not going anywhere with you. I'm not marrying you, and I'm not moving to Paris with you."

With that, I left him bewildered in his office, and I stormed outside into the stifling DC heat.

TWO

vendredi, le 24 septembre

Wine and girlfriends—don't leave home without them.

𝓘 stumbled over the redbrick sidewalks of Georgetown in a daze. How was it that my life had taken such a hideous turn in a matter of an hour? How was it that the man I thought I knew, the man who I thought loved me more than anything, could be someone else entirely, someone who cheated on me? Someone who was stupid enough to broadcast himself on online dating sites and think that I would never find out?

I felt like a complete idiot. Had there been other girls besides Brooke? Was Jeff still going to go to Paris? Without me? With that redheaded porn star on the website? Was he ever planning on telling me about her?

Suddenly, all I could see was the grotesque image of Jeff and Brooke having sex. In Jeff's bed. The same bed I had slept in with him only two nights before...and the bed where they had apparently slept together just last night. The thought of it made me want to double over and heave. He was *mine*, after all, not *hers* or anyone else's. I was the one wearing his ring; I was the one he had invited to go to Paris with him; and I was the one he loved.

At least I'd thought he loved me.

I hadn't even realized which direction I was walking until I turned the corner of Prospect and Thirty-Third Street, just a couple of blocks away from the university and down the street from my best friend Katie's house. Katie and I had grown up together in Ohio, shared our college years as roommates, and now Katie was in her fourth year of medical school at Georgetown. I knocked on her door, praying she was home.

"Hey, lady," Katie greeted me in her usual cheery tone as she swung the door open. But once she took a look at my red, splotchy face, she ushered me into the living room. "What's the matter, Charlotte? What happened?"

I sank into Katie's cushy gray couch and spilled all of the nasty details while she stared at me in disbelief.

"He put himself on *three* online dating sites? That's disgusting. I mean, he's thirty-two, for God's sake, and *he* was the one who was so intent on getting engaged after only a few months! This just doesn't make any sense. I'm so sorry, Charlotte."

"Why does this keep happening? Why does every single guy I date cheat on me? What is wrong with me, Katie?"

She grabbed my shoulders and looked me in the eye. "There's nothing wrong with you, Charlotte. You're wonderful. You're the best thing that ever happened to Jeff. He didn't deserve you."

"This never happens to you, though. There must be something with *me*, something that I do, that makes men want to run around on me."

Katie shook her head. "I haven't had as many long relationships as you have. And the guys I've dated...well, they're just *different* from the type of guy you usually date."

"You mean they're not assholes."

"I don't mean that you purposely *choose* assholes, Charlotte. What I mean is that you've had bad luck with the guys you've fallen for. You did the right thing, though. You can't marry that lying sack of shit." Katie's pale cheeks turned cherry red in her fury.

"But what am I going to do now? I gave up my teaching job *and* my translating job, and in two days, I won't even have a place to live."

"They already rented out your studio?"

"Yeah, like five seconds after I told them I wasn't renewing my lease."

"And your school already found a new French teacher?"

"They hired some girl straight out of college. It's too late to get it back."

"Shit."

"Yeah, I know. And I loved that job too. I would've never, ever given it up if I had known..." I buried my face into my hands, hoping Katie could give me some answers to this catastrophe. "I'm going to have to move back to Ohio with my parents like some pathetic failure."

"You're not moving back to Ohio," Katie asserted as she stood and paced back and forth across the living room, the way she always did when she was trying to figure out a solution to a problem. "You can stay here as long as you need to, you know that. I just can't believe he did this. I really can't. We'll figure everything out, but right now you need to breathe and have a drink."

She went into the kitchen and came back with a huge glass of red wine. "Did you hear from the Sorbonne yet?"

"Yeah, I got in, but I'm not going," I said before letting a huge gulp of smooth red wine roll down my throat.

I stared out the window and tried to imagine what it would be like to move to France by myself. Over the past few months, I'd imagined every single detail of what my life would be like in Paris with Jeff. "With Jeff" being the operative words there. Finally, after months of waiting, we were going to live together, and I was going to take graduate-level French teaching courses at the Sorbonne—an absolute dream come true for me.

But I was no longer the fiancée of Jeff Dillon, a high-powered DC attorney whose firm was paying for our lavish Parisian apartment while I went to school full-time. I was back to being Charlotte Summers, the meagerly paid high school French teacher. And hell, I wasn't even an employed French teacher anymore. I had even given that up for him. So the thought of moving to France on my own with no plan and barely any money didn't sound too appealing at the moment.

Katie sat back down next to me and looked me in the eye. "Charlotte, this is what you've always wanted to do. You love France. You've been saving your money since we graduated just so you could move to Paris, study at the Sorbonne, and teach over there. You'll regret it forever if you don't at least give it a shot. Screw Jeff. I know you loved him and never imagined things would turn out this way, but maybe going to Paris will get your mind off him and help you move on. And it will be all about *you* this time, not about some asshole guy."

"But what if Jeff goes to Paris too?"

"He doesn't deserve to go, that bastard. Paris is yours!" Katie declared, as if Paris were one of our communal possessions, and it now belonged to me, since Jeff was the reason we were breaking up. "Is he still going?"

"I don't know, I didn't ask him. I didn't want to know at the time. All I could think about was that disgusting girl and what he did with her."

"Don't even go there right now. It's not going to do any

good. Either way, whether he's going or not, it doesn't mean you couldn't still go. It's a big enough city; I doubt you'd run into him."

I took another gulp of wine, hoping the numbness would set in soon.

"It's just a thought," she continued. "Maybe it's a bit much to worry about right now, though. I think we need to get you another glass of wine and watch a movie. Something to take your mind off this."

Just as I was about to agree to spending the afternoon at Katie's and drowning my sorrows in wine and television, Katie's phone rang.

"Shoot, it's the hospital. I have to go. I'm so sorry. Are you going to be okay by yourself tonight? Maybe we should ask Hannah to come over."

"No, please don't tell Hannah yet. This is so humiliating. I mean Hannah and Mike are the ones who introduced me to Jeff in the first place, *and* we just agreed to be in their wedding next spring. Jeff's the best man." I downed the last of my wine as I stood up. "What a mess."

Katie hugged me once more. "Don't worry about the wedding. I'm sure Hannah will disinvite Jeff altogether once she finds out what he did to you. I won't say anything to her yet, though."

"Thanks Katie. For everything."

"Of course. Think about what I said, though, will you?"

"Yes, I promise."

"It's about *you* this time, Charlotte, not about him."

Katie gave me one more squeeze, then sent me back out into the oppressive heat. I trudged down to M Street to catch the bus home to my modest studio apartment off Dupont Circle, where I had been living alone since I graduated from Georgetown a couple of years earlier. As I took a seat on the bus, I glanced down at my watch. It was already four p.m. One hour since my life had taken the plunge from engaged bliss to pathetic singledom.

It hit me then, like a ton of bricks—I was single again. I wouldn't have the comfort of saying "my fiancé and I" anymore. Waves of sadness and rage flowed through me in spurts as I rode home in silence, staring out the window of the bus, realizing that my world didn't look nearly as shiny as it had only a couple of hours before.

When I made it back home to my Massachusetts Avenue apartment building, I walked through the shabby maroon-carpeted lobby and into the mailroom. I opened my mailbox to find one thin white envelope from the Sorbonne.

I didn't have the energy to find out what was inside, so instead of tearing it open like I would've done if the past hour had never happened, I took the elevator up to the eighth floor, walked into my sweltering studio, and tossed the envelope in the trash. What did it matter at this point, anyway?

I made my way through the large stacks of boxes to crank up the air-conditioning. As I passed by the bathroom, I caught a glimpse of myself in the mirror. My big brown eyes had evolved into two mascara-smudged, swollen messes, and strands of my long, dark-brown hair were plastered to my face and sticking up in every direction. I was normally so put together—never a hair out of place, and *never* crying in public. Ever. But as I stared at myself in the mirror, I realized this wasn't exactly a normal situation. It wasn't every day that I discovered my fiancé was a nasty, sleazy, cheating piece of crap.

After I emerged from the bathroom, I took off my three-inch heels and envisioned shoving them up Jeff's perfectly toned ass. Instead I hurled them across the room. I ripped off my sweaty black skirt and my stupid, uncomfortable thong and threw on a pair of cotton underwear, a tank top, and some comfy shorts. I grabbed a bottle of red wine off the kitchen counter and curled up on my couch.

Unwilling to face the prospect of my now-unsettled life, I chugged the last half of the bottle in desperation (who needed a wineglass?), lost myself in *Sex and the City* reruns until I couldn't keep my eyes open any longer, and finally fell asleep wrapped around the empty bottle. Pathetic, but I needed something to hold on to.

THREE

samedi, le 25 septembre

It's time to throw love out the window for good.

I woke up the next morning with a raging headache and the shocking realization that everything that had taken place the day before was real. That my fiancé whoring himself out on online dating services wasn't a bad dream. It had actually happened. Unbelievable.

I checked my phone to see if Jeff had called. He had. Three times. Wow, I must've really passed out. I listened to my messages to see what the pathetic liar had to say for himself.

"Charlotte, I don't know what to say. I screwed up. I really, really screwed up bad. I love you, and I know we can get through this. It will never happen again, I swear." *Damn right it won't.* "Please call me when you get this."

Yeah right. I wanted him to sit and smother in his misery. I knew he would miss me, no matter what was going on in his gross online dating life. My anger rose as I mulled over the situation.

Since I was thirteen, I'd had a never-ending string of long

relationships, one folding right into the next, barely leaving me time to breathe in between. And as I scanned through my dating history, I thought again about the fact that *every single guy* I had ever dated had cheated on me, right down to my first real boyfriend in junior high. It was an epidemic! I had truly believed that Jeff was different, but he was just like the rest of them. How many guys cheating on me was it going to take for me to realize that men don't commit?

My friends were no strangers to heartbreak either. With the exception of my two closest friends, Katie and Hannah, nearly *all* of my other girlfriends had dated at least one, if not several, scummy cheaters. We'd all had our hearts torn apart by men, yet we willingly jumped into the next relationship, hoping, believing that this guy would be "the one," that he would be different from all the rest.

Meanwhile men, especially gorgeous men like Jeff, were able to have a constant string of women coming in, so that even if they got their feelings hurt by one of them, the hurt was insignificant because they had ten more women waiting in line, or waiting *online* in Jeff's case. If I was ever going to make it in this world without experiencing continuous heartbreak and endless dramatic breakups, I needed to treat them the way they'd all treated me!

I sat down at my computer with the intention of spilling all of my anger onto an empty page, when I remembered the blog I'd created to keep in touch with family and friends back home. As I pulled up the website, there at the top of the page was a picture of me and Jeff, our heads pressed together in that annoying pose that couples do when they're totally in love. Or at least when they appear to be in love. I'd titled the blog "Charlotte and Jeff's Parisian Adventures." It almost made me gag to look at it. I needed to delete everything on this page immediately.

Just as I was about to hit the Delete button, though, I stopped. Katie's words from the day before resonated in my head. I'd already given up both of my jobs, I was about to lose my apartment, I had a plane ticket to Paris leaving the next day, and I'd already been accepted to the Sorbonne.

I *could* still go to Paris.

I jumped up from my desk, ran over to the trash can, and fished out the letter from the Sorbonne. I tore open the envelope to find a note from my new advisor, Madame Rousseau, letting me know that we had our first meeting in three short days.

I had to go.

Back in college, when I was studying abroad in Lyon, a gorgeous city a few hours south of Paris, I'd traveled up to Paris for a week to visit a friend who'd just started this exact teaching program at the Sorbonne. That week, I fell in love with her life. Morning classes at the Sorbonne. An adorable apartment on the left bank of the river. Afternoons spent drinking wine with friends at cafés on beautiful cobblestone streets. I'd made the decision right then and there that after college, I would save every spare dime, get into that program, and move to Paris.

The problem was, as a private-school teacher in an expensive city, I hadn't had too many dimes to spare.

I signed on to my bank account and felt my stomach drop as the $5,000 balance on the screen mocked my life's dreams. My meager savings *might* get me through two or three months at best, but what was I supposed to live on for the rest of the year as a full-time student? As I racked my brain trying to figure out how in the hell I was going to pull this off, my eye caught the stack of wedding magazines in the corner of my apartment.

And then I remembered it—the joint bank account Jeff had opened to put money aside for the wedding and, more specifically, for the gorgeous designer wedding dress I'd fallen in love with.

I pulled up the bank website and typed like a madwoman

to sign in. To my relief, a beautiful balance of $10,000 remained untouched. I began to set up a transfer to my personal account when my conscience nagged at me. Technically, this was Jeff's money. Did I really have the right to take it? Some of this money *was* supposed to go toward my wedding dress, so what was the difference if I just transferred it into my account? But, the whole $10,000? No, I couldn't take all of it…could I?

I tapped my pen against the desk and stared at the screen. I thought of what he'd done to me—how he'd trampled on my dreams to move to France with him. How he'd betrayed me. How he'd been sleeping with another woman and telling me he loved me all in the same day.

I couldn't contain myself. I hit the Transfer button and sent the entire $10,000 straight to my bank account. Screw him. I was going to Paris. With the low exchange rate, $10,000 more wouldn't even stretch *that* far…unless I found a really inexpensive apartment and lived on bread, cheese, chocolate, and cheap wine. I could manage that.

So, with a plane ticket, an acceptance letter, $15,000, and a broken heart, I was still on my way to Paris.

I pulled up the blog again and stared at it for a few minutes. I thought about the cheating epidemic and how horrible it was that I had to go through this. That any woman ever had to feel this low, this unloved. Why should we all keep making the same mistakes? There had to be a better way.

Instead of hitting the Delete button, I hit the Edit button. I trashed the picture of me and Jeff and hoped I'd never have to look at it again. Then I deleted the cheesy title and typed:

Rule # 1: Men are bastards.

Rule # 2: Do not fall in love with one of these bastards. Ever again.

Rule # 3: Date like a man—use men for sex when necessary but do not get attached.

I read over my entry, felt deeply satisfied, and hit the Publish button. I sent a mass e-mail to all of my girlfriends with a link to my blog, telling them I would write more once I got to Paris. I also included a side note about how Jeff was sleeping with some whore and that I was moving to Paris alone.

After leaving a voice mail for my parents to inform them that Jeff was a cheating son of a bitch, the wedding was off, and I was leaving the next day for Paris, I spent the next hour man-bashing with my friends over the phone while frantically searching online for apartments or sublets in Paris. Anything to get me out of DC and away from this hellish situation.

One of my friends who had studied abroad in Paris told me to contact the Fondation des États-Unis, a large dorm for American students located in the fourteenth arrondissement, at the southern border of the city. Apparently, it was dirt cheap compared to everything else in Paris, and it was situated on a campus called the Cité Universitaire, which housed tons of international students. I wasn't having any luck finding an affordable apartment online, so I pulled up the website to the Fondation and called the office.

To my surprise, a cheery woman answered the phone and told me that yes, in fact, they did have rooms available. She e-mailed me the application, I faxed it back, and within an hour I had secured a room at the Fondation des États-Unis. I wasn't too thrilled about the idea of dorm life at this point, but I'd take it. After all, beggars can't be choosers. Plus, it would provide a great opportunity to meet guys and get the research flowing for my blog.

I managed to finish packing up all of my things and say my good-byes to friends without too much worry. There was one last thing that was eating at me, though—I wasn't sure what to do about the ring. Seriously, what do you do when something like this happens? Of course, I'd already transferred $10,000 of Jeff's money into my account, but for some reason the ring was different. It was more personal. And I had no idea how much he'd spent on it. I knew it wasn't cheap, though, not by a long shot.

I felt like he owed it to me to let me keep it after what he had done. But at the same time, did I really want to keep a ring that would only remind me of the life we didn't have together? I decided that I at least needed to talk to him about this one thing, and, more importantly, I needed to find out if he was still going to Paris.

Before picking up the phone, I took several deep breaths to force myself to stay calm. I wanted to be cold, heartless, and cruel. I wanted to make him feel as worthless and unloved as he had made me feel. I would not break down on the phone with him.

I would not.

So, with my little speech ready to go, I dialed Jeff's number and felt the queasiness pile up inside of me like a toxic poison.

"Charlotte?" he answered, breathless.

"Hi, Jeff. I'm calling because I want you to know that I've decided to go to Paris alone, and I'm leaving tomorrow. I don't want to hear your excuses or your apologies; I just want to know if you want the ring back."

Nothing but silence on the other end. Surely he had thought of this.

"I don't know, Charlotte. I've been so upset."

Oh, poor baby. Really, cry me a river.

"Whatever. Do you want it back?" I demanded, determined to keep my ruthless tone even though my insides were crumbling.

"No, keep the ring, it's yours. I would never take it back." His voice quivered. "I really need you to know that I still love you, Charlotte."

"What does Brooke think about that?"

Ouch. He could definitely feel the sting of my bite through the phone.

"I know you're angry with me, but I wasn't going to talk to her anymore once we moved to Paris. Nothing was going on with Brooke, really, she was just a—a friend." Jeff stammered his way through his pathetic excuse and actually sounded like he might cry. "I want to be with *you*, Charlotte... I can't imagine being with anyone else."

That's it.

"Stop it, Jeff. Just stop! Do you think I actually believe you? That you were going to stop cheating on me just because we moved? I'm not that stupid, Jeff. And don't even try to make *me* feel bad for *you*. You're such an asshole. I can't believe you."

Silence.

My hands trembled so fiercely I could barely hold the phone to my ear. "I just need to know one more thing, and then you can go live your life with some other dumb girl who'll fall for your crap. Are you still moving to Paris?" I held my breath, waiting for his reply.

Jeff took what seemed like a year to answer me.

"No, I'm not going."

All of the pain from the previous day flooded right back to me. Amid all of my man-bashing, part of me had actually hoped that he would say he was still going to Paris, that somehow we'd still be going together, and that this was all just a nasty dream. But it wasn't. It was real. Jeff wasn't going to Paris with me. He wasn't going to Paris at all.

"I have to go," I mumbled, having lost my desire to destroy him over the phone.

"Charlotte, I'm sorry. Please—"

"Jeff, I have to go."

And that was it. I hung up the phone. I couldn't bear to hear another word out of his mouth.

It was over. My engagement to Jeff was over.

FOUR

lundi, le 27 septembre

Don't judge a French man by his tight jeans.

"*Bonjour, Mademoiselle,*" the Parisian cabdriver said as he heaved the weight of my life into the trunk of the cab. Even he was struggling with it.

"*Bonjour, Monsieur,*" I responded with a tired smile. "*Quinze boulevard Jourdan, au quatorzième, s'il vous plaît.*"

I asked him to take me to my new address in the fourteenth arrondissement, where I would begin my new life. I rolled down the window and rode along in silence, taking in the early-morning hustle bustle of the city.

Miniature cars buzzed in and out of the skinny, winding roads, their drivers not paying any attention to road signs or stoplights. Rows of black balconies with splashes of pink and white flowers lined the endless view of gray apartment buildings. Slim Parisians donned long sleeves and dark pants, despite the humidity that weighed down on the city like a ton of bricks. Puffs of cigarette smoke billowed from their mouths as they strolled toward the metro, not seeming to be in any kind of hurry. As we passed by a *boulangerie*, the scent of warm, buttery croissants drifted into the cab, but even so, I didn't feel an ounce of hunger.

It had been almost five years since I'd last visited Paris, and as I sat alone on the sweaty leather seat of the cab, listening to the bizarre sound of French sirens race past, my stomach churned. I didn't feel good about being here. It felt forced and wrong. In my rush to get away from Jeff and the hurt he had caused me, I hadn't dealt with any of it. And now here I was—alone in France, with no friends, no fiancé to go home to, and the thought that Jeff probably had someone to go home to tonight. Brooke. How depressing.

After an hour of nauseating stop-and-go traffic, we pulled up in front of a massive brick building on Boulevard Jourdan. Happy to rid my lungs of the stale taxicab air, I handed over the equivalent of my life savings in cab fare, lugged my bags up to the information desk, and collected the key to room number 360. God, I hoped it was nice.

As I let myself into my new abode, I dropped my suitcases onto the dirty tile floor and scanned the room. It was tiny. So tiny that it wasn't even half the size of my studio apartment in DC, and the "bed" was actually a flat little cot with a thin plastic mattress. A grungy sink stuck out of the pale-blue wall, and a rusty mirror stared back at me, making me realize I didn't have my own bathroom. Ugh. I couldn't believe I was going to have to fit all of my stuff into this space *and* try to get a good night's sleep on that cot while sharing a communal bathroom with complete strangers. The pictures of the building on the Internet had given the illusion that the rooms would be nicer than this. Or I'd been in such a rush to get away from Jeff that in my delirious state, I'd agreed to the first place I could find. Not the best planning I'd ever done.

My room did have one thing going for it—a giant window framed by a set of deep red curtains. I stuck my head through the wispy drapes and spotted a few other international dorms and a sprawling lawn filled with students playing soccer, or *"le foot"* as the French called it. It was charming, but it didn't matter at that moment—I was exhausted and alone.

And despite everything, I missed Jeff. Maybe I had acted rashly, never giving him a chance to explain, never even considering working things out. I lay down on my rock-hard cot-bed thing and wallowed in self-pity for a while. I felt horrible. Why did this have to happen to me? I was supposed to be with my fiancé, lying in a cushy, king-size bed in a beautiful apartment overlooking the Seine. Not miserable and alone in this dingy little room on this piece-of-crap bed.

My desperation was reaching new heights. I needed to talk to someone, so I reached for the phone and dialed home.

"Hello?" my mom answered anxiously, clearly hoping to hear my voice on the other line.

"Hi, Mom," I greeted her wearily.

"Charlotte!" she said in her panicky-mom voice. "Are you okay? Where are you? What happened?"

"Don't worry, Mom, I'm in Paris. I made it here just fine."

"Where are you living? You're there all alone?"

I explained my change of plans to her so she would stop flipping out.

"Well, I'm just glad you're okay. Your father and I have been worried sick since we got your message a few days ago. You are okay, aren't you, dear?"

"Mom, I'm fine," I lied. Hearing the concern in her voice made me miss her immensely.

"Charlotte, are you crying?"

Only one stray tear had made its way down my cheek, but moms always know.

"Mom, I don't know what I'm doing here…I have no one. I'm totally alone."

"Oh, honey, you're going to be okay. You're not alone. I love you."

"Jeff's such a bastard."

"Yes, he is, dear." My poor mom tried to comfort me, but I was past the point of help. I needed to go back to bed. After I hung up the phone, I passed out on my rock-hard mattress. I didn't even care that it felt like a rock. I just needed to sleep.

~

I woke abruptly to the sound of high-pitched sirens racing down the street. I shot up in my bed, not realizing where I was for a second. As the blaring noise made its way past my building, I remembered. I was in Paris. Alone.

I checked my watch—it was eight p.m. Paris time. I had slept for twelve hours. So much for adjusting to the time zone and going to sleep later that night. I peeled myself off the hot, sticky plastic bed, hung up some of my clothes, and decided to go exploring. I refused to sit alone in a puddle of my own tears on my first night in Paris.

After dragging my weary body down the hall, I found the world's smallest and nastiest set of showers. Fabulous. Not having a choice in the matter, though, I battled with the ice-cold water until, with no warning, the high-powered stream became boiling hot. Once I'd had enough, I wrapped myself as tightly as I could in my skimpy bath towel. As I emerged from the steamy shower cell, I bumped smack into another wet, towel-wrapped body.

I took a step back to have a look at the man who I'd just lunged my half-naked body at and found a tall, lean, muscular guy with light-brown hair and a sexy five o'clock shadow. He was gazing down at me with a devious grin.

"*Oh, pardon,*" he said as he checked to make sure his towel was still wrapped around his waist.

I was at such a loss for words that, like an idiot, I let out a burst of high-pitched laughter, bolted out of the bathroom, and booked it as fast as I could down the hallway.

Back in my room, I blow-dried my long hair, dabbed on a

touch of makeup, and threw on my favorite pair of jeans and a silky black tank, all the while replaying my intimate encounter with the hot, half-naked French guy over and over in my head. I wished I had said something even remotely intelligent instead of letting out that horrible laugh and running out of there as if he had cooties or something. On the bright side, if all the guys around here looked like him, this communal shower thing might not turn out to be so bad after all.

As I left my room, I spotted a guy locking his apartment door two doors down from mine. As he turned around, he caught my eye and grinned. It was the shower guy. I almost didn't recognize him with clothes on.

"*Bonsoir, Mademoiselle,*" he said politely.

"*Bonsoir,*" I responded as I blushed from head to toe.

I could hear the French hottie walking toward me as I pushed the Down button and waited for the elevator.

"*Vous êtes française?*" he asked with a bold grin on his face.

"*Non, je suis américaine,*" I answered, excited that my hint of an American accent hadn't seeped through and that he had actually thought I was French.

"Oh, you are American. You look very French to me. My name is Luc," he said in an adorable accent. "And you?"

"I'm Charlotte," I said, letting a smile slide across my lips.

He leaned in for the obligatory greeting kisses on both cheeks—the *bisous* or *bises* as the French call them. His little bit of stubble brushed up against my cheeks as he kissed me. Jeff never had stubble. He always shaved, every morning, no matter what. He had to be perfect and clean-cut every day. No surprises. I had liked it at the time, but today, as I thought about it, it infuriated me. I was glad that Luc had some stubble. I could use some spontaneity in my life. Plus, I loved the kisses. Well, I especially loved them when I was meeting a nice-looking French guy.

"I am sorry about earlier, in the shower. I hope I did not scare you."

"Oh, it's no problem. I'm not used to showering in a communal shower like that and seeing other naked…um…I mean, guys wrapped in towels…You know what I mean," I bumbled.

He laughed. "Yes, I can imagine. You must be new here. Did you come to Paris today?"

I caught him checking me out from top to bottom. Guys, especially French guys, had no shame. But, it did make me feel better after the embarrassing shower incident.

"Yeah, I flew in this morning and slept all day. I'm feeling a little more energetic now, though. So, have you lived here awhile?"

"Euh," he hesitated. "No, not long. Only two months. You will like it here. Zee…how do you say, people zat live here?" he asked, as he pointed to the other doors in the corridor.

"Neighbors?" I suggested.

"Yes, zee neighbors are very nice. You will like them. You are staying for a long time?"

"Yeah, I'm planning on staying for at least a year, but we'll see."

"You are here alone?"

Bad question.

"Mm-hmm, just me!" I said, running my hand through my hair, trying to sound happy about it, but sounding desperate in the process.

Thankfully the elevator came just then, because I really didn't feel like getting into all of the depressing reasons why I was here alone. We crammed into the rickety 1950s elevator that shook all the way down as it transported us to the ground floor. I tried not to stare, but the more I looked, the more I noticed that Luc was exceptionally cute. His hair was about an inch long and was tossed around on his head as if he had just run his hands through it. His chestnut eyes and charming smile were much warmer than Jeff's, and he had a nice summer tan going on. As most French guys are, he was thin, but he wasn't like those guys that are so skinny they make you feel fat just standing next to them. His white T-shirt showed off the right amount of lean muscles, and his almost-baggy jeans and brown euro sneakers were just plain sexy. He looked like a soccer player. Most of the guys I had met in France had played *le foot*. I bet Luc was a kick-ass *foot* player. Mmm.

"So, Charlotte, what are your plans for your first night in Paris?"

"I'm not really sure, actually. I was going to grab a glass of wine and some dinner maybe. What about you? Where are you headed for the night?" *Please, please ask me out.* I realized that I really did not want to be alone. All I would do was think about Jeff and how much I hated him...and how much I missed him.

Come on, Luc.

"Well..." he started, "I am going to meet friends at a bar to have a drink..." He paused and looked bashfully at his feet.

Oh, come on...just ask me! I've already seen you in a towel, for God's sake!

He gazed back up into my eyes and smiled. "Would you like to come?"

Thank God!

"Sure, I'd love to come!" Whoa, that definitely sounded desperate. Oh well, I *was* desperate. Who cares?

"Okay, zat's great. You will like my friends. They are very nice," he said as he continued to smile in my direction.

"So, where are we headed?" I asked as we stepped outside into the warm night air.

"We take zee RER train to Saint-Michel by Notre Dame. Then we are going to a boat, a bar boat...a bar...on a boat. Excuse me, I do not speak zee...euh...English very often." His cheeks flushed a bright shade of red.

"Don't worry, your English is great. We can speak French if you want actually. I'm a French teacher back home in DC, so I do speak the language."

"Maybe next time. I need to practice my English, and what better way zan to practice with a teacher from zee United States?"

"Very true." I smiled at my newfound French cutie. "Thanks for bringing me along…It's nice not to be alone on my first night here."

"Well…" He paused for a few seconds and then looked me intently in the eye. "A woman as *beauteeful* as you should not be alone in your apartment tonight."

Luc was so handsome and sweet that I didn't mind hearing the typical French man "you are so beautiful" comments so soon after we met. I needed a nice guy who was nothing like Jeff to dote on me that night. And what better way to get my research started for my blog than to go out with a cute French guy?

Which reminded me, under *no* circumstances was I allowed to fall for this guy just because he was hot, charming, and happened to live two doors down from me.

After buying me a ticket and running with me to catch the train, Luc pushed through the car to get me the only seat left and shielded me from all of the greasy men, who, if he hadn't been there with me, would've undoubtedly been bursting through their tight, tapered pants while trying to catch shameless glimpses of my cleavage. I definitely caught Luc gazing down there a few times, but oh well. I just wished Jeff could've been there to see another guy checking me out. Humph.

Only a few short stops later, I followed Luc through the underground labyrinth of the Notre Dame metro stop, and we emerged to the bustling Place Saint-Michel.

The sweet aroma of hot Nutella crêpes wafted past me and made my stomach growl as I took in my surroundings.

Bright-yellow awnings of Gibert Jeune bookstores lined the busy square, which held the towering Saint-Michel fountain at its center. The elegant sound of the French language flowed from the sidewalk cafés as Parisians sipped red wine and laughed with their friends. Chatty groups of tourists speaking every language possible weaved in and out of the cobblestone streets toward the Seine.

The excitement was contagious, and, before I knew it, I found myself thinking that there was no other place in the world that could possibly be as thrilling or as beautiful as this.

This was the Paris I'd remembered.

How had I managed to stay away for so long? And what reason would I ever have to go back to the States?

Luc placed his hand on the small of my back and guided me across the scooter-filled streets to the Seine. We strolled along the deep-blue sparkling river together in a comfortable silence until Luc led me down a flight of stairs to the riverbank. Adjacent to the gothic Notre Dame Cathedral, a dinner boat floated calmly on the quiet waters. We climbed on board, and, with his warm hand still firmly pressed into my back, Luc took me to the rear of the boat where a couple was sitting, their arms and legs draped all over each other, seductive whispers passing back and forth between them.

"Zose are my friends," he said, pointing in their direction.

He introduced me to Benoît, one of his close friends, and Lexi, Benoît's date. Benoît was taller and thinner than Luc, but strikingly handsome. Likewise, Lexi was absolutely gorgeous. Taller than me, she had perfect, thin legs, long, wavy black hair, iridescent amber eyes with neatly waxed eyebrows, a naturally dark complexion, and enormous breasts. I mean enormous. The two of them—Benoît and Lexi, that is—were quite a sight. They could've easily been a pair of sexy models on some high-fashion Parisian billboard.

Bisous were exchanged around the table, and before I

knew it, I was enjoying a tall glass of Merlot and chatting up a storm with Luc's friends.

"So, how do all of you know each other?" I asked the group.

"Luc and I grew up in Paris together, and then studied finance together in college. And Lexi and I just met about a month ago," Benoît said with a perfect American accent.

"Wow, your English is really good. Did you study in the States?" I asked him.

"Yes, actually, I lived in New York City for a year, right after college."

"You are saying that Benoît speaks zee English better zan me?" Luc asked as he aimed his flirty eyes at mine.

"No, not at all. I could tell that maybe he'd spent some time in the US, that's all." I giggled as I took another swig of my wine.

"Sure," he said as he tapped my foot with his underneath the table.

Just then, Luc's cell phone rang. His eyebrows furrowed inward as he looked at the name on the caller ID. "*Pardon,*" he said as he shot up from the table, gave Benoît a knowing glance, and jetted toward the door.

"I'm going to have another beer. Do you ladies want another drink?" Benoît asked.

"I'll take a dirty martini, and get this girl another glass of red wine. We need to show Charlotte a good time on her first night in Paris," Lexi said as she gave Benoît a sexy wink.

We both watched as Benoît walked over to Luc, who was talking on the phone near the door. Luc lowered his phone, then leaned toward Benoît to tell him something. Both of their expressions darkened before Luc got back on the phone and Benoît headed over to the bar.

"What do you think that's all about?" I asked Lexi.

"Damned if I know. This is the first time I've met Luc. And all I know about Benoît is that he's *amazing* in bed."

I grinned. I liked this girl already. "Do you think Luc has a girlfriend or something?"

"Oh, girl, all the men over here have girlfriends, fiancés, wives, lovers—you name it. That's why you have to play the field and not take any of it too seriously."

"Cheers to that," I said as I clinked my glass with hers. "So, what brings you to Paris? You're American, right?"

"Yeah, born and raised in New York City, but my family spent every summer in Paris in our little *pied-à-terre*, and I just fell in love with it, you know? So I moved here three years ago, right out of college, and I haven't looked back."

"So you don't think you'll ever move back to New York?"

"Not really. I mean, I travel back and forth a lot, so I still get to see my friends and all of my New York boys, but Paris is…well, it's Paris. What more can I say? New York doesn't even hold a candle to this city."

"What about the men here? Do you like French men better?"

"Oh, honey, you have so much to learn. The men here are cheesy, yes. But wait until you get one in bed. They are the most incredible lovers on this planet. Take Benoît, for example. Too thin? Yes. Pants a little too tight? Absolutely. But I'll take a bony ass and tight jeans any day when I know that once I get those tight little babies off him, he's going to keep me up all night begging for more."

I felt a flush creep over my cheeks as I laughed at Lexi's candor. "Wow. I had no idea. I had a boyfriend back home when I was studying abroad in France before, so I didn't get to experience any of this firsthand."

"Well, you've got a hot one taking you home tonight," she said as she nodded her head toward Luc, who was walking back to the table. "Don't be afraid to test the waters."

"Thanks for the advice." Lexi was exactly the kind of girl I needed to be hanging out with to make me forget about my lowlife, scum-of-the-earth ex-fiancé back home, and to advance my research...so to speak.

After Luc and Benoît made it back to the table with our drinks, Luc didn't mention anything about his mysterious phone call, and I didn't ask. He was probably seeing lots of other women, but I was here to play that game too, so what did I care?

At about one thirty in the morning, after five glasses of wine, several uncontrollable fits of laughter, and endless drunken conversation in franglais with my new friends, we decided it was time to head home. Lexi and I exchanged numbers, and she promised to call me later in the week so that we could have a girls' night out.

Once Luc brought me out into the refreshing night air, which had cooled considerably, I realized just how drunk I was. I had forgotten how easy it was to get drunk on French wine—it goes down so smoothly that you don't realize how much you've had. Luc placed his arm around me as I stumbled up the stairs and strolled with him along the river, its dark waters now shimmering underneath the moonlight.

"Thanks so much for taking me out tonight...I really needed this," I stammered, stifling a giggle. I always broke into uncontrollable giggles whenever I was drunk. I hoped I wasn't annoying Luc and tried to get the laughing fit under control.

"What is so funny?" he asked as he burst into laughter. I realized then that Luc was drunk too.

He kept his arm squeezed tightly around my shoulders as we crossed the bridge that led us back over to Place Saint-Michel. In my drunken state, Luc's arm around me suddenly made me sad. It made me think of Jeff and how this easily could've been my first night in Paris with him—strolling down the Seine, his strong arm around me, gazing out at the city lights glistening along the river and getting ready to start our adventure in Paris together. But we weren't together anymore. Jeff didn't love me anymore.

And maybe he never really had.

A few salty tears escaped and rolled down my cheeks.

Luc turned to me, shocked. "What is the matter?"

"Nothing, nothing." I wiped the tears away. "I'm so sorry. I didn't mean to do this."

"What happened? Why are you sorry? I do not understand," he replied, looking a little scared. After all, he had just met me, and we had spent a great evening together. Poor guy. I was sure he was looking for a little action—not a drunk, sobbing American girl.

"It's just that I…" I tried to regain composure. "I miss home." I thought about stopping there, but the alcohol got the best of me. "The truth is, my fiancé left me. Well, I left him. But he deserved it…that bastard," I howled. "He was cheating on me, and we were supposed to move to Paris together, but I just found out about it…so I came alone."

"Come here, sit down with me." Luc held on to me and led me over to a bench facing the river. "Zis just happened?"

"Mm-hmm," I mumbled.

Luc hugged me tightly and held on for a while. He let me cry on his shoulder while he stroked my hair.

"That is horrible. I am so sorry," he said, shaking his head.

"Thank you." I hiccupped again and tried my best to stifle the tears.

After the embarrassing cry session, which Luc handled extraordinarily well seeing as how he had only known me for five hours, he led me back to the metro station, and we took the train home together. I don't remember much of the ride or the walk back to our dorm (I think I was fading in and out of consciousness), but I do remember that Luc kept his arm around me the entire way home. By the time we made it back to my room, I'd calmed down. I was still really drunk, though.

"Thank you so much, Luc…I'm really sorry. I had so much fun with you tonight," I blabbered.

Just as Luc was starting to say something back, I leaned in and kissed him like a crazy woman right there in front of my door. Despite my puffy, swollen eyes, which, no doubt, had streaks of mascara pouring out of them, and my bright-red, irritated nose, he kissed me back. I had no idea what made me do that. Maybe it was the alcohol, maybe it was Lexi's words about French lovers, maybe it was the way he'd taken care of me that night, or maybe it was because I felt totally and utterly desperate. Whatever it was, before I knew it, I had unlocked my door and was making out with Luc inside my little dorm room.

FIVE

mardi, le 28 septembre

Jet lag + Broken engagement + Cute French guy + Five glasses of wine = Disaster

All thoughts of Jeff flew out the window, and all that existed was Luc pushing me up against the wall and kissing my neck. Then my mouth. Then my shoulders. His hands were all over me, roaming over my hips, my thighs, and my waist. We made our way two feet over from the door to my sorry excuse for a bed, which was draped in a cheap white sheet, and Luc pulled me down on top of him. Within seconds, our shirts were off, and even in our drunken state, we both knew where this was headed.

But then, as soon as it had begun, it was over. Luc sat up all of a sudden and looked at me.

"We cannot do this, Charlotte. You are sad...You are drunk. It is not right."

I wanted him so badly in that moment. All of this buildup for nothing! All of the tears, all of the crap from Jeff, the trip to Paris, this great night out, and then Luc was going to leave me here alone in this godforsaken bed with no covers!

Luc must've noticed the look on my face, and, probably out of fear that I would start crying again, he lay back down with me. But then, instead of making some lame excuse to flee the scene like most guys would've done after the way I had acted, he wrapped his arms around me, kissed me on the cheek, and stroked my hair.

His hand was so soothing that within minutes, I passed out like a baby.

∼

I woke up in a cold sweat in pitch darkness and realized that someone else's sweaty arms were wrapped around my bare chest. Oh, dear. What had I done?

I checked for my pants. Still on. Whew. At least I didn't sleep with him. I tried to recall the events of the previous night as my head pounded. I remembered drinking wine (clearly I had surpassed my limit), meeting Benoît and Lexi, and then crying. Oh, God, that's right, I had cried in front of Luc. I had cried really, really hard in front of Luc. In public! What a disaster I was becoming.

The scene of me attacking him at my apartment door flashed through my mind. Well, we'd already covered several major stages of a relationship in one night: seeing each other half-naked in the shower, meeting his friends, crying over a past event, hooking up, and spending the night together. I just couldn't believe he was still here. I was certain I wouldn't be hearing from him after he woke up and bolted back to his room.

I tried to fall back asleep, not wanting to wake Luc after the night I had put him through, but my head was pounding something fierce. I wondered what time it was. I needed to take something for this headache and put a shirt on. I lifted

Luc's arm up off my chest, set it ever so gently on the bed, and tried to climb over him without bumping him or making any noise. I successfully took a couple of steps until, a few feet from the bed, I tripped over my gargantuan suitcase. Damn.

Luc began to stir. "What time is it?" he groaned. I found my watch on the nightstand. It was only five a.m.

"It's early. Sorry to wake you...I have a headache."

"Are you okay?" he asked. Jeez, does this guy ever stop being nice?

"Yes, yes, go back to sleep. I'm fine," I murmured as I groped around in the darkness for my bra, a T-shirt, anything.

Luc got up, put his shirt on, and walked over to me just as I managed to find my tank top from last night curled up in a ball on the floor.

"I think I should go to my bed now to sleep," he said as he let out a big yawn.

Good idea. "Thank you for everything last night. Go get some sleep, okay?" I urged as I threw on my tank top.

Luc gave me a kiss on the cheek and left. I fumbled to turn the light on and grimaced from the brightness. I quickly found my trusty bottle of Aleve buried in my purse, took one for my splitting headache, and switched the light back off. I lay back down on my bed and cringed again as I thought about how I'd behaved the night before.

What was wrong with me?

I remembered then that it was only eleven p.m. in DC. I needed to talk to someone from home—someone who could remind me who I used to be before my life was flipped upside down. I reached for my phone and dialed Katie's number.

"Hey," I croaked.

"Charlotte!" she practically screamed. "How are you? How's Paris? I miss you!"

"Well, things started off with quite a bang...Luc, my

French neighbor, just left my room, and I'm pretty sure he won't be coming back anytime soon."

"What? What time is it there? Isn't it, like, really early in the morning?"

"Yeah, it's five a.m. here."

Katie laughed. "What is going on? You just got there! Who in the hell is Luc?"

I proceeded to give Katie the whole Luc story, being careful not to miss the half-naked shower encounter, the embarrassing drunken cry, and the near-sex disaster.

"Is he cute?"

"Yeah, he's definitely a looker. But, now that I've made a complete fool out of myself, I doubt we'll be spending any more time together…well, not that it matters anyway."

"You did just break up with Jeff a couple days ago. I'm glad you found someone to distract you, but you might want to give yourself some time to get over things, you know?"

"I know, I know. I was a total drunken disaster. I really hope I don't run into him again in the shower or something."

"Don't be so hard on yourself. You've had a terrible week. I think you need to get some rest and maybe take things a little slower from here on out."

"Katie, what am I doing here? Do you think I made the right choice? Moving to Paris by myself? I miss you, and…I miss Jeff. I miss him so much. Do you think I should've at least tried to work things out with him?"

"After what he did to you, he doesn't deserve a second chance. Of course you miss him—everything happened so fast. But give it some time. You'll be starting school soon, you'll make friends, and things will get better. And in the meantime, I'm always here to talk. And if, after a little while, you don't like it over there, you can always come back home."

"Thanks, Katie."

"Of course. You're going to get through this. It's just going to take time. So, when do you meet with your advisor?"

"Oh shoot. I'm meeting with her at eight o'clock this morning. I'm glad you reminded me—that's in three hours."

"This is the woman who will potentially help you get a teaching job in Paris after the program ends, right?"

"That's the plan."

"Well, good luck and let me know how it goes. I hate to run, but I have to be at the hospital at four a.m. tomorrow, so I need to get to bed. I'm so glad you called, though. I miss you already!"

"I know. I miss you too. I'll call again soon. Bye, Katie."

"Bye, Charlotte."

I felt a little better after talking to Katie, but it also made me realize how badly I wanted to talk to Jeff. I wanted to hear his voice, hear him tell me that he was sorry and that he was coming to Paris to get me. That he'd given Brooke a big fat kick to the curb and that she was a huge mistake. But even if he wanted to call me here, he'd have no way of getting my number. Katie sure as hell wouldn't give it to him.

I thought about calling him. I could tell him that I was having a wonderful time in Paris and that I already had a new guy in my life. He'd be so jealous. Or I could tell him the truth. That I missed him and loved him and that my heart was totally and utterly broken.

I couldn't call, though. It would seem desperate, especially after I'd already blocked him on every possible social media outlet. If he really wanted to get in touch, he could always e-mail me. After all, he had been spending a lot of time on the Internet these days. Just the thought of that website with his picture on it made me sick to my stomach. Or was it the five glasses of red wine from the night before?

To avoid making any more desperate drunken moves, I fished out my laptop and signed on to my blog. I had had a few hits on it already but was hoping to build this up to epic proportions. I had to reach as many women as possible. It was time to stop this smart-women-falling-for-cheaters phenomenon. I wracked my brain for a catchy title and began typing my second post.

Sleeping with Paris
A Girl's Guide to Dating Like a Man in the City of Love
by an Américaine in Paris

Two days after finding out that my fiancé has been cheating on me through an online dating site, I sit wondering how I got here. How did it come to this? If you're a woman, you've probably had this exact experience. Okay, maybe you didn't discover your fiancé's online dating profile two days before you were supposed to move to Paris together, and have an online chat with the girl who he just slept with, but you've most likely found out one way or another that a man you loved has cheated on you with another woman. And you're sick of it. You're tired of the games. You want the next man who walks through your front door to be Mr. Right so you don't have to keep putting yourself through all of this misery. So you keep on plugging away, hoping and dreaming that someday, somehow, there will be a man out there who loves you enough not to cheat on you.

Well, ladies, I'm here to tell you that it's all one big crapshoot and we've been on the wrong end of the shoot. It's time to turn the tables and take control of our lives.

Good-bye, Charlotte York. Hello, Samantha Jones.

If you've had enough and want to start having some fun, here are a few key rules:

Rule # 1—Cut ties with all cheating, desperate exes (switch continents if necessary) and find a rebound. Rebounds are key to getting over the dreaded ex.

Would your ex be sitting around, eating chocolate and wondering what went wrong? No, he'd be out there finding his next victim. So get your butt out of that cozy recliner, put down your self-help book, call your girlfriends, and hit the town.

Rule # 2—It's okay to make a fool out of yourself in front of a new guy since you don't care anymore if he calls you the next day. Remember, you're dating like a man here. Don't call. Don't expect a call. Avoid disappointment.

Case in point: Do I care that I pummeled straight into a hot, half-naked guy in the communal shower in my dorm, only to then spend the night out with him and his friends, get way too drunk, cry to him on the way home about my cheating fiancé, and then proceed to make out with him in my bedroom only minutes later? No, I don't. Because I don't need him to call me tomorrow or the next day, or the day after that. The old me would've been mortified, but really, who cares? I may never see this guy again.

So go all out. And if you end up making a mockery of yourself, at least have fun doing it. Because, and repeat after me: "It doesn't matter if he calls me tomorrow, and actually, I'd prefer if he didn't so I can go out and keep having fun."

Rule # 3—All guys are sketchy, so don't get worked up about his other girlfriends or weird phone calls. Just use him for a kiss…or more…and call it a night.

Case in Point: While I was out with Half-Naked French Hottie tonight, he bolted from the table to answer a mysterious phone call, then mentioned nothing about it when he came back.

It could be completely innocent. Or not.

He may have a girlfriend. He may have a wife. He may have several of them. But, in the end, none of that matters when you are out to whoop it up and have a good time. Let the man screw up his life however he wishes, because you're out there to date like a man. And that means no overanalyzing and no caring if the dude you happen to be out with seems to have other priorities. Guys are sketchy, and that's all the more reason not to fall in love with one.

Rule # 4—And finally, if you do switch continents as suggested in Rule # 1 above, you may find yourself feeling scared and utterly alone, which, in turn, may make you want to call your ex. After all, you did have a lot of wonderful times together. And despite how badly he hurt you, you may still love him so much you can actually feel your heart breaking without him.

Stay strong, though, ladies, and don't make that call. Remember that millions of other women have been in your shoes, and they've gotten through it, so you will too.

SIX

vendredi, le premier octobre

French men aren't like American men—they still like us after we cry.

I rolled over in my bed and pried my eyes open. The red lights on my alarm clock were flashing noon. Noon! I'd missed my appointment. Shit, shit, shit.

After I'd hung up with Katie, I'd set my alarm for six thirty a.m., but I didn't even remember hearing it go off. I checked the clock to see if it had malfunctioned. No, the alarm was still set for six thirty. In my half-drunken state, I must've turned it off. I had no recollection of doing that, though. I never, ever missed appointments. What in the hell was going on with me?

I jumped out of bed and fumbled through my unpacked suitcases to find my acceptance letter—the only piece of paper that had any sort of contact number on it. I dialed and got through to a program assistant who gave me Madame Rousseau's number.

As her phone was ringing, I thought about telling her that

my plane had been delayed, or that I'd been hit by a car, or anything so that this woman still liked me. I needed her to help me get a job in Paris after this year was over, and I definitely wasn't starting off on the right foot.

"*Allô?*" she answered.

"*Bonjour, Madame Rousseau? C'est Charlotte Summers—*"

I couldn't even get another word out because she stopped me short and let me know that she was *not* happy, not by any stretch of the imagination. She didn't even give me a chance to make up a fake excuse. After rambling on in French about how she hated when students wasted her time and about how rude and unprofessional my behavior was, she did at least set up another appointment with me for the following Tuesday at the same time. She made sure to tell me that I better be early.

This was the woman I'd be relying on to help me find a teaching job in Paris?

I got out my planner and made a note to leave two hours early for the appointment. Wasting Madame Rousseau's time was not something I would ever do again, not after that phone call.

After an entire day of mentally berating myself for being such an idiot, I finally gave up on the self-loathing and went back to bed.

∼

Going through a breakup is hard enough, but trying to muddle through it in a foreign city where I didn't have any of my closest friends nearby to distract me was proving to be more trying than I had thought it would be.

It was my fifth morning in Paris, and, as I glanced at the clock and saw that it was already noon, I realized I still had not even begun to adjust to the time change. The last few days had been a blur of staying up late at night, sleeping for a few hours, waking up again, calling home, and then sleeping again for half the day. I was hoping that by today, or this weekend at the very least, I would be able to sleep through the night and wake up at a decent hour.

I rolled over in my bed and pulled the covers up to my chin. The truth was that besides being a physical wreck, I also felt sadder than I could ever remember feeling in my entire life. I missed Jeff so much I could hardly breathe sometimes. Mostly, I missed waking up with him in the mornings. Whenever the alarm went off, he would wrap his strong arms around me and bundle me up into his chest so that I never wanted to get out of bed.

But as I lay painfully alone in my bed that morning, the thought that I would never again wake to see Jeff's face next to mine on the pillow was devastating. What was crushing me even more, though, was the thought that he had so carelessly thrown our love away to have sex with another girl. And that *she* was the one who probably saw his face every morning now.

As I envisioned the two of them waking up in bed together, I squeezed my eyes closed and willed myself to fall back asleep. What was the point of getting out of bed anyway? I didn't have any friends to hang out with, and I'd already screwed things up with the only guy I'd met since I'd arrived.

Luc hadn't stopped by at all after "the incident." While I was relieved I hadn't run into him in the hallway in my no-makeup, baggy pajamas getup, the fact that he hadn't wanted to see me made me feel even worse than I already felt.

Like Katie had said, though, I needed to deal with my broken engagement before jumping into another dramatic guy situation.

But his body was so nice. And his kisses were...well, not that I could remember all that well, but I thought they were pretty nice too.

Shaking away the memory of Luc's soft lips on mine, I forced myself up to a sitting position, climbed out of bed, and sat down at my computer. Just as I was logging in to my blog to gather strength from my own advice, my phone rang.

A jolt of hope coursed through me as Lexi's name appeared on the screen. A friend!

"Hey, Charlotte," she said. "Just wanted to see if you're up for a girls' night out on the town tonight?"

I peered around my room at the mess of unpacked suitcases, my clothes strewn over the top of them, the empty box of tissues at my bedside, and my unmade bed.

"I would love to," I told her as I smiled for the first time in three days.

"So, did anything good happen with Luc after you guys left the other night?" she asked.

I filled Lexi in on my disastrous evening, then spilled the whole story about Jeff and why I'd moved to Paris alone.

"Girl, you really need to get out and get your mind off that no-good son of a bitch," Lexi said after I'd explained my newfound disgust with online dating sites. "I have just the place for you."

I loved Lexi already. "I can't wait," I told her.

We worked out the details before she told me she had to run to get her hair done. I wondered then if Lexi had a job or any other real-life responsibilities. She hadn't mentioned them to me if she did. It seemed as if she frolicked around Paris by day, then hit the town each night. I hoped I'd be able to join in on her fun and live such a carefree life during my year here.

After talking with Lexi, I felt something I hadn't even remotely experienced in the past week—hope. I had made a new friend, I would make more friends, I would meet more guys, and things would get better. I decided to get my act together and stop sleeping all the time. Granted, I had only been living in my pajamas and littering tissues around my mess of a room for four days, and I was certainly entitled to at least a few weeks of moping, but it had never been like me to sit around and feel sorry for myself. It was time to get up off my butt and get moving.

I spent the afternoon cleaning, unpacking, and organizing my room. I turned on some angry-girl music, sang my heart out, danced around my room, and got things together. No more tears, no more wallowing in self pity.

In the midst of my cleaning frenzy, while I was bellowing out a high note, there was a knock on the door. I was so excited at the thought of a potential visitor that I ran to the door and swung it open with a huge smile on my face, forgetting that I was wearing a skimpy white tank top and inappropriately short shorts, not to mention that I was sporting a cheerleader-style high ponytail and sweating from head to toe.

It was Luc.

He smiled his gorgeous smile and leaned in to give me a kiss on the cheek. Wow, in my drunken stupor, I must not have remembered how incredibly adorable he was.

"Hi, Luc," I greeted him in my cheeriest tone. I couldn't believe he was here. I wanted to make sure there were no traces of the damaged girl he'd taken care of a few nights before.

"Bonjour, Charlotte. You are feeling better?"

"Yes, much better. I'm so sorry about the other night. I had such a great time with you and your friends, and you were so sweet to take care of me like you did."

"*Pas de problème.* I am glad you are feeling better. I was wondering if you would like to come over for dinner this week. I am a very good...euh...how do you say...in the kitchen?"

"Cook? You're a good cook?"

"Yes, cook! I am a very good cook. You will let me cook for you?"

"Sure, that would be wonderful," I said as a memory of the last time Jeff had tried to cook for me flashed through my mind. I had walked into his apartment to find him wafting clouds of smoke out of the kitchen with an exasperated look on his face. Jeff was usually good at anything he set his mind to, but in the kitchen, he'd always been a complete disaster. I'd given him a hug before we both broke into uncontrollable laughter and Jeff reached for the phone to order us a pizza.

How could we have gone from so happy, so in love…to this?

"Tomorrow night at seven is good?" Luc's voice snapped me back to reality.

"Um, yeah, that sounds great."

"Okay, I see you then." And with two more *bisous*, my charming French neighbor was off. And while I should've been elated that this sweet, handsome guy actually wanted to spend more time with me, instead I felt empty and wondered if I would ever feel truly happy again. Luc was great, but there was only one man I wanted, and that man had broken my heart.

I logged back in to my blog to take my mind off Jeff. I had several more hits than last time, which gave me hope. How horrible that so many women were probably going through exactly what I was feeling right at that moment. I sent another mass e-mail to my girlfriends to remind them to check out my blog and to forward it along to women everywhere.

∼

As a follow-up to my last post, I have a few new lessons to share:

Rule # 1—French men couldn't care less if you make a fool out of yourself. Crying, desperate American women don't scare them one bit. So, ladies, if you're sick of being called "crazy" and "too emotional" by all of those American men, pack it up and move to France.

Case in Point: Half-Naked French Hottie just showed up at my door, only a couple of days after the drunken crying incident, to ask me over for dinner at his place later this week. Which brings me to my next lesson:

Rule # 2 — Do allow men to take you out on dates, cook for you, and dote on you. This is where we, women, have the upper hand. Why spend our own hard-earned cash when we could let the man pay for it? I say, make them pay! Because why the hell not?

Rule # 3 — Remember that when you are fresh out of a breakup, you will probably still think about your ex. A lot. I don't have a fool-proof remedy for making all of your memories of him disappear, but if you are charging ahead without him, making a life for yourself, and meeting new people, those heart-ripping thoughts should, over time, become fewer and farther between.

And, if all else fails, have a glass of wine (or two), call one of your girlfriends, and remember that he is the one who's missing out on the fabulous woman that you are.

～

Later that night, I headed out on my own to meet Lexi at Le Violin Dingue, a bar in the Latin Quarter. She told me that it had a good mix of Anglos and French guys and that the dance floor was wild. It sounded perfect—I was more than ready for a crazy night out on the town.

As I left the Fondation des États-Unis, I joined the large groups of international students herding down the sidewalk toward the RER station. Ahead of me, three bubbly young girls spoke Italian, and two skinny French guys, clad in tight jeans and white tennis shoes, eyed them up. I smiled to myself. Everyone here was so different from the polo-sporting, collar-popping preppy kids back in Georgetown. It was refreshing.

We waited at the crosswalk while the spiffy new tramway that ran down Boulevard Jourdan stopped and picked up a load of students. I crossed the street behind the Italian girls, admiring their long, silky black hair and the way they looked so confident, all dressed in their tight skirts and low-cut tops, excited for a wild night of study-abroad debauchery.

As I climbed into the red, white, and blue RER train that smelled of car exhaust and body odor, I squeezed into a free pocket of space and steadied myself against the metal railing until the bumpy train came to the Luxembourg stop.

On my way up the stairs, I breathed in the humid night air as I filed past the same two tight-jeans guys, who were now laughing like hyenas and shoving each other around.

"*Mademoiselle!*" I heard one of the boys shout in my direction.

I swiveled my head around to find them both staring at me with goofy grins.

"*Comme vous êtes sexy. Vous voulez coucher chez moi ce soir?*"

I took one last glimpse of their excruciatingly tight pants, and, instead of giving in to my urge to laugh, I shot them a look of disgust before making a beeline in the other direction.

To give DC *some* credit, the preppy, collar-popping boys back in Georgetown did not stop random girls in the street to tell them how sexy they were and ask them to spend the night.

I forgot all about the French boys' immature advances as soon as I had a chance to gaze around at the lively Parisian streets. I weaved past one of the leisurely cafés that lined Boulevard Saint-Michel and fixed my eyes on a group of four French women feasting on a meal of cheesy crêpes, colorful salads, and my favorite ham-and-cheese sandwich—the *croque-monsieur*. Across the street, a tall iron gate surrounded the Jardin du Luxembourg, and a group of high-school-aged girls and boys lingered at the entrance, tossing French slang and flirty glances at each other.

As I turned the corner onto rue Soufflot and spotted the towering Panthéon building at the end of the street, I realized

I'd been in such a jet-lagged haze over the past week that I'd barely left my dorm room. There was so much life in this city, so much excitement. I made a pact with myself right then and there that no matter how bad I felt about losing Jeff, I wouldn't waste my year in Paris by moping around by myself.

After performing a balancing act with my heels on the uneven cobblestone streets that wound past the Panthéon, I spotted Lexi smoking a cigarette and showing some leg underneath the blue-and-white awning of the bar. I felt cute in my favorite red strapless top, my dark skinny jeans, and my black strappy heels. But Lexi was dressed to the nines. She had on a short black skirt and a skimpy, metallic-blue tank top that showcased her outrageous cleavage. She definitely wasn't leaving much to the imagination.

Inside the smoky bar, Lexi led me downstairs, and we pushed our way through the crowded dance floor over to the bar, where we ordered two rum and cokes.

"So, have you heard from that scumbag ex-fiancé of yours since you got here?" She took a swig of her drink, then a puff of her cigarette.

"Nope, not a word."

"And you're not trying to get in touch with him, are you?"

"No way," I assured her.

"Good, because you don't want to look pathetic. And you don't want to be the one crawling back to him. I mean, you're in Paris, you're hot, and you're going to meet other guys, so you have nothing to worry about."

I surveyed the dance floor and didn't see anyone even remotely interesting. Oh, God, did I really have to play this game again? Dress up, try to impress some stupid guy at a bar, take him home, hook up, wake up, and do it all over again? What in the hell was I doing?

Then I thought of Brooke. Jeff having sex with Brooke

while I was wearing his ring. And suddenly, my motivation to go buck wild in Paris came roaring back.

"Wanna take a shot and get moving on this meeting-new-guys thing?" I asked her.

"Hell yeah, girl."

And with that, we ordered two shots of tequila, downed them like they were water, and hit the dance floor.

Not more than ten seconds after we started dancing, two decent-looking French guys made eyes at us from across the room, bolted across the dance floor, and started dancing with us. They were both superskinny (surprise, surprise) and had short, military-style haircuts. Lexi immediately gravitated toward the dark-haired one and wrapped her arms around him. The blond one closed in on me, gripped my waist, and pushed me farther into the center of the dance floor. I rested my arms on his bony shoulders and let all thoughts of the past week drift away as the alcohol numbed me.

After I danced with the random, nameless French guy for about two songs, he finally spoke to me.

"*Vous êtes française?*" he shouted into my ear. The bass was bumping so loud, it was hard to hear anything other than the music.

"*Non, je suis américaine.*"

"Oh, you speak zee English? You are...euh, how do you say...very pretty."

As I laughed at his typical corny response, he shouted, "You want a drink?"

He took my hand and led me over to the bar. For a split second, I remembered how Jeff had taken my hand and led me to the bar the night we first met. I didn't feel any butterflies this time, though.

We ordered two shots each and took them one right after the other. After the second shot, Nameless French Boy led me back out onto the dance floor so we could really start heating the place up. He slid his hands up and down my back as he pressed his body close to mine. I didn't even notice if he was a good dancer because those shots had hit me pretty hard. Before I knew it, his lips were on mine, and we were making out as if we were alone in my room and not in the middle of a crowded dance floor.

I caught a glimpse of Lexi and the other nameless French boy next to us. They were doing the exact same thing.

I wasn't sure how long the dancing and kissing continued, but it felt great to relax in another man's arms and forget about everything that had been happening.

At the end of the night, Nameless French Boy finally told me his name.

"Frédéric," he said with a grin. "And you?" he asked with his arms still wrapped around my waist.

"Charlotte," I stammered, giggling.

"I love zat name. So beauteeful. And you, you are so beauteeful too. Maybe we can see each other zis week?"

"Sure, when are you free?"

"Well, I am an officer of zee police, so I work at zee daytime. But maybe at night I can see you? I can have your phone number?"

After I scribbled my number on a napkin for Frédéric, he leaned down to give me one last passionate bar kiss. How romantic. I couldn't say I didn't enjoy it, though.

"I go to find my friend now...but I will miss you," Frédéric said as he looked down at me longingly. Then he wiped a fake tear out from under his eye and said almost incomprehensibly, "I tear without you."

I laughed out loud. Come on—*I tear*? What the hell was that supposed to mean? He was going to cry because he had to leave me?

"I'm sure you'll be okay, Freddy boy," I said as I grabbed his hand and led him over to the corner of the bar where Lexi and her French dude were still going at it pretty hot and heavy. It was definitely time to go home.

"Mm-hmm," Frédéric grunted, trying to get their attention.

Lexi disentangled herself from Frédéric's friend's lips and shot us a devious grin. If we had waited any longer to come over here, they probably would've been kicked out of the bar for indecent exposure. This dude looked like he was just dying to rip her clothes off.

"*On y va?*" Frédéric asked Lexi's new boy toy if he wanted to get going.

"*Ouais*," he answered reluctantly before he went in for another long, passionate kiss, much like the one Frédéric had just given me. Having already completed our make-out-and-dance session for the night, Frédéric and I shuffled around and surveyed the steamy bar for what seemed like an eternity while the horny lovebirds wrapped things up.

Finally, they came up for air, and the boys were off. A wave of exhaustion swept over me as Lexi and I headed for the door. My feet were killing me. It was time to go home and get some sleep.

"So, it looks like you had a pretty hot time. I told you that you had nothing to worry about," Lexi said as she put her arm around me. We laughed as we stumbled out of the bar and split a cab ride home.

The alcohol had worn off by the time I reached my dorm, and suddenly I wasn't feeling that tired anymore. I hated going home alone and trying to fall asleep by myself. While it had been fun to distract myself for the night with a new guy, the whole bar scene made me feel even more desperate and alone than I already felt. I missed home. I missed my friends. And most of all, I missed the feeling of security that I had felt with Jeff. But here I was, back in the singles scene again, back out at the bars, making out with random guys. Acting like I was in college. But what other choice did I have?

I glanced at myself in the mirror. My black eye makeup had smudged, my lipstick had worn off, and the circles under my eyes had grown to epic proportions. I looked like a drunken mess.

What in the hell was I doing?

I sat down at my computer, hoping to find some e-mails from home that could take away this empty, sickening feeling.

But there, at the top of my in-box, was an e-mail from Jeff.

SEVEN

samedi, le 2 octobre

When the ex comes knocking, lock your heart in a vault and don't answer the door.

Charlotte,

How are you? How are things in Paris? I hope you're okay. I miss you more than you can imagine. I wish you would've let me explain so we could've worked things out. Can you e-mail me your number over there so we can at least talk? I need you, Charlotte.

I love you,
Jeff

Patches of heat stung my face as I stared at the screen. What in the hell was he thinking? Did he forget that he'd *cheated on me*?

At the same time, I felt elated that he had written to me, that he missed me, that he still loved me. I loved him so much and just wanted to be with him, talk to him, feel his arms around me. Anything to make this emptiness go away.

And still, I was so furious with him. Furious at everything he had done and at his insensitive e-mail. I needed to move on and get over him, but reading his words on the screen made me want to fly back to DC and forget that any of this had ever happened.

I started typing.

Dear Jeff,
I miss you like crazy and I love you too. I'm coming home tomorrow. Let's just forget about everything and move on.
Love,
Charlotte

I read my e-mail over and over again, wanting to hit the Send button so that I could erase everything and go back to the way things used to be before he had hurt me so badly. But that's just it—he had hurt me, more than anyone had in my entire life, and I knew in my heart that there was no way I could move on and pretend it had never happened. I deleted my e-mail and started over.

Jeff,
After everything you've put me through, how can you expect me to want to talk to you? Please just leave me alone.
Charlotte

～

I woke up the next morning to the sound of my head pounding inside my skull. My mind raced to remember the night before. The shots, Frédéric, and as if I could forget, Jeff's e-mail. As soon as I remembered our e-mail exchange, I shot out of bed and turned on my computer to see if Jeff had replied.

Nothing. No response. I guess I *had* told him to leave me alone. Still, I was hoping for a response. I wanted Jeff to fight for me. To not take no for an answer. But there was nothing except the pounding inside my head and the silence in my lonely room greeting me when I awoke that morning.

I took an Aleve and downed two glasses of water while I gazed out my window at the tree-lined path behind my dorm. The leaves on the trees were just starting to change colors, making the view even more charming and beautiful than it already was. I was having a hard time appreciating it, though.

I had wanted to live and study in Paris for so long, and now here I was, feeling miserable and lonely in the most romantic city in the world. Plus, I'd already started off on the wrong foot with Madame Rousseau. I wanted to believe that she was a nice woman, that she'd recommend me to a wonderful school, and that a year from now I'd be happily teaching at my dream job in Paris. But after the stunt I'd pulled and the wreck of a phone conversation we'd had afterward, I wasn't too hopeful.

I checked the clock; it was already two p.m. I couldn't believe I had slept that late. I picked up my cell phone to see if I had missed any calls but saw that I had a text message instead. It was from a number I didn't recognize. It read:

I kissed you baby. I love the American girl. More kisses this week. I call you soon. Hope you had the good night.

I burst into laughter. No doubt it was from Frédéric. Nothing like a hilarious text message from a random French boy to brighten my mood. I immediately called Lexi.

"Hey, babe," Lexi said as she yawned into the phone. "I'm so hungover from last night, but it was totally worth it. That guy was such a sweet kisser. How are you?"

"I'm tired too. I just woke up, actually. Speaking of those

guys, I just got a text message from mine. Wait until you hear this."

I read her the message, and we both laughed hysterically into the phone.

"You better get used to it. I have a whole slew of absurd foreign-boy text messages saved on my phone. He was pretty hot, though. Are you going to see him again if he calls you?"

"I think so. He was a lot of fun, not that I remember too much. But I need all I can get right now, so I'm open to whatever."

"You definitely need some sexy man action after everything your ex just put you through. You poor thing, how are you holding up?"

"I'm doing okay for the most part, I guess. I have these moments where I miss him so much, and I just want to forget about everything and go back to him. But I know I can't do that, and I know things will be fine here." I lied just a little bit. I wasn't really sure if I'd be okay or if that gnawing feeling in my stomach would ever go away. But I did know that I couldn't go back to Jeff. I'd been known to hold a grudge or two, and cheating was one of the offenses I'd never been able to forgive. If I did go back to him, I'd hold it over his head forever.

"Yeah, honey," Lexi continued. "It's just going to take some time. Plus, you have me now, and we're going to tear things up in Paris, so don't you worry," she assured me.

"Thanks, Lexi. Hey, so what's the story with you and Benoît? Are you guys still dating?"

"Yeah, we're still seeing each other. It's not serious, though, and definitely not exclusive. I'm just not that kind of girl. I like to go out and have my fun, you know? There's no point in tying yourself down when shit happens like what just happened to you. No offense or anything."

"None taken. I totally agree. Men are pretty much good for sex and…well, that's about it!"

"You got it, girl. And, like I told you, that's the one thing that Benoît is extremely good at. I'm sure Luc isn't so bad himself."

"Really, you think he's good in bed?" I remembered then that I was supposed to go over to Luc's for dinner that night.

"Oh yeah, no doubt about it. Have you seen that ass? Get a move on it! It's obvious that he likes you."

"Well, he's cooking me dinner tonight. At least that will help me get my mind off everything."

"Well, there you go. It's in the bag. I gotta run, but keep me posted on how tonight goes, and let's definitely go out again soon. Talk to you later, Charlotte."

Lexi was a wild woman. Much wilder than Katie, or any of my other friends for that matter. But, a wild relationship-hater friend was just what I needed right now.

I thought about what Lexi had said about Luc. I wondered how she knew he was good in the sack. Probably just a rumor through mutual friends...but, it wouldn't have surprised me if she'd slept with him at one point. On the other hand, though, Lexi didn't really seem like Luc's type. Not that I knew him that well...or really at all. Oh well, it didn't matter. I needed to focus on having some fun with Luc tonight and moving on. Yes, Jeff and I had just broken up, but what was the point of sitting around and feeling sorry for myself when I knew I wasn't going to go back to him? I decided to get moving and start primping for my dinner with Luc that night. Before any of that, though, I had to sign in to my blog to share the latest.

I was surprised to see that I had five new comments. Three were from my friends, and two were from girls I didn't even know. All five of the women were right on board with my train of thought. A woman named Jill from Indiana had commented on my very first post:

"This is better than any self-help book. Keep the adventures flowing and the lessons coming. I'm sending this to all of my girlfriends. You're definitely on to something here. Can't wait to read more."

Another woman, K.T. from New York, wrote:

"I just found out that my boyfriend of six years has been sleeping with another woman for the past year. I'm devastated. One of my friends forwarded me your blog. I love this idea—dating like a man, but beating them at their own game. Count me in. You hang in there too—I know you must be hurting."

Inspired by my new online friends, I composed a new post:

Rule # 1 — Have no shame and treat it like a game.

Horny, drunk guys will approach almost any woman in a bar, give them a corny line, get shot down, and do it again. They clearly have no shame. Because to them, it's all a game of who they can score next.

We can do the same thing, ladies, but of course we'll do it with a finesse that men could never possess. Don't be afraid to talk to a cute guy in a bar. After all, if he disses you, he's not worth your time anyway. And remember, we don't care if we ever see him again. Put yourself out there to meet new guys, and don't expect any of them to be your Mr. Right. Who is that dude, anyway? I know I've never met him.

Rule # 2 — Resist all temptation to get back with sleazy exes.

To do this, you must follow lesson # 1 above. If you're sitting at home alone remembering all of the good old days, this is a perfect time for your nasty, cheating ex to sneak up on you and attack. This is dangerous.

You must be meeting other men to counteract an attack of this sort. Because, believe me, after those cheaters have had a little bit of time to sit with the weight of their actions, they will come crawling right back to you, begging for mercy.

Don't. Give. In.

Rule # 3 — Protect your heart at all costs.

After you've put your ex in his place, you may still secretly hope he will continue fighting for you. In these moments of desperation, remember that he was the one who chose to give you up when he cheated, and that even though you are hurting more than you ever thought possible, protecting your heart should be your number-one priority. Don't let him or your overwhelming emotions convince you otherwise.

EIGHT

samedi, le 2 octobre

Always bring a to-go box on a dinner date—you never know if you'll have to flee the scene.

At seven o'clock on the dot, I was ready to go. I had thrown together a casual but sexy outfit. I was wearing my favorite dark jeans paired with a pretty light-pink tank that showed off my cleavage. No need for modesty at this point. It was time to go for it.

I walked the five steps down the hall to Luc's place and knocked on the door. A whiff of butter and tomato sauce wafted past me as his smiling face appeared in the doorway.

"*Salut, Charlotte,*" he said sweetly as he kissed my cheeks.

Oh, my gosh, Luc is so incredibly gorgeous. Maybe we can just skip dinner?

"*Salut, Luc,*" I said as I returned the kisses.

Luc's place was much roomier than mine. It was more like a studio apartment than a teeny dorm room. He had it sectioned off into two separate spaces: a living room with a couch and a small kitchen table, and then a bedroom area with a real bed (not a plastic cot mattress like the one I had). The bare walls and limited color scheme screamed bachelor pad, but it was clean and comfortable, and it smelled of basil, garlic, and Luc's cologne. I liked it.

He poured me a glass of red wine and led me over to his miniature kitchen table to have a seat. He had made a dish of linguine, fresh tomatoes, and mozzarella, a colorful salad, and of course, a baguette. I was impressed. Most men had no idea what they were doing in the kitchen.

"This looks delicious," I said as I took in the smell of the meal. "I love Italian food."

"You do? You like zee, euh, pasta? I am so happy because I did not know what you liked, but I thought to myself today, this…this will be good." He raised his glass and clinked it with mine as he flashed a warm smile my way. He was such a sweet guy, not at all cocky or pretentious. I couldn't have asked for a better rebound after my broken-engagement disaster.

"So, Charlotte, you have lived in France before?"

"Yeah, I lived with a host family in Lyon for a semester in college."

"Really? I have family in Lyon. It is beautiful there, is it not?"

"I loved every minute of it. I can't wait to go back and visit this year…but I'm not sure when I'll be able to go. This whole being-a-poor-student thing doesn't really lend to traveling around Europe."

"I know. I am a poor student too. I'm getting my master's degree in education right now. I want to be a teacher, like you. That is the only reason why I live here in the dorm."

"You'll love teaching, and I'm sure you'll be really great at it. I did think you looked a little old to be living in a dorm, though," I poked at him.

"Hey, hey. Well, yes, I guess I am kind of old."

"How old are you?" I asked as I savored a bite of linguine and basil.

"I am twenty-nine. I will be thirty in March. And you?"

"Haven't you learned that rule? You can never ask a woman how old she is."

"That is a silly rule. Come on, tell me."

"I know, I'm just kidding. I think it's silly too. I'm twenty-five."

"You are so young. Only twenty-five?"

"What, did you think I was a lot older or something?"

"No, no, it's just that life was so different at twenty-five." Luc stared off in the distance for a second.

"What were you doing when you were twenty-five?" I asked him, curious to find out what he was thinking about.

"Euh...well, I was living in a nice apartment in the sixth arrondissement, working in finance, and making a lot of good money."

"Sounds like fun. I bet you were going out a lot too— probably a heartbreaker," I flirted as I took a sip of my plum-flavored wine.

"Actually, no, that was not the case." Luc shifted uncomfortably in his chair.

"No?" I was curious to see where this was heading.

"No, I was married."

Now, there's a conversation stopper. I wasn't sure what to say to that. But, of course, being a girl, I wanted to know the *whole* story.

"Oh, really?"

"Yes." Luc's eyes darted around the room, avoiding my glance.

"Did...are you...still married?" I thought I'd throw that question out there just in case.

"*Mais, non.* Of course not."

Of course not, because all marriages end in divorce, that's why.

"Right. So, how long have you been on your own?"

Luc got up from the table to grab the bottle of wine. "*Un peu plus?*"

"Sure, thank you."

"Enough about me. How do you like Paris?" he asked as he filled up my glass. Guess he didn't want to talk about it anymore.

It didn't look like I'd be getting any more juicy information out of Luc for the night. Even though I wanted to know every little detail (Like who is your ex-wife? Where does she live? Why did you get a divorce? Was it your fault or hers?), I had to remind myself that I wasn't here to get involved with him. I was here to date and have fun. So, just because my instinct was to grill him (or to run for the hills), I relaxed back in my chair, enjoyed my second glass of wine, and continued our discussion.

"It's been a little hard adjusting, but I think I'm really going to like—"

Luc's phone interrupted me. He checked the number on the screen, scrunched up his eyebrows exactly as he had done the other night at the bar, and said "*Excuse-moi, Charlotte*, I have to answer this." He bolted out into the hallway, leaving me alone in his room.

What in the hell was going on with this dude? First he tells me that he used to be married, then he jets out for another mysterious phone call. I wondered if he was, in fact, single?

I surveyed the room to see if I could find any evidence of another woman. It was totally fine with me if he was seeing other people since I was on a strict no-relationship policy, but I was annoyed that he needed to take calls while we were having a nice dinner. I walked around his room looking for clues but found nothing. Maybe he wasn't talking to another woman, but then why couldn't he take the call in here? Or better yet, hit the Ignore button and call back later?

After a few minutes, I inched closer to the door to see if I could hear him talking in the hallway. I heard his muffled voice speaking quickly in French, and he didn't sound happy. I couldn't make out what he was saying, though, and I didn't want to wait at the door like a crazy woman in case he came back in.

Ten minutes later, Luc resurfaced with an exasperated look on his face.

"Is everything okay?" I asked him as he reached for his wine glass and took a huge gulp.

"Yes, yes, everything is fine," he said unconvincingly.

"Do you want to talk about it?"

"No, everything is fine," he said more forcefully this time. "But I have to go."

"You have to go?"

"Yes, I am sorry. I have to leave now. But thank you for coming to dinner. I hope you liked the pasta. We can talk more next time."

I hadn't even finished my pasta. I wondered if he'd let me take it in a to-go box.

"Oh...okay," I responded as I began clearing the plates off the table.

"It's okay, I will clean later. I really have to go."

"Sorry, okay. Well, thanks for dinner. I guess I'll see you around."

Luc opened the door for me, and instead of a long night of mind-blowing French sex, he gave me two *bisous* on the cheeks and ushered me out.

Back in my room, I plopped down on my bed in confusion. This was *exactly* why I would not get hung up him or any other man.

NINE

lundi, le 4 octobre

Nothing goes better with sex than a hot French man feeding you chocolate.

On Monday I had my first class at the Sorbonne. Even though I had studied at a French university in Lyon during my semester of study abroad, Georgetown had put the program together, so I'd had a team of people helping me navigate through the disorganized French university system.

Today, though, my stomach knotted up at the thought of going to a foreign university totally alone. No one was here to guide me through my study-abroad experience this time around…well, except for Madame Rousseau, and I wasn't sure how much help she was going to be after I'd thoroughly pissed her off.

My palms were sweaty and my heart pounded as I exited the RER train at the Luxembourg stop and headed north on Boulevard Saint-Michel. I was set to take courses at the Université de la Sorbonne Nouvelle, Paris III, in their Enseignement du FLE (Français Langue Étrangère) program, which was centered on learning how to teach French as a foreign language. There are tons of universities scattered around Paris, but this one is in a prime location. Situated between the Jardin du Luxembourg and the Panthéon in the fifth arrondissement, it's just a short walk away from the Seine and Notre Dame Cathedral and only a few blocks from the wild bar that Lexi had taken me to on Friday night.

I took a right onto rue Soufflot, the same street I'd taken on my way to the bar, but found the mood in the Latin Quarter to be much different in the daytime. Professionals and students wound through the streets with newspapers and baguettes tucked under their arms. Gone were the aggressive groups of French guys, flirting with every girl that walked past. Parisians sat alone at sidewalk cafés, sipping their tiny cups of French espresso and nibbling on fluffy croissants.

As I passed by a *boulangerie* and breathed in the sweet smell of freshly baked French bread, I tilted my head up to the blue fall sky and felt myself calm down. I was in Paris, the most beautiful city in the world, on my way to do what I'd been dreaming about doing for so long. It was time to let the nervousness go and enjoy the moment.

I continued toward the massive Panthéon building, then turned left down rue Saint-Jacques. A couple of short blocks down the street, I found two armed police officers guarding the entrance to the department where I was supposed to take all of my courses. At least I thought this was my department. What was with the huge guns?

I double-checked the sheet of paper where I'd jotted down the address. Forty-six rue Saint-Jacques. This was it. I smiled as I approached the guards.

"*Carte d'étudiant, s'il vous plaît,*" the shorter one stated with a blank expression on his face.

They wanted me to show them my student ID card for the Sorbonne, but there was one tiny glitch. I didn't have one yet.

And how would I get one if they wouldn't let me into the building in the first place?

I rummaged through my bag and pulled out my DC driver's license.

The taller guard eyed it suspiciously. *"Vous n'avez pas votre carte d'étudiant?"*

"Pas encore. Je suis désolée, Monsieur," I responded.

After apologizing and letting them know that I didn't have one yet, I smiled my sweetest, most innocent smile, and the straight-faced police officers let me pass. Whew.

As I wound my way up three rickety flights of stairs, I thought back to my study-abroad days in Lyon. There had never been armed officers guarding the doorways at the universities there. How bizarre.

I peeked into the classroom and was relieved to see that I was the first one to arrive. I took a seat at one of the long wooden tables, and as I was pulling my notebook out of my bag, a superskinny girl with shoulder-length light-brown hair and big green eyes walked into the room and sat down next to me. She glanced over, giving me a shaky smile.

"Bonjour," I said, smiling warmly. *"Je m'appelle Charlotte, et vous?"*

"Je suis Fiona...Do you speak English by any chance?" she asked in a strong British accent.

"Yeah—"

"Oh, thank God!" The tension left her face as she breathed a heavy sigh of relief.

"I'm really nervous, are you?" I asked Fiona, feeling immediately comfortable with her.

"Yes!" she whispered as her eyes darted around the classroom. "I just got to Paris last week, and I'm here all alone, and I was totally freaked out about coming to this class by myself."

"I was too," I commiserated. "I've studied in France before, but that was with my study-abroad program in college, so I was with a bunch of friends. I've never done this on my own."

"Same here. Are you taking all FLE courses here this semester?"

"Yeah, I am. I taught French for the past few years at a high school in DC, but I just wanted to advance a little, you know?"

"Definitely. I taught for about two years out of university, then went back to get my master's in French and had the option of coming over here to take some classes that will count toward my degree. But no one else in my program ended up coming over at the same time as me, so I'm totally alone here."

"At least we have each other now," I said. "Do you want to grab a coffee after class?"

"Sure, sounds great." Fiona smiled back as the professor entered the room and started class. "Here we go," she said, giggling a little under her breath.

The class had filled up with what seemed to be a mix of French students (I could tell they were French when they pulled out their nifty pencil cases), a few English speakers, and other students from all different countries. I started to relax. This is what I wanted to do, and I was finally here doing it. Screw Jeff. I didn't need him here to have a good time.

The professor was a petite French woman who spoke slowly and deliberately. She seemed nice but stern, and she didn't waste any time getting down to business. I could tell I was going to like her class a lot.

Fiona and I spent the majority of the class scribbling down notes like crazy, which made the hours whiz by. I understood everything the professor said, which made me relax even more. Teaching French at the high school level didn't necessarily mean that I was sharpening my advanced speaking and listening skills on a daily basis. I was teaching a lot of "hello, my name is, how are you, where are you from?" type stuff. So, it was comforting to realize that I hadn't totally lost my ability to understand what was going on in an advanced French class.

After class, Fiona and I strolled back over to Boulevard Saint-Michel and took a seat at a quaint little café called Paul.

"Un café, et un pain au chocolat s'il vous plaît," I ordered.

"Un pain au chocolat et un café pour moi aussi," Fiona added.

"Oh, man, gotta love the *pain au chocolat!*" I let out a giggle.

"Seriously, I haven't stopped eating them since I got here," Fiona said as she relaxed back in her seat.

"So, you're from England, right?" I asked her.

"Mm-hmm. Liverpool originally, then moved to London for uni. I taught for a few years at a dreadful high school in the city, then got dumped by my boyfriend of five years for another woman, and that's when I realized my life was total and complete shit. So, I quit my job and went back to school for my master's. Life's still been crap without him, but I'm hoping Paris will be better. God, you didn't even ask all that, did you? You just wanted to know if I was from England, so to answer your question, yes, I am." Fiona's cheeks blushed as she let out a nervous laugh.

"Don't worry. I completely understand." I briefly filled Fiona in on the online dating debacle.

"Oh, God, that's *awful.* I can't believe that all just happened to you last week. Andrew broke up with me a year ago and I'm still a pathetic mess. I can't even imagine how you must be feeling."

"Yeah, sad, pathetic, and pissed off pretty much sums it up. But I'm keeping a blog to reach out to other women who are going through the same thing." I was eager to change the subject—Jeff didn't deserve any more of my attention.

"Sounds like something I should read. I haven't had the energy to even go on a date since the bastard dumped me.

Even though he was awful, I always find myself comparing everyone to him."

"We're going to have to get you back out there. I just met another girl here, Lexi, and we had a lot of fun going out last weekend, plus we met some pretty cute guys. You'll have to come out with us soon."

"I'm not too big on the bar scene...but yeah, I guess I do need to get out and meet some people. It'd be a shame to come to Paris and keep my head in the books the whole time." Fiona's shoulders relaxed as she gave me a warm smile.

She definitely needed to read my blog. I made a mental note to send her the link later that night. After a year, she was still hung up on her ex. So help me God if I was still pining over Jeff in a year.

We sipped our *cafés* together and devoured our buttery croissants filled with melted dark chocolate while we chatted some more. After talking with Fiona, it became clear that she was much more innocent and reserved than me or Lexi in the man department, but she was sweet and supportive. I definitely empathized with her on the whole breakup issue. Granted, we seemed to have different coping methods, but we both understood what it felt like to get our hearts broken, and that made for a strong connection.

"Do you have any plans this afternoon?" I asked her.

"No, not really. You're the first person I've met here, so my social life is pretty nonexistent at this point," she joked.

"Do you want to take a stroll around the city? I haven't explored at all since I got in last week. Between adjusting to the time zone, trying to get over my breakup, and going out, I haven't made any time for it."

"That sounds great. Where to?"

"Want to walk down the river for a bit?"

"Perfect."

As we headed up Boulevard Saint-Michel toward the

Seine, we ended up at Place Saint-Michel, where Luc and I had gotten off the train on my first night in Paris. I spotted the yellow awnings of the Gibert Jeune bookstores again while delicious aromas of cheese, bread, chocolate, and coffee wafted out of the crowded sidewalk cafés. We took a left, dodged the never-ending groups of fanny-pack-sporting tourists, and headed down the quai des Grands Augustins, taking in the view of the sun beating down on the sparkling river and passing by one of the famous bridges in Paris, the Pont Neuf.

We continued along the *quai* for a little while, chatting the whole time, and soon reached the Pont des Arts, a delightful little pedestrian bridge that stretches across the Seine and leads to the Louvre.

"God, I love it here," Fiona said as we strolled along the bridge, admiring the artwork on display. "I mean, where else in the world could we admire outdoor art after stuffing ourselves with chocolate-filled croissants?"

"Nowhere," I responded.

And that's when it hit me—I was in Paris. Paris!

I had wanted to move back to France for so long, and I was finally here. When I'd arrived the week before, I was so afraid that all I would have the energy to do was to hole up in my room and cry over Jeff. What would've even been the point of coming here if I'd continued on that pathetic streak? My stroll around Paris that afternoon made me remember why I loved France so much and why this was the right decision—no matter how distraught I was over my broken engagement.

Fiona and I talked our way all the way down the river to La Tour Eiffel. As I marveled at the impressive structure, a feeling of bubbly excitement came over me. I couldn't have cared less that the French thought it was tacky—it made me feel like a little girl at a carnival.

We crossed the Seine and walked underneath the tower to

the Champ de Mars, an immense field packed with tourists and locals eating and reading in the sun. We found an open spot on the grass, stretched out on the lawn, and stared up at the deep-blue sky and the fluffy white clouds that brushed the top of the Eiffel Tower as they floated by. As I was enjoying the view, I heard my phone beep. I dug it out of my purse and was surprised to see that I had a text message from Luc. It read:

Want to watch movie tonight?

I didn't have anything else going on that night, and despite his sketchy behavior, I found myself still wanting to hang out with him. He was so damn handsome—just the thought of his sweet smile and his sexy five o'clock shadow gave me butterflies. Plus, I needed to collect more stories for my blog readers. So, really, I had to say yes.

I wrote back: *Sure, what time?*

Luc wrote back quickly: *19h, I bring Netflix.*

Excited, I texted back: *Sounds good, see you then.*

Fiona had fallen asleep in the grass, so she didn't notice my text exchange. I could always tell her about Luc later on. I didn't want my new friend to get the wrong impression of me —fresh out of an engagement and already hanging out with a new guy on my first week in Paris—a divorced guy at that. Not that anything had even happened, since he kept answering his damn phone. Hopefully tonight would be different.

~

At seven o'clock, Luc knocked on my door. He greeted me with the usual *bisous* and then handed me a huge bar of chocolate.

"You like *le chocolat*, right?" he asked sweetly.

"Of course. Thank you, that's so thoughtful."

"No problem. I...euh...bring...brought my laptop so we can watch Netflix."

"Perfect."

I poured us each a glass of red wine, and then we tried to make ourselves comfortable on my hard cot thingy.

After Luc started up his computer, he grabbed my hand and said, "Listen, Charlotte, I am sorry for the other night. I was rude, and I want to apologize."

"It's no problem at all. I know that things can come up. It's no big deal, really."

"Yes, I know, it's just that..." Luc gazed down at his wine, then back up at me with a serious expression on his face. "I wanted to spend more time with you, and I really like you... so there is something I want to tell you."

Oh no. Not this. Was he going to tell me he wanted to be in a relationship? Was he going to tell me he was still married? Whatever it was, I didn't want to hear it. I was here to have fun. To meet charming, good-looking men and have my way with them. I was *not* here to have a serious discussion.

So, instead of giving him time to spit out whatever it was that was bothering him, I leaned over and gave him the most passionate kiss I had in me. I could tell he was taken aback at first, but he soon got over it and returned the favor.

"But, Charlotte." He pulled back, trying to continue the talk.

"Shhh," I said as I placed my finger firmly on his lips. "You don't need to worry about anything." I leaned in to kiss him again and felt his body relax into mine. Guys are so easy to distract.

After enjoying the feel of his soft lips on mine for a few minutes, I pulled back and looked him intently in the eye. "So, Luc, I hear that you may be good in bed. Is this a true statement?" I wasn't going to let any phone calls get in the way of our night this time.

He laughed and responded, "Well, that depends. Who told you this?"

"Oh, no one important...just something I may have heard recently," I said as I shot him a flirty smile.

"Well, I would have to say that I am very good in the bedroom." He grinned from ear to ear.

"I think you'll have to prove it."

Thankful that I had diverted Luc from "the talk," and delighted to have a hot French man in my bed, I let Luc remove my tank top and jeans, while I all but tore his T-shirt over his head, then pulled his pants to the ground.

Luc stopped for a moment and gave me his most devious smile. "You are sure you want to find out if I am good in the bed, as you say?"

I laughed at his adorable accent. "Yes, I want to know. Right now," I said as I yanked on his boxers.

Luc slipped off my underwear and unhooked my bra with the ease of a professional, while I, much less gracefully, pulled off his boxers. Then he reached down into his jeans pocket and pulled out a condom. But instead of putting it on right away, he laid it on the stand and wrapped me up in his tan, lean body. He caressed my breasts with his strong hands while he kissed my neck, sending tingles down my spine. Then, he knelt over me and kissed me firmly on the lips as his hands roamed down my stomach and still farther down until he made me quiver with pleasure. Suddenly, I couldn't take it anymore. I wanted him. I reached over for the condom and shoved it into his hands. He grinned at me, rolled over on his side, and as soon as I had caught my breath, he was back on top and inside me.

Goose bumps ran down the entire length of my body as he continued kissing every spare inch of my bare skin. He grabbed my hands and held them over my head as he moved forcefully over the top of me. Then he flipped me over on top of him and ran his hands over the curves of my hips and up to my breasts as he let me slide slowly up and down.

Lexi hadn't been lying. This man definitely knew what he was doing.

It was more than that, though. There was something different about the way he touched me. The way he gazed into my eyes. An intensity. A spark I'd never felt before.

I wasn't sure if it was just his smooth French-man moves, or if our connection was unique, but either way, Luc got me so worked up that I had an orgasm after only a few minutes. He kept going, moving me into all different positions, each with the purpose of pleasing me as much as possible, all the while holding me, kissing me, and moving so deeply into me, I couldn't help but surrender to the intensity of the moment.

After the second orgasm sent me through the roof, I was spent. I lay down on my back and let him work his magic. He pressed his glistening body deep into mine as he tenderly kissed my neck, and then my lips. He wrapped me up in his arms as his breathing intensified, and suddenly, I felt him pulsating inside of me. A groan escaped from his lips before his breathing slowed down, and he collapsed on top of me.

We lay in bed together breathing heavily until Luc interrupted the silence.

"I did not expect that," he grinned slyly at me.

"Sure," I teased him.

"I didn't, really, Charlotte."

"I'm just joking."

"So you liked?" he asked.

"Yes, I liked." I giggled.

Luc reached over and grabbed the bar of Lindt milk chocolate he had given me. "*Un peu de chocolat?*"

"Chocolate, after sex?" I asked, a little puzzled, even though it did sound wonderful.

"Why not? Sex, chocolate, all good things," he responded as he peeled open the wrapping.

"Okay, why not." I couldn't argue—sex and chocolate *were* two of my favorite things.

So my new French lover and I lay naked in bed and savored square after square of the creamiest, softest, milkiest chocolate I'd ever tasted.

These French guys really knew what they were doing.

As I was eating my fourth square of chocolate, my phone beeped. I rolled over and discreetly checked it to find a text message from Frédéric. It read:

Can't stop thinking about you, American girl. Friday night, I take you to dinner? Bisous, Frédéric.

"You got a message?" Luc asked as he peered over my shoulder.

I tossed the phone down, hoping he hadn't seen it. "Yeah, it's from one of the girls I became friends with at school."

"Frédéric is a girl?" he asked as he looked at me suspiciously.

Damn. Why did I have to go and look at my phone right after having amazing sex? Stupid, stupid, stupid.

"Oh, it's nothing. It's just a friend from school," I mumbled.

"Oh, I see." He obviously didn't believe me. But, what was I supposed to do? Tell him the truth after he just gave me two orgasms? *He* was the one taking weird phone calls all the time *and* he used to be married. He could have ten other women right now for all I knew, so I didn't need to feel defensive about getting a simple text message.

In an attempt to distract him, I fed him another square of chocolate and asked if he wanted to stay the night. He seemed hesitant at first, but with a little coercion (in the form of another sexy make-out session and a couple more glasses of wine), he seemed to forget all about the text message.

∼

In the middle of the night, I woke up feeling sweaty and uncomfortable from being stuffed in my tiny bed with Luc draped all over me.

Still buzzed from the excessive amount of wine I had drunk, I stumbled out of bed and decided to check my e-mail. I found one from Katie and a few others from friends, but still nothing from Jeff. I pulled up the oh-so-polite e-mail I had sent to him a few days back. As I read it over a few times, a rip-roaring vengeance swept over me. So, in my half-asleep, drunken state, I composed another one.

> *Jeff,*
> *I just wanted you to know that I have a handsome, sexy French man in my bed at this very moment. Besides being attractive and sweet, he is AMAZING in bed…much better than you ever were. We had sex three times tonight, in fact.*
> *Just wanted you to know how it feels.*
> *Your ex-fiancée,*
> *Charlotte*

Okay, so maybe three times was an exaggeration, but what the hell. Without hesitation, I hit the Send button and off went my bitter e-mail to Jeff. Immature? Maybe. But did it feel good? Oh yes, it did.

I signed on to my blog and found that my hits were rising, and several more women had commented. How exciting. I began composing a new post:

Rule # 1—Avoid all serious "talks" with men who you are just having fun with. Think of the last time you told a man, "We need to talk." Do you remember the expression on his face? How he looked like he'd rather jump off a twenty-story building to his imminent death than sit there trapped in a "talk" with you?

In our new method of dating like a man, the same thing applies to us, ladies. Since we're not looking for love, there is no need to have serious talks with guys we're seeing. The less you know, the better.

But you don't want to seem heartless either. We are sweet, caring women, after all. In the following example, I will show you how I successfully distracted a man from having "the talk" with me earlier tonight, without acting like a heartless bitch.

Case in Point: After telling me he used to be married, then ditching me halfway through our date after another sketchy phone call, Half-Naked French Hottie came over tonight to redeem himself. Just as we were about to enjoy a movie, he apologized for the other night, then proceeded to say that he had something to tell me.

A few possibilities ran through my mind. He's still married. He has a girlfriend. Or, even worse, he wants to start a relationship. We've only hung out twice before this, so the relationship talk seems premature, but who knows? I am in a foreign country.

Whatever he had to say was irrelevant, though. I'm here to have fun, remember? Not to get into a relationship, have serious talks about issues, and become all emotionally involved.

So, to shut him up without making him feel bad, I kissed him. Which brings me to my next rule:

Rule # 2 — Do have mind-blowing sex with no strings attached, and then eat chocolate immediately afterward. Who cares if you gain a few pounds? It's all about pleasure here, ladies.

Think about it. What motivates a man's every decision? Pleasure. That's all they're looking for. They'll have a beer when they feel like it. They'll have a great night of sex whenever they want (or whenever they can get it). They'll sit around in their underwear scratching their balls, just because they can.

We women, on the other hand, are always in the pursuit of love. But, as we throw our hearts on the line, guys are just wondering when they'll get their next lay.

So, I am calling on each and every one of you to make a dramatic shift in your thought process. Remember this: pleasure just for the sake of pleasure is a good thing. We don't need to be madly in love with a guy to have amazing sex and feel satisfied. In fact, it's quite the opposite. If we're not worried about what happens after the sex, the sex is more fun, more carefree, and definitely more orgasmic. Plus, if we don't care about the next-day callback, we can eat a big fat chocolate bar in bed with our hot new catch and not feel bad about it one bit.

And just in case you're all wondering, Half-Naked French Hottie is currently sleeping in my bed, after having hot sex and sharing a bar of scrumptious chocolate. See, all that and no dreadful "talk" was necessary. What could be better?

This brings me to my final lesson of the night:

Rule # 3—After being cheated on, there's nothing like a little revenge to lift a girl's spirits. If you need to experience the sweet taste of revenge in your efforts to get over your ex and move on to bigger and better things (no pun intended), go for it. Granted, it won't erase the pain or the hurt he caused you, but trust me, it will make you feel a hell of a lot better.

TEN

mardi, le 5 octobre

Smiling won't get you very far with a French woman.

When my alarm buzzed at six o'clock the next morning, I sent Luc back to his room and hurried to get ready for my appointment with Madame Rousseau. There was no way I would mess up another meeting with her. I was hoping that by being early and by telling her how dedicated I was to this program, she would forgive me for standing her up and actually turn out to be a nice person. One could only hope.

As I crossed the street to get to the train, masses of students were exiting the station and cursing. What the hell was going on? I pushed through the crowds to the message screen inside only to find out that there was a *grève*, otherwise known as a strike. The French were famous for their *grèves*, as I remembered all too well from my semester in Lyon. Back then, though, the transportation strikes were a great excuse to skip class. But today of all days? *Seriously*?

The transportation workers were striking for the entire

day, so the only way to get up to the Sorbonne would be by cab. I checked my wallet to see if I had any cash on me, and of course, I didn't. I sprinted back across the street to the student center ATM, waited in line behind one unbelievably slow Spanish student, withdrew some euros and ran back out to Boulevard Jourdan to hail a cab. Everyone else had the same idea, though, so it didn't look promising. I jogged down to the corner to get away from the masses, and after showing a little leg, I snagged one. Sometimes it helps to be a girl.

As we wound in and out of the busy Parisian streets, I checked my watch. I had twenty minutes to get there. I would make it on time. I would. I closed my eyes and willed the traffic to be clear.

The cab pulled up in front of the Sorbonne at exactly seven fifty-eight a.m. I thrust the bills into the driver's hands and bolted up the stairs.

With their massive guns in tow, the same two police officers stood guard at the entrance. I'd forgotten to get a student ID card the day before, so I handed them my driver's license, hoping they would let it slide once more.

The taller one shook his head at me, but his expression remained blank. It made me want to scream. I *could not* be late.

I explained to them in French that I was terribly sorry, and that I would be sure to get my student ID today. I told them that I had an important meeting at eight a.m., and that I absolutely had to be on time.

By the time they let me through, I had less than ten seconds to fly up those wobbly stairs or take the minuscule, ancient elevator that was already packed with too many students. I opted for the stairs.

I had seen Madame Rousseau's office after my class the day before, so thankfully I knew where to go. I arrived at her door at eight a.m. on the dot, out of breath, with beads of sweat pouring down my face. But, hey, I was on time.

I knocked on her door as I wiped my brow with my forearm. No response. I waited a few seconds and knocked again, a little harder this time. Still no response.

Then, I heard a set of high heels clanking down the hallway. I turned to see a miniature gray-haired woman marching toward me. She wore a black turtleneck paired with a long black skirt, and she had her hair pulled back into the tightest bun known to man—so tight that the corners of her eyes were actually stretching to accommodate the pull of the bun. I didn't even have to ask—*this* was Madame Rousseau.

Without smiling, she locked eyes with me, walked right in front of me, unlocked her door, then closed it in my face.

What was I supposed to do with that?

I waited a second or two, then knocked again.

A full five minutes later, she opened the door, peered down at her watch, and in a flat tone said, "*Vous êtes en retard.*" *You're late.*

Was this woman for real? First of all, I wasn't late. And second of all, since when were the French so keen on timeliness?

I walked into her tiny but pristine office and noticed the rows upon rows of French pedagogy books packed into the bookshelf above her desk. She motioned for me to sit down as she took a seat at her desk.

"So, *you* are Charlotte Summers," she scowled in French.

"Yes, thank you so much for meeting with me today, Madame Rousseau. You have no idea how honored and excited I am to be a part of this program."

"Yes, well, we will have to work on your timeliness, won't we?" She tapped her pen on the desk and peered at her watch once more.

"I'm terribly sorry about last week. My plane—"

"I do not have time for this, Mademoiselle Summers. Let us discuss the program and what will be expected of you. As you know, I am the professor appointed to help you find a teaching position after you complete your year of study at *la Sorbonne*. But, this is not to say that it will be so easy. You must prove yourself this year. Not only academically, but you must show yourself to be of good character and of sound judgment. I work with some of the most prestigious, elite private schools in Paris, and it is my responsibility to make sure that the teachers I place in these schools are not *stupide*, but rather outstanding, brilliant role models for these young children. *Vous comprenez?*"

"Yes, I totally understand."

"You will meet with me two or three times each semester to go over your progress, and you will turn in copies of your final papers to me as well as to your professors. I will personally monitor your work, and if I see fit, I will recommend you to one of the private schools in Paris. And trust me, Mademoiselle Summers, the schools look very highly on my recommendation. Without it, well…*bonne chance*." Madame Rousseau stood abruptly, opened her door, and gestured for me to leave. "I have class in twenty minutes. We will meet in December, at which time I expect you to turn in your final papers. You must contact me by e-mail to schedule the meeting."

"Thank you so much for meeting with me today," I said as she ushered me out of her office.

Just as she was about to close the door, she peeked her tight little face out and shot me her sternest look yet. "And Mademoiselle Summers, when we meet in December, I expect you to be here fifteen minutes early." With that, she closed the door in my face, and I stood there wondering how in the hell I was ever going to make this woman like me.

∽

During my first week of classes, Frédéric sent me three more hilarious text messages, but I didn't hear a word from Luc, nor did I hear from Jeff after the ruthless e-mail I had sent him. While I couldn't help but admit that I was disappointed Luc hadn't called or stopped by after our great night of sex, it was Jeff who I couldn't get off my mind.

I had so many mixed emotions swimming around in my head. I wanted to see his reaction when he read my e-mail. I wanted to see the pain on his face. I wanted to know that I had hurt him as badly as he had hurt me. Then I wondered if I *had* even hurt him. If he was able to run around on me so easily, did he even care what I was doing now?

On the other hand, I did think there was a slight chance that Jeff still cared for me or he wouldn't have written that e-mail begging to talk to me. Maybe I should've agreed to talk to him. Maybe he could've explained things so that we could at least be friends.

I tried to envision Jeff and myself as friends. We weren't the kind of couple who had, in addition to being lovers, become best friends over the course of our relationship. I always assumed that would happen later on as we matured as a couple. After all, we hadn't even been together a full year, and for most of that time, we were still in that lovey-dovey, sickening stage that made our friends want to vomit. But, as I imagined what it would be like to be friends with Jeff now, in the aftermath of our breakup, only a few key images came to mind: Jeff telling me over the phone what a phenomenal lover Brooke is, then me screaming, "Bastard!" into the phone and throwing it across the room...or even better, Jeff introducing me to Brooke, and me pulling her hair out while kicking Jeff in the balls.

No, it didn't look like the whole "friend" thing would work out after all.

I wasn't capable of being friends with him at this point, and I probably never would be. The hurt was too deep. At times, I felt like I couldn't breathe without him. The only thing that made me feel better was to keep busy and to not think about the whole disaster.

~

Late Thursday night, while I was sitting alone in my room, wishing I could be with Jeff at that very moment, the phone rang. It was Katie.

"Hey, lady!"

"Hey, Katie, what's up?"

"I don't have long to talk because I'm on my way to the hospital for my superdepressing ICU rotation, but I just wanted to tell you my news."

"Good news, I hope."

"Yes, very good." She took a long pause. "I met a guy."

"You met someone? Where? When? Give me the details."

"Well, I met him during my ob/gyn rotation, of all things."

"Oh, my gosh, don't even tell me he's a gynecologist."

"Yep, you got it."

"That's hilarious...I mean, not to be immature about it, but doesn't it bother you that he's staring at other women's judies all day?" Back in high school, Katie and I had coined the term "judy" as an alternative to all the other vulgar expressions referring to the female anatomy. However immature, the name stuck throughout the years...until I met Jeff's mom, who, as it would happen, was named Judy.

I got a hard laugh out of Katie for that one. "After doing that rotation, I'm pretty sure there's nothing sexy about it, so I'm not too worried."

"Hmm...I'm surprised," I said sarcastically. "I thought you'd fall in love with it and want to become a gyno yourself."

"Ha! Yeah right," she said. "It's definitely not my thing. I'm not even going to go into all the stories I have from that one." Katie was known to have extraordinarily gross stories from all of her medical experiences; I was too queasy to handle most of them.

"Mmm...I can only imagine."

"Anyway, his name is Joe, and you're going to love him. He took me out on our first date last weekend, and...I just have a good feeling about this one."

The thought that Katie may have found the love of her life just one week after I had lost mine made me feel just the slightest twinge of jealousy. Okay, it was a pretty large twinge. I knew I should've been happy for her, and it was only their first date, but Katie didn't really date as much as I did, so when she found someone she liked, they usually stuck around for a while. Which meant that if all went well, Katie would be experiencing that perfect, blissful (sickening) beginning of a relationship where you love absolutely everything about the other person. And after my love life had taken a plunge down the gutter, the last thing I could handle was listening to all of the wonderful things this new guy would surely do for her.

But Katie was my best friend. I needed to be happy for her, no matter how shitty I was feeling.

"That's awesome, I'm so happy for you. Any more dates on the horizon?"

"Yeah, he's taking me out in the city again this weekend, so we'll see..." She trailed off, sounding dreamy and hopeful.

I remembered when I first felt that way about Jeff. Those early butterflies and the hope that this is really it. That you've finally found the guy you're going to spend your life with. I hoped that this was it for Katie, but my loss made me feel bitter at the same time. Along with losing Jeff, I had lost my faith in love, in marriage, and in relationships in general. I wasn't going to be heading back down that road for a long time. But Katie hadn't been burned like I had, so she was allowed to be hopeful and excited.

"Keep me posted on how it goes. I can't wait to meet him."

"I'll try to give you a call next week so we can catch up again. I just got to the hospital, so I have to run. I want to hear all about how you're doing, though, so let's talk soon."

"Definitely. Good luck in the ICU."

"Yeah, I'll need it. Bye!"

In an effort to distract myself from the feelings of loneliness that had been creeping up on me every night this week, I logged in to my blog. Since my last post on Monday night, I'd had tons more hits and several enthusiastic comments. This gave me hope. At least we were all in this mess together. A lot of the comments were from women asking what was going on with Half-Naked French Hottie. I hadn't seen him around in the dorm (or the showers), and I hadn't heard from him at all since we'd first slept together on Monday night. The old, desperate me was threatening to scratch her way to the surface and ask all of those scary questions, like why hasn't he called? Wasn't the sex good for him too? It was definitely some of the best I'd ever had—I mean, what man feeds you chocolate in bed *after* giving you two orgasms? But maybe I didn't do enough to reciprocate. Was he angry about the text message from Frédéric?

But then I remembered my purpose here in France. To have fun. To like being single. To not care if I ever heard from him again. As I sat alone in my room that night, though, it seemed like this whole not-caring thing might end up being more difficult than I'd expected.

ELEVEN

vendredi, le 8 octobre

Dating multiple men at once keeps life interesting.

The next morning, I woke up feeling refreshed and alive again. Yes, lonely nights in my little dorm room weren't the most fun (especially when I knew there was a gorgeous man just two doors down who *wasn't* calling me!), but I had class at the Sorbonne in less than an hour, plus a busy weekend ahead of me, so all was not lost.

As I exited the train at the Luxembourg stop, my stomach growled at the tempting aroma of croissants and coffee emanating from the Brioche Dorée café across the street. The Brioche Dorée is one of the closest things the French have to a fast-food restaurant, except instead of hamburgers and fries, they carry tasty pastries, sandwiches, and salads. I couldn't resist as I walked past, so I stopped and grabbed a croissant to go. I smiled as I took my first scrumptious bite. How do the French stay so thin? I could easily eat ten of these a day.

As I approached the Sorbonne, I took the last bite of my buttery pastry before grabbing my new student ID and presenting it to the gun-wielding French police officers. I expected them to at least show *some* appreciation that I'd finally obtained the proper identification to enter the building, but the corners of their mouths didn't so much as move an inch. After I passed through the giant doors, I gazed down and noticed a pool of croissant flakes covering my chest. I laughed to myself as I realized that even *that* hadn't made them smile.

I spotted Fiona immediately upon entering the large classroom. No more than a minute after I'd sat down, our tiny professor began her lecture on French teaching methodology. As I scribbled down notes, I thought about the glorious fact that we'd had an entire week of class but not one single assignment. Instead of assigning weekly homework like the professors did back in the States, our Sorbonne instructors required us to complete one final paper, presentation, or exam, which constituted our entire grade. Granted, I had to make sure to perform well on my finals since those were my only grades for each class—and *especially* since I would be handing them in to Madame Rousseau—but it was so nice not to have much work to do during the semester. More time for going out and doing research for my blog!

After class, Fiona and I peeked into all of the colorful boutique windows as we walked up to Boulevard Saint-Germain and took a seat outside at a *brasserie*. I ordered my first *croque-monsieur* since I'd been in Paris and a glass of *vin rosé* while Fiona ordered a bowl of *soupe à l'oignon* and a glass of *vin rouge*.

"So, have you heard from Jeff at all this week?" Fiona asked while she struggled to bite the long strings of cheese dangling from her spoon.

"No, I haven't heard from him..." I hesitated as I took my first bite of the soft, fluffy bread and melted Emmental cheese.

I wasn't sure if I wanted to tell Fiona about the callous e-mail I had sent on Monday night. She didn't seem to be the kind of person who would do something like that. Then again, she *had* gone through a tough breakup, so what the hell. "But, I did get in touch with *him*, actually."

"You did?"

"Well, I sent him an e-mail on Monday night...a nasty e-mail." I snickered.

"Really? What did you say?"

I hadn't told Fiona about Luc yet because I was worried about her reaction, but I figured if we were going to be friends, now was as good a time as any.

"I told him that I had another guy in my bed who was better than he ever was. Basically I wanted to make him feel as awful as he made me feel."

"So you just made up a story to get him back?" she asked innocently.

"Well...not exactly. There really was a guy in my bed." I held my breath in anticipation of her response.

Fiona's eyes widened. "Whoa, seriously? Who? Are you seeing someone here?" Fiona was clearly surprised at this revelation, but she seemed interested, so I kept talking.

"His name is Luc, and he lives in my dorm—on my floor, actually. I met him my first night here, and he's *so* cute. But, we're not dating. He just spent the night that one time. And I have to admit, it felt really good to throw it back in Jeff's face."

"I bet. Did he write you back?"

"Nope, nothing. But I can't really expect him to want to talk to me after that, I guess. It *was* a tad bit immature."

"Maybe...but he started it in the first place—not you." Fiona seemed to identify with the situation and wasn't judgmental at all. I was relieved.

"You're right, he did. He deserves it, then."

"That's right." Fiona grinned in agreement.

We clinked our wineglasses to that and kept on chatting.

"Do you have any plans tonight?" Fiona asked, still struggling to eat the massive amount of melted cheese topping her French onion soup.

"Yeah, actually I do. I'm going on a date."

"With Luc?"

"No, Frédéric. I met him out at a bar last weekend with Lexi."

"You're not wasting any time here, are you? I guess I need to start going out with you!" She giggled and took a sip of her wine.

"I know, I just need things, or guys really, to take my mind off Jeff, you know?"

"Oh, I completely understand. School has been my main distraction, not that it's the most fun distraction, but it's something." She paused to take another bite. "Well, you'll have to let me know how your date goes tonight."

"Definitely. Oh, I wanted to ask if you'd be up for going out with me and Lexi tomorrow night."

"What do you have in mind?" she asked, shooting me an apprehensive glance.

"We'll probably just go to a bar, have some drinks, and meet some boys. You know, the usual."

Fiona's wavering smile told me she was unsure.

"Come on, you were just saying that you needed to get out more. We're going to have so much fun." I wasn't sure how Lexi and Fiona would get along, but if they were both going to be my friends, then I figured there was no harm in giving it a shot.

"I know, you're right. Okay, I'm in. Where do you think we'll go?"

"I don't know all of the good bars around here yet, but I'm sure Lexi will have something fabulous in mind. She's lived here a little while, and she goes out a lot. I'll call you tomorrow with the details. Sound good?"

"Sounds good," she said, sounding only a tad more convinced.

After Fiona and I took off in separate directions to go home, a wave of fatigue hit me. I headed home, changed into a pair of comfy shorts and a loose T-shirt, and lay down for a nice afternoon nap. That was one good thing about being single—I could do whatever I wanted, when I wanted. Not too shabby.

I jolted awake to the sound of techno music blaring from the room next to me. The walls here were a little too thin. I rubbed my eyes and peered over at the clock—it was already six p.m. Whoa, I'd slept for a whopping three hours. I needed to get a move on it if I wanted to be ready in time for my date with Frédéric.

I rinsed my face off in my minisink, brushed a bit of powder and blush onto my cheeks, then peeked inside my little closet to pick out an outfit. It was still nice and warm outside, so I threw on a denim skirt, a dark-violet tank top, and a pair of flip-flops before heading out the door.

As I was crossing the street to go to the RER stop, I spotted Luc walking a few steps ahead of me on his cell phone. Of course I hadn't heard from him all week, and then he would magically appear while I was on my way to a date. It figured. I trailed close enough behind him so I could catch part of his conversation without him seeing me. Yes, I was being nosy.

"*Je t'aime, Adeline. À demain,*" he said sweetly into his phone.

I *knew* there was another woman. After telling this Adeline girl that he loved her and would see her tomorrow, he snapped his phone shut. I slowed my pace, hoping he wouldn't see me, but no such luck.

"Charlotte," he called, flashing his charming smile in my direction.

"*Salut, Luc,*" I said, not sure how I felt about this little run-in. I had just confirmed my suspicion that not only was he seeing at least one other woman, but he was in love with her.

At least I didn't need to feel bad about being on my way to a date.

Luc leaned in to give me *bisous*, and we continued walking toward the metro together.

"So, where are you going tonight?" he asked.

None of your business, dude with a girlfriend who just slept with me on Monday night.

"Oh, just meeting up with a friend at Odéon. You?"

"Me too. I'm meeting Benoît there for a drink. *C'est parfait.* We can take the train together."

Damn. Why did I have to tell him where I was going?

A few minutes later, we squeezed onto the packed, smelly train. Apparently the entire world had decided to travel into the city that night. Luc's body was smashed up against mine, which, despite the fact that I had just heard him tell another woman that he loved her over the phone, wasn't all that uncomfortable.

With his face about an inch from mine, Luc said, "You and your friend can come for a drink with us if you want."

"Um, well, thanks for the invite, but I'm not really sure."

"Why not? It will be fun."

"That's really sweet, but maybe another time."

"Oh okay," Luc said as he lowered his eyes to the floor.

We rode along in silence, pressed up against each other in the smoldering train car, and without even realizing it, I found myself wondering what it would be like if Luc were my boyfriend. If I could just take his hand, rest my head on his shoulder, and make the whole world disappear.

The train jolted to an abrupt stop and jerked me back to reality. Luc's woman situation seemed like a mess, and it was a mess I did not need to be jumping into. Jumping into bed with him was a different story. That was acceptable in my new dating-like-a-man plan. But thinking about him as potential boyfriend material was so not in the plan.

As we exited the train together at the Odéon stop, my

stomach tightened. How was I supposed to find Frédéric with Luc in tow? I gazed up at the top of the stairs and spotted Frédéric waiting for me. Or was that him? I suddenly realized that I didn't really remember what he looked like. All I could remember was that he had short blond hair and that he was cute. Or at least in my drunken state, I had thought he was cute. The guy at the top of the stairs had short blond hair and was kind of attractive.

I made eye contact with the mystery man to test the waters. He grinned slyly in my direction. Okay, I was pretty sure it was him. As we walked closer, his grin spread wider across his face. Definitely him.

"I think I see my friend there, so have fun with Benoît, and I'll see you around." I tried to bolt from Luc without making a scene, but he didn't get the hint and instead stayed right by my side as I approached Frédéric.

But, just as I was about to say hello to the guy I *thought* was my date, I felt a tap on my shoulder.

I turned around to see a familiar face. It was Frédéric. Shit.

Note to self: don't get so drunk that I can't remember what a guy looks like after I've made out with him in a bar. Maybe a better rule of thumb would be to not make out with guys in bars in the first place.

I beamed at him in an attempt to make up for the mistake. "*Salut, Frédéric,*" I said as I noticed Luc still attached to my side, his expression turning from one of confusion to confrontation.

Frédéric looked from me to Luc and back to me with a puzzled expression on his face. "*Salut, Charlotte.*"

"Um, Frédéric, this is my friend Luc. Luc, this is Frédéric."

Luc gave Frédéric a firm handshake as he sized him up. Frédéric was clueless.

"Well, tell Benoît I said hi, and have fun tonight," I said to Luc as I tried to start moving in the other direction with Frédéric.

Luc did not budge. Luckily, Benoît appeared just then and saved us all from the awkward moment. He slapped Luc on the back, and as Luc turned to talk to him, I took the opportunity to grab Frédéric's hand and make a run for it.

"Bye, Luc," I called as I pulled Frédéric down the street. Luc locked eyes with me as I was walking away, and he made no attempt to mask the hurt expression on his face.

A pang of guilt crept up inside me until I remembered that I had just heard him tell another woman that he loved her over the phone. What was I feeling sorry for? He had no right to be jealous. He had no claim on me. He hadn't even tried to hang out with me or call me after having sex, so I refused to feel bad that I was going on a date with another guy.

"You are hungry?" Frédéric asked eagerly.

"I'm starving. Where are we headed?" I tried to switch gears and focus on Frédéric. He was much better-looking than the guy who I'd originally thought was my date. Granted, he was no Luc, but there was definitely potential. He was thinner than any other guy I'd ever dated, but I couldn't expect a lot of meat on the bones when skinny was the norm in France. It was his face that caught my eye. He had a perfect, light complexion, charcoal-gray eyes, dimples, and a warm smile that melted me the minute I laid eyes on him.

"I take you to my favorite restaurant. It's *magnifique*," he said with a swoop of his arms. "You will love it. We will be there in just one minute." Frédéric took my hand and led me across the crowded Boulevard Saint-Germain back through the winding cobblestone streets.

This area of Paris was buzzing with people, but even so, the neighborhood seemed much less touristy than the Notre Dame area where Luc had taken me. We must've passed ten outdoor cafés, and the only language I heard people speaking as they sipped their wine and their tiny cups of coffee was French. I didn't spot a single group of fanny-pack-clad tourists in this part of Paris.

I felt energized and excited just by walking down the street here. Who needed a cheating fiancé when I could have all this? Not to mention the fact that I had an attractive man on my arm. Life was really starting to look up.

After a few minutes, Frédéric stopped in front of an Italian restaurant, whose bright neon sign read *Ristorante*. A short, hairy man with a giant potbelly greeted Frédéric with a hearty *"buona sera"* as we walked in. When he saw me appear, he winked at us and led us over to a table in the back corner of the restaurant. Clearly Frédéric came here a lot. I wondered how many other girls he had sat in this back corner with. I realized though that I didn't really care. It was fun to have a new guy taking me out to dinner, and what he did before or after this date was of no concern to me. Maybe I'd write Jeff an e-mail about this one too. Humph.

We ordered a bottle of Bordeaux before Frédéric focused his big gray eyes on me and smiled.

"I am so happy you come with me to dinner," he began in his strong accent. "I have been waiting to see you again since we meet."

I felt my cheeks redden as the blackberry taste of the wine tingled on my tongue. "Thanks for inviting me out. This is a really beautiful restaurant." I broke Frédéric's gaze and glanced around the room, taking in the quiet, candlelit tables and the flirty couples sitting at each one.

Frédéric reached across the checkered tablecloth and placed his hand firmly on mine. *"Oui*, yes, it is very nice here. But tonight, Charlotte, it is *you* that is *beauteeful."*

I giggled. "You're not so bad yourself."

Frédéric's eyebrows furrowed inward. "I am sorry, I do not understand. You think I am so bad?"

"No, what I mean is that you look very nice tonight."

"Oh, thank you. I am sorry, my English is...euh...well, I do not study it since zee university, and that was a very long time ago. But will it be okay for me to practice with you?"

"Of course," I answered, even though I knew the conversation would be smoother if we could just speak French together.

"So, where did you go to college?" I asked him.

"I study at zee Sorbonne for a time, but...euh, then I have *des problèmes*, and, well, I do not finish."

"Problems?" I asked.

"Euh...yes. It is a long story. So I decide to become a *policier* with my brother, and I do this for zee past eight years."

Just then, a suave, dark-haired waiter appeared at our table and winked at Frédéric.

"*Vous désirez?*" he asked us.

As I quickly skimmed the menu, I heard Frédéric ordering in French for both of us.

"I hope you do not mind," he said, pouring himself another glass of red wine as he'd already managed to finish his first. "I order you zee best plate on zee menu. You will love it, I promise."

Jeff had never ordered for me when we'd gone out to dinner. In fact, no guy had ever done that. I'd always thought it was kind of old-fashioned. But maybe it was normal in France?

I smiled at him. "That's fine. I'm sure it will be wonderful."

Frédéric downed his second glass, then scooted his chair closer to mine and slid his hand onto my thigh. My cheeks burned as I drank a few more sips to catch up with him.

"So, Charlotte, what do you do in zee United States?"

"I was a French teacher at a private high school back in DC before moving to Paris."

His eyes lit up. "Oh, you are a teacher. So will you teach me some words?"

I laughed as the wine warmed my stomach. "I'm not sure

there are any French words I could teach you that you wouldn't already know."

Frédéric scooted his chair even closer to me. "No, it is not French words I want to know. It is English words."

"Okay, what kinds of words?"

As his clean-cut face and intense eyes narrowed in on me, he brushed his lips against my neck and whispered in my ear, "Dirty words."

I giggled again, then choked so hard on my wine that tears streamed out of the corners of my eyes.

Frédéric wasn't fazed in the slightest. "I know some expressions already, like 'You are so sexy,' and 'I want you, baby,' and 'Kiss my ass…with shit.' Do you know this one?"

Oh, God. Between the wine and the dead-serious expression on Frédéric's face, I couldn't hold it in any longer. My choking fit morphed into a loud burst of laughter.

"What is so funny?" he asked, a genuine look of surprise washing over his face.

"It's just that, well, that last one you said—"

"Kiss my ass with shit?" he repeated again, louder this time.

"Mm-hmm. That one. That's not *exactly* the way we use the expression. You can leave out the last part."

"The 'with shit' part?"

"Yes, don't say that. Ever."

"Why not? I do not understand."

"Just trust me on this one. Don't say it."

Thankfully, the waiter brought our meals then, because I was not looking forward to further explaining why he should *never* say that again.

As I drank my second glass of Bordeaux and enjoyed a delectable bowl of pasta smothered in a peppery pesto sauce and topped with sun-dried tomatoes and shaved parmesan, Frédéric used one hand to feed himself and planted the other firmly on my thigh. He didn't stop there, though. That hand inched higher and higher throughout the meal until it couldn't go any farther.

I didn't mind too much, though. I was just happy to be finished with the dirty-words conversation.

After dinner, Frédéric didn't hesitate to take care of the check before leading me back out to the lively Parisian night.

"Do you like the movies?" he asked. "There is a cinema close to zee metro at Odéon if you would like to go."

After Frédéric's obvious physical advances over dinner, I had been sure he was going to ask me back to his place, but I was impressed that he wasn't attempting to jump right in for the sex. Nice display of willpower.

On our way to the theater, I noticed dying couples everywhere. "Dying couples" was another term that Katie and I had coined when we studied abroad in college. It was basically referring to couples who were all over each other in public, ready to have sex on a park bench or at any given metro stop. They were "dying" because they would hang on each other and act outrageously serious as if one of them had just been diagnosed with a terminal illness. As if this moment —right then and there—would be the only chance they'd ever have again to hold each other, make out, and dry hump. So, be it on the sidewalk, in the middle of the street, on the metro, or outside at a café, they were unavoidable—those damn dying couples.

I only minded them when I was walking around alone. *Get a freaking room*, I always thought to myself. But tonight, as Frédéric pulled me close to him and ever so slightly brushed his lips on my neck right there in the middle of a crowded Parisian street, I couldn't have cared less about all of the other dying couples. Maybe we looked like a dying couple too. Oh well, so be it.

Frédéric took my hand as we walked into one of the movie theaters on Boulevard Saint-Germain and chose a movie that neither of us had seen. After paying for our tickets, he wrapped his arm around my shoulders and led me to the back of the dark, empty theater.

The minute we sat down, Frédéric was all over me. Hands on my thighs, mouth on my neck, kissing me and whispering things in my ear that I couldn't quite understand.

I was still somewhat tipsy, so I didn't mind all that much, but as the theater filled up a bit, I really hoped he would calm down.

But oh no, he seemed to get even hornier as the movie began. Luckily we were in the back row and no one was sitting close to us, so I don't think anyone witnessed the thirteen-year-old—no, wait—the *thirty-year-old* breathing heavily and sucking on my neck like it was a lollipop.

As I felt his fingers inching up my skirt, I grabbed his hand and smoothly directed it back to his own lap while trying to nudge his head up off my neck. That skinny little police officer was persistent, though. He took my hand and placed it right on his crotch so that I could feel his boner. Okay, that was it. I wasn't cool with being a dying couple anymore. I was seriously grossed out. We had eaten a nice dinner together...well, minus the dirty-words lesson, and now he wanted me to service him in a movie theater?

In an attempt to gain control over the situation, I leaned toward him and whispered, "Let's watch the movie. I really, really want to see this one."

"We are watching zee movie, but it is more fun this way," he whispered seductively as he stuck his slimy tongue down my throat and just about gagged me. I thought I remembered him being a good kisser the other night at the bar. I must've been hammered. He sucked. Plus, he was acting like a horny teenage boy, and that wasn't really working out for me.

I pushed his face off mine and grabbed his chin so that he would look at me.

"I'm serious. I want to watch the movie."

He must've heard my don't-mess-with-me tone of voice,

because he stopped his desperate attempts to undress me and have sex in the back of the movie theater. I should've left after his major display of immaturity, but I didn't feel like making a scene, so I stuck it out.

After the movie, Frédéric walked me across the street to the metro.

"I think I'm going to head home. I'm really tired," I told him as I faked a yawn.

Frédéric leaned down, wrapped his arms around my waist, and just as I thought he was going to kiss me again, he stopped and stared straight into my eyes.

"There is something I want to tell you," he whispered intently.

"Okay," I said, thinking he was just going to give me some line about how beautiful I was or that he wanted to see me again or wanted me to come home with him—the usual crap.

"I love you," he declared in a dramatic attempt to sweep me off my feet.

"Oh," I stammered, not really sure what to say. Who says "I love you" on the first date? After trying to jump you in a movie theater? After saying "kiss my ass with shit" at the dinner table?

I pulled away from his grasp and blurted, "Thanks for dinner, have a great night!" Then I bolted for the metro. I don't think I've ever run away from a date so fast in my life. Come to think of it, I don't think I've ever actually run away from a date, period.

I sprinted to catch the metro, hoping he wasn't following me. Who knew what tricks this guy had up his sleeve? I plopped down in an isolated seat on the train, and as I mulled over what had just happened, I burst out laughing. What a weirdo! It made me realize how much I missed being in a normal, functioning relationship. Like the one Jeff and I had shared before his online dating escapades.

At the end of the night, no matter who I was with, it

always came back to Jeff. I guessed that was normal since it had barely been a few weeks since the breakup. But after this most unsuccessful date, I truly missed him. I would not be writing him an e-mail to boast about the horrible date I'd just had, though. Instead, I called Lexi when I got home to dish about the ridiculousness of the night.

She laughed so hard she could barely breathe when I told her about the "I love you."

"What a freak!" She laughed heartily into the phone. "Get used to it, though. Guys pull some weird shit over here."

"Seriously."

"Hey, so we're still on for tomorrow night, right?"

"Yeah, I'm really excited. I'm going to bring my friend Fiona from class, if that's cool with you."

"Just make sure she's ready for a wild night. It's going to be crazy."

"I have no doubt it will be," I said as I smiled to myself.

Before bed, I logged in to my blog. My hits were soaring, with more comments from women I didn't know. Most of the women were loving it, but I did get a comment from Janie in Georgia calling me a "man-hater." Wow. At least I was provoking some strong emotions in my readers. I began typing.

More lessons on how to avoid love in the City of Love:

Rule # 1 — Date lots of men and don't apologize for it. Until a commitment is clearly stated on both ends, you have no obligations to any of the men you are seeing. If one of them tries to make you feel guilty for seeing another one, forget him. Do you know for sure that he isn't seeing other people too? Remember, this is all a game to them, and instead of being a victim of the game, you are now an active player. That means playing the field, seeing what's out there, and having a damn good time in the process! This brings me to my next point:

Rule # 2 — Do not, under any circumstances, allow the men you are dating to meet each other. This is an extremely awkward situa-

tion that should be avoided at all costs. Since we're smart women, this shouldn't be too difficult to pull off, but every once in a while, even a smart woman can find herself in an unpleasant run-in with two of her prospective men.

If you do find yourself in this situation, don't guilt yourself to death. They probably have other women waiting in the wings too.

Case in Point: As I was on my way to the metro to meet a French police officer for our first date, I spotted Half-Naked French Hottie ahead of me. I overheard him telling another woman that he loves her over the phone. Of course he was going to the same metro stop as me, so he ended up meeting my date, then giving me a sad, desperate look as I left with my handsome police officer. What right did he have to make me feel guilty after I had just overheard the end of his lovey-dovey conversation with some other woman? Not to mention the fact that he hadn't even tried to get in touch with me after the mind-blowing sex-and-chocolate experience a couple of nights ago.

And last but definitely not least:

Rule # 3—Don't put up with crazy behavior. Period. If a guy pulls something weird, get out now. Remember, you're in this to have fun, not to be sketched out and uncomfortable. You are too fabulous and smart for that.

Do guys ever put up with crazy behavior from us? No, never. They run for the hills as fast as their little penises will carry them.

So, if a guy acts like a horny teenage boy and tries to accost you in a movie theater, or if he expresses his undying love for you after your first date, he's a goner. Yes, both of those things happened to me tonight. I'm exhausted.

TWELVE

samedi, le 9 octobre

Climbing onto a bus with a wild rugby team in the middle of the night is never a good idea.

Fiona called me the next morning sounding nervous. "What are you wearing tonight?" she asked.

"I'm not sure...I haven't really thought about it yet. Probably just jeans, a tank top, and heels. It's still pretty warm out."

"So you're not getting really dressed up or anything, right? I just don't want to be underdressed or overdressed, you know?"

"Yeah, I'd just go for jeans and a cute top—nothing too fancy." It was clear that Fiona didn't get out much, and I was starting to worry that asking her to come out with Lexi may not have been the best idea.

"I know. I just haven't been out in a while. Andrew and I were together for so long that I think I've forgotten how to go out and have a good time...pathetic, I know."

"It's not pathetic," I assured her, "but it's time to get back out there and start meeting some new people. I mean, we're in Paris! What have you got to lose?"

"I know, you're right. Tonight's going to be fun," she said, sounding a little more convinced. "Oh, I almost forgot to ask, how did your date go last night?"

"Ugh, don't ask!"

"That bad?"

"Well, let's just say that I literally ran away from him after he told me he loved me because I think he was about to propose marriage."

Fiona gasped. "What? He told you he loved you? On the first date?"

"Mm-hmm…*after* he tried take off my pants during the movie."

"What a creep! That's disgusting. See, that's why I haven't wanted to meet anyone—they're all freaks."

"I know…some of them are pretty bad, but at least it makes for a good story."

"Did you tell him you don't want to see him again?"

"No, I didn't have time. I ran away too fast."

"What are you going to say if he calls you again?"

"Um, I probably won't answer the phone, or I'll just tell him to leave me alone. That date was totally ridiculous; I don't even feel bad about blowing him off."

"And what about the other guy you've been seeing…" She paused, probably wondering just how many guys there were.

"Luc?"

"Yeah, Luc. Is he normal at least?"

"Well, normal for a guy, I guess. They all seem to be a little messed up. But don't let it discourage you from going out. We're going to have fun tonight, and if there are any crazies, we'll stick together. Don't worry." Between Fiona being worried about stepping foot in a bar and Lexi, who would probably go home with any guy in the bar, I could tell we had an interesting night ahead of us.

~

I left my place at ten o'clock to meet up with Fiona and Lexi at a bar in the fifth arrondissement called The Long Hop.

After exiting the metro, I'd no more than stepped one high-heeled foot into the crosswalk on Boulevard Saint-Germain before a man on a cherry-red scooter raced past me and just about ran me over.

"Hey!" I shouted after him as I stumbled backward over the curb and slammed into someone.

I swiveled around to find three young French guys, as slim as the cigarettes they were smoking, sizing me up.

"*Vous êtes américaine, ma princesse?*" one of them asked me as a dirty grin spread across his bony face.

My princess? Was he serious?

Without responding, I looked both ways to make sure there weren't any more drag-racing scooters and jetted across the street to the bar.

I realized that walking around Paris at night by myself wasn't the best idea. Not that I felt unsafe here. It just seemed that whenever a pack of French guys spotted me walking alone, all dressed up to go out, they couldn't keep their comments to themselves. Maybe next time I'd take a cab straight to the bar.

Michael Jackson's "Billie Jean" pounded through the speakers as I shoved my way across the packed dance floor and finally spotted my friends.

Lexi, as usual, had on a hot little number which made every guy in the bar stop, stare, and drool as she walked past. And Fiona surprised me. I thought she'd show up in a pink polo shirt with a khaki skirt or something equally conservative, but instead, she was sporting a tight fluorescent-pink tank top with a pair of slim dark jeans and sexy black strappy heels.

I introduced the two girls as we strutted our stuff over to the bar to buy our first round of drinks. The bar was packed with way more guys than girls, and it was a wild crowd. Lexi and I downed our drinks while Fiona sipped hers, and then we made our way out to the dance floor together.

We danced for a good half an hour, just the three of us, in the middle of a booming dance floor. Lexi and I fought to keep our space on the floor, throwing elbows to keep scummy guys away from us. Fiona's eyes darted around the room as she stepped her feet from side to side in time with the bumping bass. I hoped she'd loosen up a bit once the alcohol hit her.

"I'm heading to the ladies' room. Anyone else need to go?" Lexi yelled over the music.

"Yeah, I'll come with you," Fiona yelled back.

"I'll stay here and hold down the fort," I assured them while busting a move to a Madonna song. The French definitely had a thing for American eighties music.

Right after the girls left, two French guys approached me. They were both sporting painfully tight black jeans and skin-hugging blue T-shirts that showcased their thin builds, and they had military-style haircuts. I wondered if they were in the police force with Frédéric and if they were going to tell me how much they loved me after five minutes of talking to me.

"We heard you speak English," one of the boys yelled over the music in a strong French accent.

"Yes, that's right, I was speaking English," I said sarcastically. I wasn't really feeling it. These boys were not my type.

"So, you are American or English?" the other one asked, giving me a slimy smile.

"American," I said dryly as I kept dancing, hoping the girls would come back soon so I could get rid of them.

"Oh, zee American girl. I love zee American girl." They both grinned at me while they attempted to dance in their ball-hugging jeans. Oh, dear. This was quite the sight.

"Where are you from?"

"California." I lied. No reason to tell the truth here. Might as well have some fun with the situation.

"Oh, Caleefornia, I love Caleefornia!" one of them replied, while the other one did a hysterical raise-the-roof gesture with his hands. I held in my laughter.

"Zat is why you are so beauteeful; all of zee Caleefornia girls are beauteeful," Raise-the-Roof Guy said as he tried to take my hand to dance with me.

I yanked my hand away and asked them, "So, are you guys police officers?"

"Oh no, we are in zee army, and we are brothers. You like zee army man, no?"

What? The army man? Normally, yes, I like the army man, but our military guys at home wear baggy pants. In this instance, the army men were wearing jeans so tight that they were probably becoming more sterile by the minute.

"Mmm...yes. Army, very nice," I replied, not really knowing how to respond to that.

"You are zee perfect girl...you will have my baby?"

Okay, that was it. They were kind of funny at first, but now they were getting a little too out of control. Have their baby?! Where did Fiona and Lexi go? I turned around to search for my friends so I could escape. And that's when my gaze landed on an even more hilarious sight than the one I was currently trapped in.

Fiona and Lexi were surrounded by the most massive group of guys I'd ever seen. And I don't mean massive as in numbers. I mean massive as in huge. As in giant-size men.

Lexi danced up a storm in the center of the group while all of the enormous boys whooped, hollered, and chugged pints of beer. Fiona just stood there with wide eyes, staring up at the giants towering over her.

"Sorry, guys, I have to go meet my friends," I told the army men with the ball-hugging pants as I fled the scene to find out who in the world these mammoth hunks were.

I pushed my way past one of the giants to get to Fiona, who breathed a sigh of relief when she saw me.

"Who are these guys?" I yelled into her ear.

"English rugby players. They're crazy!" Fiona yelled back.

"Well, hello, gorgeous girls," a tall, handsome rugby player said to me and Fiona as he shook our hands.

"Hello, tall, handsome man," I replied back.

He flashed a charming smile. "I'm Dean, and you are?"

Wow, I loved, loved, loved his accent. And his huge muscles.

"I'm Charlotte, and this is Fiona."

"It's wonderful to meet you, Charlotte and Fiona. What can I get you two lovely ladies to drink?" Dean was less barbaric than his rugby buddies, who were now chanting some unrecognizable song and stomping their feet so hard that the floor was actually trembling.

"I'm fine," Fiona said, trying to avoid the drink.

"Oh, come on, you've only had one drink so far tonight!" I prodded her toward the bar as Dean led the way.

"I know, but I just don't want to get too out of control."

"Fiona, that"—I said, pointing to the group of grunting giants—"is out of control. You, my dear, would have to try very hard to get out of control. You're having another drink."

"What can I get you two?" Dean placed his heavy arms around us as we reached the bar.

"Two vodka-and-cranberries, please." I took the lead since Fiona was clearly intimidated by the madness all around us.

"Coming right up, darling." Dean winked at me, then ordered our drinks.

After that point, the night could pretty much be summed up like this:

Dean was all over me the minute we made it back to his group of friends. We danced and made out all night on the dance floor. It was overwhelmingly hot.

Lexi continued to dance in true stripper fashion in the middle of a group of about five rugby boys who took turns groping and grinding on her.

As for Fiona...well, I thought she was going to stand in the corner the whole night with the same wide-eyed, terrified look on her face. But after that vodka and cranberry hit her, she proceeded to take dance lessons from Lexi and ended up dancing with the absolute hottest player in the bunch, Matt. He was about a foot and a half taller than Fiona, but that didn't stop him from leaning down to make out with her for the rest of the night.

When you have an insane night like that, sometimes it's better to stop while you're ahead. Otherwise people get too drunk and crazy things happen. In our case, we opted for the latter.

With an entire English rugby team in tow, Lexi, Fiona, and I stumbled out of the bar as it was closing. It was one of those drunken, debauchery-filled study-abroad nights where we were all laughing so hard we could barely move, let alone walk to the nearest cab. So we leaned on the boys for support and walked with them through the empty Parisian streets for blocks and blocks without even asking where in the hell we were going.

After who knows how long of stumbling, laughing, and even falling on the hard cobblestone sidewalks, we rounded a corner and spotted a big blue bus.

Dean pointed up ahead. "That's our bus, and you, my dear, are getting on it with me."

In my giggly, drunken state, I smiled, took Dean's hand, and got right on that bus. Fiona and Lexi weren't far behind.

The rugby boys grew rowdier once they boarded the bus, if that's even possible. I think that at least five of them simultaneously kissed Lexi, while Fiona and Matt bolted straight to the back and disappeared behind the seats.

Before we knew it, we were on a long bus ride to an unknown destination with a hormonally charged group of rugby players.

"Where are we going?" I asked Dean as the bus took off, suddenly feeling alarmed that we'd climbed on with no clue where we were headed.

"Oh, I don't know, love...some hotel outside the city."

"How far outside the city?"

"An hour, maybe? But relax, you're with me," he said as he pushed me down into the seat underneath him and stared into my eyes. "Wanna snog?"

"Snog?" I asked, confused, thinking he wanted to have sex with me on the bus. I admit I had been a little crazy since I'd arrived in Paris, but I wasn't *that* easy.

Dean leaned down and kissed me. "That's snogging, my dear," he explained as he pulled me closer to him.

"Oh well, in that case, yes, I would love to snog," I replied as Dean planted his lips on mine.

The Rugby Sex Bus arrived at a random hotel in the middle of nowhere about an hour and much snogging later. I grabbed Fiona and Lexi on our way into the hotel and asked them if they were both okay. Granted, I was having a great time myself, but this could've been a really sketchy situation, and we girls needed to stick together.

"Daaaarling, don't worry," Lexi replied in her best English accent. "This is a fabulous night!"

Fiona was grinning from ear to ear with Matt's arm wrapped tightly around her.

"I'm fine," she squeaked as we all piled into the hotel.

Dean led me to his room while Fiona followed Matt down the hallway, and Lexi followed...well, a group of three guys into one room. I didn't even want to know what was going to go down in there.

When we got into the room, Dean didn't waste any time. He pushed me up against the wall and kissed my neck, face, and lips—basically any bare skin he could reach. He then found a way to get both my tank top and bra off in one swift movement, unbuttoned my jeans, and yanked both his shirt and pants off. His roaming hands were all over me, making it hard for me not to want to take things further as he pulled me down on the bed on top of him.

His upper body was amazing. He was more finely cut than any guy I'd ever seen. Yes, better than Jeff. Humph. Suddenly I wished I had a camera to take a picture of Dean to send off to Jeff. How nice it would've been to throw yet another one in his face.

My buzz began to wear off, though, as Dean buried me underneath him on the bed. All of a sudden, I wasn't sure how I felt about being alone in a hotel room with this random, huge dude on top of me. Who knew where this guy had been or how many drunk girls just like me he had been sleeping with all over Europe?

Of course, it would've been easy to just sleep with him. He was attractive, and he was probably really good in bed. But the truth of the matter was that I didn't want to rack my numbers up that high with a guy who I knew nothing about. A guy who cared nothing about me, and who I would never see again. If I were a man, I would just have sex. But I wasn't. I was a smart woman, and I suddenly knew for certain that I did *not* want to have sex with this guy. So, before things got too out of hand, I pulled the ultimate girl excuse.

"I'm sorry, I can't. It's a bad time of the month."

"It's okay, I don't mind if you don't mind. We can still do it."

What? I had never heard that one before. Gross.

"Um, I think you will mind. It's just not going to happen tonight, okay?"

"Really, Charlotte. It's not that big of a deal," he said as he thrust his hand down into my jeans.

I grabbed his hand and placed it firmly on the bed. "No, really, I'm not okay with it."

Dean pressed his groin hard on top of me and groped my breasts. "But I want you so bad."

As Dean began dry humping me, and I could feel his erection pressing hard into my inner thigh, I wanted out. I struggled to roll out from underneath him, but he was too heavy and too drunk.

"Dean, seriously, I can't do this. You need to stop," I shouted in his ear.

He rolled his eyes at me, shot up and stalked over to his clothes. He threw his T-shirt back on and gave me a harsh glare. "Fine. I just don't understand why you came in here in the first place then. What did you think was going to happen?"

"I told you it's a bad time of the month, and I don't want to do it, okay? You don't need to be such a jerk about it."

"Whatever. I'm going to bed." He walked over to the bed in his tighty whities and a T-shirt, buried himself under the covers, and within seconds began snoring.

I was so shaken up by the way he had acted that I just wanted to go home. But I knew that Fiona and Lexi were probably having the time of their lives, and I didn't want to ruin it for them.

Even though I was pretty certain that a tornado couldn't get the sleeping giant out of bed, I didn't want to risk waking Dean up, so I locked myself in the bathroom and slid down the wall onto the cold tile floor.

I closed my eyes and buried my head in my hands. As the alcohol swished around in my stomach, I felt disgusted with myself. Was *this* what life without Jeff was going to be like?

Getting wasted at bars and ending up in strange hotel rooms with scary men who wanted nothing more than sex?

My new plan to date like a man was supposed to empower me. It was supposed to make me feel confident and happy.

But instead, as I curled up on the hard tiles and wished for morning to come, I felt more empty, scared, and alone than I ever had in my life.

∼

At nine o'clock the next morning, a bunch of hungover rugby boys pounded on our door.

"Dean, the bus leaves in ten minutes. Get your arse out of bed!"

I peeled myself up off the bathroom tile and opened the door, dreading having to face Dean again. I wanted to get out of there as quickly as possible.

"Bugger," Dean muttered under his breath as he scrambled to get his clothes on and throw his things in his giant rugby bag.

When he saw me grabbing my purse and heading for the door, he called out, "Wait, Charlotte. Where are you going?"

"I'm leaving."

"You're not even going to say good-bye?"

Who the hell did this guy think he was?

"Not after the way you acted last night, no."

"I'm sorry, what do you mean? I had so much fun with you last night. I guess I don't remember…Did I say something wrong?"

"You don't remember what happened?"

"No, I'm sorry, I don't," he said as looked shamefully at the floor.

"Well, we'll just say it wasn't pretty. And I'm ready to get the hell out of here."

"Listen, for whatever it's worth, I'm sorry. I'm not always the best drunk."

"Yeah, maybe you shouldn't have so much to drink the next time you bring a girl back to your hotel room." And with that, I stormed out of the room and slammed the door behind me. After a long night alone on a cold bathroom floor, I had no sympathy for him. I needed to find my friends and go home.

I spotted Lexi strutting down the hall with the same three boys still trailing behind her, and Matt and Fiona walking out of their room cooing at each other like two lovebirds. It seemed as if everyone else had had a successful night but me.

"Hey, chick, did ya have a good night?" Lexi asked me with a wink.

I shot her a look that showed that I most definitely did *not* have a good night.

"Ohhh, we'll talk soon. Are you okay?" she whispered.

"Yeah, let's just get out of here."

Apparently the Rugby Asshole Bus was heading down to Lyon next, which was not where we needed to be going, not that I would've ever stepped foot on that thing again anyway. Fiona kissed Matt good-bye while Lexi kissed all three of her drooling boys on their cheeks. The girls waved as their men pulled off toward their next destination in search of more women and more trouble.

"Where in the hell are we?" Lexi asked after the bus drove off.

"I have no idea, but let's figure it out so we can get home." I led the way back into the hotel so we could talk to the concierge and figure out where we were. It turned out that an RER stop was just a few blocks away from the hotel, so we caught the next train and dished the entire way home.

Fiona put her arm around me. "Are you okay? Did something bad happen?"

I filled them in on the stunt that Dean had pulled.

"You should've come and found us, Charlotte. Don't ever sleep on a bathroom floor again. That's horrible," Fiona said as she squeezed my shoulder.

"Thanks. I just didn't want to ruin your night. Enough about that, though, I'm fine. Lexi, what happened with you and all your men?"

"Wouldn't you like to know?" A devious grin spread across her face before she changed the subject. "What about you, Fiona? You and Matt seemed pretty into each other. Did you do the deed?"

"We had a nice night," she answered curtly, trying to avoid the question.

"Oh no, you don't! We want the details, girl, the dirty details. How was he?" Lexi wasn't going to let her get away with it.

Fiona blushed, and then she finally let it all loose. "He was...amazing. Oh, my gosh. He's the most gorgeous guy I've ever seen! And he was so sweet about everything."

"And?" Lexi prodded.

"And what?" she answered innocently.

"Did you sleep with him?"

She paused, blushed an even darker shade of red, and finally spit it out. "Mm-hmm."

It was the most excited I'd seen Fiona since I met her. She was always so studious and controlled; it was nice to see her let down her guard a little bit.

"It was *so* good," she cooed.

"It's been a little while, hasn't it?" I asked her. I was fairly sure that she hadn't been with anyone since Andrew.

"Yes, over a year!"

"Oh, honey, you're killing me. A year?" Lexi gasped in disbelief. Not having sex for an entire year was probably more than Lexi could ever imagine, seeing as how she could get laid just by walking down the street. "Well, it's a good thing you came out with us, then!"

In the midst of our laughter, one by one, we fell asleep on the train. As I was dozing off, I thought of Jeff. And for the first time, instead of hating him and wanting to cut off his balls, I thought about the fact that if he hadn't cheated on me, and if I hadn't come to Paris alone, I would never have met Fiona and Lexi. Plus, I was only twenty-five years old—way too young to be marrying a pathetic, lowlife scumbag. I had my whole life to make those kinds of mistakes. Why start now?

Back in my room, I logged in to my blog. More hits than last time, but still, I wanted to reach even more women. I forwarded the blog to Fiona and Lexi, hoping they could pass it around and spread the word. I began typing:

I just got back from a disastrous all-nighter, and I have an extremely important lesson to share with all of you:

Rule # 1—Sleeping around is okay, but don't act like a manwhore and sleep with anything that walks. Yes, we're attempting to date like men, but that doesn't mean we should do everything they do. We're smarter, remember? So, just because they would sleep with anything that has a pulse does not mean we should copy that behavior.

If you have a hot, sexy man in your bed and you feel comfortable taking the plunge, by all means, go for it. (And do be safe about it, ladies.) But if for any reason, at any time, you decide you're not feeling it, don't be afraid to say no. Then, if he acts like an asshole about it, call your friends, talk about what a jerk he is, and move on.

Case in Point: Even though I just spent the night alone on the bathroom floor of a random hotel because the guy I was with became angry after I told him I didn't want to have sex, I am still happy that I stuck to my guns. Would I really have wanted to sleep with such a prick just because he was good-looking? No. Trust your instincts, ladies, and you'll be one step ahead of the game.

THIRTEEN

dimanche, le 31 octobre

Ex-boyfriends should be quarantined on a deserted island.

Three weeks, ten dates, and four missed classes later, Fiona, Lexi, and I were becoming inseparable. We went out together every weekend and lunched at cafés in the city a few times a week. Luc had stopped over once to say hi but had completely disappeared after that. In a desperate moment one night, I knocked on his door to see if he was around, but he didn't answer. I figured it was better off this way. The sex was fantastic, and I couldn't say I wasn't hoping for it to happen again, but Luc was dangerous. He was handsome, sweet, and amazing in bed, but sketchy and divorced and in love with someone else. Exactly the kind of guy I should avoid. So, even though I found myself thinking about him and wishing he'd knock on my door with that sweet smile and another bar of creamy chocolate, I reasoned that it was better to steer clear and keep seeing other men.

I still thought about Jeff a lot, and some days I missed him terribly, while other days I hated him with all my heart and soul. Amid all of my mixed emotions, though, a small part of me was beginning to realize that leaving him was possibly the best thing I could ever have done for myself.

Of course, one of the major disadvantages to not having Jeff with me in Paris was the effect it was having on my bank account. Being a full-time student in an expensive European city where the dollar wasn't worth a whole lot was seriously draining my funds. So, one beautiful autumn day in Paris, before heading out for a jog at the scenic Parc Montsouris across from my building, I wandered into all of the international dorms at the Cité Universitaire and posted some English-tutoring flyers.

Later that evening, I was checking the hits on my blog when my phone rang.

"Hello?"

"Yes, hello. My name is Marc. Is zis Charlotte, zee English teacher?"

I smiled. Already a potential student! "Yes, this is Charlotte. Are you interested in taking lessons?"

"Yes, very much so. I am looking for an American to speak with a couple hours each week to hopefully become fluent. I lived in zee States for five years when I was young, but I have lost much of my accent."

Marc was already a pretty strong English speaker, so this would be fun. "Great, I'd love to help you out. Where do you live?"

"I am in zee Italian house at zee Cité Universitaire, although I am not Italian. I am a French medical student, and I am trying to save money by living here. But just because I am a student, I do not want you to think I will not pay you well for zee lessons. It is hard to find a good English teacher who is American, so I am willing to pay a lot for zee right person."

Lucky for him, I was willing to charge a lot for the right student.

"That sounds great, Marc. I live right around the corner at the American house, so would you like to have our first lesson tomorrow at Parc Montsouris across the street? We can meet at noon at the big gate on the corner of Boulevard Jourdan and rue Gazan if that works for you."

"That is perfect. I look forward to it."

The next day, I waited anxiously at the gate for Marc, hoping he would be normal and easy to work with. Even though he'd sounded professional over the phone, in my past experiences with tutoring, students tended to flake out and cancel a lot, making it difficult to maintain a steady stream of cash. To sustain the fun lifestyle I was leading in Paris, I really needed this to work out.

After waiting for about five minutes, a scary-looking middle-aged man stumbled up to me. Oh no, this couldn't seriously be him.

"*Excusez-moi, Mademoiselle, vous êtes ravissante,*" the scary dude said to me while drooling on his musty, olive-green T-shirt. This definitely wasn't him. Marc wouldn't walk up to me and tell me I'm ravishing when he's about to pay me to teach him English. Plus, he didn't sound this old, or drunk, on the phone.

"Sorry, I don't speak French," I lied as I scanned the sidewalk looking for Marc. He needed to hurry up.

The weird dude advanced toward me and tried to grab my hand. That was where I drew the line.

"You need to back up right now," I said sternly as I turned around to walk away from him but, instead, ran straight into some other guy. What in the hell was going on?

"*Pardon.*" I apologized as I pushed past him to get away from the weirdo.

"Wait, are you Charlotte?" the guy asked.

"Oh, Marc?"

"Yes, are you okay? Do you know zis man?" he asked, gesturing toward the scary man hovering over us.

"No, I don't, so let's walk!" I raised my eyebrows and gave him a this-guy-is-scary-look, hoping he'd catch on.

Luckily, Marc took the hint and held on to my arm as if we were a couple, leading me down the tree-lined walking path. The weird man yelled something incomprehensible at us, but then got bored and walked the other way. *Whew!*

"Thank you!" I sighed as Marc let go of my arm and turned around to make sure the guy was gone.

"No problem. I thought zat was you, and zat man, well… euh…he was not normal."

"I appreciate it," I said as I smiled at him.

Marc had just scored major points as my new, normal English student by saving me from the scary French drunkard. As we walked farther into the lush, green park together, I immediately relaxed. As much as I loved the hustle and bustle of the city, it could be overwhelming at times. The Parc Montsouris, in contrast, was a peaceful haven full of shady trees, open grassy hills, fresh beds of flowers, meandering pathways, and, well…the occasional drunk.

I breathed in the scent of freshly cut grass while I sized up my new student. Marc was almost a foot taller than me and had a lean, firm build. His dark, straight hair sat in a messy pile on his head and was still a tad wet, as if he'd just toweled off. He had captivating hazel eyes and a warm, friendly smile. He wore a plain navy-blue T-shirt and a nice, baggy pair of jeans. (Well, baggy for a French guy, that is.)

"So, I would like to meet with you one or two times each week to work on English. If zat is too much, I understand, but I have extra time in zee weekend and zee evenings to study English." Marc's English was very formal, but grammatically, it was practically spotless. Just like Luc, he had problems making the *th* sound. Overall, though, this was going to be easy.

"Sure, I have a lot of spare time, so we can meet as much

as you'd like. It's great that we live so close; it'll make meeting up a lot easier."

"Yes, definitely. Zee Parc Montsouris is a great place to meet when zee weather is so beautiful."

"I agree," I said as I gazed down the hill at the glistening lake below and noticed the red and golden hues that shimmered on the trees.

"So, what would you like to work on in our lessons each week?"

"I want to speak, speak, speak. Like I told you on zee phone, I lived in zee US when I was young, and back then, I spoke perfectly. Now, I feel zat I have lost zee accent and I forget zee...euh...vocabulary. I don't have anyone to talk to in English. So if we can just talk about things, like everyday things, zat would be great. And I need to work on asking questions and understanding zee answers. It is hard, you know, when you speak fast, to understand zee English."

"It can be really difficult. How about we get started, then?"

Marc and I took a seat on a green wooden bench facing the lake as a pack of men in obscenely short shorts ran past.

"Okay. I will ask you some questions first," Marc said, a look of determination on his face. "Where are you from?"

"I grew up in Ohio, and then I went to college in Washington, DC." I was anxious to hear how Marc pronounced Ohio. Most French speakers dropped the *h* making it sound like "Oio," and it always made me giggle.

"Oh, you are from Oio...What is in Oio? I have never been there."

I suppressed my laughter. "It's actually O-*hi*-o, don't forget that *h* in there." I smiled at him to make sure he felt comfortable with my corrections.

"I know...Zat is one of zee most difficult letters for me to pronounce. Let me try." Marc made a very serious face and then spit it out. "O-*hi*-o!"

"Yes, that's it!"

"So, what is in O-hi-o?" he asked, a proud look on his face.

"Um, not a whole lot. I was raised in a small town surrounded by cornfields. It snows a lot, and the weather kind of sucks, truthfully. It's nothing like Paris. But it was a nice, safe place to grow up, and the people there are really sweet and down-to-earth."

"Sucks?"

"It's a slang word. It means that it's not good."

"I see. And what are you doing here in Paris? You are a student, no?"

I filled Marc in on the program I was completing at the Sorbonne and on my plans to teach in France.

"There's only one problem, though," I continued.

"What is zee problem?"

"I was assigned an advisor at the Sorbonne, and she's *awful*. She's worse than awful, actually—she's mean and uptight and she already hates me after only one meeting." I figured if I was going to help Marc with his English, there was no need to sugarcoat it.

"Must you have this woman's approval, though?" he asked with a laugh.

"Unfortunately I do. If I want to get a teaching position at a good private school in Paris, I have to get *her* recommendation. And you should just see her. She wears these black turtlenecks that stretch up to her wrinkly chin, and she pulls her hair back in this tiny little bun with her beady eyes squinting at the sides. Oh, and you should hear the way she says my name in her stern voice—'Mademoiselle Summers,' like she's about to slap me on the wrist with a ruler. God, she's terrible."

Marc's pleasant smile faded into a blank stare. I figured he was having a hard time understanding words like "uptight" and "wrinkly chin." Maybe I should've taken things a little slower.

"Sorry, I'm probably speaking too fast. It's just that she really infuriates me."

"No, I...I understood perfectly." Marc shifted uncomfortably and refused to meet my gaze.

Was I making him uneasy? I decided to change the subject. "What about you? Where did you grow up?"

"Oh...euh...I grew up in Lyon. You know Lyon? It is south of Paris." Marc stared off into the distance, clearly distracted.

I immediately lit up. "Yes, I love Lyon! I lived there for six months, actually."

"Zat is nice. My father still lives there."

"What about your mom?" I asked him.

"Euh..." He hesitated while he kicked at some branches on the ground. "She is a professor in Paris."

"That's cool. Where does she teach?"

Marc kicked the branches a little harder this time and fixed his gaze on a tall swan floating on the water. "At zee Sorbonne."

"Oh, cool. Maybe I've seen her around. What subject?"

"She trains students in how to teach French as a Foreign Language."

As I hoped this wasn't heading where I thought it was, I suddenly remembered something. When Marc had first called to introduce himself, he'd said his full name—Marc Rousseau.

Oh shit.

"Marc, are you related...?"

"Zee woman, your advisor. Her name is Madame Rousseau? No?"

I nodded in agreement while my stomach twisted up in knots.

"She is my mother."

I bowed my head in shame as my cheeks went up in flames. I wanted to crawl under the bench, cover myself up in leaves, and never come out.

What a disaster. I couldn't lose my first student already. I really needed the money, and Marc was so nice. Speaking of which, how was Madame Rousseau capable of producing offspring as polite and handsome as Marc?

Regardless, I had to fix this. I couldn't let that woman ruin everything for me.

I looked Marc in the eye. "Marc, I'm so, terribly sorry. I had no idea she was your mom, and I should never have said all of those horrible things about her. I normally don't talk like that about people. I'm sure she's a wonderful mother. I just had a bad first meeting with her, that's all. I'm so sorry."

"I know you did not know. But if you have such a hatred for my mother, I am not sure if you will want to work with me."

"Hatred? I don't hate her, Marc. We just haven't gotten along that well, that's all." God, I hoped he was buying this. "But I know it will get better. I definitely want to continue working with you, if you still want to work with me, that is."

"I don't know. I do not want to be in the middle of you and my mother. I do understand how she can be, though...I grew up with her, you know. She is a very strict woman. She has a long reputation at zee Sorbonne...and sadly, it is not always good. Even still, I am quite close with her."

How could he be close with *her*? He was so sweet. So normal. And she was so strict and mean. But it wasn't his fault she was like that. Plus, I genuinely liked him.

"You won't be in the middle. You don't even have to tell her you know me." I couldn't believe this was happening. That freaking woman!

Marc stared up at the wispy tree leaves above us and squinted in the sunlight. When he lowered his gaze back to mine, I noticed the warmth in his eyes had returned.

"I have tried so hard to find an English tutor, and each one of them has been weird and difficult to speak with. I feel comfortable with you, so maybe we can try to have a lesson today and forget about my mother."

Whew. "That sounds wonderful, Marc."

I was amazed that Marc was still able to be decent to me after I'd just verbally trashed his mom. He must've been adopted. There was just no way that *he* came from *her*.

Despite our rough start, Marc and I found out that we had a lot in common, which gave us more than enough topics to cover during our first lesson. We chatted about Lyon, about growing up as only children, and about his plans to become a pediatrician and, thankfully, didn't speak another word about his mother. He was really easy to talk to and open to corrections, which made him great to work with. After a little over an hour of talking, he needed to head back to his place to get some studying done, so we planned to meet a few days later back at the park to pick up where we left off.

As I walked back to my dorm, I tried to remember the exact words I'd used to describe Madame Rousseau to Marc. As my furious rant came back to me, I felt mortified. Marc was actually someone I could see myself being friends with. I hadn't had a solid male friend in a while.

How was it, though, that I would meet Madame Rousseau's one and only son? It must've been a virgin birth because I could not imagine any man getting into bed with her. Ugh. That was not a mental image I had any desire to conjure up.

Back in my room, I tried to distract myself from the thought of Madame Rousseau procreating and my horrible start with Marc by checking my e-mail. I saw the usual ones from my mom and Katie and then a new one from my friend Hannah, with "Bridesmaids" written in the subject line. My stomach churned as I remembered that Hannah's wedding to Mike, Jeff's best friend from law school, was coming up this spring. It was Hannah who had first introduced me to Jeff, at her engagement party last year.

After that night, my story changed. Instead of being an eternally dating bachelorette, I was going to be the girl who had met the love of her life a few years after college, traveled the world with her handsome husband, had a couple of kids, and lived happily ever after. But in the blink of an eye, my happily ever after had turned into unhappily ever after. My prince charming had turned out to be a lying, cheating, filthy piece of crap. Ugh.

I closed my eyes and shook away the memories. I'd been so consumed with my issues that I had completely forgotten about my bridesmaid commitment. I opened her e-mail to find an exhaustive bridesmaid to-do list complete with dress-ordering instructions and detailed descriptions of the shoes and jewelry she wanted us to wear, as well as a possible timeline for the big wedding weekend which would be held in April, back in DC. Hannah was one of my closer friends from Georgetown, but I hadn't heard much from her since I'd arrived in Paris. I knew she was busy planning the wedding, and, truthfully, I didn't want to talk to her that much since I knew that she and Mike probably still hung out with Jeff. How either of them could still stand the sight of him after knowing what he had done was beyond me, but I figured I should give her the benefit of the doubt and call her to talk things over.

"Hannah?"

"Oh, my gosh, Charlotte! How are you? How's Paris? I'm so sorry I haven't been in touch. I've been going out of my mind planning this wedding! I mean, we've had the longest engagement ever, but you know me…always procrastinating. Now I'm scrambling to get it all booked in time." Hannah had a way of babbling really quickly on the phone so that it was hard to get a word in edgewise.

"Don't worry, I'm sure it will all come together. I just got your e-mail about all of the bridesmaid stuff, so I'll make sure to get on it."

"Oh, thank you! I didn't mean to come off as a crazy

bridezilla in the e-mail, I just want everything to be perfect, you know?"

I did know. I had felt the same way when I had envisioned my wedding to Jeff. We had also decided to have a long engagement and were planning on getting married after we got back from Paris. But just because I hadn't actually booked the church or the reception hall yet didn't mean that I didn't have it all perfectly planned out in my head.

"No, I completely understand, so just let me know what you need me to do and it's done, okay?"

"Thanks, you're a doll. So, how are things? Are you doing okay since…you know, since everything happened?"

I didn't want Hannah to know how much Jeff had really hurt me. Even though she was one of my close friends, it could get back to Jeff. So I tried to play it cool. "Yeah, you know, of course it sucked, but Jeff just wasn't the right one for me in the end."

"So, you're really doing okay, then? Have you met anyone new?"

"Yeah, I've met a few nice guys over here."

"Oh, I'm so glad to hear you say that, Charlotte…" She paused hesitantly. "So you won't mind, then, that Jeff's still in the wedding?"

"What? Well, I mean I knew he would be there of course, but I didn't think that after what he did to me that you, or Mike, would actually keep him in the wedding," I said as I tried to keep the shrillness out of my voice.

"I'm sorry, Charlotte. I tried to convince Mike to leave Jeff out of the wedding party because I knew it would be awful for you, but we ended up having a huge fight about it. Even though Jeff cheated on you, he's still Mike's best friend, and Mike isn't going to budge. Plus, it sounds like you're moving on, so maybe it won't be that bad in the end." Hannah was so naïve. She was the sweetest, most wholesome girl I knew and had never been cheated on (well, to her knowledge anyway—hopefully Mike wasn't as big of a scumbag as Jeff).

"Yes, I'm moving on. But Hannah, we were engaged to be married, and we were about to move to Paris, and he cheated on me! What if that happened to you? What if you had this whole wedding planned and you found out that Mike was sleeping with another woman?"

Hannah was quiet for a moment. "I would be devastated."

"And what if I married Jeff and we had Mike in the wedding so you had to see him and hang out with him all weekend and have the whole embarrassing situation shoved back in your face in front of all of your friends?"

Hannah stayed quiet for a few more seconds before speaking. "I know this is going to be hard for you, Charlotte, but it's not my fault that Jeff cheated on you. And I can't help the fact that Jeff is Mike's best friend. He's going to be there, but I need you here for me. You can totally ignore him all weekend. Just focus on me and seeing all of the girls again. We really miss you."

Hannah was right—I was freaking out at the wrong person. As much as I wanted her to kick Jeff out of their lives, or at least out of their wedding, she was stuck in a tricky situation.

"Is he bringing a date?" I asked.

"I really don't know."

"Is he still seeing that girl Brooke?"

"This isn't going to help you get over him. I think we should change the subject."

"Hannah, I'm coming to the wedding, and I'll calm down...I'm sorry. It's not until April anyway, so I'm sure things will be even better by then. But please just tell me, is he still with that girl?"

She paused for a long time. "I think so."

I suddenly felt so defeated that my body went limp, and I could almost hear my heart dropping to the floor.

"So, tell me more about Paris, don't you just love it?" Hannah made her best effort at changing the subject, but I wasn't in the mood to chitchat anymore.

"Hey, listen, I actually have to run. I have a date tonight, and I have to hop in the shower so I'm not late." I didn't have a date, but I didn't want her to go blabbing to Mike about what a maniac I was on the phone. I just needed to go.

"Oh, that's great! Well, have fun, and we'll be in touch over e-mail…" She paused and then sighed into the phone. "I'm sorry, Charlotte, please don't be mad at me."

"I'm not mad at you…I just need to get going, all right?"

"Okay." Hannah's voice dropped.

"I'll talk to you soon, though. Bye." I hung up the phone without giving her a chance to say good-bye and instantly felt the tears welling up.

Damn him.

I thought I was getting over my broken engagement. But hearing that Jeff was actually still with Brooke brought all of those unbearable feelings back to the surface.

I'd thought I'd found my soul mate in Jeff, but he clearly had never loved me the way I'd loved him. Had I been nothing more than a means to an end? The catalyst in helping Jeff to find Brooke, his true soul mate?

What if I never found anyone I loved as much as him? What if I was destined to be single and alone forever? Because, at this point, with my insides ripping to shreds just at the mention of his name, I wasn't sure if I'd ever be able to truly give my heart over to another man.

As my tears transformed to anger, and I wondered how I would face Jeff and Brooke together at the wedding, I threw on my running clothes, raced outside, and sprinted like a madwoman around the park. I silently cursed all of the dying couples who had invaded the tranquil space in the last half hour since I'd been there with Marc. On every bench I passed, they were kissing, groping, and cooing at each other with serious, dramatic looks on their faces.

I diverted my eyes and focused on the dirt path ahead while the pounding of my feet echoed throughout my tired, beaten-down body.

Once my lungs were sufficiently deflated, I collapsed in the grass, gasping for breath. I stared up at the dark-gray clouds that pushed their way through the sky, blocking the sun and darkening the world with their heaviness, and wondered when, or if, I would stop caring about Jeff.

In that moment, I felt as if all the effort I'd made to move on with my life in Paris had been for nothing. Had meeting other guys and attempting to date like a man really gotten me anywhere? I was right back where I'd started, feeling lonely, desperate, and brokenhearted.

What was I doing here? And would I really be able to pull it together in time to be there for Hannah at her wedding?

As large, chilling drops of rain fell from the sky and pelted my hot skin, I peeled myself up off the grass and hobbled across the street to my dorm. I lowered my eyes to the ground as the rain blew through me in sheets. I couldn't bear to see even one more happy couple, their eyes gleaming and their cheeks all rosy as they trotted through the rain, smashing their bodies up against each other underneath their miniature umbrellas.

Back in my room, I sank down into my bed, wrapped a blanket around my drenched shoulders, and pulled my computer onto my lap so I could sign in to my blog. I had to do something to pull myself out of this funk.

I was shocked to find that I suddenly had hundreds of hits. I scrolled through the long list of comments and saw Lexi's name at the bottom. She wrote: "Girl, I *love* your blog. Every woman needs to read this. I forwarded it to everyone I know. I'll see your hot ass soon!"

Wow. Good thing I met Lexi. Now I really *could* help tons of women going through this dating mess. I began typing:

Rule # 1 — Guy friends are good.

You don't have to be romantically attracted to every guy you hang out with. Having male friends helps to fill that companionship void we all feel after the loss of a relationship, and it ensures that we won't have to hook up or have sex with guys who we're not that attracted to just to feel validated. This is another area where we, as women, have the upper hand. We are much better at just being friends with the opposite sex than men are (obviously because we're not barbarians who think with penises). It's as simple as that. Nurturing your male friendships will help you to leave those slimy exes in the dust and move forward with your fabulous new life.

And it will help you to avoid taking desperate measures just to be in a man's company.

Case in Point: Now that I have my new, charming tutoring student to hang out with, I will (hopefully) not feel the need to knock on Half-Naked French Hottie's door just to experience male companionship. Since he hasn't attempted to see me in a month, contacting him would be desperate behavior on my part. Having a handsome French male friend in my life will keep me on track in my quest to avoid messy, sketchy men and more importantly, love. (Although the handsome part is irrelevant since he's only a friend, and more appropriately, a tutoring student whose mother turned out to be my evil advisor — but we'll get into that another day).

Rule # 2 — Do not attempt to find out what is going on in your ex's love life. Even if you think you can handle it, please spare yourself the second dose of heartache and keep moving forward with your life. Because once you hear that he's still with the woman who stole him away from you in the first place, you will feel as if someone has ripped your heart out all over again and spat on it.

Trust me, I know.

I started to type a third rule about how being a bridesmaid in a wedding where your ex is going to be the best man is about the worst thing you could ever do, but then I remembered that I had forwarded my blog to all of my friends back home, including Hannah. I doubted she was reading it, seeing as how she was busy planning a wedding and being in love and all that, but I didn't want to make the situation any more awkward than it already was. So I bit my tongue on that one and kept it to myself.

FOURTEEN

jeudi, le 18 novembre

Save yourself the drama and buy your own damn chocolate bar.

More than two weeks had passed since my phone call with Hannah, and as I closed the curtains in my room to block any light from coming in and poured myself another glass of wine, I realized I had officially plummeted to the depths of despair.

For days now, I hadn't been able to erase the thought of Jeff and Brooke from my mind. I had absurd visions where they were holding hands and frolicking through daffodil-covered fields, then stopping to make love in the grass while Jeff would whisper in her ear how happy he was that he'd finally found his soul mate. I had nightmares about walking in on them having sex in Jeff's bed, and when they saw the horrified look on my face, they simply laughed and kept at it. I woke up more than a few times that week covered in sweat, with tears streaming down my face.

I was in no state to see anyone, so I holed up in my room, ignored my friends' messages, skipped classes, slept, and drank *a lot* of cheap wine. I didn't eat much either, and the few times I did get dressed to go buy more wine, I noticed that my jeans were falling off me. I'd canceled my sessions with Marc, telling him I'd come down with a bug that I just couldn't shake off, and even when Luc had finally knocked on my door the day before, I'd stayed in bed.

I'd hit a new all-time low, and I wasn't sure how to get myself out of it. The only person I had any desire to talk to was my mom, but I couldn't get in touch with her or my dad. They hadn't answered any of my calls or e-mails. I probably should've been worried, but I was too depressed to think about anything other than Jeff and Brooke's lovemaking sessions in the daffodil field.

The only thing that gave me even a remote sense of comfort was thinking about spending Christmas back in Ohio with my parents. So on that chilly November evening, after I'd made the mistake of digging my engagement ring out of my jewelry box and slipping it back on my desolate ring finger, I downed two more glasses of wine on an empty stomach and dialed home.

"Hello? Charlotte?"

"Hi, Mom." I let out a sigh of relief at the sound of her voice.

"Hi, sweetie. I'm so glad you called. I have something very exciting to tell you!" My mom hadn't sounded this excited in a long time, so I knew it must be big.

"Really? What's going on?" I thought that maybe she and my dad were planning a trip to come see me or that she had bought a new comforter for their bed—who knew?

"I'm leaving your father," she announced, very matter-of-factly.

My jaw dropped to the floor. The two of them had been together for over thirty years now, and even though I knew they weren't "in love," so to speak, I *never* thought my mom would leave him.

"So...what are you going to do?" I asked, fumbling to come up with the right words.

"Oh, I have all sorts of plans. As a matter of fact, I'm packing right now to take a trip to Florida to visit Aunt Liza. I may just stay down there for a while. Who knows? There's a whole world of possibilities now that I won't be tied down to a man!" She sounded a little too excited, manic actually.

I really couldn't believe what I was hearing. My mom had always been the passive type who seemed like she would be content with a mediocre marriage for the rest of her life as long as Dad mowed the lawn and paid the bills. That brought me to my next concern. My mom hadn't worked a full-time job since as long as I could remember. She had held odd, part-time jobs, like working at a flower shop and a bakery, but she had never gone to college and instead had become an expert at spending my dad's money on making the house perfect. It's what all the women in her family had done before her, so it's all she knew, and she did it well. Without my dad's money to support her, what on earth was she going to do? Plus, Aunt Liza was a wild woman. She had never settled down or had children, she was always dating someone new every time we talked to her, and, for all I knew, she had more sex than I did—which, at this point, since I wasn't having any sex, wasn't that difficult to do. My mom had never approved of her lifestyle, so they'd never gotten along too well over the years.

I tried to calm the frenzied thoughts that were zipping around in my head, but I couldn't. I felt like a needy little girl at the thought of my parents separating, and as I struggled to think of the right thing to say, I decided I was entitled to ask questions. This was my family too, after all.

"You're going to live with Aunt Liza? But you hate her! Are you going to work? How are you going to make money? What does Dad think? Did you tell him you were leaving?"

"Yes, of course your father knows. It's been coming for

quite some time, you know. I just didn't have the courage to go before now. And money isn't an issue; your father and I will split everything equally. You don't need to worry about me, dear. I'm happier than I've been in years!"

"What about the house? Dad will stay there while you're gone, right?"

"Um, not exactly," she answered hesitantly. "We put it on the market last week."

"Where's Dad going to live?" The thought of losing the house I'd grown up in made me feel frantic. I'd already lost so much this year, I couldn't lose my home and my family too.

"He'll be moving in with Joan," she said in a dry tone.

"Who the hell is Joan?"

"Joan is...well, she's Dad's *friend*."

"Friend? Mom, I'm not five years old anymore. You can tell me. Is Dad already dating someone else?"

She paused and took a deep breath. "Your dad has been seeing her for quite some time now."

"And you knew?"

"Of course I knew, Charlotte. A woman always knows."

"But I didn't know that Jeff was cheating on me. I had no idea."

"Well, I've been with your father for over thirty years now, and I just knew. What made me finally realize that it was time for me to leave, though, was when I read your blog. You gave me the strength to do this, Charlotte. You're such an inspiration."

"What? My blog? How did you even know I was writing a blog?"

"You sent it to me in a mass e-mail with your friends. Don't you remember, dear?"

I plopped my forehead into my hands. I must've added her to the e-mail by accident. I *never* wanted my mom to see those posts.

"You're taking *my* advice?" I asked.

"Of course, dear. Why not? You're absolutely right. It's time to throw love out the window and get in the game!"

I couldn't believe what I was hearing. "But mom, I'm *twenty-five*. You're fifty-five. That advice isn't meant for parents! You can't use that as a reason to break up our family."

"Charlotte." My mom's voice was stern over the line. "*I* am not the one who has broken up this family. Our marriage has been broken for years now. Don't you remember what happened when you were a teenager?"

I closed my eyes, the memories I'd stifled for so long threatening to burst to the surface. But no matter how hard I tried, I couldn't stop them.

My mom had been out of town visiting her best friend, and I'd come home sick from school one day only to find my father climbing into his car with a tall blonde woman, kissing her on the lips, then driving away with her.

With the secret of my father's infidelity ripping away at my insides, I'd confessed what I'd seen to my mom the next week. After an entire month of knock'em-down screaming fights in our house, and my fearing that my little family would forever be torn apart, Dad finally realized what he needed to do. He sent Mom flowers every day for a month, cooked her dinner, took her to the theater, wrote her love letters. He even flew her to Italy for their anniversary. But after about a year, the grand gestures died down and life returned to normal.

Except it wasn't normal. It was never the same again. All of the flowers, the dinners, the letters, even the trip, couldn't earn Mom's trust back again. She never looked at Dad with that adoring gaze she had before. Dad stopped kissing Mom before he left the house every morning. And once I left for college, they even stopped sleeping in the same bedroom.

I guess I was naïve to ever have thought a marriage could endure in that state. But their thirty-plus years together had made me believe that they would never separate. That I would always have my quaint little home in Ohio to return to. That even though their love hadn't survived the test of time and infidelity, the *appearance* of my family would always be there.

All the while, I was unable to erase the thought that it was all my fault. If only I had kept my mouth shut, my mom's heart never would've been broken. My family would've stayed intact.

And now, to find out it was *my* blog that had spurred my mother to leave. What a disaster.

"Charlotte?" my mom said, calling me back to the present.

"Yes, Mom. Of course I remember what happened. I should never have told you what I saw that day. Maybe things would be different now."

"That's nonsense. None of this is your fault. You did the right thing. But now I've realized that I want your dad to just go and be with Joan. If she makes him happy, then so be it. The point is that we don't make each other happy anymore, and we haven't for years. You know that."

"I know. But what about you? You're going to Florida and then what?"

"Well, Aunt Liza has a few people she's going to introduce me to down there, and I'm going to start a whole new life. An exciting one! There's no time to waste!"

"Well, I...I'm happy for you, then," I said, trying to sound supportive even though I was totally lying. I decided right then and there that I wasn't going home for Christmas. The thought of visiting my mom at crazy Aunt Liza's house or going to Ohio to see my dad and his new girlfriend made me feel sick to my stomach. Neither option involved going to *my* house, having Christmas Eve dinner with *my* parents, or drinking hot chocolate and opening presents on Christmas morning like we had done every year since I was born. Instead, I'd be spending Christmas with weird people I barely knew, so it wasn't an option at this point. My mom was disappointed, but too bad. I was disappointed too. This whole situation just confirmed my feelings about marriage.

As an institution, it was a total disaster.

Not wanting to hear another word, I hastily got off the phone. I tore the giant rock off my finger and buried it back in the depths of my jewelry box. As I kicked around at the empty wine bottles littered all over my floor, I knew I had to get out of there. If I stayed in my room another minute, my life was certain to take the plunge from depressing to hopeless. Plus, even though I'd been buying cheap wine, I'd bought a lot of it and had managed to deplete a nice portion of my bank account. So I dialed Marc's number and told him my flu was gone, and he agreed to meet me at a café across the street in fifteen minutes for a lesson. It was time to work on divorce vocabulary.

Marc was sipping a cup of espresso at a tiny table in the back corner of the café when I arrived.

"Hey, Marc," I said, taking a seat across from him.

"Hi, Charlotte, how's it going?" he said as he chuckled to himself. During our first lesson, I had instructed him to use phrases like "How's it going?" and "What's up?" instead of always saying "How are you doing?"

"I'm okay," I lied. "How about you?"

"Pretty good. I—I just have a question for you, though."

"Yeah?"

"Were you really sick for the past three weeks?"

Shit.

"Yeah, why?"

"I know I told you I wasn't going to get in the middle of things with you and my mother, but after you and I worked everything out last time and had our lesson, I had a really great time. Even though I *was* offended by the way you described her, I thought about it, and I can see now how she could seem kind of mean to someone who doesn't know her like I do."

Kind of mean?

I cringed on the inside as Marc continued.

"I think you're an excellent English teacher, so I thought that if I told my mom about working with you, she might be a little nicer and actually help you get your teaching position. After all, I know she is very picky about who she recommends."

"So how did it go when you told her you knew me?"

Marc stirred a sugar cube into his espresso and, for the first time in our conversation, avoided my gaze.

"Not so good," he finally answered.

I buried my head in my hands. This was the last thing I needed right now.

"She said you have not been attending your classes this month, and so I told her you were ill. She did not believe me, though, so that is why I asked you."

I considered telling Marc the truth because I just didn't have the energy to lie anymore, but what if he told his mom? I'd be more screwed than I already was. And, in a sense, I *did* have an illness of sorts—an emotional one. And that was exactly the kind that Madame Rousseau would never understand.

"I haven't been to class because I've been really sick," I snapped.

Marc's expression darkened. "I see. Then I am sorry if I put you in a worse position. I tried my best to tell her to give you a second chance, but she was still very angry."

I immediately felt bad for snapping at Marc. Here he was going up against his monster of a mother to help me out after I'd completely trashed her during our first lesson. What guy would do that?

I softened my voice. "No, Marc, *I'm* sorry. I'm sorry for saying all of those horrible things last time. I can't even believe you still want to work with me. And I'm sorry for disappearing these past few weeks. I'm going to be more available to work with you from now on, and I'll try to do better in school so hopefully your mom will form a better opinion of me on her own. It's not your job to fix it for me, but I really appreciate you trying, after everything."

Exasperated, I let out a long sigh. My life was in shambles. I stared out the window at the Parisians all bundled up in their long coats and scarves. I wondered what it would be like to jump into another person's skin, to be someone else for the day. My mom always used to tell me that I would never trade my problems for someone else's, but I wasn't so sure anymore.

I wasn't sure if I could get through any of this. My parents' divorce. Losing Jeff to another woman. Facing them at the wedding in the spring. Finishing my semester in Paris. Even having this lesson with Marc. It was all too much.

"Are you okay?" Marc asked.

Something about the concern in his eyes made me just spit it out. "My parents are getting a divorce."

"Oh, I am so sorry. Did you just hear?"

"Yeah, I talked to my mom about an hour ago. She's leaving my dad and moving to Florida for a little while, and my dad is moving in with his girlfriend." I shook my head in disgust. "It's just so weird, you know?"

"Yes, I know. My parents are also divorced."

I thought of Madame Rousseau and instantly understood. How could anyone have stayed married to *her*?

"They got divorced two years ago. It was really difficult," he continued. "I completely understand how you feel."

A wave of sadness swept over me as I realized that this was real. That I was never going to have holidays or even simple weekends at home with both of my parents in the same room. A knot caught in my throat as I stared down at the table in silence. Marc reached over and gently placed his hand on my shoulder.

"I know it is difficult, but you have to let them live their lives and you have to live your life here in Paris. They will be okay, and you must take care of yourself."

I glanced up and managed a smile. Marc was so sweet. How could he be so nice to me after I'd started off our relationship by being so offensive?

"Let's go into the city and have a drink," he said as he squeezed my shoulder. "You need to forget about all of this mess and have fun." I noticed then that Marc must've been working on perfecting his *th* sound during our three-week break.

"Really, you're not busy tonight?" I asked him.

"No, I was going to study, but I can do that tomorrow. It's a yes?"

A drink, or maybe ten, sounded wonderful right about now. "That sounds great, let's go."

Marc paid for his coffee, and we headed down the chilly, student-filled Boulevard Jourdan toward the RER station.

"Charlotte!"

I turned around to find Luc walking right behind us and smiling his huge grin. But when Luc met eyes with Marc, his smile faded.

"Hey, Luc. Haven't seen you around in a while," I said.

"I know, I am sorry. I have been out of town for the month. I had to see family and take care of some things. I knocked on your door yesterday, but you did not answer."

So that's why I hadn't seen him around—if he was even telling the truth. I thought he was just avoiding me after the run-in with Frédéric. Not that I would've wanted to see him anyway in my pathetic state.

Luc glanced over at Marc and then back at me, until I realized that I should probably introduce them. "Luc, this is

Marc, my English student. And Marc, this is my friend Luc. He lives in my building."

The tension in Luc's face faded, and he reached out to shake Marc's hand.

"You are walking to the RER?" Luc asked us.

"Yeah, where are you headed?"

"I am going to take a drink with Benoît. Do you want to join me?" He aimed the question at me and didn't seem to be including Marc in the invitation.

"Well, Marc and I were in the middle of our lesson and were going to go grab a drink in the city while we continued, so...I'm not really sure," I replied, looking to Marc to see if he would be opposed to the idea.

"Oh," Luc said as his shoulders hunched just the slightest bit. "The two of you can come, that is no problem. And we will speak English for the whole night. No?"

I wasn't sure what to do, but a "yes" popped out of my mouth, and the three of us were off. We piled onto the RER together, which thankfully was becoming more pleasant to ride as the weather cooled down. Luc and Marc made awkward small talk, which made me feel even more uncomfortable, so I pulled out my phone and sent Lexi and Fiona a desperate text message:

On way to Rhubarb with Luc, Marc, and Benoît. Awkward! Please come!

As Marc, Luc, and I climbed the stairs at the Luxembourg stop, we emerged to the moonlit Latin Quarter, where groups of friends, every age, strolled down the narrow sidewalks, skimming over the fallen leaves in their Euro sneakers and walking with an extra skip in their step as the night air chilled around them.

As I wrapped my thin red jacket tighter around my waist, I noticed all of the hard-core Parisians sitting outdoors at the cafés, not fazed in the slightest by the sudden drop in temperature. And each time we passed by a group of hormonally charged French guys, bopping around in their skintight jeans and white Reebok high-tops, they didn't toss any of their immature remarks my way.

I would have to bring Marc and Luc into the city with me more often.

The girls showed up at Rhubarb, a hole-in-the-wall bar in the fifth arrondissement, no more than ten minutes after Luc, Marc, and I had arrived to meet Benoît. Lexi strutted in and planted a big one on Benoît right in front of everyone. I had thought that Lexi wasn't all that into him since she hooked up with tons of other guys every time we went out, but she attached herself to him the minute she got there. Fiona made a more modest entrance and, after greeting all of the guys, came over to chat with me.

"I'm so glad you invited me out. Is everything okay? I haven't heard from you in a few weeks, and I haven't seen you in class."

"I'm really sorry. I've just been having a hard time lately." I filled Fiona in on the wedding, my newfound drinking habit, and my parents' divorce.

"I'm so sorry you're going through all of that. Next time, you can call me, though. You don't have to hide in your room, you know."

"I'm sorry. That was really shitty of me."

"It's okay. I do understand. I didn't leave my flat for practically six months after Andrew left me. At least call me next time so I know you're alive, okay?"

"I promise I will."

"Speaking of Andrew, he called me today and tried to stir things up again, so I needed to get out and get my mind off him."

Underneath the dim lights of the bar, I noticed then that Fiona's eyes were bloodshot and puffy like she'd been crying.

"Does he want to get back together?"

"No…yes…I don't know. He's still with that other girl, but

he told me he misses me." She shook her head and dropped her eyes to the floor. "I'm so confused."

After having the divorce talk with my mom earlier, I was even more convinced that all relationships were doomed to fail. "Don't fall for it, Fiona. Your life is here now, and he's still with that other girl. You need to have a few drinks and forget about that bastard."

Fiona laughed. She always giggled like a little girl whenever I called guys rotten names. "So, who's Marc?" she asked as she gave him the once-over.

"He's my English student, and you'll never believe this, but he's Madame Rousseau's son!"

Fiona's eyes widened to the size of quarters. "That old hag at the Sorbonne?"

"Mm-hmm."

She glanced over at Marc then back at me. "It's not possible. He seems so normal, not to mention good-looking, and she's so...*dreadful*."

"I couldn't believe it either. But you'll see; he's nothing like her." I watched Fiona glue her gaze on Marc as he and the rest of the group walked over to us.

Luc had ordered everyone a drink, so we all clinked our glasses together and got started. In an attempt to drown our sorrows, Fiona and I downed our first two drinks. I hadn't eaten dinner, so the alcohol hit me right away. There wasn't too much space to dance at Rhubarb, but we made room. Before we knew it, our whole group was out on the dance floor busting a move, except Lexi and Benoît, who were draped all over each other in the corner of the bar. Luc took my hand to dance with me, so Fiona and Marc ended up dancing together.

"It's so nice to see you again. I missed you," Luc said as he wrapped his arms around my waist.

"It's nice to see you again too. So you've been out of town for the whole month?"

"Yes, but it is good to be back," he said as he brushed his stubble up against my cheek and pulled me closer to him.

I inched my face back and asked, "Is everything okay with your family?" I knew I was breaking one of my own rules by starting a serious talk when I should just enjoy the moment, but I wanted to know what in the heck was going on with this guy and why he had disappeared for a month.

"Euh…well, it will be okay," he said unconvincingly. "But for tonight, I just want to forget about it and enjoy this time with you." He pulled me in even tighter while his hands roamed down to the small of my back.

I became intoxicated by the smell of his cologne and the feel of his body pressed up against mine. He made me forget all about Jeff and Brooke's frolics through the daffodil fields, not to mention my dysfunctional family situation. Plus, I hadn't had any physical contact with a guy since the night of my phone call with Hannah, and it was starting to take a toll on me.

The news of my parents' divorce was still ringing loudly in my ears, though, telling me to sleep with Luc and nothing more. No feelings, no attachment, no falling in love.

So, when we got back to our dorm and Luc invited me into his room, without hesitation I said yes.

Luc led me over to his bed and pulled me down on top of him. I relaxed into his arms as his hands wandered all over my body. He kissed my neck and shoulders and slowly made his way up to my lips. His scruffy face scraped against my soft cheeks as his lips pressed harder into mine and he rolled over on top of me. Our hips ground together as Luc moved back and forth over my pulsing body.

Jeff's face flashed unwelcome through my mind as Luc's hands slipped underneath my bra. I tried to forget about Jeff, but then I thought of Brooke. Stealing my fiancé. She probably thought she'd won the jackpot with him, just as I'd thought when we'd first met.

As Luc's hands groped my breasts and his breathing grew heavy, I snapped back to reality. *Screw them*, I thought. I was here, in bed with this gorgeous, sweet guy who wanted every square inch of me. I didn't need Jeff. I had Luc.

As rage and passion boiled inside of me, I reached down to unbutton Luc's pants. He grinned at me as he let me remove his pants and shirt, and then he tore off all of my clothes. He reached into his bedside stand for a condom and put it on in record speed. He kissed me again as he pushed himself inside of me and moved forcefully on top of me. He groped my ass, my waist, my breasts, and moaned deeply in my ear as our bodies moved violently in sync. I dug my nails into his back as he rolled me over on top of him and made me cry out in pleasure. Then, no more than a few seconds later, he finished and we collapsed in each other's arms, barely able to breathe.

We lay in bed together for a few minutes, my head resting on his chest, listening to his rapidly beating heart. He ran his hands up and down my back and kissed the top of my head. I looked up at him and smiled, and he leaned down and kissed me softly on the lips. Once we caught our breath, Luc stepped out of bed and sauntered, naked, over to the counter to pour us each another glass of wine. I admired his lean, sculpted body as he grabbed a small bag of Ferrero Rocher chocolates and cuddled up next to me once again.

Luc unwrapped one of the golden truffles and held it out for me to take a bite. An explosion of luscious hazelnut and creamy milk chocolate met my tongue. Luc popped the other half of the truffle into his mouth.

"Mmm." I closed my eyes and took a sip of the smoky red wine. "This is delicious."

"See, you agree with me now. There is nothing better than chocolate after sex."

I smiled as Luc fed me another truffle, his warm, bare skin pressing up against mine.

"I am sorry I did not tell you I was leaving for a while. I didn't know I would be gone that long," he said after unwrapping another piece of chocolate for himself.

"That's okay. It's just nice to see you again."

"You too. Are you having a good time in Paris?"

I opened my mouth, ready to lie, to tell him what a fabulous time I was having here. But with the exception of spending this wonderful evening with him, life had been pretty tough lately. I knew that if I opened up, I would be violating my rules—no serious talks and no emotional involvement. But lying there in bed with Luc, I felt myself wanting to let him in and show him the real me...even the not-so-glamorous parts.

So, I ignored my rules, my blog, my promise to myself to stay detached, and instead, I started talking.

"To be honest, the past few weeks here have been kind of rough."

Luc pulled the sheet up over us and cuddled even closer to me. "I'm so sorry to hear this. What has been going on?"

As I began to tell Luc about my parents' soon-to-be divorce, the knot that had been lodged in my chest since that talk with Hannah finally released. It felt so amazing to open up to someone who cared, someone who listened without judging, without trying to fix everything. And as I started in on the story of what happened with my dad when I was a teenager, I realized that I'd never told any of my friends about that incident. Not even Katie. I'd been so mortified that my dad would do something so deceitful to both me and my mom that I'd never told a soul. I'd let everyone believe that my parents were happy, that my family was perfect.

But they weren't perfect, and Luc seemed to get that. He understood that I wasn't perfect either. So, as I ignored all of my rules and spilled my guts to this man, who somehow had managed to draw me in like no other, I wondered if, in Luc,

I'd actually found a man who could be different from all the rest. Different from my dad. Different from Jeff.

A man who wouldn't hurt me.

After I finished talking, Luc squeezed my hand and kissed me on the forehead. "Divorce is ugly," he said. "And even though you are an adult, it is never easy to see your family falling apart. Trust me, I know."

Just as I was opening my mouth to thank him for listening and to ask how *he* was doing and why he'd been out of town for so long, his cell phone rang.

He jumped out of bed naked, took one look at the caller ID, and scowled. "I'm sorry, Charlotte. I have to take this...alone."

I sat up in Luc's bed, only a sheet draped over my naked body. He was seriously kicking me out? After we'd just had sex, and after I'd told him the entire story about my family splitting up? Unbelievable.

I shot out of bed, feeling like an idiot to have thought for even one second that Luc would be different. When would I learn? I threw on my clothes and let the door slam on my way out.

Back in my room, I could almost feel the steam puffing out of my ears as I flipped open my computer. I didn't want to waste any more tears over a dumb man, so instead, I poured all of my rage into my next blog entry:

Rule # 1—Avoid relationships at all costs because they may eventually lead to marriage, and marriage is doomed to fail. Over half of marriages will end in divorce and heartache. Do you really want to be fifty years old and reinventing your life all by yourself while your husband is off sleeping with a younger model? I know I may be coming off as a pessimistic man-hater, but I'm just telling you how it is, ladies.

Case in Point: After finding out that my parents are getting a divorce and my dad is sleeping with another woman, I have to reinforce this point. How could it be possible to be with someone for your entire life and never want to be with anyone else? I'm not even blaming it all on my dad here. Marriages take two people, but those two people are human, and humans get bored easily. So why even enter into such a faulty institution in the first place?

Rule # 2—Guys are sketchy. I know, I've already told you this, but hear me out.

Case in Point: After disappearing for a month, Half-Naked French Hottie shows up, we have a wonderful night out dancing in Paris, then we come back to his place and have orgasmic sex followed by chocolate and wine in bed.

Then his phone rings, and he bolts up out of bed to answer it before telling me to leave. Totally unacceptable, not to mention rude. Tell me, who exactly do you think is calling him at two in the morning? It's not his mother, that's for sure.

I'm not saying that you can't hang out with guys who demonstrate sketchy behavior (because, let's face it, they all do something weird at one point or another). I'm just saying that you shouldn't get emotionally attached to these guys. They're dangerous, and, as I've said before, taking care of your heart should be your number-one priority.

Rule # 3—It's okay to hole up in your apartment and hide from the outside world from time to time. Sometimes you just can't take another setback, and it's better to close the door on all of it and hope that the drama has disappeared by the time you're ready to come out.

As I was about to hit the Publish button, I thought about the fact that my mom was reading my blog now. I didn't want to add even more fuel to her fire, but I knew that it didn't matter what I said at this point. The house was on the market. She was leaving Dad. My small family was officially broken.

I published my blog post, then signed in to my e-mail. There, I found a message from Madame Rousseau at the top of my in-box. My insides twisted into knots before I even opened it.

Mademoiselle Summers,

After checking in with your professors, I have learned that you have not been attending your classes. In addition, you have not yet contacted me to schedule our required meeting in December. My schedule is extremely busy, so if you are serious about being a teacher at a private school in Paris, I suggest you make more of an effort. The fact that my son seems to be keen on your abilities to teach English does not mean you have earned the privilege to miss your classes and act like an irresponsible teenager. If this behavior continues, I, for one, will not place you in a teaching position at the end of the academic year, and I will advise my son to discontinue his English lessons with you.
Madame Rousseau

Why was this woman so freaking unreasonable? It was only the middle of November. Did I really have to schedule our meeting a full month in advance?

I e-mailed her back and informed her I'd been deathly ill with a contagious flu. At least I'd told Marc I'd been sick, so if she asked him, he would confirm my lie. Then I asked her if we could meet the second week in December, when all of my final papers were due to my professors.

I was so not looking forward to that meeting.

At this point, I was sure Madame Rousseau would never recommend me for a teaching position in Paris. I'd have to kick some serious ass on my final papers to even begin to prove to her that I was worthy. What if I didn't get a teaching job when the school year was over? What would I have to go home to? Reminders of my broken engagement and divorced parents—that's what.

I had to stay in Paris and I had to get a job. And if impressing that time-obsessed old French hag was what I had to do, then that's what I was going to do.

FIFTEEN

vendredi, le 10 décembre

A straight man who takes you to the ballet is like a rare gem—once you give it up, regret inevitably follows.

In early December, after two weeks of avoiding Luc's calls, texts, and knocks on the door by locking myself up in my room to write my final papers, I received an e-mail from an editor at *Bella Magazine*, a popular women's magazine back in the US.

> *Dear Charlotte,*
> *My friend Lexi passed your blog on to me, and we here at* Bella Magazine *think you're on to something. If you're interested, we'd like for you to write an article for our April issue on the top ten lessons you've learned on how to date like a man in Paris. You can include your personal anecdotes, just as you do in your blog.*
>
> *I, personally, am hooked on the Half-Naked French Hottie story line, and I think our readers would love to see how it*

all turns out. Please let me know if you're interested. I look forward to hearing from you.
Beth Harding
Editor, Bella Magazine

I couldn't believe what I was reading. *Bella Magazine* wanted *me* to write an article? I could reach thousands and thousands of women this way. I could save many of them from heartbreak. This was incredible.

I hit the Reply button without so much as giving it a second thought. I told her I was thrilled to write an article for them and that I would begin working on it immediately. I figured I should probably finish writing my final papers first, but I couldn't help but draw up a blank document and start drafting. I had so much to share. How would I condense it all into just one article?

∽

After another week and a half of nonstop writing and the occasional break to shower, sleep, and have lunch with the girls, I hit the Print button for my final papers. The article was still a work in progress. Then I decided to get out of my room and take a walk. I needed some fresh air. I peeked down the hallway first to make sure I didn't see Luc, and then sprinted down the corridor. Just as the elevator reached my floor, a door clicked shut down the hall. As the elevator door was opening, a man's voice yelled, "*Attends*, Charlotte!"

Damn. I almost made it. It's not that I didn't want to see Luc because I didn't like him. It was exactly the opposite. I was afraid that the more I hung out with him, and the more fantastic sex we had, I might really start to care about him. But he would keep answering his damn phone in the middle of our dates (while we're naked, no less) and disappearing for weeks at a time, and I wasn't willing to put up with all of that nonsense.

Luc caught up to me and leaned down to kiss me on the cheeks.

"I've been trying to talk to you," he said as we stepped onto the elevator together. "But, I cannot get in touch with you. You are okay, right?"

"Yeah, sorry, I've just had a lot of work to do for finals. I've been really busy."

"I want to apologize for the last time we were together. For asking you to leave when the phone rang. That was rude of me. I want to explain—"

"Luc, seriously, whatever you do in your free time is your business," I said, cutting him off. "You don't need to tell me about it. In fact, I don't really want to know. I've got my own stuff going on too."

"Oh okay." He shifted his eyes to the floor. "Well, I wanted to give you something."

It was then that I noticed the envelope he was holding with my name written across the front. He handed it to me as we stepped out of the elevator.

"Open it," he urged. "It's your Christmas gift."

With all the writing I'd been doing, I'd practically forgotten that Christmas was coming up in just a little over a week. I slipped my finger through the flap in the envelope and pulled out two tickets to the Paris Ballet at the Opéra Garnier. I was speechless. Why would he do this for me?

"How did you know I liked the ballet?"

"I saw that photograph in your room of you and your friend doing ballet when you were little girls, plus it is one of the most beautiful things to see in Paris, and I wanted to do something nice for you. So will you go?"

I couldn't believe Luc had noticed that picture. It was of me and Katie in our little pink tutus at our first ballet recital in second grade. It was my absolute favorite picture of the two of us. I'd had it in my studio in DC the entire time I'd dated Jeff and he'd never once asked me about it.

The little voice inside my head told me to say no. Saying yes could open the door to a relationship, to drama, to potential heartbreak.

But his gesture was so kind, so touching, I couldn't listen to that damn little voice. Instead I smiled at him. "Of course I'll go with you. And you're actually going to sit through the ballet with me?"

"*Bien sûr*, I love the ballet. And at the Opéra Garnier, there is nothing better."

Whoa, French men were seriously cultured. I couldn't have gotten Jeff to sit through a ballet with me if I'd paid him a million dollars and promised to give him a blow job a night for the rest of his life.

∼

I had my next meeting with Madame Rousseau at eight o'clock on Friday morning. I had set my alarm for five a.m. and had already verified that there was no *grève* planned for that day. I had worked so hard on these papers, I wasn't about to let the disgruntled transportation workers ruin it for me.

At seven thirty on the dot, I was waiting on a bench outside of Madame Rousseau's office, trying not to fall asleep. I must've dozed off at some point, though, because I was startled awake at the sound of her little black heels clicking down the hallway toward me. I straightened my posture and did my best imitation of a genuine smile.

"I see you are getting quite comfortable there, Mademoiselle Summers." She scowled.

My smile faded. *Can't a girl close her eyes for a minute? Jeez.*

She opened her door and actually let me in this time instead of shutting it in my face. Progress.

I handed her my stack of final papers.

"Well, I certainly hope *this* won't be a waste of my time," she said coolly as she thumbed through my work.

This woman was getting on my last nerve. I forced myself to remain calm as she continued.

"Your professors have informed me that you have returned to their classes. I suspect your *deadly flu* is gone now?" she asked sarcastically.

"Yes, I'm feeling much better, thank you."

"And about my son."

Oh, God. I really didn't want to talk about this.

"Yes, Madame Rousseau?"

"As you know, he has informed me that you are now his *English tutor*." The corners of her mouth turned down into a frown after she'd said the words, as if there were nothing worse in the world she could think of than having *me*, the untimely American, tutor *her* son. "Do you possess formal English tutoring qualifications, Mademoiselle Summers?"

"Well, I *am* a native speaker, and I've been a French teacher for the past three years, so I'm certainly familiar with—"

"So you do not have any formal qualification?"

"Well, um…not a formal qual—"

"Do refrain from stuttering in my presence, Mademoiselle Summers. Tell me, then, would the *professional* description of a tutor include taking your student to a bar and introducing him to your drunken friends?"

God, did Marc tell her *everything*?

"No, I—"

"Stuttering, Mademoiselle Summers!" she shouted suddenly.

I jumped in my seat. I really wanted to leave. Now.

"My son has informed me that you introduced him to a friend of yours, Fiona?"

"Yes, I introduced them during our last lesson."

"Your last lesson at a *bar*." Her eyes burned a hole in me, daring me to respond.

I kept my mouth shut.

"This Fiona girl, where did she get her degree?"

"She went to college in London, and she's a wonderful person."

"I did not ask what kind of person she is, Mademoiselle Summers. I want to know if she is intelligent."

"Yes, she's very sma—"

Madame Rousseau's face boiled red as she cut me off. "Because if you think that you can introduce *my* son, who is going to be a *doctor*, to just any girl, you are very wrong, Mademoiselle Summers. By the way he spoke of this *Fiona*, though, I can tell that he is interested in a...well, a *relationship*, if you will, and I will not have my son marrying an unintelligent British girl!"

Who said anything about marriage? I didn't even know that Marc was interested in Fiona to begin with. Come to think of it, though, they were dancing pretty close that night at the bar. And they didn't leave each other's side the whole night.

"I assure you, Madame Rousseau, Fiona is very intelligent."

"Coming from you, that doesn't say much."

I willed myself to stay planted in my seat. I so wanted to smack her across the face and slam the door on my way out.

"Very well," she said as she tossed my final papers into a large bin on her desk, as if they were nothing more than a piece of trash. "Since my son is of a mature age, I unfortunately cannot force him to find a new tutor, but I assure you I will not hold back my opinion when it comes to his choice in a future mate."

A future mate? God, he'd just danced with Fiona for one night at a bar. I couldn't imagine that Madame Rousseau had ever set foot in a bar, though. "Fun" was probably a punishable word in her household.

"I will contact you after the holiday to discuss whether or not I will be proceeding with a recommendation. In the meantime, please refrain from falling asleep outside of professors' offices. It does not matter if you are early when you are out there sleeping like a cat, Mademoiselle Summers." She stood up and ushered me out the door without letting me say a single word.

I hated that woman.

~

After sharing my less-than-desirable encounter with Madame Rousseau over the phone with Fiona and confirming that Fiona was, in fact, interested in Marc, I began getting ready for my night on the town with Luc. I had been looking forward to it all day.

He showed up at my door that night wearing a crisp, sangria-colored collared shirt, black pants, and a classy overcoat to match. He looked incredible. I had on a beautiful short red dress that plunged down the back...and down the front. I had splurged on it the day after Luc had invited me to the ballet. I spotted it in a store window on rue de Passy, and despite my budget restrictions and the fact that it may have been a little too risqué for a night out in the frosty winter air, I just couldn't resist.

When Luc saw me, his eyes widened. "Charlotte, you look beautiful."

My cheeks flushed and my stomach fluttered as I leaned in to give him *bisous*. Luc dodged my cheeks and went straight for my lips. I plummeted into the depths of his warm, sweet kiss, knowing this was dangerous. But as his lips brushed over mine, I told myself that I was following one of my rules—allowing a guy to pay for a nice night out on the town. That's all this was. A nice, innocent night out in Paris. After we came up for air, Luc helped me on with my coat, and we were off to the ballet.

As we emerged from the Opéra metro stop, the excitement in the air was palpable. Couples dressed in fancy evening attire dashed across the busy street toward the grand old opera house, its pillars and golden sculptures towering over the square like a castle over its kingdom. To the left was the famous Café de la Paix, its deep-green awning and gold lettering all lit up under the lampposts that lined the crowded sidewalks.

My heartbeat quickened as Luc took my hand and led me up the stairs and into the opera house. It was my first time inside the theater, and I was speechless. An endless sea of burgundy seats stretched out before us, while rows of golden balconies climbed up to the ceiling. Once we took our seats, I fixed my gaze up to the immense chandelier overhead and the hues of blue, yellow, green, and red that swirled around it, forming a uniquely modern canvas against its majestic surroundings.

As the lights dimmed and the red velvet curtain lifted off the stage, Luc turned to me, took my hand in his, and winked. I smiled back at him, feeling overwhelmed with warmth.

I glanced over at Luc about halfway through the performance and admired his handsome, sweet face. As I felt another butterfly flutter in my stomach, I wondered if he was still seeing the girl I had heard him talking to on the phone that one day. I wondered who kept calling him at all hours of the night and why he just *had* to take those calls. And more importantly, why he had to take them alone.

Inside that cozy, gorgeous theater, with the sound of the ballet dancers' pointe shoes tapping away on the stage and the feel of Luc's warm hand wrapped around mine, I wanted to forget about all of that. I wanted to lay my head on his shoulder and just be with him for a while.

Later, after the curtain had gone down, and we were walking toward our dorm, Luc wrapped his arm tightly around me and asked, "You are going home for the holiday, no?"

"Actually, I'm staying in Paris," I told him as the bitter night air ran a shiver down my spine.

"You are not going to see your family?"

"No, I don't feel like dealing with that whole mess. Plus, my parents won't even be in the same state. So I'm just staying here."

"If you do not already have a plan for the holiday, you can come to stay with my family for Christmas. There is someone…euh…some people who I would really like you to meet."

I opened my mouth, the word "yes" dangling so heavily at the tip of my tongue, I could almost taste it. I liked Luc…I liked him a lot. And I wanted to place my trust in him. But despite the enchanting evening we'd just spent together, I knew firsthand that life wasn't a fairy tale like the one we'd seen on the stage. The images of Jeff's online dating profile ingrained in my head were solid proof of that.

Plus, Luc was still hiding something…or someone.

Even though I was about to violate my rule of not having serious discussions, I had to find out some answers.

"That's really sweet of you to offer, but I have to ask you something first. Do you have a girlfriend…or are you still in love with your ex-wife?"

"No, of course not. My ex-wife is…well, she is not a nice person. And no, I do not have a girlfriend. Do you have a boyfriend? That guy who I met some months ago?"

"No, I'm not with anyone. That was just a date. It's just all of the phone calls and everything with you. What is going on, Luc? I've told you about my engagement, my breakup, my parents' divorce. What are you not telling me?"

Luc took a deep breath and avoided my gaze for a few

seconds. "It's complicated, Charlotte. I know this will be difficult to understand, but I can't tell you right now. Not yet, anyway. I'm sorry."

"If you can't even tell me what's really going on with you, I don't understand why you would ask me to spend Christmas with your family."

"I am asking you to spend Christmas with my family because I like you, Charlotte. I love spending time with you. You make me happy. And I do not have another woman in my life, I promise you."

If I took one step closer, I was going to fall even harder for Luc than I already had…which was exactly the reason why I couldn't say yes.

I couldn't bear to be hurt again.

"Luc, I like spending time with you too. But I'm not looking for a relationship right now, especially one where we can't be completely honest with each other. I'm sorry, but I can't do this."

Luc removed his arm from my shoulders while the corners of his mouth dropped into a full-out frown. And even though I knew I shouldn't have felt bad for turning him down, I kept babbling to soften the blow. "Plus, I already told Lexi I'd have Christmas dinner with her and her brother. Her parents are off traveling, so her brother is flying in for the holidays, and they invited me to spend Christmas with them." This was only partly true. Lexi had mentioned to me that she wanted to introduce me to her brother, Brad, who would be in Paris over Christmas, but she hadn't actually invited me to have dinner with them. I assumed that she would, though, and even if she didn't, I couldn't say yes to Luc's invitation.

Luc didn't say a word as we took the elevator back up to our rooms.

When we reached my door, I turned to him. "Thank you

so much for tonight. The ballet was beautiful. I…I'm sorry if I've hurt your feelings."

Luc gazed at me, his big chestnut eyes not masking their hurt. "It's okay. I understand. How can I expect you to want to come home with me when I cannot tell you everything about myself? I guess I had hoped that you would trust me anyway. But it was stupid of me to think like that. I am glad you liked the ballet, and I hope you have a good Christmas." Without kissing me good-bye, he turned around and let himself into his room.

I collapsed on my hard bed, wondering if I had made the right choice. Wondering if I should've just said yes. I felt torn, but I knew, deep down, that I wasn't ready to meet Luc's family. We weren't even together, and there was so much he hadn't explained to me. So he said he didn't have another woman in his life, but how would I know? I gave him a chance to explain the phone calls, and he refused. How could I trust him? I had to follow my own advice. So, instead of feeling bad about the situation, I pulled up my blog, read through my past posts and all of the encouraging comments I'd received, and then kept working on the draft of my article for *Bella Magazine*. Thousands of women were going to read this article in a few months, so I had to stay strong. I couldn't cave in to the pressure to be in a relationship just because one guy liked me and wanted to be with me. How did I know he wouldn't turn out to be just like Jeff in the end?

SIXTEEN

vendredi, le 24 décembre

Even the brightest lights in Paris cannot fill the void you feel when spending Christmas alone.

Thankfully, Lexi did invite me over to spend Christmas with her and her brother. What she didn't tell me until Christmas Eve, though, was that we weren't spending the holiday in Lexi's fancy little apartment off the Champs-Élysées. Instead, her parents had reserved a two-bedroom suite at a hotel as a special Christmas present for their privileged children.

I took the metro to the Franklin D. Roosevelt stop on the Champs-Élysées and bounded up the stairs past the herds of tourists, all bundled in their thick hats and gloves, giant cameras dangling from their necks.

Once I reached the top and set my eyes upon the magical, wintery wonderland of the avenue des Champs-Élysées at Christmastime, I wished I had brought my camera too. White twinkling lights encircled the never-ending sea of trees that lined the avenue and led the way to the majestic Arc de

Triomphe. The enticing scent of *chocolat chaud* drifted out into the sidewalks, where tourists and Parisians alike popped from Louis Vuitton over to Sephora, lugging their heavy shopping bags, trying to cross those last few gifts off their Christmas lists.

I took a left down avenue Montaigne, warming my hands in my coat pockets as I passed by the decorated store windows of Dolce&Gabbana, Chanel, and Christian Dior. I picked up the pace as a bitter burst of cold air whipped past me, blowing strands of my long hair across my pink nose. I spotted the red awnings of the Hôtel Plaza Athénée and smiled as the doorman let me into the lobby.

Before leaving my dorm room earlier, I'd been in a depressed funk, missing Luc and thinking that I was going to be spending Christmas in some random hotel with people I didn't know very well. None of it sounded like the cozy Christmas I was used to back in Ohio.

But as I gazed around at the sparkling crystal chandeliers, the fresh flowers circling the tall, creamy pillars, and the swirling marble floors, I realized this was no ordinary hotel. A wave of excitement swept over me as I rode the elevator up to Lexi's suite. Maybe turning Luc down hadn't been such a bad idea after all.

"It's about time, chick. I was starting to get lonely sitting in this palace all by myself," Lexi said before giving me *bisous* and ushering me in the door.

"This is gorgeous!" I beamed as I placed my bag on the plush white carpet and walked over to the floor-to-ceiling window, which boasted an astonishing view of the glittering Eiffel Tower.

I turned to Lexi who was now lounging on one of the gray velvety sofas, a glass of champagne in hand, looking calm and collected as usual. As if it were completely normal to spend Christmas in a luxury hotel suite that probably cost more than an entire year of rent on her apartment.

"Is this a typical Christmas present from your parents?" I asked as I gazed around at the lush silver drapes, the pink pastel lamp shades, and the fresh white roses that were sprinkled around the suite. In the adjoining room, I spotted a stunning grand piano that sat underneath a crystal chandelier, its lights glistening in the gold-rimmed mirror.

"Well, they went all out this year since they couldn't spend Christmas with us. They're off gallivanting around the world as usual, so they're flying Brad and his friend Dylan in to keep us company tonight."

"Wow…well, thanks for having me." I was speechless. Lexi had one of *those* families. One of those families who could afford to travel the world *and* pay for their children to stay in lavish hotels with a perfect view of La Tour Eiffel. I couldn't even imagine having a life like that. But at least I'd get to pretend for a night.

"No problem. I'm glad you could come. So, how was the ballet? Seems like things are getting a little serious with Luc, no?" she instigated as she poured me a glass of Bollinger champagne.

"The ballet was awesome…but afterward…well, he asked me to spend Christmas with his family." I sat down on the couch next to Lexi and sank back against a cushy pink pillow while I sipped my bubbly champagne.

"No!" Lexi's eyes widened in horror.

"Yeah, I know. So I asked him about all of those weird phone calls and if he had another woman in his life. He refused to explain the calls, saying it was *complicated*, but he still swore that he isn't seeing anyone else. How can I trust him, though?"

"That's just it. You can't. We all know that 'complicated' in man code means 'I'm fucking someone else.' Listen, girl, you can't let yourself get attached to this dude and his family when you don't know what's going on behind the scenes."

"So you think I made the right choice?"

Lexi lifted her eyebrows, then gestured to our luxurious surroundings. "Um…ya think? Besides being able to spend Christmas with *me*, which is obviously better than spending it with some dude's family, you're absolutely right about Luc. Don't change a thing. You have the perfect situation right now. You have all the fun, but none of the relationship mess to deal with, so why would you want to take things to the next level? We all know how that ends."

"You're right. I can't let him persuade me. Does Benoît understand that the two of you aren't in a relationship—that you're just having fun together?"

"Not exactly." She took one last gulp to finish her glass of champagne. "He wants things to be more than they are. But I've never verbally committed to him, so the way I see it, I have no obligation to him. We go on dates, have sex, and have fun together, but he's not my boyfriend. I don't call him my boyfriend, and I'm not planning on it. If he gets any ideas, then I'll just move on. There are plenty of other fish in the sea who are up for this sort of arrangement. It's just like your blog, really—I'm dating like a man and having the time of my life."

I hoped that we could keep these types of "arrangements" going on without someone getting hurt…but I knew by the way Luc had left my room the other night that it was too late for that. I had already hurt him.

Just as I was finishing up my first glass, there was a knock at the door.

"I have just the cure for you," she said as she crossed the suite. "You won't be worrying about Luc once you meet my brother." She opened the door to reveal two incredibly handsome men. Christmas wasn't going to be too shabby after all.

Brad, who, as it turns out, was Lexi's stepbrother (their parents got married when the two kids were really young, so Lexi just referred to him as her brother), was a lean six-foot-four with short, jet-black hair, coal-black eyes, and muscles in all the right places. He was the male version of Lexi in the looks department. One of those men who undoubtedly left trails of drooling, gawking women in his wake wherever he went. Dylan, his friend, was about six feet tall with messy, sandy-blond hair, green eyes, and pearly white teeth. When he hugged Lexi, he held her for an extra few seconds, leading me to believe that something had gone on between them in the past. And if they hadn't already slept together, they certainly would tonight.

"Charlotte, this is my brother, Brad, and his friend Dylan." Lexi walked over to the bar to pour them each a glass of wine as the two men greeted me with *bisous*. They were both American, so I was impressed that they went in for the kisses instead of the more impersonal American handshake. How culturally aware of them.

The four of us relaxed in the elegant living room and enjoyed the incredible view of the Eiffel Tower while working on the never-ending supply of wine and champagne in our suite. Feeling light-headed and giddy from all of that expensive alcohol sloshing around in my empty stomach, I was relieved to hear another knock on the door. This time, it was room service, bringing us our Christmas Eve dinner.

As two polite French men dressed in spiffy red-and-black uniforms placed the silver platters on a candlelit table, I tried to hide my childlike excitement in front of Lexi, Brad, and Dylan, who acted like this was just another average Christmas—as if.

Dinner was amazing. As an appetizer, we all started with a bowl of *soupe à l'oignon* that had about an inch of gooey melted gruyère cheese layered over top of a hot, bread-filled broth. Next, I dug into a small *salade niçoise* topped with tuna, juicy red tomatoes, crisp cucumbers, and some type of small unidentifiable bird egg that I tried just for the hell of it. Finally, I nibbled on a juicy chicken breast with buttery *carottes fondantes* on the side.

For dessert, we feasted on seven different types of cheeses, from the light and creamy Camembert to the pungent Roquefort. And, just when I thought I couldn't take anymore, Lexi lifted the lid off a platter of chocolate praline cake.

Brad scooted his chair closer to mine and smiled deviously in my direction as he dipped his fork into the fudgy icing and held it out for me to take a bite.

"Do you like chocolate?" he asked.

I nodded as I opened my mouth and let the thick, sugary icing melt on my tongue.

After he fed me another bite of the moist cake, I took a sip of champagne to wash it down and smiled.

"I don't want to eat your whole piece," I told him.

"It's okay," he said. "I'm not a big chocolate fan. It's too rich for me."

Just then, a memory of Luc lying naked and feeding me chocolate in bed flashed through my mind.

"Here you go," Brad said, luring me back to the present moment as he held another bite out for me to taste.

I suddenly wasn't that hungry for chocolate.

I waved his hand away. "Thanks, but I think I'm all set. You're right—it is a little too rich."

As Brad led me over to the living room, I noticed that Lexi was now cuddled up with Dylan in a corner of the suite, her legs draped over his lap, their eyes locked in a lustful gaze.

Brad and I relaxed on the sofa together, his arm stretched loosely behind my shoulders. "So, how long have you been living in Paris?" he asked as his penetrating black eyes met mine.

"About four months now. I'm taking some time off work to take classes at the Sorbonne."

"Oh, so you're a smart one, eh?" He winked at me as he edged a little closer.

I laughed as a flush crept up my neck and cheeks. I wondered if it would be weird to do something with Brad, considering the minor detail that he was Lexi's stepbrother *and* that Lexi happened to be staying in the same hotel suite.

But I knew it was more than that. No matter how incredible this night was turning out to be, and no matter how gorgeous and sexy the man sitting next to me was, I couldn't ignore the one thought that kept flashing through my mind.

I wanted Luc to be the one feeding me chocolate.

I missed him.

"So, what about you?" I asked Brad, shaking Luc's sweet face from my memory. "Lexi hasn't told me where you live or what you do."

"I'm living in Rome right now, but I'm thinking about moving up here, actually. I spend a lot of time traveling in France for work, so I'd rather have a place in Paris anyway...but enough about work. Let's get you another glass of wine." Brad didn't actually say what he did, but I got the feeling that whatever it was earned him a lot of money. Or maybe "work" was traveling and meeting women. Who knew?

He came back with two glasses of port, took my hand, and led me toward the master bedroom.

As I followed Brad's broad shoulders and felt his hand wrapped around mine, my stomach churned. Something didn't feel right about this.

I glanced over my shoulder to see what Lexi and Dylan were doing, hoping Lexi would sense my hesitation and stop me from doing what I knew would happen if I followed Brad into this room...but they were nowhere in sight. They must've disappeared into the other bedroom.

Brad gestured for me to take a seat with him on the king-size bed that spread out before us.

"Cheers," he said as he clinked his glass with mine and shot me a mischievous grin.

I drank two large gulps of the rich dessert wine, hoping it would relax me and help me to push aside the gnawing feeling in my gut that I had made a mistake in turning down Luc's invitation.

Brad reached over and took the wineglass out of my hand, gently set it down on the bedside stand, then led me over to the bedroom window. The streets below now appeared cold and desolate, all of the last-minute shoppers having returned home to spend the evening with their families. The Eiffel Tower stood alone, far out in the distance, lighting up the frigid night sky.

As Brad's warm body pressed into my back, and he wrapped his muscular arms around my waist, Luc's hurt face from the night of the ballet flashed through my mind. A pang of guilt swept through me as I thought of how I could've been with him at that very moment, meeting his family and drinking hot chocolate.

Brad may have sensed that I was somewhere else, because he grabbed my hips, turned me around to face him, and pressed his lips against mine while he explored my body with his strong hands. I pushed Luc's face out of my mind. I could feel bad all I wanted, but that wouldn't change the past. I was about to spend the night with a sexy, attractive man in one of the most expensive and beautiful hotel rooms in Paris. As far as the Charlotte on my blog was concerned, this was *exactly* what I needed to reaffirm my decision to stay away from relationships. If I had committed to Luc, I wouldn't have gotten to experience this. And the Charlotte on my blog would think that would've been a damn shame.

So even though my instincts weren't agreeing with my blog, I pushed my doubts aside and allowed Brad to take me.

He slid my slinky black dress over my head, took off his shirt, and kissed me from head to toe. After slipping off my lacy black bra-and-panty set, he picked me up, laid me down on the bed, and buried me beneath his tan, cut body.

As his hands roamed over my skin, I felt disconnected from myself, as if it were some other girl—a girl I didn't know anymore—lying there under the weight of his touch, going through the motions.

Brad leaned down, and as he grabbed a condom from his jeans pocket, two more condoms spilled to the ground. It was clear that he hadn't been planning on feeding me hot chocolate and giving me presents all night long.

After slipping on condom number one, Brad lifted his muscular body back on top of me, then pushed into me with the force of a Clydesdale. After a few strokes, I started to adjust to the feeling of him inside of me, and I forced myself to get into it. I replayed the lessons I had laid out on my blog over and over in my head. Every time Luc's lovable smile entered my mind, I pushed it out. I tried to focus on Brad, on his intoxicating scent that threatened to envelop me as he thrust farther and farther into me. On his eyes, burning into mine as he pleasured himself.

But, no matter how hard I tried to enjoy the feeling of Brad's hands all over me, I couldn't. It just didn't feel right.

"Charlotte, you're so damn sexy," he whispered in my ear. And then, not long after he'd begun, he moaned and collapsed on top of me.

Moments later, once he caught his breath, he rolled over to his side and closed his eyes. I held my breath, hoping he would just fall asleep. Lo and behold, after about two minutes, Brad began snoring.

I tiptoed out of bed and into the bathroom. As I flipped on the light and leaned into the porcelain sink to wash my face, I caught a glimpse of myself in the mirror. I didn't see the sexy, confident woman that Brad had seen earlier in the night. I saw a scared, sad shell of a woman. I wasn't sure what would fill this shell, or if it would ever be filled.

∼

On Christmas morning, I awoke not to the sound of a fire

crackling in the hearth or to the scent of pine needles and sugar cookies and cinnamon, but instead to the sound of Lexi sobbing in the hotel suite. I was jolted out of bed, her cries startling me from my sleep. The dim morning light beaming through the window revealed an empty side of the bed where Brad would've been.

Lexi's muffled cries grew louder as I ran, disheveled and disoriented, through the suite. In the second bedroom, I found Brad leaning his forehead against a closed bathroom door, Lexi howling on the other side. Dylan was nowhere in sight.

"Lexi, open the door," Brad said.

She didn't respond. Instead she wailed louder.

"Lexi, open the door *now*." Exhaustion outlined his profile as he closed his eyes and let out a long sigh.

"Brad, what's going on? What happened?" I asked.

Brad turned to me, his eyes bloodshot, his face pale and sunken. He shook his head. "It's best if you leave, Charlotte. I'm sorry."

"Is she going to be okay? Did something happen with Dylan? Maybe I can talk to her."

Brad walked toward me, wincing as another anguishing sob emanated from the bathroom. "Trust me, she won't want you to see her like this. I can handle her. I...I'm the *only* one who can handle this."

"But—"

"Please, just go, Charlotte."

By the time I gathered my things, Lexi's cries had only intensified, and she still hadn't opened the bathroom door. I tried one more time to see if I could help, but Brad only waved me away.

As I rode the pristine elevator down to the ground floor, I wondered what in the hell was going on. What could've happened to Lexi to make her so upset? And where was Dylan? Had he tried to hurt her? What did Brad mean when he'd said that only *he* could handle this? Was there something I didn't know about Lexi?

Even as I walked through the gorgeous lobby, I could still hear Lexi's loud, gut-wrenching sobs ringing through my ears. I really hoped that whatever had happened, she would be okay. I only wished I could've helped.

"*Joyeux Noël, Mademoiselle,*" the doorman said with a smile as I exited the lobby.

"*Et vous aussi, Monsieur,*" I responded, realizing that today would probably be the *least* merry of Christmases I'd ever had.

I checked my phone to see if Luc had called or sent me a text message. He hadn't. In fact, I had no missed calls. No text messages.

I wandered alone down the deserted Champs-Élysées, the bitter-cold air stinging my fingertips and turning my nose bright red. On the busiest street in Paris, there was hardly a soul in sight. The hordes of miniature cars that normally sped up and down the avenue had disappeared. The tourists had vanished. Even the rows of trees that had been so lovely and magical the night before now appeared barren, their skinny branches reaching in vain toward the cloudy, gray sky.

It seemed that everyone in the world had somewhere important to be on Christmas morning.

Everyone but me.

I thought of my parents and wondered where they were, and if they were feeling as hollow as I was. Even though it was the middle of the night in Florida, where my mom was now living with my aunt, I dialed her cell.

After five rings, she picked up, but instead of hearing her voice, I heard booming bass and men shouting.

"Mom?" I yelled into the phone. "Mom, are you there?"

"Hello? Charlotte, is that you?" she yelled back over the raging music.

"Yeah, Mom. It's me. Where are you?"

"Oh, Charlotte! I'm so glad you called. Hold on, let me just get around the pool so I can hear you. This DJ is amazing!"

She was at a pool party on Christmas Eve? With a DJ? Was this really my mom?

"Whew, okay, that's a little better. Can you hear me?" she screamed into the phone.

"Um, yeah, I can hear you now. What's going on?"

"Oh, Aunt Liza threw a big Christmas Eve bash, and you should just see all the beautiful men that came out. You know Aunt Liza, she always knows how to have a good time."

But you hate Aunt Liza.

"Isn't it like four in the morning there? You're still up?" I asked her.

"Oh, is it that late? I didn't even notice, I've just been whooping it up all night! Oh, dear, my bikini is falling down. Hold on just one sec. Oh—oh, there we go. All set. Gotta keep those babies in place."

Oh, dear. My fifty-five-year-old mother, who was usually wearing a red-and-green Christmas tree sweatshirt for the holidays, was wearing a bikini? I had *never* seen her wear a bikini. Ever. I had no words.

"It's so much fun here, Charlotte. You really should've come out for Christmas. I could've introduced you to Frank. He's Dave's son, and you would love him. He's a real hottie."

"Who's Dave?"

"Oh, this wonderful man that Aunt Liza introduced me to. But don't worry dear, I'm not getting married again or anything silly like that. Just dating around and having my fun. I can't believe I've been missing out on this for the last thirty years!"

You missed out on this because you had me and Dad. Remember?

"I just wanted to call to wish you a Merry Christmas."

"Thanks, dear. You too. I miss you so much and wish you

were here. Oh—oh!" she squealed into the phone. "Dave, stop it. I'm on the phone with my daughter."

That was enough of that.

"Okay, Mom. It sounds like you're busy there, so I better let you go."

"I'm so glad you called, sweetie. Do come visit soon, okay? I'd love for you to meet everyone. I'm sure you're having a glamorous Christmas in Paris. Love you lots! Toodle-oo!"

Toodle-oo?

"Bye, Mo—" I started, but she had already hung up.

I picked up my pace as I headed for the metro. After a few seconds I broke into a full-out sprint. What the hell was going on? Where did my mom go? Who was this woman? Running around in a bikini at pool parties on Christmas Eve? I'd never felt so angry in all my life. My parents had thrown away our family so they could run around and have sex with other people. It was sick.

I slowed down and caught my breath as I reached the metro. I waited alone in the drafty underground station for fifteen minutes before the next train came, and as I climbed on board, I realized I was the only passenger.

I rode home in silence with my head in my hands, listening to the sound of the train barreling down the tracks, its doors opening and closing, but no one climbing on.

I felt so alone in that clattering, godforsaken train all by myself. I would've given anything to have a hug from my mom. Not the Florida pool-party mom I'd just spoken with, though. I wanted my sweet, innocent Ohio mom. I wanted to tell her what was going on in my life. That I wasn't sure if I was making the right decisions with Luc. That I felt empty and confused after what I'd done with Brad. That I couldn't get the sound of Lexi's cries out of my head. And that I was scared. I wanted to feel my mom's soft hands stroking the back of my head like she always used to do, and hear her soothing voice telling me everything was going to be okay. And that even if it wasn't, she'd be here for me.

But she wasn't here for me anymore. It was Christmas, and she didn't even seem to care.

As the train rattled to a stop, I wrapped my violet peacoat tighter around my waist and ran across the windy, abandoned Boulevard Jourdan, the masses of students having evaporated, leaving me to confront the day alone.

What was I going to do by myself on Christmas Day? I wanted to be with Luc and his family, but there was still so much I didn't know about him. What if I committed to him and fell in love with him, only to have it end in disaster, just like my parents' marriage? I was sure that my mom and dad hadn't envisioned a divorce in their future when they stood up at the altar saying their vows. I was sure they'd never thought there would come a time when they wouldn't even care to talk to their own daughter on Christmas because they'd be out partying instead.

I wouldn't let that happen to me. Ever.

When I reached my dorm room, I cranked up the heat and bundled up in as many layers as I could pile on. I sat down at my computer, pulled up my blog, and began typing.

Merry Christmas, ladies. As I sit here shivering at my computer, I realize that I don't have any magical formulas for you today. Just a few things I've picked up over the past few weeks that may help you along your journey.

Rule # 1—Avoiding relationships at all costs, as I have advised you to do, doesn't necessarily give you a warm and fuzzy feeling at the end of the day. I still stand by my earlier statements that you should go out, date like a man, and have fun without being in a relationship. It is inevitable, though, that at some point, one of the men you're dating will try to take things to the next level. And you may actually like this man. If you can continue having fun with him without committing, by all means, go for it. If you can't see that happening because of the feelings one or both of you may have for each other, this is where you'll have to trust your instincts. If you like him but instinctively don't trust him, then it may be best to take a step back. Beware, though: taking this step back may make you feel awful. Take comfort in remembering that marriage is likely to fail and that you may have just saved yourself from heartache.

Case in Point: After Half-Naked French Hottie took me to the ballet, he invited me to spend Christmas with him and his family. As enticing as a cozy family Christmas sounded, especially right after hearing the news of my parents' separation, I said no. I don't fully trust this guy. I gave him a chance to tell me that he has another woman in his life, and he denied it. But of course he would deny it. That's what guys do. Once, when I confronted an old boyfriend the day after he had cheated on me, he actually replied to me, "No, I could never, ever cheat on you. I love you so much. I can't even believe you would think I could do such a thing." See what I mean?

The downside of saying no to Half-Naked French Hottie's invitation is that I'm spending Christmas alone in Paris, and to be honest, I feel miserable. The upside is my next point:

Rule # 2—If given the chance, do spend a night in a lavish hotel suite with a gorgeous man, but please enjoy it more than I did.

Case in Point: Because I denied said invitation, I had the privilege of spending last night in one of the most luxurious hotels in Paris, with a male model. Okay, he wasn't actually a male model (or maybe he was—he didn't tell me what he did for a living), but either way, he was hot. Because I had just hurt Half-Naked Hottie's feelings this week, I wasn't feeling that great during what should've been one of the hottest, most unbelievable nights of my life. If you get this chance, please just let loose and have a kick-ass time. And then e-mail me about it. I want to hear all the juicy details.

My next point has nothing to do with how to date like a man, but it's Christmas, so give me a break.

Rule # 3—If you're a mom, act like one. Period.

What I don't mean by this is that if you're a mom, you should chop all your hair off and wear boring mom clothes (no offense to all you moms out there with short hair—I'm sure you look gorgeous). What I do mean is that if you've had children, remember that they are always your children and you are always their mom. If you go through a midlife crisis or get a divorce and are in the process of reinventing your life, that's fine. But don't forget that you're still a mom, and you still have children who need to hear your comforting mom voice over the phone when they are spending Christmas alone in Paris.

Rule # 4—Consider disregarding Rules 1 and 2 above and, instead, take a chance on what your heart really wants so you won't end up feeling sad and utterly alone on Christmas.

SEVENTEEN

mercredi, le 19 janvier

True friends are like chocolate—they're always there when you need them, and they rarely disappoint you.

Since the entire country of France loves taking vacation almost more than they love drinking wine, I didn't have any classes for the whole month of January. Luc had disappeared completely. Each night, I found myself walking back and forth to the bathroom several times, just so I could creep past his door and see if any light was peeking out. But the only thing peeking out was darkness. I figured he was staying with his family for the month. Or maybe he had even met someone new. It wasn't any of my business anyway.

Fiona was out of town, having flown back to England for winter break, and Lexi hadn't answered any of my calls. Instead, she sent me a text message saying she'd be staying with Brad in Italy for the next month, then visiting with her parents. I wrote back and asked if everything was okay, and she responded in typical Lexi fashion:

Hell yeah, girl. Couldn't be better. Have a fab month! See you in February.

No mention of the Christmas-morning sobbing incident. As if it had never happened. I'd convinced myself that Lexi had just gotten too drunk and emotional, but every time I thought about the wary look in Brad's eyes that morning, as if he'd fielded Lexi's cries many times before, I wondered if there wasn't more to the story. I was at least happy she was going to spend time with her parents. Maybe all she needed was a good dose of family time to help her feel better.

The lack of men, classes, and a social life allowed me tons of time to fine-tune my article for *Bella Magazine*. I wanted it to be perfect. I wanted to inspire as many women as I could.

One night, while I was sitting alone in my room, trying to crank a few more words of wisdom onto the page, Fiona called me.

"Hey, Charlotte!"

"Hi, Fiona!"

"Oh, it's so good to hear your voice. I miss you so much," Fiona said.

"I know, I miss you too. Did you have a good Christmas?"

"Yeah, you know, the usual. Family, presents, snow, all that good stuff. It's nice to be home, but it's making me realize how much I love my life in Paris."

"And how much you like Marc?"

Fiona laughed. "Yeah, he's okay."

"Just okay? I thought you were really interested in him. Plus, he's been talking about you nonstop during our lessons."

"It's a little complicated."

"Complicated? Have you been talking to Andrew since you've been back?"

Fiona hesitated. "Yeah, he came over on Christmas, actually."

"Whoa, really? What's going on, did he break up with his girlfriend?"

"No, I guess they're still together, but they're having problems. Or so he says. And he keeps saying how much he misses me."

"Fiona, don't fall for it. He's still with her."

"I know, I know. Don't worry. I'm not going to sleep with him or anything. It's just so hard seeing him again. We were together for so long, and he was a huge part of my family. Even my parents miss him. It felt so normal to have him here for the holidays. But then when I think about him with that cow he's dating, it makes me sick."

"I can identify with that. Thinking about Jeff with Brooke still makes me nauseous. But unless Andrew is going to break up with his girlfriend and really be with you, you're just torturing yourself by letting him come around." I was worried about Fiona. She was a huge pushover and was bound to get herself hurt.

"I know, you're right. You are. But you know how it goes...It's not that easy."

"Well, promise me you won't sleep with him...at least until he's single again."

"I promise," Fiona said, sounding unsure of herself. "So, I read your latest blog post. What's all this about Luc trying to be in a relationship and then you and some hot guy in a hotel suite?"

I filled Fiona in on all of the details, and on the latest with my mom. I almost told her about what had happened with Lexi, but I stopped myself. No need to spread embarrassing gossip about a friend.

"Jeez, that's a lot. Are you doing okay?" Fiona asked.

"Yeah, I'll be fine. I've just been working on the article to keep myself busy. I can't wait until you come back. Hurry your butt up, okay?"

She giggled. "I will. Only two more weeks, and then we'll have a girls' night out. It sounds like you need it."

"You can say that again. Well, have a great time at home, and call me if you need motivation to stay away from Andrew. I'm always here to help."

After I hung up the phone, I checked my e-mail and spotted Madame Rousseau's name at the top of my in-box. I'd been waiting to hear from her since I'd turned in my final papers, hoping and praying that after reading my work, she'd change her mind about me and help me find a teaching job in Paris.

With my heart racing a little faster than normal, I double clicked on her e-mail.

Mademoiselle Summers,
Please meet me at eight a.m. in my office tomorrow morning.
Madame Rousseau

That didn't sound good. What was it going to take to get this woman to pull the stick out of her ass and just help me?

∽

The next morning, at seven forty-five on the dot, I was waiting outside of Madame Rousseau's office. I had stopped on the way and downed a double shot of espresso so that I wouldn't doze off on her bench again. I was not about to give her yet one more reason to despise me.

A few minutes later, I heard her black heels pounding down the hallway and turned to find her stalking toward me in her typical black uniform with her bun pulling at the sides of her face, as usual.

"Mademoiselle Summers." She nodded as she let me into her office.

"Bonjour, Madame Rousseau," I replied in my sweetest tone possible. I had no clue what she was going to say about my papers, but I didn't think it was going to be pretty. And I figured a little politeness couldn't hurt.

"Well, I have read your work," she began.

I lowered my eyes to the floor to ready myself for the blow.

"And it is quite good."

What? Good? Did I hear her correctly? I lifted my eyes up off the floor to make sure I was getting all of this.

"You are a strong writer, and it is clear that you put a great amount of effort into your courses. You have a brilliant grasp of French teaching methodology. I can see that your past three years of teaching experience in Washington, DC have taught you well. Bravo, Mademoiselle Summers."

I was dumbfounded. Flabbergasted. I couldn't have heard her correctly. But I did, and she liked my work. She liked my work!

Then, shock of all shocks, Madame Rousseau smiled at me. I hadn't thought those dry, brittle lips were capable of such kindness.

"Thank you, Madame Rousseau. Thank you so much."

"I have decided that I will put in a recommendation for you at a private Catholic school that I am very fond of. It is the school my niece attends, and I used to teach there myself. I trust that you will show the utmost respect and *timeliness* as you go through the application process."

"Of course, Madame Rousseau, of course. Thank you so much."

"You're welcome. The job openings for the schools usually come out in March, and interviews will take place in April. So, in the meantime, you must continue to perform well in all of your courses, and I will do my best to secure an interview for you."

"I really appreciate your help, Madame."

"*Pas de problème*...but do not forget, Mademoiselle Summers, nothing is guaranteed. You must continue to prove yourself to me and to this program as a responsible, intelligent student and educator. I can revoke my recommendation at any point."

"I understand."

"Well, that is all." She stood up and ushered me out of her office.

I skipped out of the building with a huge grin on my face. This was going to work out. I was going to get my dream teaching job in Paris! Madame Rousseau kind of liked me! And she hadn't even mentioned anything about Marc or Fiona—what a relief. I trotted down to a café on the corner of Boulevard Saint-Germain and treated myself to a big fat *pain au chocolat*. Nothing better than a fluffy, buttery pastry crammed with rich dark chocolate to top off an already fantastic morning.

∽

My meeting with Madame Rousseau had brightened an otherwise dreary January in Paris, but as I bundled up in my frigid dorm room one snowy afternoon and munched on a warm baguette and some creamy Camembert cheese, I thought about how nice it would be to have someone there to share this giant wheel of cheese with.

As I pulled up my blog to begin writing about how to stay sane during a man drought in winter (namely—eat as many fattening pastries and as much cheese and bread as you want), I glanced out my window and noticed a cute couple all bundled up in their thick coats and chunky scarves, their noses pressed together as they stopped to kiss underneath the miniature snowflakes that floated from the sky. Then, as they continued down the path hand in hand, the girl turned her head to the side, revealing long locks of strawberry-red hair that spilled out from under her hat.

I snapped my face away from the window and focused on the computer screen. But no matter how hard I tried to ignore the unwelcome images that were now racing through my head, all I could think of was Brooke's long red hair, Jeff's arms wrapped around her, the two of them kissing against a lamppost in Georgetown, the snow gathering at their feet.

I wondered if they were as happy as the couple underneath my windowsill.

I shook my head, then tore off another piece of the crispy bread and smothered it in cheese. So what if they were? I bit into the bread and washed it down with a sip of hot chocolate. I was just fine here on my own. Well, if I ignored the feelings of loneliness and boredom eating away at my insides, that is.

And just as my hands hit the keyboard to begin my next blog post, there was a knock on the door.

I opened it up to find Marc on the other side, his teeth chattering and his nose bright red from the cold.

"Hey, Charlotte. I was just walking past your building and thought I'd come to see if you were free for a last-minute lesson."

"I've never been more free." I smiled as I ushered him into my room. "Here, have a seat." I took Marc's coat, then poured him a cup of hot chocolate.

"Mmm, thanks," he said, taking a big gulp. "It's freezing out there, is it not?"

"It is," I agreed as I handed him the baguette and a slice of cheese. How nice that I had someone to share it with now.

Marc had been my only human contact for the entire month of January. With my funds still diminishing, we'd been meeting three times a week since the holidays. His speaking was much more relaxed now, making him even more fun to hang out with. Plus, the fact that his mother and I had patched things up seemed to ease any remaining tension left over from all the mean things I'd said about her.

"So, let's pick up where we left off last time," I said as I settled into a cross-legged position on my bed. "You were telling me about how you and Delphine first met."

I'd decided that the best way to teach Marc how to speak English like a native was to bypass the surface talk and get personal. So I'd filled him in on the Jeff fiasco (Marc learned a lot of colorful vocabulary that day), and during our last lesson, Marc had begun to tell me about his last girlfriend, Delphine, who'd broken his heart. He'd also worked on his question-forming abilities by asking a million and one questions about Fiona, not even trying to hide the fact that he was interested in her. I'd originally let on that she was interested in him too, but once I'd spoken with her on the phone and found out that Andrew was coming around again, I didn't want to say too much for fear of leading Marc in the wrong direction.

As Marc shared my wheel of cheese with me and searched for the right words to tell his story of Delphine, I forgot all about Jeff and Brooke, all about the cute couple kissing outside my window, and all about my loneliness.

And later that night, as I curled up in bed, I thought about how wonderful it was that Marc and I had established a real connection. It was the first time in a while that I'd made a solid male friend.

I knew though that while my friendship with Marc was fulfilling some aspects of that strong urge I felt to have a man in my life, he was still just a friend, and I had other needs that could not be met in a friendship—specifically, the need for a man's touch. And as much as thoughts of Jeff still haunted me from time to time, it wasn't *his* touch I was craving anymore.

It was Luc's.

∽

February in Paris rolled around in a haze of rain, snow, and nasty cold weather. My consumption of fattening, delicious French pastries was at an all-time high. So now, instead of tightening my belt buckle so my jeans wouldn't fall off me, I had to release the top button by the end of each day so I wouldn't have to suck it all in.

It was totally worth it.

Just after I'd submitted the final draft of my article to *Bella Magazine*, Fiona and Lexi had finally arrived back in Paris. Despite the wintery weather, the three of us planned a fun night out on the town to catch up and to celebrate me finishing my article. We met at La Suite, a posh club off the Champs-Élysées, near the George V hotel. It was the kind of swanky place where you would get turned down if you weren't dressed to the nines. Luckily, Lexi had told us to spice up our attire, or else Fiona and I might have gotten the boot. I usually didn't go to places like this. They were overpriced and too stuffy in my opinion, but tonight, I didn't care so much. I was happy to have the girls back in town and was dying to meet some new guys…and take my mind off the one I'd let go.

Inside the neon-lit club, we ordered a couple of dirty martinis and squeezed into a cushy black booth.

"So, how was your trip? Aren't you so glad to be back?" I asked Fiona over the booming techno music that blared from the speakers.

"It was great, and…well, I have mixed feelings about coming back, actually," she replied, looking weary-eyed.

"Don't even tell me. You totally slept with Andrew, didn't you?" Lexi chimed in as her usual devious grin spread across her full red lips. With her smoky black eyeliner, a glint in her eye, and a slinky black dress hugging her body, I found no traces of the broken girl I'd heard crying in the bathroom on Christmas morning. It seemed Lexi was back to normal.

Fiona's cheeks turned a shade of red I hadn't seen since she'd slept with Matt the English rugby player. "Um…"

"Come on, it's no big deal. I used to sleep with my ex all the time," Lexi assured her.

"Andrew and I are back together." She smiled hesitantly, expecting a choir of disapproval.

I couldn't believe she had gotten back together with him after he broke her heart and was with some other girl all year. And what about Marc? "Wow, so he broke up with that girl, and then he asked you back?" I asked.

"Something like that," she said, her eyes darting toward the dance floor.

"He did break up with her, right?" Lexi asked before taking a huge gulp of her martini.

"Oh yeah, they're not together anymore. It just didn't happen in that order. We kind of…um…slept together first. Then he broke up with her."

"That a girl!" Lexi laughed as she clinked her glass with Fiona's.

Fiona relaxed back into the booth. "Yeah, I know it wasn't necessarily the right thing to do, and I know I *promised* I wouldn't do it, but you know how it goes. A few days after I talked to you, Charlotte, Andrew invited me over to his place. He cooked me this really fancy dinner, one thing led to another, and before I knew it, I was back in his bed."

"How was it?" I asked, a little jealous that she had been having sex for the past month when I'd been lying alone in my room with visions of male strippers dancing in my head.

An intense expression splashed over Fiona's face as she took another sip of her drink. "It was *so* good…the best it's ever been, actually."

"Good for you, honey, you totally deserve it. So then what? Did he break up with that girl right after you slept together?" Lexi asked.

"Yup, he called her the next morning and broke it off for good."

"Well...congratulations!" I said, faking my enthusiasm.

"Thanks. It's brilliant that we're back together, but it was really hard to leave him. I mean, we spent a whole month together, and now we have to be apart for four more months."

"Yeah, but you'll be here with us in Paris, so it won't be that bad," I assured her.

"I know, I didn't mean that I'm not happy to be back here with you guys, but I'm going to miss him, and..."

"And the sex," Lexi finished for her.

"Yeah, that too." Fiona giggled.

I'd had enough relationship talk. Fiona was back with Andrew, and that jerk would probably just hurt her again. There was nothing I could do about that, though.

"Want some more drinks?" I asked the girls.

"Yeah, another martini—this is really good," Fiona said, already looking tipsy.

"I'll get the next round. Be right back." As I squeezed past a group of college-aged girls, their tall, thin legs protruding from their skimpy dresses and their perfectly manicured feet wrapped in fancy stilettos, I heard a guy call my name. I turned around to find Marc grinning at me.

"Marc, oh, my gosh! I can't believe you're here."

He placed his hand on my waist as he leaned in and kissed my cheeks. "Are you going to get a drink?"

"Yeah, I'm just getting a few drinks for Fiona and Lexi. They're sitting over there," I said as I pointed over to our booth.

I noticed Marc's gaze resting on Fiona and immediately felt bad for him. He was such a great guy. Why did she have to go and get back with her sleazy ex?

"What are you having? Let me," he offered.

"That's so nice, but really, you don't have to." *But please do*, I thought. Paying for a round of martinis was going to be expensive. And I wasn't exactly swimming in cash after forking over that cover charge.

"No, I insist. What are you drinking?"

"Martinis."

Marc grabbed my hand and led me to the bar. He was being really touchy-feely, which surprised me until he stumbled on the way to the bar, and I realized he was drunk. I let out a quiet giggle as he stumbled once more, then paid for our martinis. What would Madame Rousseau think?

"Look who I found at the bar," I said to Lexi and Fiona as Marc handed them their drinks.

Fiona's cheeks blushed as she met eyes with Marc. Uh-oh. I *knew* she still liked him.

"Marc!" Lexi yelped as she stood up to kiss his cheeks. "Here, have a seat." She scooted over to make room for Marc in the booth, then leaned toward him, exposing her cleavage.

"I haven't seen *you* in a while," she chirped.

What was Lexi talking about? She'd only met him briefly at the bar that one night when she'd been all over Benoît, and she knew that Marc was interested in Fiona.

Marc gave her a goofy, drunk smile. "I think I have only met you one time. Is that right?"

Lexi leaned closer to Marc, actually resting her right breast on his arm. "Mm-hmm, but we should hang out more."

Fiona gave me a what-the-hell look, which I echoed back. Even though Fiona had just told us she was back in bliss with Andrew, Lexi knew that Fiona had liked Marc not so long ago. And, in the Girlfriend Etiquette Handbook, until Lexi had a conversation with Fiona, clearing the way for her to hit on Marc, it wasn't technically okay.

And Marc, while he was trying his best to give Fiona some attention, was totally mesmerized by Lexi and her boobs. Who could blame him? She was a total knockout, and she was throwing herself at him. She was one of those friends who was difficult to go out with because no matter how pretty you were, she was prettier, and all of the guys would inevitably flock to her. The problem was that she knew it and didn't hesitate to use it to her advantage.

Fiona gulped down her martini, then inched closer to Marc until he had Fiona draped over one knee and Lexi dry humping the other. As I sipped my drink and watched the competition unfold, I wanted to smack all three of them. Why did everything have to be all about a guy? I knew I was one to talk, but still, why couldn't the four of us spend a nice night out as friends? Why did Lexi have to jump all over every man with a pulse? And if Fiona hadn't gotten back together with Andrew, she could actually *be* with Marc instead of fighting this immature fight with Lexi.

Before I had a chance to snap them all out of their ridiculousness, Lexi grabbed Marc's hand and pulled him up to the dance floor.

Fiona stayed silent as she watched the two of them grind all over each other.

"Let's go dance," I said to Fiona, hoping to snap her out of her jealous trance.

"I'm not really in the mood," she said before downing the last of her drink.

I turned to face her in the booth. "You still like Marc, don't you?"

She hesitated, her eyes darting from the dying couple back to me. "Okay, fine. I'm a little jealous. Lexi is...well, I know this is going to sound awful, but sometimes she's a sodding slut!" Fiona's strong English accent deepened the angrier she became.

"I mean, why does she have to throw herself all over every guy? I know she's our friend, but you know how she is, Charlotte. Marc won't mean anything to her. She'll just sleep with him and be done with him."

I'd originally decided to keep my opinions to myself, but with Fiona's heart so clearly hung up on Marc, I needed to say something. "I knew you still liked Marc. So what are you doing back with Andrew? Do you really think this is a good decision, Fiona?"

Fiona's emerald eyes flashed underneath the strobe light. "Yes, Charlotte, I do. Just because I'm annoyed with the situation tonight doesn't mean I should break up with Andrew. We have a history together. And I can't just throw that away over Marc, who clearly can't even keep any semblance of self-control when Lexi the Sex Goddess casts her spell over him."

"But just last year, Andrew was willing to throw your relationship away without a second thought. And honestly, what do you think he's going to be doing while you're in Paris the rest of the year?"

Fiona's cheeks flushed crimson. "Just because your fiancé and your father are cheaters does not mean that all men cheat."

Her tone stung, but the alcohol fueled my fire. Why was Fiona being so naïve? "Didn't you just tell us that Andrew cheated on his girlfriend with *you* only a few weeks ago? So how is that any different?"

Fiona avoided my gaze, then huffed out a breath as she reached for her purse. "I'm really not in the mood for this. I'm going home."

I grabbed Fiona's arm. "Listen, I'm sorry. I just don't want you to get hurt, that's all."

Fiona jerked her arm away. "I can take care of myself just fine. Besides, do you really think you should be..." Fiona trailed off as she bit her lip.

"What were you going to say?"

"No, forget it. It's not worth it."

"No, really. What were you going to say?"

Fiona sighed, her eyes suddenly appearing tired. "All I was going to say is that you can't spend your whole life running away from relationships, Charlotte. Hiding from love like it's the plague. If you do, you'll end up alone and desperate." She nodded toward the dance floor, where Lexi was rubbing her butt in Marc's crotch and reaching around to massage his thighs. "You'll end up like Lexi."

Fiona turned and left me alone in the bar, her words ringing loudly in my ears.

I drank the last of my martini and let the alcohol wash their truth away from my consciousness. I didn't want to hear it.

~

Back in my room, I poured myself a huge glass of red wine and cuddled up on my bed, unable to erase Fiona's words from my mind. She was right. I *was* alone. I *was* desperate. And even though when I first met Lexi, I'd believed I'd wanted her life of glitz and glamour, hot guys and steamy sex, I was beginning to see the emptiness of that lifestyle. And while Lexi would never admit to it, I knew she felt it. That hole. That void that comes with being alone, with never letting anyone in. I'd heard it in her cries on Christmas morning. Those weren't the cries of a drunk, sobbing girl. Those were the cries of someone who, deep down, was broken and afraid to love.

I shuddered to think that Fiona had seen that same girl in me tonight. That maybe she'd seen her in me all year long, and she'd just been too sweet to tell me.

Real friends tell you the truth, though, even when it's difficult to hear. And that's what Fiona had done tonight. She'd held the mirror up, and although I didn't want to look, I couldn't help but see the broken-down, fearful face staring back at me.

I opened my laptop and felt a pang of sadness as I thought about Katie back at home. She was a true friend too, and she always had been. Yet all year I'd been jealous of her relationship with Joe, meanwhile prattling on and on about how relationships are doomed and the smartest thing a girl can do is to avoid them altogether.

Then when I thought about Lexi's advances on Marc, and her obsession with men and sex in general, I realized I felt bad for her...but I also knew that if I didn't get a grip on my life and on my priorities, I would *become* her.

In that moment, I wished I was back in DC so I could just call Katie and take the bus over to her place like I always used to do.

But I wasn't home. I was alone in France, sitting with a person I wasn't liking all too much at the moment—myself.

I pulled up my blog and began typing.

Rule # 1—Relationships with men are fleeting, so it is important to surround yourself with true friends who you know you can always count on.

If I've learned anything this past year, it's that guys will come and go. So while you're out having a good time, don't forget to be there for your friends. This means remembering that friendships come first and guys come second. No exceptions.

At the end of the day, ladies, if you're down and out, will the new guy you just met out at a bar be the one listening to you vent on the phone about your latest catastrophe?

No, he most certainly will not.

It will be your friends—your true friends—who will pick up the pieces and make you feel loved again. And, more importantly, your true friends will be the ones to tell you the truth about yourself, even if you're not willing to hear it.

After publishing my blog post, I wrote Fiona an e-mail to apologize. I told her that I was genuinely happy for her and Andrew, and that I appreciated her honesty with me. Then, as I switched off the light in my bedroom and curled up underneath my comforter, missing my friends from home and wishing they weren't an ocean away, my phone beeped.

It was a text message from Lexi. It read:

The sex with Marc was just so-so.

Which in Lexi language meant that she'd never be talking to Marc again. He was just another notch on her bedpost. And while Lexi was exactly the type of friend I'd needed to get over my broken engagement when I'd first arrived in Paris, I wondered how deep the friendship could really go when her main priority was sleeping around.

EIGHTEEN

samedi, le 12 mars

Until you have all the facts, don't go judging a French man by his skinny cover.

As February rolled into March, I noticed the light peering out from under Luc's door every night. He was back.

Whenever I heard a door close in the hallway, I jetted up to my peephole and peered through to see if he was walking down the hall. I hadn't had any luck, until one day when I was leaving the showers. I was all wrapped up in my skimpy towel, with another towel wrapped like a turban around my wet hair, when I spotted Luc locking his door. Even though I'd been doing a little more than just hoping to run into him (spying—*moi*?), I considered turning around and running back to the showers. What would I say to him? "Hey, I know I turned you down, but could we still have sex and eat chocolate in bed together?" It seemed perfectly logical to me, but I didn't know if he'd buy it. And besides, I knew it was more than that. Just the sight of him released a flock of wild butterflies in my stomach.

Before I had a chance to decide what to do, Luc turned around and spotted me standing at the end of the hall, dripping wet.

"Charlotte, hey."

"Hi, Luc." I shuffled toward him, making sure my towel didn't fall down. Not that he hadn't seen what was underneath it anyway, but still.

"I always see you coming out of the shower. Are you planning this?"

I laughed. "No, of course not. I think you're following me around, waiting to see me in this hot towel."

That got a laugh out of him. "Yes, I love that towel wrapped around your hair. It is so sexy."

"So, how have you been?" I asked.

"Good, very busy. I am close to finishing my master's degree, you know...and I have a lot of other things going on too, so yes, I have been very busy. And you? You are still enjoying life in Paris?"

"Yeah, it's been good, you know. I...I've been meaning to stop by. I knew you were probably busy, though, and..." I trailed off, not really knowing where I was going with this, just knowing that I was happy to see him.

Luc shifted his weight back and forth a few times, then finally looked me in the eye and smiled. "I would like to take you out tomorrow. It is my birthday, so we will go out and have a drink, no?"

"That sounds perfect. It's your thirtieth, right?"

"No, I will only be twenty-two. What are you talking about?" he said as he winked at me. "I will knock on your door at eight o'clock."

"Sounds great, I'll see you then."

I scuttled back to my room and realized that I felt more

excited about hanging out with Luc the next night than I had about anything in a long time.

∼

Always punctual, Luc knocked on my door just as the clock turned eight. He smiled flirtatiously as he slid his hand around my waist and leaned in to give me *bisous*. The smell of his cologne and the feel of his warm breath on my skin gave me goose bumps. God, I'd missed him.

Instead of taking me to the RER station, Luc led me to his car—a blue Renault Twingo, which was just slightly larger than a Smart car. We climbed in, and after winking in my direction, Luc sped off through the city as its night lights twinkled underneath the full moon. He cranked up a French radio station as he whizzed in and out of the winding streets, and whenever he wasn't shifting, Luc reached his right hand over and placed it gently on my thigh. My heartbeat picked up as we passed by the Opéra Garnier, where we'd had our last date. Before I had a chance to think about how badly that date had ended, though, Luc rounded the corner and zoomed into a tight parking spot on a busy side street.

After opening the door for me, Luc took my hand and led me down rue Daunou to a bar called Footsie. A blast of warm air welcomed us into the dimly lit pub as we walked up to the long wooden bar and squeezed in between two packs of rowdy French guys.

"Tonight, we are having beer," Luc told me before ordering us two tall glasses, then leading me over to a booth in the corner of the bar.

"Happy thirtieth birthday," I said as I clinked my glass with his. We both took a big, long sip, and to my surprise, the beer actually tasted great going down. I took a second giant sip just to loosen up. I'd been nervous all day, wondering what we would talk about, how this night would unfold. I wasn't sure why Luc would want to spend his thirtieth birthday with me, but then again, I wasn't sure why I wanted to spend his thirtieth birthday with him either if I was so antirelationship. All I knew was that I was happy to be in his company again, and my hormones hadn't shut off since January. It had been a two-month buildup, and something had to give.

"I can't believe I am thirty. It goes so fast. One minute you are twenty, you're young, you're at the university with no bills to pay, no responsibilities, and then, the next minute you are thirty. Tell me, Charlotte, how does this happen?"

I laughed. "Oh, come on, thirty isn't that old. I thought men weren't supposed to care about age."

"You are right, it is the women who are supposed to feel sad and depressed when they are thirty, not the men."

"That's right, so cheer up and drink some more of that beer," I said as I nudged him in the side. "I'm sure I'll be depressed enough for the both of us when I turn thirty."

He grinned at me, then took a huge gulp of beer. "No, you will be even more beautiful when you are thirty than you are now."

I felt my cheeks blush all the way up to my ears. How was it that he could always get me with those corny French-man lines?

Luc downed the last of his beer and headed back up to the bar to get two more. When he sat back down, he wrapped his arm tightly around my shoulders and pressed his thigh up against mine.

His hot breath blew across my neck as he leaned in to my ear. "So, why did you want to come out with me on my birthday? I didn't know if I would see you again."

I gazed up into his handsome chestnut eyes and knew I wouldn't be able to keep my guard up any longer. I had to tell him the truth. "I missed you."

Luc pinned his serious gaze on me as he lowered his face

to mine, and just as I thought he was going to kiss me, he ran his finger down my neck, then picked up my necklace instead. "Your necklace is all tied up," he said as he rested his hands above my chest and untangled the silver chain.

My body temperature rose. With Luc's hands so close to my breasts and the alcohol taking its hold on me, I wanted to kiss him. To feel his arms around me. To be naked in bed with him.

I wanted another chance to be with him.

But had I said too much?

"There, all better." He ran his hands over my shoulders, then smiled at me—that warm, sweet, sexy smile that melted me, that made me lose all my defenses. Then, just before his lips met mine, he whispered, "I missed you too."

He laced his fingers through my hair and held the back of my head as he kissed me in the corner of the crowded bar. I didn't even notice the noisy crowd yelling and laughing around us. All I could think about was how insanely wonderful it felt to be kissing Luc again. And how I never wanted it to stop.

"Want to get out of here?" he whispered in my ear after letting me come up for air.

I didn't even answer him. I grabbed his hand and pulled him out of the booth. We raced for the door, and once we were back in the car, Luc kissed me again before we sped off into the Parisian night. As we rounded Place de la Concorde, with its tall obelisk lighting up the circle, Luc stopped at a red light and placed his hand on my inner thigh. He massaged it higher and higher until I thought I would explode. It seemed like it took an eternity for us to get back to his room, where he stripped me naked within seconds of walking in the door. I tore off his shirt and pants before he picked me up, wrapped my legs around his waist, and slammed my back up against the wall. He pressed tightly into me and began thrusting so deeply that I cried out in pleasure. I didn't care that my back would be covered in bruises the next day. I needed him inside of me, and the pleasure was almost unbearable.

I gripped Luc's shoulders as he carried me over to the bed, laid me down, and rolled me over onto my stomach. Then he reached his hands up in between my legs, spread them ever so slightly, and pushed his fingers inside of me. He straddled me and kept pressing his hand deeper as he kissed the length of my back. I felt his hand pull out as he pressed his groin on top of me and entered me from behind. He went so deep, I could hardly breathe.

He lowered his body against my back as he slid in and out of me.

"Charlotte, I missed your body," he whispered into my ear as his hot breath sent tingles down my spine. *"Je veux te faire l'amour toute la nuit."*

There's nothing sexier than a hot French man telling you *in French* that he wants to make love to you all night long. I flipped onto my back, pushed him over, and climbed on top of him. He grinned as he let me take control. I slid back and forth on top of him until I couldn't hold my pleasure in any longer. I moaned as I collapsed on top of him. Luc kept pushing deep inside of me as I held on to his shoulders. Finally, I felt him throbbing as he let out a groan and collapsed onto his back.

We lay tangled in his sheets for a while until we caught our breath. I wondered how another man could ever compare to this. I'd never felt so pleased, so deeply satisfied, as I did when I was with Luc.

Then, as if the sex weren't amazing enough, Luc reached into his nightstand and pulled out a bar of Lindt dark chocolate.

I burst out laughing.

"What, you think eating chocolate after sex is funny?"

"No, I love it. It's just you. You're cute, that's all."

"Cute?"

"Okay, you're a sexy, hot man who loves chocolate. You're not cute."

"That's better." Luc unwrapped the bar of chocolate and fed me square after decadent square until my pleasure meter had hit its max. As I was drowning in delight, the taste of rich, melty chocolate swirling around on my tongue, a thought crossed my mind. Hannah's DC wedding was coming up in a month, and I still didn't have a date.

"Luc, I have a question for you."

"Yes?"

"Would you be interested in coming with me to a wedding back in DC next month?"

"Really? You want me to be your date?"

"Yes, I'd love to have you there with me."

Luc's grin widened as he leaned in and planted a kiss on my lips.

"I take that as a yes?"

"Yes, I would love to go with you."

"Happy Birthday, Luc," I said as I kissed his neck and wrapped my arms around his sexy, naked body.

And just as we were starting to roll around under the sheets again, Luc's cell phone rang.

He shot up out of bed to answer it while I tried to remain calm. Who in the hell was always calling him this late, and why did he have to jump out of bed to answer it? This was bullshit. I started to get up and put my clothes back on, but Luc walked over to me and grabbed my shoulders. "Charlotte, I have to take this call, and then I will explain. Please don't leave."

I sat back down on the bed, shaking my head. I thought Luc would put some clothes on and dash out into the hallway to take the call like he had the first time this had happened. But, he didn't. Instead, he threw on his underwear, sat down at his kitchen table, and answered his phone.

"Coucou Adeline," he started.

After he said hello in a sickeningly sweet voice, I grew increasingly impatient.

"*Oui, tu me manques aussi, ma fille.*"

Wait, had I just heard him right? *I miss you too, my little girl*?

What?

"*Tu es allée au zoo? Tu as vu des lions? Ah, des tigres aussi? C'est super, ma petite chérie.*"

Oh, my gosh. Luc was definitely *not* talking to a woman.

It was a child—a daughter.

Luc had a daughter.

I wasn't even sure what to do with this information. So, this is who had been calling him at all hours of the night? This is who he'd been running out on me to talk to? Why was a little girl calling him at one in the morning, though? And why did he have to hide it from me?

Before I had a chance to digest what was going on, Luc finished his conversation with, "*Je t'aime aussi, Adeline. À demain.*"

He gazed up at me with a worried expression on his face.

"So you have a daughter?"

"Yes, her name is Adeline."

"So why didn't you just tell me about her? All this time, that's who's been calling you? Why does she call you in the middle of the night? What is going on?"

"Calm down, please. At first, I tried to tell you about her, but you weren't interested in letting me explain."

Then I remembered all of the times when he'd said he had something important to tell me, and I'd cut him off or kissed him, or done whatever I had to *not* to have that conversation.

"I'm sorry for not letting you explain. But what about after the ballet, when you asked me to come home with you for Christmas? I asked you then to explain the calls, and you said you couldn't tell me. That it was complicated. Why wouldn't you have just told me the truth at that point?"

"I wanted you to know about her, but things never went right with us, and then suddenly things became very complicated with my ex-wife. It wasn't something I wanted to drag you into. And also, I was afraid that if I told you the truth, you wouldn't want to see me anymore."

"Why would you think that?" I asked.

"To be honest, at the time, you didn't seem like someone who would want to date a man with a child."

He had a point.

"My daughter calls late at night because she lives in Australia now, and there is a big time difference."

"Australia?"

"While I was married, Adeline's mother cheated on me with another man. An Australian man. Then during the divorce, she got custody of Adeline and took her to Australia." I noticed the weariness in Luc's eyes as he told the story. "She is only three years old, and she has been gone for a year. I miss her so much, and I am trying to get her back. The man her mother is with is not a nice man. Adeline is scared of him, and she wants to come home to me. So all year, I have been going to court, and even traveling to Australia, trying to get her back."

"Oh, my gosh." I was speechless. Luc had been cheated on too. He'd had his heart broken just like me. And here, all this time, he was simply trying to get his little girl back.

"I am sorry that I didn't tell you right away. Besides the way things were with us, and besides the complications of the court battle, I have to be careful, you know, about who I allow into my daughter's life. This situation is already messy enough. I hope you understand."

"I should've let you explain the first time. But I do wish you would've told me sooner." I ran my hands through my hair, shaking my head. "I can't believe you've been going through all of this."

"That is why I wanted to take you home for Christmas.

Adeline flew home, and we all stayed with my parents for a few weeks. I wanted you to meet her in person, but you told me you didn't want a relationship, so I let it go."

My gaze dropped to the floor, the guilt settling in. "I'm sorry, Luc. I'm so sorry."

Luc walked over to his bookshelf and grabbed a photo album. "Here, let me show you." He flipped open to a picture of him holding an adorable little girl in his arms. "This is Adeline."

"She's beautiful. She looks just like you."

As we climbed back into bed together, my mind reeled from the revelations that had just been made.

Luc had a daughter. Luc was a *father*.

I wasn't just sleeping with some random sexy French man now. This was a man who had been hurt. A man who had a child and who was fighting to get that child back. A man who had more on his plate than sleeping with a bunch of women and finishing up a master's degree.

And then I remembered my article. The article where I had verbally bashed Luc and all of his attempts to be with me. Where I had droned on and on about his stupid phone calls and his sketchy behavior to prove to women that all men are liars and that they can't be trusted. My article that would be published in a major US women's magazine in April, right in time for the wedding.

Oh shit.

NINETEEN

vendredi, le premier avril

No amount of primping will prepare you for the first time you lay eyes on the man who broke your heart and the woman who stole his.

"*Bienvenue.*" The perky flight attendant welcomed the passengers as Luc and I buckled our seat belts in the cramped airplane seats. Hannah and Mike's wedding had snuck up on me, leaving me completely unprepared for what I would have to face.

The April issue of *Bella Magazine* with my article, "How to Date Like a Man in the City of Love," had hit newsstands in the US the week before. I had called Beth, the editor, the day after Luc told me about his daughter. I begged her to let me rewrite the article, but she said it was too late for revisions. I pleaded again, but she stayed firm. She said she had no choice.

Once I knew there was no going back, I thought about telling Luc, but I hadn't been able to build up the courage to just sit him down and spill it. How would I even begin to justify all the hurtful things I'd written about him?

So I bit my nails, hoping, praying that Luc wouldn't get wind of the article. I had never worried about my blog because my name wasn't on it, plus it was a blog specifically written for women. It was the same thing with the article, I reasoned. It was a women's magazine, so what reason would he ever have to pick it up? I had already warned all of my girlfriends who would be at the wedding to keep their mouths zipped, so it would be okay. It had to be okay.

I downed two of those minibottles of wine they give you on the plane, because not only was I nervous about the article, but in less than twenty-four hours, I would be seeing Jeff and his girlfriend, Brooke, in person. Katie had confirmed that Brooke was, in fact, attending the wedding, and she'd promised to trip her or spill red wine on her. What else are best friends for?

Despite the dread that had overcome me the minute we boarded the flight to DC, I had decided that no matter what vengeful feelings I felt when I saw Jeff and Brooke together, I would keep my cool and focus on Hannah. As one of her best friends and as her bridesmaid, I owed it to her to put my feelings aside and to support her on the biggest day of her life. After more than eight months in Paris without Jeff, in theory, I should've been totally and completely over him. In a way, I was looking forward to seeing him so that I could show him just how over him I was. Having an attractive, sweet French man on my arm all weekend should do the trick. But the attractive French man sleeping next to me on the plane had no clue that Jeff was going to be at the wedding. And since I wasn't planning on being all buddy-buddy with Jeff, I didn't see the need to tell Luc. It would've just made him feel uncomfortable and out of place, so I figured that what he didn't know wouldn't hurt him.

Hours later, we arrived at a Marriott hotel in northwest DC, right by the National Zoo. The wedding reception was going to be held at the hotel, following a ceremony on

Georgetown's campus. We didn't have much time to relax before we had to get ready for the rehearsal, so Luc and I sped up to our hotel room to shower and change. But before I hopped in the shower, I had to find Katie. This was the longest time we'd gone without seeing each other in our entire friendship of twenty years. Plus, she had a copy of *Bella Magazine*.

While Luc was showering, I raced down to Katie's room and knocked on the door.

"Is that who I think it is?" Katie said as she peeked her head out. "Charlotte!" she screamed as she hugged me.

"Oh, my gosh, it's so good to see you! You look great!" I stood back for a minute to look at my best friend. She did look fabulous. She was wearing an adorable blue-and-white summer dress, and her short blonde hair had grown all the way down her back since I'd last seen her.

"Thanks! You look great too!" she shrieked with excitement.

"Oh, stop. I just got off the plane and haven't even taken a shower yet."

"Well, you could've fooled me, hot lady," she said with a wink.

"So, where's your man?" I asked in anticipation. Katie was still dating Joe, the gynecologist, and I was excited to meet him and see what all the fuss was about. Plus, I wanted Katie to know that I supported her relationship, no matter how antilove I'd been all year long.

Katie grinned sheepishly as she led me into their hotel room. Joe stood at the window looking all spiffy in a crisp white shirt paired with a dark-red tie. I immediately understood what all the fuss was about—and it wasn't just about the looks. He was definitely handsome, with his full head of dark-brown hair and his muscular physique, but it was his warm personality that shone through right off the bat. Instead of just shaking my hand, he gave me a big bear hug. And at six-foot-five, he was definitely a big cuddly bear.

"So this is the wild single gal in Paris who Katie's told me so much about. It's good to finally meet you," he said as he smiled warmly at me.

"What has she been telling you? Hopefully not all the bad stuff," I said jokingly, but I was really a little serious.

"No, no, only good things. So, where's your man? Luc, right?"

"He's good," I said to Katie, pointing at Joe. "Remembering names already. I'm impressed." I turned to Joe. "He's getting ready back in our room, which is what I need to be doing if I don't want to be late."

As Katie walked me to the door, I whispered in her ear, "Do you have the magazine?"

"Um, let's see. My best friend publishes an article in my favorite magazine and I don't have it. Come on, lady, obviously I have it." She walked over to her suitcase, grabbed the latest issue of *Bella Magazine*, flipped the pages to my article, and handed it over to me. Joe stepped into the bathroom and closed the door, leaving us alone.

Inside the glossy magazine, I spotted my picture at the top of the three-page feature article that I had written for women everywhere. I felt so excited at the sight of my byline that I almost forgot about the fact that if Luc saw it, he'd never want to see me again.

"Charlotte, it's awesome. I've talked to all the girls, and everyone loves it. I mean, can you believe it? *Your* article is in *Bella Magazine*. It's freaking ridiculous!"

"Thanks, Katie. Yeah, it does look pretty great, doesn't it?"

"Yes, and don't you worry your little butt about a thing. There's no way Luc will find out about it. This is a women's magazine, for God's sake. Why on earth would he pick this up?"

"You're right. But still, after everything he told me, it would just be awful."

I filled Katie in on Luc's evil ex-wife and her Australian boyfriend who'd stolen Luc's little girl away.

"Yeah, but you didn't know all of that when you wrote this, or you would've written it differently. It's great the way it is, and it's not like the whole article is about you and Luc. Only some of it."

I raised my eyebrows at her.

"Okay, you do relate most of your points back to him. But he's not going to see it, Charlotte. All of us girls have it tucked away in our suitcases, okay?"

"Thanks, Katie."

"Oh, I picked you up like ten copies. I figured you could sneak them back with you."

"You're the best," I said as I gave her a hug.

"I know," she said with a shrug. "Just kidding. All right, lady, you better get a move on it so we're not late."

"See you in a few," I said as I jetted out of their room. I so needed more than half an hour to get ready, but it would have to do.

"Hey, Charlotte, wait!" Katie hissed down the hallway.

"What is it?"

"Come here for a minute. I just want you to be prepared. Jeff and Brooke are staying in the hotel too…I saw them a few hours ago." She peeked down the hallway to make sure no one was listening.

My stomach churned. "Why are they staying here when they live in the city?"

"Same reason as us, I guess: so they don't have to drive home after the reception, and so everyone can party together tonight probably. He *is* the best man." She rolled her eyes. "I still can't believe Hannah and Mike left him in the wedding party."

Knowing that Jeff and Brooke were in the very same hotel

at that moment made me feel sick to my stomach. And the fact that I was standing in the hallway looking like a tired mess after a long flight made me want to get the hell out of there before they happened to walk by. "Thanks for letting me know...I'll be fine, though. I better go get ready."

Katie didn't look convinced, and, truthfully, I wasn't convinced myself. In less than an hour, I was going to see Jeff and the redheaded girl who had made my life a mess. As much as I wanted to kick and scream and tell them that this wasn't fair, that they'd caused me so much pain and didn't deserve to be here sharing this special time with me and my friends, I had to accept that this was the situation I'd been dealt, and there was nothing I could do about it. Acting like a maniac would make Jeff feel like he had made a good choice in cheating on me, and it would make me look like a fool.

Instead, I wanted him to squirm.

My plan of attack was simple: I would look strikingly beautiful and act incredibly calm and sophisticated throughout the entire event. And I would *not* hide my growing feelings for Luc. I wanted Jeff to see for himself that I'd found a new, wonderful man, and that our old relationship was completely dead to me. I would even be sugary sweet to him and Brooke, showing them both just how much I had moved on. My hope, of course, was that this would drive him completely insane.

After a quick shower and blow-dry, I put on my makeup and threw on a sexy raspberry-colored dress that I had bought just for this occasion and was ready for action. When I walked out of the bathroom, Luc grabbed me around the waist and kissed me. His desire sent tingles down my spine. I could see that he was ready for action too, and if we weren't in such a time crunch, I would've taken him up on it. Ever since we'd spent his thirtieth birthday night together, we hadn't been able to keep our hands *or* our lips off each other.

Luc settled for a quick make-out session inside our hotel

room before whispering a promise for more in my ear and taking off with me toward Katie and Joe's room.

The four of us rode down to Georgetown University together, then wound our way through the familiar, beautiful campus toward Dahlgren Chapel, where the ceremony would be held. As I breathed in the sweet scent of the red and yellow tulips lining the towering statue of John Carroll, I grasped Luc's hand a little tighter and led him through Healy Hall. We emerged into Dahlgren Quad, my absolute favorite place on campus. With its trees boasting lush pink blossoms, and a peaceful fountain flowing in the center, this tranquil little spot immediately calmed my nerves.

But, as we walked around the fountain, an unmistakable voice shattered my peace.

It was Jeff.

There he was after all this time, standing with Mike in the middle of the square, laughing his hearty laugh and looking as handsome as ever. Ugh. Katie raised a subtle eyebrow in my direction. I shot her a tense smile in return as I dug my fingernails into the palm of my hand and silently gritted my teeth. My eyes frantically scanned the quad for a redhead with big boobs. No such creature in sight. Hmm...hopefully Jeff had caught her sleeping with some other sucker and had broken up with her on the spot. Or better yet, maybe *she* had dumped *him*.

I linked my arm through Luc's, hoping we could bypass Jeff and Mike and jet straight into the church.

"Charlotte!" Mike called.

Damn.

As Jeff jerked his head around to face us, the look that splashed across his chiseled, clean-cut features was priceless. I couldn't have hoped for more, really. His perfect blue eyes widened and his mouth dropped open as he looked from me to Luc and back to me as if in disbelief that I had actually brought a date. Did he honestly think I would show up here alone? He clearly had no idea who he was dealing with.

"Hey, beautiful!" Mike ran over to me and gave me a huge hug and a kiss on the cheek. "Man, what are those French men doing to you over there? You look amazing. Hannah's going to be so happy you're here. She's a little stressed with all of the wedding stuff...to say the least."

"Weddings tend to have that effect on people," I said as I smiled coolly in Jeff's direction. I thought I could see him squirming under his shirt and tie. "Guys, this is my date, Luc," I said proudly.

Mike reached out and shook Luc's hand. "I hope my crazy bride in there doesn't scare you off from American weddings," Mike said with a grin. "Glad you could make it."

"Thank you," Luc said before innocently reaching his hand out to Jeff.

Jeff didn't seem to notice Luc's hand, though, because he was still staring at me with that same flabbergasted look plastered across his face. Almost the same expression he'd had when I'd discovered his online dating profile.

I grabbed Luc's dangling hand and smiled back at Mike. "So where is this stressed-out bride-to-be? I'm sure she could use a little help."

Mike pointed toward the chapel. "Watch out—she's in rare form."

Jeff shot one more pointed glance at Luc and me before we broke free from the intense awkwardness and headed into the chapel.

"That went well," Katie whispered into my ear.

"Were you worried?" I whispered back.

"I just didn't know what was going to happen when you guys saw each other again. You really held it together. And he was definitely uncomfortable. Nice work," Katie said as she winked at me.

I glanced over at Luc to find him marveling at the clock

tower atop Healy Hall. "I cannot believe you went to college here. This campus is amazing. There is nothing like this in France."

Whew. He didn't seem to have any clue as to *whom* he'd just met.

I squeezed his hand. "It *is* gorgeous here. But, don't forget, nothing this beautiful comes without a heavy price. At least the schools in France don't bankrupt you."

He chuckled as we walked down the main aisle of the chapel and found Hannah running around like a madwoman.

"Charlotte! Luc! Katie! Joe! You're here, you're finally here!" she yelped as she gave us all huge, desperate hugs.

Sensing Hannah's frenzy, Katie took charge. "You need to relax, lady. What do you need help with? We're the bridesmaids, so that's our job. Give us something to do."

"You don't mind if I steal your dates, do you guys?" Hannah asked Joe and Luc as she took our hands and whirled us away into the land of prewedding craziness. She kept us busy right up until the rehearsal started. So much so that I barely noticed Jeff sitting with Mike in the front row, staring me down. Brooke was still nowhere in sight. I knew I would recognize her the minute she arrived. I still had that image of her red hair and her tight, slutty top with her boobs bursting out etched in my mind like a nightmare.

As Jeff and I took our places at the altar performing our best man and bridesmaid duties, respectively, I caught his eyes glancing over my way more than a few times. Each time his gaze landed on me, I forced myself to look away and to focus on Hannah and Mike, on Luc, on anyone other than Jeff.

But I couldn't ignore the overwhelming emotions boiling over inside of me at the sight of my old love, my ex-fiancé, the man who'd broken my heart.

How was I supposed to face him for two days straight? With Luc as my date, no less? And what would happen when the redheaded vixen entered the picture?

Spotting the wine chalices at the back of the chapel, I wished I could fill one of those babies up and chug it right about now. But I didn't think Hannah *or* the priest would especially appreciate that gesture.

After the rehearsal, fueled by my intense need for alcohol, I practically dragged Luc over the brick sidewalks of Georgetown down toward the waterfront, where the rehearsal dinner was set to be held.

"Why are you walking so fast?" Luc asked. "Your friends are behind us. Don't you want to visit with them? It's been so long since you've seen them."

I tugged on Luc's hand to make him keep up. "We'll have plenty of time for chatting this weekend. I need a drink."

Luc raised an eyebrow, then laughed. "You American women like the alcohol a lot, no?"

"And French women don't?" I asked as we headed toward the entrance of Tony and Joe's.

Hannah's voice came loud behind me. "Charlotte, wrong restaurant!"

I flipped around, confused.

"Dinner is next door, at Sequoia. Tony and Joe's flooded last week, so we had to rebook."

I opened my mouth, but no words came out. Sequoia was the infamous restaurant where Jeff had proposed to me, just last year.

Could this night get any worse?

Inside the restaurant, I held Luc's hand and led him over to a beautiful table next to the floor-to-ceiling windows which overlooked the Potomac River, all the while trying to block out the memories of the last time I'd taken in this view...with Jeff down on one knee, asking me to be his wife.

As the waiters served us our salads and I downed my first glass of Chardonnay like it was water, I peeked down the table and noticed that Brooke still hadn't arrived. I was beginning to think that she wouldn't be gracing us with her presence tonight, which would've been just fine with me.

Luc leaned in and wrapped his arm around my shoulders, making me forget about Brooke for the moment.

"You look beautiful tonight, Charlotte. I cannot take my eyes off you," he whispered in my ear.

Out of the corner of my eye, I noticed Jeff spying on us from a few seats down. He narrowed his eyes at me, then shook his head and turned away.

Humph. Take that, asshole.

My cheeks flushed as I returned Luc's gaze and smiled. He lowered his face to mine and brushed my lips with his before taking my hand and turning back toward Katie and Joe.

"I am so glad that I was lucky enough to be invited to meet all of you here in DC," Luc said to them. "You Americans are all so friendly. Much different than the Parisians."

Katie grinned. "Well, I've been hearing about you for so long now, it's about time she brought you over here."

Luc laughed and continued to chat with them about the differences between France and the States. Katie flashed me a look of approval from across the table. I could tell she was a huge Luc fan.

We were just finishing our salads when I spotted Jeff standing up and turning around. Suddenly the hairs on the back of my neck stood up as if a ghost had just entered the room. My stomach started doing somersaults, and as I glanced over Jeff's shoulder, I knew why.

There she was. The woman who'd stolen my fiancé. There in the flesh.

Brooke was actually prettier than I had remembered from the online photo. The picture had screamed slut, whore, what have you, but what I was seeing here was a totally different picture. Silky, strawberry-blonde hair ran the length of her back. Her arctic-blue eyes sparkled against a pale complexion, and a stunning diamond necklace cradled her bony little neck. As if that weren't enough, a slinky black dress hugged her perfect figure.

I knew I shouldn't have cared. I should've been over it. But seeing her in person, in the same room where Jeff had proposed to me not long ago, was a whole different story.

I hated her.

As Jeff slid his arm around her waist and kissed her on the cheek, I felt the blood rush to my face while every muscle in my body tensed up. I took a huge gulp of water to cool down. Katie shot me a concerned glance, so I arranged a smile on my face and pretended as if I were doing just fine. Having the time of my life.

It took all my strength not to lunge across that table and yank those diamonds off Brooke's neck and pull her hair out. Suddenly Jeff wasn't the criminal in the situation—it was her. I mean, look at her. What guy wouldn't go for her? *Slut, slut, slut.* I chanted it over and over in my head until I started to feel dizzy. I needed to get away from here before I did or said something I would regret.

"I'm going to use the ladies' room," I told Luc and Katie before dashing away from the table as fast as I could.

I stood in the bathroom, splashing cold water onto my steaming-hot face and stared at myself in the mirror. I knew rationally that I shouldn't have been so upset by this. I should've been confident and strong enough to handle seeing Jeff and Brooke together. But all the rationalizing in the world couldn't take away the anger that had resurfaced, the jealousy that even after all this time, ate away at my insides, and the feeling that in the end, I would never be enough for any man. Maybe not even for Luc.

And even though Luc was so amazing, and I'd actually begun to let my guard down again and trust him, the truth of the matter was that tonight, he was the furthest thing from my mind. How could I focus on my feelings for Luc when Jeff and Brooke were sitting across the table from me? At the very same restaurant where Jeff had proposed?

No wonder my mom had left Ohio the minute she and my dad had separated. How could she have stayed, knowing my dad was living just down the road with his girlfriend? What if she ran into them at the store? Thinking about Jeff and Brooke and my broken family made me feel nauseous all of a sudden. I rushed into one of the stalls and got sick.

After that ghastly experience, I popped in a stick of gum, touched up my makeup, and stared at my reflection in the mirror.

Get it together, Charlotte. Get it together.

I couldn't let Jeff and Brooke see how they were making me feel.

Determined to keep my shit together for the rest of the night, I turned to leave the bathroom. But just as I was walking out the door, I crashed right into Jeff.

"Oh, sorry," I stammered as I pushed past him.

"Charlotte, wait," he called as he followed me down the hallway. "Are you okay? You look a little pale."

Probably because the sight of you with your online girlfriend literally just made me get sick.

"Yeah, I'm fine. Are you okay?" I asked, noticing that Jeff was flustered and out of breath.

"Yeah, I just..." He paused and looked into my eyes. "I can't believe they chose *this* restaurant for the rehearsal dinner. And, well, it's just so good to see you again. You look beautiful, Charlotte. Really, you're stunning."

"What about that girlfriend of yours? She's quite the looker, Jeff. Well done," I said curtly as I rounded him to flee the scene.

Jeff grabbed my shoulders and turned me around to face him. "Wait, I just want to talk to you for a minute. We haven't talked in months."

"What is there to talk about?" I asked, wanting to smack him across the face so badly I could've screamed.

"You just look so...so happy. Are you really happy with that guy? That *French* guy?"

"That French guy has a name, and it's Luc. And yes, I am happy. He's amazing. And you...you seem happy with... what's her name again?" *Like I could ever forget.*

"Brooke," he replied as he gazed shamefully at the floor.

"Oh yes, Brooke, that's right. I almost forgot. You two are lovely together. I'm so glad you found each other."

He lifted an eyebrow, clearly not buying my fake sincerity.

"I'm over us, Jeff, totally and completely over us. So you can stop feeling bad and trying to see if I'm okay. I'm fine. Luc and I are really happy together. It all worked out for the best." The words flew out of my mouth just as I had practiced them, and I was hoping they were believable.

"Oh...well...that's great," Jeff stammered as he glanced down at his feet. "I'm glad you're doing so well. I mean, you seem so happy...you really do."

"Thanks, I am," I said as I turned to walk away.

Jeff grabbed my hand one last time and pulled me back toward him. "Charlotte, one more thing...Did I make you that happy?"

I hesitated, knowing that before I'd found out that Jeff was cheating on me, I'd never felt happier. I'd never fallen in love so hard, so fast, as I had with Jeff. But he'd broken that love. He'd broken my heart. And I couldn't stand here and look into his big blue eyes for another second. "I'm sure Brooke is wondering where you are. You better get back." And with that, I pulled away from his grip and walked back through the restaurant, leaving him alone to question his decisions.

Luc was walking toward me as I approached the table. "I was just coming to find you. You are okay? You were gone for a while."

"Yes, I'm fine. Thanks for checking, though," I said as I kissed him on the cheek.

My entire body ached after my run-in with Jeff and my purge in the bathroom. I did my best to act happy. Happy to be with Luc, happy to be with my friends again, and happy for Hannah and Mike. But with Jeff and Brooke just a few seats down, happiness was not on tonight's menu. I averted my eyes from the dreaded couple throughout the remainder of the meal, but I could feel Jeff's eyes on me all night, burning a hole through my heart.

TWENTY

samedi, le 2 avril

Nothing good can come from mixing alcohol with a wedding, an ex-fiancé, and a big-busted redhead.

The hotel alarm clock roared loudly in my ears before the sun had even risen the next morning. I rolled out of bed half-awake and climbed into the shower. Dread gripped my stomach as I thought about spending one more full day in the same room as Jeff and Brooke. I had to keep it together, though. This was Hannah's day, not mine. Plus, things were going so well with Luc. He really cared about me. And even though I was still hesitant to commit to someone for a *lifetime* per se, I cared deeply for him too. It wasn't fair to him for me to be focused on Jeff and Brooke's antics all weekend.

After all, I was over Jeff. Completely over him.

Wasn't I?

I shook off my doubts and met the girls down in the lobby at six a.m. on the dot. We spent the entire morning at a classy salon on Connecticut Avenue, Katie, Hannah, and I sitting side by side while stylists pulled, combed, curled, and sprayed our hair into typical wedding 'dos.

"It's so great to have you home from Paris, Charlotte," Hannah said. "We've missed you so much. And your Parisian boyfriend is just scrumptious!"

Katie giggled. "And such a better guy than Jeff ever was. Not to mention the fact that he's totally in love with you."

"I wouldn't take it *that* far, Katie." *Could Luc really be in love with me?*

"He flew with you from Paris to DC to come to Hannah's wedding. He didn't come all the way here to see what an American wedding was like. Or to have sex with you. He came here to *be* with you."

"I know he really has feelings for me, Katie. And I like him too. A lot. But he has a *child*. And I haven't even met her yet. Plus, I can't help but wonder, what if I fall for him and then it ends in disaster like the rest of my relationships? And like my parents'?"

"Charlotte, Jeff broke your heart, yes. But Luc isn't Jeff."

"Speaking of Jeff," Hannah cut in. "Is everything okay with you guys this weekend? I know you weren't looking forward to seeing him...or meeting his girlfriend."

"Everything's fine, Hannah. Please don't worry, okay? This is your day. I would never do anything to ruin it."

"I didn't mean that you would," Hannah replied. "It's just...I was on my way to the bathroom at the rehearsal dinner last night and noticed the two of you talking really close. I know this is nuts to even ask, but is he trying to get back together with you?"

"God, Hannah, no. Don't be ridiculous. I think he's just getting all nostalgic and rethinking his actions now that he's seen me here with another guy. I'm not going to fall for it, though, so you have nothing to worry about."

"I'm sorry, I know that was a dumb thing of me to ask. I'm just nervous about the wedding, that's all," Hannah said, wringing her hands in her lap. "I don't want any drama on my big day, you know. I want this to be the best wedding everyone has ever been to. I want it to be perfect. Plus, I've gotten to know Brooke a little bit, and well, she's not as horrible as you guys might think. She doesn't know that Jeff was engaged when she met him. She thinks you guys broke up a while before they started dating."

I clenched the arms of my chair and forced my expression to stay neutral. If Hannah didn't want any drama, she shouldn't have told me she was fraternizing with the enemy, or that Jeff had continued his lying streak with his new girlfriend.

"I'm not surprised he didn't tell her," Katie said, glancing over at me nervously. "But I think we should drop the subject. Everything will be fine today, right, Charlotte?"

"Yes, you guys. Seriously. I'm not going to do anything stupid. Jeff was the one who approached me last night after I came out of the bathroom. I'm doing my best to avoid him. Plus, I haven't spoken to Brooke, and I don't plan on it."

It seemed that my friends had forgotten *who* had been the one to begin this drama eight months ago with his disgusting online dating profile. But now wasn't the time to remind them of that.

Hannah and Katie stayed silent, so I lifted the corners of my mouth into a smile and kept talking. "Like I said, Hannah, this day is all about you and Mike. I'm so happy for you two, I really am. There won't be any drama tonight, and if Jeff even tries to start anything weird, you can count on me to put an end to it. Okay?"

"Thanks, Charlotte. I didn't think I could count on Jeff to behave, but I knew I could count on you. It was silly of me to think otherwise. It's just the wedding jitters talking."

And while we didn't speak of Jeff or Brooke for the rest of the morning, those two unwelcome lovebirds made themselves cozy in the back of my mind and refused to leave.

∽

Hannah's wedding jitters made several more appearances throughout the day, and with only a half an hour until go time, *Bridezilla* had officially come to town.

"Mom and Kelly, you need to stop crying! You're making *me* cry, and I can't have makeup smearing down my face like a clown when I walk down the aisle!" Hannah snapped at her mother and sister after they'd helped her slip on her wedding gown.

Hannah's mom dabbed at her eyes with a tissue. "A few tears on your wedding day aren't going to make you look like a clown, dear. It shows character. And besides, you look so beautiful. I can't help it."

"*Mom.*" Hannah parked her hands on her skinny hips. She looked like an angry cream puff in her poufy wedding gown.

Katie raised her eyebrows at me. "Maybe we all need to give Hannah some air. This is a big day."

"Yes, that's exactly what I need," Hannah said. "Would everyone just stop ogling me and give me some freaking room to breathe?"

Hannah's sister ushered their mother out of the Healy Hall classroom, dabbing at her eyes the whole way, while Katie and I followed suit. But Hannah grabbed hold of my arm just as I was about to leave.

"Charlotte, you can stay."

I didn't dare argue with *Bridezilla*. Instead, I closed the door and turned around to face my friend, wondering why weddings made girls turn into crazy women.

"Are you okay?" I asked as Hannah paced the room in her sparkly white princess gown, the short train swishing at her feet. With her sandy-blonde hair pulled back under an elegant, lacy veil, I'd never seen her look more beautiful...or more nervous.

She stopped and gazed up at me, tears rimming her eyelids. "I need to tell you something, Charlotte."

"What is it?" I asked, taking a step toward her.

Her eyes darted to the floor as she squeezed her hands together. "You have to promise not to judge me."

"Of course I won't judge you. Whatever it is, you can tell me," I said, laying a hand on her shoulder.

She let out a long, shaky breath. "Oh, God. I can't believe I'm going to say this out loud, right before I'm about to walk down the aisle. But I have to. I have to get this out."

"What is it, Hannah?"

"You swear you will never tell anyone? No matter what. This goes to the grave."

"I swear."

"Okay, here goes...I cheated on Mike."

I stared at my innocent, beautiful bride-to-be friend, not believing my ears. Hannah was so perfect. So naïve. So prudish. Had I even heard her correctly? "You...what?"

"You heard me, Charlotte," she hissed. "I cheated on him! On my fiancé! A week before my wedding. What the fuck was I thinking?"

She never said "fuck" either. In fact, Katie and I had never heard Hannah so much as utter a "shit" or even a "damn" in all of our years as college roommates, or after college for that matter. She was a classic good girl. And classic good girls did *not* sleep with men *other* than their fiancés, and they certainly didn't shout the F word while standing in their wedding gowns about to commit to the supposed love of their life.

"Charlotte!" she snapped.

"Okay, I'm sorry. I just had to let that register for a minute. So this just happened last week?"

Hannah plopped into a chair, smashing a big white pouf underneath her butt, then gazed up at me with her huge green eyes. "Yes."

I swallowed, trying not to show the shock on my face. "And who was it with?"

"A coworker."

"Do you have feelings for this guy?"

"No."

"Then why...?"

"Oh, God, I don't know." She stood and resumed her frantic pacing. "I've been reading your blog all year, you know. Jeff and Mike really aren't that different, and it got me worried. Like what if what happened to you happened to me, but *after* I got married? What if Mike and I end up like your parents? Over fifty percent of marriages end in divorce! I can't ignore that statistic. And then your article came out, and it got me thinking about the flip side of the coin, about being with *one man* for the rest of my life. I mean, you know I've only ever *been* with Mike. He was my first everything, and he was *going* to be my last. And I guess I just kind of freaked out about it. So last weekend, while Mike was out at his bachelor party, I went out for drinks with a few coworkers. At the end of the night, it was just me and this one guy, Chris, and we were both really drunk. He's liked me for years, and I've always wondered what it would be like...and, well, now I know." Hannah gazed at the floor as a tear rolled down her cheek.

I couldn't believe that Hannah, my seemingly perfect friend with her seemingly perfect life, had actually been listening to my advice. And worse, she'd acted on it.

Before I could form a coherent response, Hannah started up again.

"At first it was kind of fun. But then I felt guilty. So guilty it almost made me sick. I could barely look at Mike the next day. That's why I've been such a crazy woman all week. I thought if the wedding was absolutely perfect, it would erase what I'd done. But nothing can erase it. What should I do,

Charlotte? I mean, am I making the right decision getting married in the first place?"

I grabbed Hannah's shoulders and looked her in the eye. I'd created this mess, and despite my own personal doubts about marriage, I had to make it right.

"Do you love him, Hannah? Do you love Mike?"

"Yes, of course I do. I love him so much."

"And do you have any doubts about his love for you?"

She shook her head. "No, he's wonderful. He loves me. He's never given me reason to think otherwise. But what if I'm just being naïve?"

"You're not being naïve. Mike *isn't* like Jeff, Hannah. He's been completely committed to you for years now. And besides, I've seen the way he looks at you. He's totally and completely in love."

"Thank you…but please don't sugarcoat it just to say what you *think* I want to hear. I know your beliefs on relationships and marriage. And I think you have valid points about all of it. I mean, look at what's happened to you, and to your parents. Excluding what I've just done, do you think my relationship, my future marriage, even has a shot at lasting?"

I reached out and wiped the tear from Hannah's rosy cheek. "If anyone's relationship has a shot, it's yours, Hannah. You guys are going to last. I know it." I hoped I was right, I really did. All I knew *for sure*, though, was that I couldn't allow her to cancel her whole wedding based on my antirelationship ramblings.

"But now I've gone and ruined it. I've betrayed him. How can I go through with the wedding after what I've done? Should I tell him?"

"Hannah, if you tell Mike you slept with another man, you know the wedding will be off."

Hannah's eyes widened. "Oh, my God. I didn't *sleep* with Chris! I would never do that. How could you even think I would do that?"

"Wait, what are you talking about? You said you cheated on Mike, right?"

"Yes, but we didn't have sex. God, what kind of a slut do you think I am?"

"Then what did you do with him?"

"We kissed."

"This is all over a kiss?"

"Yes! A kiss is very intimate. A kiss can be even more intimate than sex."

Oh, thank God. I hadn't *completely* corrupted her.

"Even so, you said you don't have any feelings for this Chris guy, correct?" I asked.

"None."

"And you're totally in love with Mike?"

"Totally."

"Okay, here's what you're going to do. You're going to take all of that guilt you're feeling and pass it over to me. This is my fault anyway, Hannah. I had no idea what I'd written would make you doubt your relationship. That was never my intention." I reached out and grabbed Hannah's hands. "Now close your eyes and squeeze. Squeeze as hard as you can and give me all of that toxic guilt."

"Charlotte, this is ridiculous."

"*Hannah.* Just do it."

"Fine." She squared her shoulders, closed her eyes, then squeezed my hands so hard I thought my fingers would break. But that's okay. I would take a broken finger if it meant Hannah would walk down that aisle in ten minutes.

She released her grip on my hands, opened her eyes, and let out a long sigh. "Thank you, Charlotte. Thank you so much."

I smiled. "Now you're going to walk down that aisle and marry the love of your life."

She lunged forward and hugged me as I breathed out my own sigh of relief.

I made a mental note to edit my blog content when I arrived back in Paris. I didn't need any more friends using *my* antilove propaganda as an excuse to break up their perfectly good relationships.

God, weddings are *drama*.

~

A few minutes later, with my bouquet of pink calla lilies in tow, I lined up with Katie and Hannah's sister in the back of the chapel while Hannah took her dad's arm and the both of them tried not to cry.

"What was that all about?" Katie whispered in my ear.

"Just a little wedding drama." *Drama that originated with my freaking blog.* "I handled it, though."

Katie winked at me. "Nice work, lady."

I leaned back over and whispered one more thing in Katie's ear. "If I ever *do* get married, please remind me to elope. Weddings make people do crazy things."

Katie stifled a giggle as the massive wooden doors at the back of the chapel swung open. Then, as a string quartet serenaded us with a gorgeous rendition of *Canon in D*, she began her march down the aisle.

When it was my turn, I took a deep breath and walked slowly through the packed church, scanning the crowd for Luc. I needed to see his face. I needed to be reminded of his sincerity, of his support, of his feelings for me. But I couldn't find him.

Instead, without meaning to, I met Jeff's intent stare at the front of the church. I tried to pull my gaze away from his, but I couldn't. I couldn't take my eyes off him. And despite the ill feelings I'd touted all year about marriage, relationships, and love, in that moment, as I walked toward the man who I would've married, I knew that it was all just a front.

What I'd really wanted all along was to have exactly what

Hannah and Mike had (well, minus the prewedding kiss and freak-out). But I had. I'd wanted *this* more than anything. I'd wanted to walk down this exact aisle, gazing into Jeff's beautiful blue eyes, knowing that I was the only woman in the world he'd ever want. The only woman he would ever love.

But I wasn't the only woman he'd wanted. And his love for me...well, I wasn't sure how true it had ever really been.

The hardest part today, though, was taking in the regret that traced Jeff's sad eyes.

I wanted to stop the wedding and shout at him. *Why, then? Why did you do it, Jeff? And why did you have to bring her here and shove it in my face one more time? And stop looking at me like that!*

Because the more he gazed at me with that sorrowful look in his eyes, the more I missed him. The more I missed us.

Real life isn't as grand as the movies, though, so I kept my mouth shut, tugged a smile onto my lips, then quietly took my place at the altar.

Hannah appeared at the back of the chapel, glowing and gorgeous and white, swishing down the aisle with her teary-eyed father by her side. I remembered then that even if it had been me walking down the aisle to marry Jeff, my parents wouldn't have even been here together. My family would've been broken.

Why did some people get their happily-ever-afters, and others didn't?

I bit my bottom lip, telling myself not to cry. But as I watched the way Mike gazed at Hannah, I couldn't help but let a tear slide down my cheek. Hannah was making the right decision. Mike would never betray her. He wasn't like Jeff. He wasn't like my dad.

I felt horrible for inciting such doubt in her when she really did have one of the good relationships. One that would last. Or that at least had a real shot.

But as Hannah's father gave her away, I wondered how

you could ever really know for sure. If a good girl like Hannah could stray—even if for a brief moment—anyone could. Marriage vows certainly weren't a foolproof guarantee that you wouldn't get your heart broken. And an engagement ring wasn't either.

I wiped the tear from my eye, knowing in my heart that there were no guarantees. Falling in love was a risk. A messy one.

I searched the crowd once more for Luc's face. For his chestnut eyes, his sweet smile.

But I couldn't find him.

Instead, I felt Jeff's gaze on me for the entire ceremony, the regret radiating off him like he was on fire.

~

Back at the hotel, the reception hall was decorated like a mini-wonderland. Bunches of pink and white calla lilies adorned the guest tables, which were each surrounded by chairs wrapped in smooth, shimmering white covers with thick pink ribbons flowing down the backs. Underneath the glittery white lights that draped from the ceiling, the DJ played a Frank Sinatra tune while guests mingled with flutes of champagne in their hands.

Luc and I wove through the sparkly pink maze to our assigned table. As I plucked a glass of champagne off the waiter's tray, I surveyed the guests and spotted Jeff and Brooke across the room. Whew. At least Hannah's wedding planner hadn't made a blunder and seated us together. After standing across from Jeff at the altar for the past hour, I couldn't bear to face him for another second.

A fancy five-course dinner and way too many Frank Sinatra tunes later, Luc excused himself to go to the restroom, and Katie and Joe headed up to the dance floor. I used my fork to swipe a glob of icing off the delectable raspberry-and-vanilla wedding cake, but just as I was about to drown my hurricane of emotions in another blast of sugar and alcohol, a familiar scent wafted past my nose.

Jeff's cologne.

I lifted my face to find Jeff standing before me.

"Charlotte, can we talk?"

I dropped my fork onto my plate. "What? Right now?"

Jeff took a step closer. "Yes, just hear me out for a minute, okay?"

I glanced nervously around the reception hall, but when I saw that no one was paying any attention to us, I nodded. "Fine. You have one minute."

Jeff sat down next to me, his big blue gaze intense as he began speaking. "Charlotte, I miss you. I made a mistake. A huge mistake. I don't love her. I love you. I always have."

My stomach twisted in knots as I tried not to hear him. Tried to block out his words. Tried to think of Luc. But it was all too much.

"I can't do this right now, Jeff." I shot up from the table and raced out of the reception hall.

Just as I stepped into the elevator, though, I heard someone rush in behind me. And as I flipped my head around, I found Jeff staring at me breathlessly.

The doors closed, and we were alone.

TWENTY-ONE

samedi, le 2 avril

Your instincts will always know the difference between a good man and a bad one; the trick is in listening to your gut before it's too late.

"What are you doing?" I asked him frantically. I was done pretending to be calm, cool, and collected. I felt anything but.

He charged toward me and laid his hands on my shoulders, the feel of his skin against mine fueling my wild torrent of emotions for him.

"Please, Charlotte, hear me out. I'm different now. I've had a lot of time to think about what went wrong, and the mistakes I've made. And if you'll give me a second chance, I promise things will be different."

"You're crazy! You're here with Brooke, and I'm here with Luc. What do you think you're doing?" I hissed as I willed the elevator to open up on my floor. I needed to get away from him. I could already feel myself falling, plummeting into the depths of his gaze, his touch, his voice.

Jeff took a step closer to me, his grip on my shoulders

tightening. "I love you, Charlotte. I've never stopped loving you." Then, without warning, he leaned in and pushed his lips onto mine.

I struggled to shove him off me. "Stop it, Jeff, stop!" I cried. But my efforts weren't strong enough. He pushed me up against the wall of the elevator and kissed me even harder.

And even though I hated what he had done to me, and I loathed the fact that he had brought Brooke to this wedding, somewhere deep inside of me, it felt good. It felt good to know that he still had feelings for me.

That tonight, given the choice, he had chosen *me* over her.

And so, after fighting his kiss for a few more seconds, I finally gave in and kissed him back.

The elevator opened up on my floor, jolting me from the trance Jeff had put me in with his passionate kiss. I broke from his grasp and took off down the hallway. "We can't do this. Not now, not here. You have Brooke here, and I have Luc."

"You don't really want to be with *Luc*," he said in a demeaning tone as he tailed me. "I can tell by the way you look at him. You're not in love with him."

"And what about Brooke?" I asked as I opened the door to my room. "You're not in love with her either, I suppose?"

"No, I'm not!" Jeff practically yelled as he followed me into the room. "She's not you. I made a huge, huge mistake, Charlotte…" Jeff paused as he looked straight into my eyes. "But after you sent me those e-mails, I really thought you were gone for good. So I tried to make things work with her. But I don't love her. I would never marry her. I want you. I want to marry *you*." He leaned in and kissed me again as the door slammed shut behind him.

He said what I'd wanted to hear all year long—that I was the one for him, that he had made a huge mistake, and that he loved me, not her. That he wanted to marry *me*. And in another moment of extreme moral weakness, I collapsed into him and ignored the feeling that this time it was me who was making the mistake.

It was clear that we hadn't been intimate in a long time. Jeff all but ripped my dress right off my body, and I couldn't unbutton his shirt and pants fast enough. His lips tasted so good, I could hardly stand it. His arms felt even stronger than I remembered as he picked me up and laid me down on the bed.

But, as I let all of the perfect things he had just said to me sink in, I thought of Luc. Luc, who'd flown across the ocean to be with me at my friend's wedding. Luc, who'd been there for me all year, so patient, even though I was avoiding commitment like the plague. Luc, who was a real man who fought to keep his daughter. Luc, who treated me better than any man in my life ever had.

Luc...whom I was beginning to fall in love with.

I gazed up at Jeff and realized with sudden and absolute clarity that even though he'd gotten me all stirred up again, he was the *last* person I wanted to be looking at, let alone climbing into bed with.

I pushed Jeff to the side, bolted out of bed, and scrambled to get my bra and underwear back on. What was I thinking? I had to go find Luc. I had to tell him how I felt.

"Charlotte, what's the matter? Come lay with me for a minute."

"What's the matter? What's the matter? Oh, you have some nerve!" I yelled as I slipped my dress over my head. "If it was me that you had wanted all along, then why did you put yourself on three online dating sites? Why did you cheat on me with Brooke? Why did you let me leave for Paris without even trying to come see me? Why didn't you fight harder to keep me if you really knew that it was me and only me that you wanted to be with for the rest of your life?"

Jeff sat up naked in bed and stared at me with that same

bewildered look he'd had on his face when I first confronted him in his office last summer.

"You want to know why?" I answered for him. "Hmm, let me think. Because you're full of shit, that's why. You think you can come in here with your puppy-dog eyes and have sex with me and tell me all these romantic things and that'll make it all go away? That it'll make me forget that you humiliated me by cheating on me with that girl and then bringing her to *my* friend's wedding to throw it all back in my face?"

Jeff stood up and paced toward me.

"Put your clothes on and go find your girlfriend. I'm sure she's waiting for you," I said dryly as I turned around to leave the room.

"Charlotte, wait, you've got it all wrong!" he yelled after me as he pulled his pants on and followed me out the door.

As I raced out of the room, I ran straight into a fuming little redhead—Brooke.

"I knew it! I knew you were going to do this to me, with *her*!" she yelled, pointing at me, drunk and frantic.

I tried to push past her and leave the shirtless sleaze of a man behind me to fend for himself, but Brooke wasn't having it. She grabbed me firmly by the wrist and pulled me back toward her. Her bony little arms were much stronger than they appeared to be.

She shot her furious graze right through me. "What did you do with him?"

And there, in Brooke's icy blue eyes, I recognized something very familiar. It was me, just eight months ago, when I had first found out Jeff was cheating on me. She had that same pained, hysterical look, like a deer in headlights, about to get hit.

Hannah's words from this morning rushed back to me. Brooke didn't know that Jeff and I had been engaged when she'd first started dating him.

And while I didn't want to perpetuate the drama any further, I figured she at least deserved to know the truth.

"You want to know what just happened? Your boyfriend just tried to have sex with me," I said, pointing to my hotel room. "I know what you're thinking—how could Jeff, my perfect, rich lawyer boyfriend, do this to me? Well, I've got news for you. He was engaged to *me* when he started sleeping with *you*."

"What? No, he wasn't. He told me you two had broken up a long time before we started seeing each other. You're lying. She's lying, Jeff, isn't she?"

Jeff stood with his shoulders slumped, a pathetic mess staring blankly at the ground.

"Why do you think he didn't end up going to Paris?" I asked as I pulled my arm from her grasp.

"He said his trip got canceled at the last minute." Doubt suddenly clouded her eyes like a raging storm passing through.

"It got canceled because I found out he was cheating on me with you, and *we* were supposed to be moving there together. So Jeff decided not to go once he'd been caught."

A new fire raged in Brooke's eyes. She wasn't concerned with me anymore. It was Jeff's blood she wanted. "Is that true? Is that true?" she shouted desperately, surely waking up anyone in the hotel who may have been trying to get a good night's rest.

Defeated, Jeff muttered back to her, "Yes, it's true. I...I'm sorry."

Tears streaked her perfectly made-up face as she pummeled Jeff's chest with her bony fists. She was a fiery little thing. "You piece of shit! I can't believe you tried to sleep with her! I can't believe you lied to me!" Brooke continued raging and Jeff continued making excuses as I turned around to flee the scene. But my eyes landed on someone else's gaze this time.

Luc. Oh, God, *Luc*.

He had been standing at the end of the hall watching the whole hideous scene unravel.

Then I noticed that he was holding something in his hands. It was a magazine. It was *Bella Magazine*. We made eye contact, and then, with a disgusted look on his face, he shook his head at me and turned around. I dug my heels into the floor and bolted after him.

"Luc, wait, this isn't what it looks like! Wait!" I called after him.

Meanwhile, Jeff had pushed past Brooke and was following me down the hallway.

"Charlotte, wait! What I said was true, come back!"

I turned around and stared Jeff in the eye. "Don't you think you've done enough damage for one day? Leave me alone!" And with that, I raced down the hall and jumped into the elevator with Luc just before it closed.

He glared at me with angry eyes as he shook the magazine in the air.

"What is this, Charlotte? Did you think I would never see it? Was I just a research project for you?"

My gut twisted in knots as I struggled to get the words out. "No, Luc, no, you were never a research project. I…I started writing this blog about being single in Paris, and it didn't have names in it or anything, but then the magazine contacted me and wanted me to write an article. You and I weren't together then, and you had all of those weird phone calls, and I…there's no excuse. I'm so sorry."

"It doesn't matter. I know I never meant anything to you because now I see you upstairs with that man, ruining that girl Brooke's life."

"How do you know who Brooke is?"

"She gave me the magazine," he said as he shook his head in disgust and stormed out of the elevator.

That little bitch.

I chased after him. "We didn't do anything, I swear. I don't love him anymore, Luc. I love you. I just didn't know everything about you, so I didn't understand what a great person you are. But now I know, and I'm so sorry—"

"I don't care if you are sorry. After tomorrow, you will never have to see me again." Luc shoved the magazine into my hands and took off into the DC night.

I stood in the lobby of the hotel and dropped the magazine to the floor. What had I done?

"Charlotte," Katie called. "Where have you been? Are you all right? Where's Luc?"

I turned my weary face to meet hers, and with one look, she knew.

"Oh no. He saw the article, didn't he?"

I nodded as I stared at the magazine lying on the ground. I wanted to rip it to shreds.

Katie took the elevator up to my room with me so we could talk. I opened the door to find the covers all messed about and Jeff's shirt still on the floor.

Katie bent down and picked up his crumpled shirt. "What's this?"

"There's more to the story than Luc seeing the article," I told her, the shame of what I'd just done making me want to curl up in a ball and never face the world again.

As Katie listened quietly to the latest turn of events, I noticed the sympathy slowly draining from her eyes. Finally, when I was finished, she spoke.

"Charlotte, I know that what Jeff did to you was awful, but you have to get over it. I mean, seriously, how could you have taken him into your hotel room when Luc was just downstairs? What is it about Jeff that makes you go so nuts? And this is Hannah's wedding, for God's sake. You promised her you wouldn't do anything to ruin it! Can you ever just get over yourself and all of your relationship drama and just be there for your friends?" She stood up and stormed toward the door, then stopped and turned back around to face me.

"I'm your best friend, and I know I'm supposed to be supportive of everything you do, so I wasn't going to say anything about this, but I can't hold it in any longer. All year you've been writing on your blog about how awful relationships are, how dumb it is to even think about committing to a guy, when here I am, completely falling in love with Joe. At first, I understood. You had your heart broken and you were just lashing out. But as the months went on, you'd be on the phone with me one day, pretending to be happy for me, then the very next day write a blog post about how relationships are the devil. And it hurt my feelings that you couldn't recognize that good relationships *do* exist, Charlotte. And that I'd finally found one."

"Those posts weren't aimed at you, Katie. And I *am* happy for you. I wasn't pretending."

"You can't play both sides, Charlotte. Relationships aren't all black and white, and when you brought Luc as your date for the wedding, I really thought you were starting to see that. That you were starting to calm down and be yourself again. I missed my best friend…the one I could always count on. The one I knew *before* you went buck wild in Paris and decided to sleep around like it was your job. But after what happened tonight, I don't think you're the person I used to know. In fact, I don't even think *you* even know who you are anymore. I sure as hell don't."

Katie gave me one last glare, then left me alone in my mess of a hotel room with no one to answer for my despicable actions except myself.

∽

I woke to the sound of someone knocking on the door and sprang out of bed thinking it was Luc. He'd never returned to the room after Katie had left, and I'd finally passed out in my bridesmaid dress and heels, waiting for him to come back.

I ran to the door and swung it open, but to my dismay, I found Jeff on the other side. I started to open my mouth to tell him to leave, but he held his hand up to quiet me.

"I didn't come here to fight with you anymore. I knew you were probably in here alone, and I just wanted to see if you were okay." He looked genuinely concerned, even though I didn't really believe that was possible.

"I'm fine. And what makes you think I'm alone?" I shot back.

"Luc and Brooke are downstairs at the bar together."

I felt the blood rise to my head. If that redheaded little monster was trying to steal Luc now, it was on.

"Oh well, I'm sure they're just commiserating over what assholes we are," I said, trying to act nonchalant about it while I clenched my fists and forced myself not to think about what Brooke was probably saying—or *doing*—to Luc.

"Yeah, I've pretty much messed everything up. With you, with her, with everyone." Jeff leaned against the wall and looked down. "I'm sorry, for whatever it matters at this point…" He paused and looked up at me. "I'm sorry."

"I just don't understand you, Jeff. You seemed so happy with us last year, and then you went and cheated on me with her, and now here we are, and you want me again. You can't just play with women like that and expect it to all work out in the end." As I listened to my own words, I realized I should've been giving this same advice to myself. What I'd done to Luc wasn't much different from what Jeff had done to me.

"I know I've done some really shitty things," Jeff said, "but I followed you upstairs today because I miss you and seeing you again made me realize how much I love you."

"But you didn't realize those things until you saw me with

Luc. You were just jealous. And besides, you're with Brooke now. This isn't fair to her either."

"Not anymore. We broke up, and we're not getting back together. I don't love her; I never did. And I wasn't just jealous of that French dude."

"*Luc*," I interjected, annoyed.

"Whatever," he said as if Luc were nothing more than a speck of dirt on the ground. "I've been in love with you this whole time, and I'm ready to do this, Charlotte, to really do this." He stepped into the doorway and leaned in to kiss me.

But I turned my head. I didn't want his kiss.

"I don't love you anymore." The words dropped effortlessly from my mouth.

Jeff stopped in his tracks and shot me a questioning glance.

"I don't love you anymore," I said again, firmer this time.

Jeff took a large step back into the hallway and gazed down at me with his pathetic puppy-dog eyes.

"I did love you, I really did," I said softly, "but it's too late now. Too much has happened, and as great as it would be to forget everything and live happily ever after, I think I've actually started to move on." As the words came out of my mouth, I felt them in my heart. I knew then that I really had begun to move on. I didn't love Jeff anymore. I really didn't. As wonderful as it felt to have this realization, it felt just as awful to know that I'd given up my relationship with Luc *and* lost my best friend, all for someone I wasn't even in love with anymore.

"Do you love him?" Jeff asked.

"Luc, you mean?"

Jeff nodded.

"Well, whether I do or not, that's all ruined now, isn't it?"

"Yeah, I guess so," Jeff said, glancing down at his feet and combing his hand through his wavy blond hair.

"I think you better go," I told him as I began to close the door.

Then Jeff gave me one of those looks. One of those final, parting looks where you know this will be the last time you look into each other's eyes. He lingered there for a few seconds and then slowly turned around to saunter back to his room. I closed the door and leaned against it, not even believing the day I had just experienced. Probably the worst day of my life. Maybe even topping the day I first found Jeff's online dating profile.

I got exactly what I had thought I wanted, but, in the end, it turned out to be exactly what I didn't want. And now I was here alone, and Luc was downstairs with Brooke. I felt sick to my stomach. But what was I supposed to do, go down there and tell him he couldn't talk to her when I had just been in bed with my ex-fiancé that very day? When I had totally refused to make any kind of commitment to him whatsoever? He had no obligation to me, and Brooke had no obligation to Jeff at this point.

I sat on the bed for a few minutes and contemplated going downstairs to try to talk to Luc or running down to Katie's room to tell her how sorry I was, but as my eyes grew heavy and my logic took over, I decided I needed to sit with the weight of my actions for once. And somehow, I needed to figure out how to put the pieces of my frazzled life back together on my own this time.

~

I wasn't sure what time Luc came back to our room, but he did come back. I woke up to find him sleeping on the couch on the other side of the room, with no blankets or pillow. My stomach churned just thinking that he had heard me yelling like a maniac at Brooke, and that he had seen Jeff barge out of our room without his shirt on, not to mention that he had read my article. No wonder he had chosen the cold couch over getting into bed next to me. It made me feel even worse to think about what might have happened between him and Brooke last night. At least he had come back to our room, though.

We had to catch our flight in a couple of hours, so I gently tapped Luc's shoulder to wake him up.

"Luc, we have to get ready to go," I said softly.

Luc grunted and rubbed his eyes. When he finally opened them and saw me, he promptly sat up and headed for the shower. I decided it would be better to wait to try to talk to him until he had woken up a bit. So, we showered and packed up our things in complete silence.

As we were about to head out the door, I stopped and turned around to face Luc.

"I'm so sorry about everything that happened yesterday. I—"

"I do not want to hear what you say. I know what you did, and I know that there can be no future for us. You love him, so that's good for you. Go be with him." Luc's accent and awkward wording worsened with his anger.

"But I don't love Jeff. What happened yesterday was a huge mistake. I don't want to be with him, I want to be with you," I said, searching his eyes for a hint of forgiveness and realizing even as the words exited my mouth that I sounded exactly like Jeff. Ugh.

"You didn't have sex with him as mistake. You made a choice."

"I didn't have sex with Jeff. He tried, but I stopped it."

"Why should I believe you? You wrote in your article that you are dating like a man, and that is exactly what a man would do, right? He would have sex with as many people as he could." Luc pushed past me to get out the door.

I followed him down the hallway and into the elevator

without saying a word. He was right—how was he supposed to believe me? I wouldn't have believed me either.

We rode to the airport in a thick, nauseating silence. Luc didn't so much as glance my way as we waited in the long security lines and boarded our plane. The next seven hours were agonizing—sitting next to him but knowing he was as far away from me as he could possibly be. He was clearly finished with me. He even devoured an entire chocolate bar that he had bought in the airport without offering so much as a morsel to me. Normally we would've split that bar right down the middle. That was our thing. I didn't know if Luc would ever want to share chocolate with me again.

To drown my sorrows, I guzzled two miniature bottles of wine and watched movie after movie on the plane. None of it made me forget about how terrible I had been or how disgusting I felt as a human being. And that this time, contrary to when Jeff was at fault, I was the one who had screwed up my own life. I was to blame.

After an entire day of intolerable silence, Luc and I finally made it back to our building, where he let himself into his place without saying good-bye to me. I shuffled into my room, threw my bags in the corner, and collapsed on my hard cot. I stared up at the cracked ceiling, wishing I could wipe the slate clean and start all over. Wishing I had done things differently all year so I wouldn't be lying here alone, in the aftermath of the mess I had created.

After a good half hour of self-loathing, my phone beeped. One new voice mail. I checked the caller ID and saw that Madame Rousseau had called. Probably to let me know the date of my interview. At least I hadn't screwed that up.

I dialed my voice mail and got a pen and paper ready to jot down the date and time.

"Mademoiselle Summers," her message began, "please call me immediately." *Click.*

She didn't sound happy at all. What could I have done

this time? I'd been attending all (well, most) of my classes this semester, and I hadn't had any other opportunities to screw things up. My stomach knotted into a tight ball as I dialed her number, hoping I would still have an interview. Hoping at least this one thing would work out for me.

"*Allô?*" she answered.

"*Bonjour, Madame, c'est Charlotte.*"

"Mademoiselle Summers, you have disgraced me and my profession. You should be ashamed of yourself!" Her shrill tone was reminiscent of the nuns who'd taught at my Catholic grade school. It made the hairs on the back of my neck stand up.

"My niece's friend had a copy of that filthy *Bella Magazine*, and I happened to see *your* picture next to a positively revolting article. No wonder you were always late this year. You have been running around, using men and having sex. I was wrong about you, Mademoiselle Summers. I believed you to be a young woman of integrity, of high morals. But clearly, you are quite the opposite. I have withdrawn my recommendation and have canceled your interview. If my niece's school finds out about this piece of *trash* that you have written, my reputation will be tarnished for even recommending that you teach there in the first place. An upstanding private Catholic institution has no place for such debauchery. You said you were serious about teaching at this school? Were you not?"

"Yes…I still am. I'm sorry. I can—"

"I do not want to hear your excuses. I am finished working with you, Mademoiselle Summers. You will turn in your final papers, and you will be on your own. Do not expect to find a job at a private school in Paris without my recommendation. I will not allow such a disgraceful young woman to waste any more of my time, or that of my colleagues! And I doubt my son will want to have another lesson with you once I speak with him."

"But, Madame Rousseau," I began as the dial tone rang loudly in my ear.

She'd hung up on me.

I hurled my phone across the room, and it landed right on one of my copies of *Bella Magazine*. I stood up, grabbed the magazine, tore my article out, and ripped it to shreds. Then I sank to the floor, buried my head in my hands, and cried.

TWENTY-TWO

lundi, le 4 avril

Running away from love will land you smack in the middle of nowhere.

The next morning, after a sleepless night full of tears, stomach problems, and several trips to the bathroom, I stared at my phone, trying to decide which friend to get in touch with so that I wouldn't hole up in my room and pick up a drinking habit.

Fiona had accepted my apology after our heated argument at the club back in February, but even so, we hadn't been hanging out as much since I'd started things up with Luc again. Plus, she'd been back and forth to London to visit Andrew almost every other weekend. Lexi had been completely MIA since she'd sent me that text saying that the sex with Marc was just so-so. I figured she was ensconced in her usual routine of going out and picking up a new man every night, so I stopped trying to get in touch when she hadn't responded to any of my messages. Marc had been my only consistent friend (and student) for the past two months, but I knew if Madame Rousseau had anything to say about it, Marc would be finished with me too. And right now, the last thing I could handle was to lose one of the nicest friends I'd made here.

Before I could chicken out, I sent him a text message to see if he wanted to meet up at the park for a language exchange. Within seconds, he wrote back and said he'd meet me there in thirty minutes.

As I showered and tried to make myself slightly presentable, that dreadful, sickening feeling took hold of my stomach again. I was absolutely desperate to take back what I had done. What on earth had possessed me to actually go so far as to get in bed with Jeff while Luc was just downstairs? What if he had walked in on us? How could I have been so stupid to fall for Jeff's antics after everything he had done? And to cause so much pain to Luc only to realize that I didn't love Jeff anymore.

Everything Katie had said was right. I'd been so obsessed with my rules, my blog, my mission of dating like a man, that I hadn't stopped to think about how my words were affecting those around me. I'd inspired my mom to leave my dad and Hannah to cheat on her fiancé. I'd made Katie feel bad about falling in love when I should've been her biggest cheerleader. I'd lost my teaching recommendation, and worst of all, I'd lost Luc.

I really was low. Lower than low. One of the lowest beings on the planet. And I was sure that was exactly how Luc saw me now. After reading my article, he was probably wondering how many other men I had slept with this year. He was surely ready to rid his life of the slut he now knew I was. But I, on the other hand, was ready to tell him how sorry I was, how I wished I could take it all back, and that I knew in my heart that he was the one for me. I had been staring love in the face all year, but didn't want to admit it. And now it was crystal clear.

Luc *had* loved me. And I loved him. I really did…I loved him.

I collapsed against the wall of the tiny shower in desperation. I had just ruined any chance of really being with the man I loved. The man who I honestly believed was different from the others. Katie was right—Luc wasn't Jeff. He wasn't capable of that kind of deception. I, on the other hand, apparently was.

After the desperation came the rage. I wanted to rip Jeff's eyes out of his head or cut off his balls, or anything else to severely harm him so he would feel the full effect of how badly he'd screwed with my life. I felt just as much rage toward myself, though, for ever falling for Jeff in the first place and for falling for him again, even though it was only for a brief five minutes in that damn hotel room. Just thinking about kissing him again made me want to vomit. I scrubbed my body until my skin was raw in hopes of washing away the filth and the guilt that had overcome me.

My hair was still wet and my eyes were bloodshot and raw from fatigue when I left to meet Marc at the entrance to the park. He leaned in to give me two *bisous*, but a look of concern quickly swept over his face.

"Thanks for meeting me here," I said. "I'm sure your mom has been in touch with you."

Marc lowered his gaze to the ground as we strolled down the dusty dirt path into the park. A cool, light breeze rustled through the blossoming tulips and the budding tree branches, making me want to lie down in the grass and listen to that sound all day long if it could make me forget about my life for even a few minutes.

"Yes, she told me about the article. And about how she revoked her recommendation. I'm sorry she—"

"Please don't apologize, Marc. I'm not here to make you feel bad about something that was my fault. I shouldn't have written that article and still expected to earn your mother's recommendation. And I just wanted to apologize to you for any drama I may have created between you and your mom. I don't expect you to want to have lessons with me anymore… but I don't want to lose you as a friend."

Marc didn't say anything. Instead he leaned forward and hugged me.

It felt so nice to have a hug after everything that had happened the past few days…or the past year, for that matter.

"Charlotte, what you need to understand is that I don't always agree with the way my mother sees the world. In her eyes, everything is black or white. Good or bad. There is no in-between. That is not the way I see things, though. I know that you have had a difficult year, getting over your ex, trying to move on. Ever since Delphine left me, I have done a lot of stupid things too."

"You? The overachiever medical student? What kinds of stupid things?" Marc and I had never discussed what had happened with Lexi that night in February, but I couldn't say I wasn't just a tiny bit curious to hear his side of the story. And I was tired of thinking about all of the ways I had royally screwed up my life. Time to focus on someone else for a change.

"Yes," Marc responded. "Like the last time we all went out. You know I was interested in Fiona, and instead I spent the evening with Lexi. And no offense, I know she is your friend, but that woman is *folle*."

I laughed. "Spending the night with a crazy woman at least made for a good time, right?"

Marc shook his head. "No, it was not fun at all. She got really drunk, and I was afraid to let her go home alone, so I took her back to my place and let her sleep in my bed while I slept on the floor. Then I woke up in the middle of the night and heard her crying in the bathroom. I tried to get her to tell me what was wrong, but she wouldn't talk to me. It was really strange."

"So the two of you didn't...?"

"No, nothing happened between us. Well, besides what you saw on the dance floor."

"Really? *Nothing?*" Lexi had clearly told me they'd slept together. So one of them had to be lying.

Marc shook his head as we strolled farther into the park. "*Je te jure.* How do you say this in English?"

"I swear."

"I swear, nothing happened. I would never do something with a girl who is that drunk. I do have a little bit of my mother's morals in me, you know. Why do you ask? You thought we...?"

"I made a wrong assumption, that's all. I'm sorry." Marc seemed sincere, so it was his word against Lexi's. And if she hadn't really slept with him, what was the point of lying to me?

Underneath Lexi's tough façade, she must've really been hurting. Over what, I wasn't sure. But girls didn't lie to their friends about who they were having sex with and lock themselves up crying in the bathroom for no reason. I didn't care that she had lied to me. I just hoped she would be okay.

I tucked my long hair behind my ears and decided to keep being nosy. "So, have you talked to Fiona recently?"

"Yes, I called her, but she seemed angry, and then she told me she was back together with her boyfriend from London." Marc frowned. "Is that true?"

"Yes, she's back with Andrew. But if it makes you feel any better, she was really jealous when you were dancing with Lexi that night." I knew I was violating girlfriend rules by revealing Fiona's feelings to Marc, especially since she was back with Andrew now, but I couldn't help it. I liked Marc, and he and Fiona would make such a cute couple. If only I could get her to dump Andrew.

"Well, it doesn't matter now if she has a boyfriend."

"True, but you never know what might happen down the road."

"Either way, my life is so busy right now. I really do not have time for a girlfriend. I have too much work to do and too much English to learn. Do you think I've gotten better?"

"So much better. You speak much more naturally now. You sound like a native."

"Really? You wouldn't know I'm French?"

"Barely. You still have a hint of a French accent, but you've come a long way."

"Thank you, Charlotte. It is all thanks to you." He wrapped his arm around my shoulders and pulled me close as we finished our walk around the park.

And for the first time all day, I smiled. At least I hadn't lost *all* of my friends.

～

On the way back to my dorm, I dialed Lexi's number. I knew I had bigger, more important fish to fry, like apologizing to Katie and trying to make Luc understand how sorry I really was, but what Marc had told me about Lexi had left an ominous feeling in the pit of my stomach. I wanted to make sure she was okay.

"Charlotte?" A deep male voice answered, making me wonder if I'd dialed the wrong number.

"Yes, who is this?" I asked.

"This is Brad, Lexi's brother. I'm glad you called."

"What's going on? Is Lexi okay?"

A heavy pause traveled through the line.

"Brad?"

"Alexis is in the hospital, Charlotte. Last night, she overdosed on antidepressants."

I stopped walking, my breath catching in my throat. "She overdosed? Was it an accident?"

I already knew the answer, though.

"No. She knew what she was doing."

I gripped the banister by my side to steady myself. This couldn't be happening. "Is she going to be okay?"

"They stabilized her last night, but she hasn't woken up yet. Can you come?"

"Of course. Which hospital are you at?"

"It's the hospital Hôtel-Dieu, right across from Notre Dame."

"I'll be there in ten minutes."

I hailed a cab on Boulevard Jourdan, my heart pounding inside my chest.

"*Hôpital Hôtel-Dieu. Vite, s'il vous plaît.*" *Fast,* I told the cab driver.

The city I'd grown to love whizzed by the window, but I only noticed it in flashes, my brain trying to comprehend the gravity of what had happened. The trees lining Parc Montsouris. The tall green fence surrounding Jardin du Luxembourg to my left. The looming Panthéon building to my right. The crowded cafés on Boulevard Saint-Michel. The Seine and its dark waters lapping up toward the gothic Notre Dame Cathedral.

Lexi had tried to kill herself.

Lexi didn't care if she saw Paris ever again.

How? How could this have happened?

Suddenly my mistakes, my rules, my blog, my grudges all seemed so trivial. So inconsequential.

As the cab pulled up to the hospital, I thrust a wad of euros into the front seat and bolted toward the main entrance. I weaved through the hallways, the scents of illness and plastic water pitchers and stale food making me nauseous.

Please let Lexi be okay. Please.

When I reached her room, I found Brad sitting by Lexi's bedside, holding her hand.

I knocked lightly on the door.

"Hey," Brad said, rising to his feet. His dark hair was a mess, his eyes bloodshot and exhausted. This wasn't the same Brad I'd met at the hotel Christmas Eve night.

I didn't say anything. I just hugged him.

"Thank you for coming."

I nodded as I peered around his broad shoulders. Lexi lay underneath a pale-blue sheet in a metal hospital bed, her cheeks chalky white, gray circles lining her sunken eyes. "Is she going to be okay?"

"Yes, she's stable, anyway. She took a lot of pills. The doctor said it was a really rough night. I just arrived from Rome this morning."

I walked up to her bed and laid my hand on hers. Her skin was so cold it made me shudder. Gone were her beautiful, smoky eyes, her olive complexion, her gorgeous, silky black hair. Instead, she looked sick and fragile, like a withered-up rose, devoid of life.

Lexi was completely broken. I squeezed her hand. I was so glad she was still here.

"I'm so sorry, Brad. I can't believe this is happening."

Brad joined me at Lexi's bedside, where we both took a seat. "This has happened before, you know. A couple times."

I opened my mouth, but I had no words.

"I'm the only one who knows about it, though," he continued. "She's never told anyone else. I know she'd be mortified if she knew you were here, but I couldn't do it alone this time."

I placed my hand on his arm. "I'm glad you asked me to come. You shouldn't be alone right now. What about your parents? Do they know?"

Brad shook his head, a look of frustration passing through his coal-black eyes. "Lexi didn't tell you?"

"Tell me what?"

"When I was fifteen and Lexi was only thirteen, our parents died in a car accident."

"Oh, my gosh, but Lexi said…"

"She doesn't like to tell people the truth. She doesn't like to open up or let people in. She's too afraid she'll lose them." Brad blinked his watery eyes as he gazed down at his sister. "It's no way to live."

As I glanced back at my friend, the tubes sticking out of her arms, the beeping machines at her bedside, suddenly everything that had happened in my life this past year came into focus. I realized that life is a total mess. And in trying to avoid love, I thought I was avoiding that mess. But the events of the wedding weekend compounded by Lexi's scary situation were both proof that avoiding love only made the mess that is life that much more unbearable. The only way we were going to get through this crazy journey was if we all stuck together. And the only way any of it would *matter* was if we opened ourselves up to love.

Even if it meant getting our hearts broken from time to time.

Because the alternative, as Brad had said, was no way to live. And Lexi, lying here in the aftermath of her attempt to end her own life, was more proof of that fact than I'd ever needed.

Brad left the hospital room to eat, so I stayed with Lexi, stroking her hair and telling her it was all going to be okay. I didn't know if she could hear me, but I wanted her to feel loved. I wanted her to know that she mattered.

A few minutes later, I noticed her eyes blinking.

"Water," she whispered as she cleared her throat.

I reached for the pitcher and handed it to her. She sucked down three huge gulps before coming up for air and meeting my gaze. "Charlotte, how did you…?"

Squeezing her hand, I smiled softly at her. "I spoke with Brad. I hope you don't mind that I'm here."

She shook her head, tears instantly spilling over her cheeks. "I'm so sorry. This is so embarrassing."

I leaned forward and hugged her tightly. "You have nothing to be embarrassed about. I'm your friend, and I'm here for you. This is what friends do for each other." I knew I hadn't always been the greatest friend to Katie, Hannah, *or* Fiona this past year, but I figured I could change that streak now.

"Thank you." She sniffled as she plopped her head back down on her pillow. "God, I can't believe I'm here again. I'm such a mess."

"You're going to get through this, Lexi. You are."

She wiped her eyes and gazed up at me, the wall she'd built around herself completely torn down. "I've lied to you a lot this year, Charlotte. I'm not a good person."

"It's okay," I said. "Brad told me about your parents. I'm so sorry."

"It wasn't only that, though. I never slept with Marc that night. I don't know why I told you I did. I just…" She paused to gaze out the window, tears still streaming down her cheeks. "I push people away. And I know it's stupid, but I don't know how else to be. Like Christmas Eve night in the hotel room with Dylan. I know you heard me crying the next morning."

"What happened that night, Lexi? I was worried about you."

"Dylan and I, we have a history. We've dated off and on for years, but I always fuck it up. It's what I do. I fuck things up. And that night, he told me he loved me. That he's loved me forever. And what did I do? I told him I didn't love him. Then I asked him to leave." Lexi's lip quivered as she continued. "I'm just so scared, you know. What if he leaves me one day for someone else? What if I'm not enough? Or what if something happens to him? I don't think I could handle it, Charlotte. I *know* I couldn't."

I handed Lexi a tissue, seeing myself in her eyes. We had a lot more in common than I'd originally thought. "I understand, Lexi. I really do. If it makes you feel any better, I realized I'm in love with Luc, but I screwed it all up this past weekend too."

"I knew you were falling for him," she said, wiping underneath her eyes. "That's why I wasn't in touch these past few months. With you and Fiona both in relationships, I couldn't handle it. But then, where did that get me? Here. In a fucking hospital. Ugh. Sorry for being so pathetic. It's so sweet of you to be here for me."

"If you're pathetic, then I am too," I told her with a smile.

"All right, so tell me what happened at the wedding? How did you screw things up with Luc? And did you trip that bitch who stole your fiancé?"

One day after an overdose, and sassy Lexi was still in there. I laughed as I told her the whole story. She seemed to cheer up as she learned that she wasn't the only one who consistently pushed people away.

After I finished talking, Lexi's eyelids began to droop and Brad returned to the room. I gave her one more hug. "You're going to get through this, and I'm here for you the whole way. You can call me anytime you need to talk, okay?"

Her lips formed a weak smile. "Thanks for letting me know that you're *almost* as big of a screwup as me. I think I still win the prize, though. But you're the best, really."

Brad stepped into the hallway with me to exchange cell phone numbers. "As soon as Lexi is a bit stronger, I'm going to take her back to New York for a little while. We have some family there, and her doctor is there too. This is going to be a long road, but hopefully she'll get better."

"Will you keep me posted?" I asked.

"Of course. Thank you so much for being here."

I hugged him once more. "Of course."

Leaving the hospital, I breathed in the warm spring air and decided to walk home. Seeing what had happened to Lexi, and even more so, seeing myself in her eyes, had really put things in perspective. It showed me that no one's life is perfect. That no matter how thick the walls are that we build around ourselves, if we don't let people in from time to time, those walls will crumble, and we will be left alone.

Katie and Fiona's words came rushing back to me as I crossed the Seine and took in the life that buzzed through Paris. I couldn't hide any longer. I couldn't keep looking at relationships as black or white.

I needed to value the people who had been there for me all along. I needed to make amends with everyone I'd hurt. I needed to get my priorities on track.

And most of all, Lexi's situation had shown me that there is no time to waste.

∽

Back in my room, with my computer mouse hovering over a round-trip ticket from DC to Paris, I dialed Katie's number.

"Hello?"

"Katie, it's Charlotte."

"Hey," she said, her usual cheery tone replaced with one of disdain.

"I know I'm probably the last person you want to talk to right now, but I hope you'll at least hear me out."

She didn't respond, so I kept going.

"I want to apologize for not being there for you this year like I should've. You've always been there for me, even when I didn't deserve it, and I'm sorry I wasn't that kind of friend for you. I should've thought about how my actions and words were making you feel. I never meant to make you feel like your relationship with Joe wasn't important, or that I wasn't happy for you. And after what I did at the wedding… well, I completely understand if you need a break from me. But, instead of just telling you how sorry I am and telling you that I'll be a better friend from here on out, I want to show you."

"What are you talking about, Charlotte?"

"I want us to spend some time together, just the girls, like the old days. And I know you have your spring break coming up, so if you don't already have plans, I'd like to fly you over to France, and then me, you, and my friend Fiona are going to take the train down to Lyon. I have the hotel and the train tickets reserved already. All you have to do is say yes, and I'll have your plane ticket too."

"Charlotte, are you serious? How can you even afford this? This is crazy."

"Don't worry about money. It's all taken care of." I planned on using the money I'd made from my *Bella Magazine* article to pay for Katie's plane ticket. I figured it was the least I could do.

"You don't have to do this."

"I know I don't, Katie. But I want to. I want to spend some time with you and show you that I'm still me. And that I'm sorry for being a crap friend. So please just say yes."

She paused, her breath heavy on the other line. "When do I leave?"

∼

Dear Luc,

I know you're not ready to talk to me yet, and maybe you never will be after the way I've treated you. I just want you to know, though, that I'm so very sorry for the way I acted this past weekend, and for writing the article. I have no excuse for my actions, and all I can do is hope that someday you will at least want to be my friend.

Even though I may not have always shown or expressed my feelings for you, I want you to know that spending time with you this year has been amazing. I've completely fallen in love with you. You are the most caring man I've ever known, and I only regret not giving you the chance to tell me earlier about your daughter. I know you will win her back.

I'll be in Lyon for the next two weeks with Katie and Fiona. I'll have my phone with me, though, so please call me if you'd like to talk. If not, I understand, but know that I'll be here whenever, if ever, you want to be with me.

Love,
Charlotte

∼

After slipping the letter under Luc's door, I lay in my bed, waiting for Katie's arrival the next day and trying to remain hopeful. People make mistakes and ask for forgiveness all the time. Maybe this would blow over. Maybe leaving for Lyon and giving Luc some space was the best thing I could do. As I began to drift off, I desperately hoped that Luc would be waiting for me with open arms when I came back to Paris. But I couldn't control the outcome. All I could do was hope.

TWENTY-THREE

mardi, le 5 avril

Don't wait for love to come find you. Buy the train ticket, make the trip, and go get him! What have you got to lose?

The next afternoon, Katie, Fiona, and I boarded the train to Lyon. After Katie and I broke a sweat loading our gargantuan suitcases into the baggage compartment and Fiona effortlessly plucked up her mini roll-on bag and tossed it overhead, we took our seats and let out a collective sigh.

Katie nudged me as she nodded to a skinny weasel of a man making his way down the aisle. "I see the French men are still sporting those excruciatingly tight jeans. What's with that?" Katie had visited me in Lyon when I'd studied abroad in college, so she'd already witnessed France's ball-hugging-jeans phenomenon firsthand.

Fiona laughed. "I thought the same thing the first time I came to France. That *can't* be comfortable."

"I didn't notice Luc wearing pants like that last weekend.

Did you make him throw out all of his pants or something?" Katie asked.

Masking the pang of sadness that ripped through me at the mention of Luc's name, I laughed. "No, Luc was an exception to the rule...in more ways than one."

Katie patted my arm. "Sorry, I didn't mean to bring him up. But while we're on the topic, has anything changed? Have you heard from him at all?"

I shook my head. "No, I left him a letter, hoping he might reconsider things. But I don't expect him to. Not after what happened...but enough about that. This weekend is about spending time with my girls. Not about lamenting over a guy. I think I've done enough of that this year." After having seen Lexi in the hospital earlier this week, I was determined to show Katie and Fiona a good time in Lyon.

As the gorgeous French countryside zoomed past our window, the three of us got cozy in our seats and split a box of scrumptious Petit Écolier cookies. "So, tell me how things are going with your men," I asked Katie and Fiona before biting into my milk-chocolate-covered biscuit. "With all of my self-inflicted drama, I haven't made enough time to get the scoop on your love lives. And I'm sorry for that. So it's time to dish up."

Katie smiled. "Well, the latest on my end is that Joe invited me to come on his annual family vacation in Lake Tahoe this summer."

"Whoa. Meeting the fam. That's serious," I said. "Are you excited?"

Katie hesitated. "Yes and no. First of all, it's not just his mom, dad, and three sisters. It's his *entire* family. I'm talking like thirty people, kids included. So that's a little overwhelming in and of itself. But the thing that really worries me is that I've met his older sister, Sophia, and she's...how can I put this nicely? Well, screw being nice. She's a raging bitch. She's really protective of Joe, like he's still a little boy or something, and she was grilling me all night. I mean, he's a grown man and a doctor, for God's sake. I think he can handle himself."

"Did he ask his sister to tone it down a bit?" Fiona asked.

"No, that was the other problem. Joe didn't seem to think she did anything wrong. He told me that's just the way their relationship is and I'll have to learn to accept it."

"That's tough," I said, holding the box of cookies out for Katie. "But maybe she'll chill out once she gets to know you. And if you and Joe keep getting serious, he's going to have to listen to your concerns on this. It's not fair for you to be treated that way when you haven't done anything wrong." I thought about how Luc had asked me to spend Christmas with his family, and how upset he'd been when I turned him down. If I had ignored my doubts and said yes, maybe things would be different now. I shook the thoughts away. There was no point in playing the what-if game. After all, I couldn't change the past...or any of the million mistakes I'd made. I could only move forward.

"What about you, Fiona?" Katie asked. "Charlotte tells me you're pretty serious with your boyfriend. Andrew, is it?"

Fiona nodded. "Things are going...*okay*." Fiona's eyes darted out the window.

"What's up? Is everything all right with you two?" I asked.

"Everything's fine, really. He's being a little weird, that's all."

"How so?" Katie said.

Fiona fidgeted with her hands in her lap. "Okay. This is really embarrassing, but I have to tell someone." She leaned forward and peered around to make sure our train neighbors weren't listening.

"What is it?" I asked.

A rose-colored flush crept up Fiona's cheeks. "Ever since

we got back together, Andrew has been wanting to do...*interesting* things in the bedroom."

I stifled a giggle. "Like what?"

Fiona buried her face in her hands. "I can't even believe I'm going to say this out loud. Please don't judge me. And if you ever meet Andrew, don't *ever* tell him I told you this. Promise?"

"Promise," Katie and I said simultaneously as we leaned forward in our seats.

"All right. He is completely obsessed with the *arse*."

Katie furrowed her eyebrows while I suppressed another laugh. "The *arse*? You mean, the *ass*? As in asshole?" Katie asked.

"Shhh!" Fiona's face turned lobster red as the flush spread up to the tips of her ears.

"So he wants to have anal?" I whispered.

"Yes, but it's more than that," Fiona whispered back. "He wants *me* to do things to *his* arse too."

"Oh, God. Like what? Finger it?" Katie asked, her eyes widened in terror.

Fiona bit her lip. "Unfortunately for me, he quite likes that. I've only done it once. And I put gloves on, of course. Oh, God. This is disgusting, isn't it? Just horrifying."

I couldn't hold it in any longer. Listening to Fiona's prim and proper British accent talking about sticking fingers in her boyfriend's arse was just too much. I burst out laughing.

Fiona smacked me on the arm. "It's not funny. This is a serious problem!"

But Katie couldn't keep it together either. She began giggling, and soon Fiona joined in until we all had tears streaming down our cheeks.

When the man in the ball-hugging black jeans shot us the evil eye from across the aisle, we laughed even harder.

"Seriously, though. I cannot and I will not do this for the

rest of my life. Something has to change," Fiona said, gaining control.

"You dated Andrew for years before this, though. Why the sudden arse obsession?" I asked, taking on my own British accent.

Fiona frowned. "The only reason I can come up with is that sodding cow he dated for the past year. *She* must've been up for it. I've asked him if she was the one who put these filthy fantasies in his head, but he denies it. I know he's lying, though. He was never this crude before."

Katie shook her head. "I don't know what to tell you, lady. That's just not acceptable. You're going to have to put your foot down. Or stop putting your fingers up."

The three of us broke into another fit of laughter as we continued our girl talk for the entire train ride down to Lyon. After everything that had happened the past week, it felt wonderful to spend time with my friends, to share in their lives once again, and especially to know that Katie wasn't angry at me anymore.

But even with all of the laughter and the silly stories we shared, I couldn't get Luc out of my head. I peeked at my cell phone at least ten times during our two-hour train ride, hoping he would call once he read my letter.

But, there were no missed calls. No texts. No word from the man I loved.

~

As we stepped into the Perrache train station in Lyon, a comforting twinge of familiarity masked my broken heart. It had been years since I'd been back, but nothing had changed. I took a deep breath and realized I was in a place that was mine. A place that had nothing to do with Jeff or Luc. A place that I had loved long before I knew either of them. And even though I so wanted to continue wallowing in sorrow and self-pity (on the inside anyway), a peculiar feeling crept up inside me—excitement.

"The metro here is so much cleaner than in Paris. I like this city already," Fiona said.

"This is only the beginning," I told her. "You'll see. Lyon is a gorgeous city." I was suddenly extremely grateful that I'd booked this trip with my girlfriends. If I had stayed alone in Paris, I would've been dangerously close to starting up an alcohol addiction while drowning in a pool of my own wretched despair.

Katie's eyes lit up. "We had so much fun when I visited you in college. Remember that crazy bar, Ayer's Rock? We *have* to take Fiona there."

"Oh, my gosh. That place was insane. I don't know if they'd let me back in after all the trouble I got myself into there."

"What's Ayer's Rock?" Fiona asked.

"It's this Australian bar that Charlotte and her friends went to *all* the time—like almost every night of the week." Katie shot me a sly grin. "A lot of table dancing and man grinding went down in that joint."

"Oh, God, table dancing. So much table dancing." I shook my head. "I don't know if I'm up for all of that this time around."

"We at least have to go once, for old times' sake," Katie said as she nudged my side. "I barely get to go out with girlfriends anymore since Joe and I started dating, and you said this trip was all about us, so you have no choice."

"All right, whatever you say. But let it be known that I am *not* going there to pick up random guys. I'm done playing that game. I'm twenty-five years old, and it hasn't gotten me anywhere."

"About to be twenty-six," Katie said in a sing-songy voice.

I sat up in my metro seat and thought for a minute. Amid all the drama, I had completely forgotten that my twenty-sixth birthday was coming up the following week. "I guess I forgot."

"Well, we're going to make this a big one, lady." Katie said as she winked at me.

Once we arrived at our metro stop, Bellecour, Katie and I dragged our oversize suitcases up the stairs while Fiona effortlessly carried her minisuitcase with one hand. Katie and I always overpacked.

Huffing and puffing up the stairs, Katie yelled up at Fiona, who was already waiting for us at the top. "How did you pack so light? We're here for two weeks!"

"I only brought the essentials, really." She shrugged and smiled.

I looked over at Katie as we neared the top of the never-ending staircase. "Fiona's way more organized than we'll ever be. Must be a British thing."

As we emerged from the metro, the bright sun shone down on the red, sandy courtyard, which, by midday, was bustling with people. I gazed up into the deep-blue sky to find that the luminous white basilica, Fourvière, stood majestically up on the hill just as it always had. The tension I'd been holding in my shoulders relaxed, and the knots that had taken up residence in my stomach dissipated as I breathed in the warm breeze and felt like I was home.

I had booked us an adorable hotel room right off the courtyard, on rue Victor Hugo. The room was as French as it could be, with a charming balcony overlooking all of the trendy shops and open-air markets that lined the cobblestone street below. After we unpacked and hung up some of our clothes in the minuscule closet, we headed out for our first afternoon of city exploration.

During our first week in Lyon, I successfully kept the three of us occupied every moment of the day so that I didn't have time to think about Luc, Jeff, my lack of future employment, or anything in between. Instead, I focused on my friends. We ate out, shopped, strolled along the rivers, rode bicycles through the city, and visited pubs and cafés in the evenings.

The only times I felt myself sinking back into self-pity mode were late at night after the two of them had fallen asleep and in the mornings before they woke up. I lay in bed tossing and turning and replaying the wedding events over and over again in my mind. Incessantly asking myself the same tiresome questions as if maybe all of the questioning would somehow change the outcome.

Why couldn't I have resisted Jeff? Why did I let him kiss me in the elevator? Did I really think I still loved him? Or was I just acting out in revenge against Brooke? I mean, no matter how nice of a person I thought I was, I certainly didn't mind hurting her in that whole process, seeing as how badly she and Jeff had hurt me. Despite my ill feelings toward Jeff and Brooke, though, my thoughts kept coming back to Luc.

Luc was the one person I didn't want to hurt. What had he ever done to me? Only wonderful things like take me to the ballet and feed me chocolate in bed after giving me multiple orgasms. Jeff didn't even hold a candle to Luc. What was I thinking? I mean, seriously, *what in the hell was I thinking*?

As these self-destructive thoughts auto-played through my mind every night, I was desperate for Luc's touch. Desperate to run my hands through his hair again. Desperate to go back and change the way it had all played out. And unbearably desperate for him to call me and accept my apology (and it wouldn't hurt if he'd also say that he was madly in love with me and that he wanted to spend the rest of his life with me—but I guess I couldn't expect all of that just yet).

So every night, I slept with my phone by my side. It was my only possible attachment to Luc. In the miraculous event that he decided he needed to get in touch with me after reading my letter, God forbid I wasn't there to pick up the phone the second he called. I hid my obsessive phone checking from Katie and Fiona because even though they said they understood what I was going through, they didn't. Neither of them had ever ruined their love lives like I had just done. Sure, they had both been burned before, but they didn't know what it felt like to be the one who had done the burning. And to regret it so badly that you would do anything—absolutely anything—to fix it.

I also thought a lot about Lexi. Brad sent me regular text updates to keep me in the know. He'd taken her back to New York City, where they were staying with their aunt and uncle for a little while. Lexi was seeing a good doctor, and as Brad had said, she was starting to come back to life. What I'd seen that night at the hospital had scared me, though. I wanted to talk with Fiona and Katie about it, but Lexi had e-mailed me and asked that I keep her situation private. So I did my best to keep my fears about Lexi and losing Luc to myself, and instead arranged a smile on my face and stayed happy for my friends…even if, on the inside, I wasn't always feeling it.

One early morning, as we kicked off our second week in Lyon, Katie and Fiona sat on opposite sides of the tiny hotel room, ears glued to their cell phones, making their daily lovebird calls to their significant others.

"I miss you so much, Joe," Katie said.

"I know, love. Only two more weeks and I'll be in London," Fiona said.

I was happy for them. I really was. But as I stared at my silent phone, I realized I was only human. And if I had to listen to any more dying-couple talk before I'd even had a chance to drink a cup of espresso, I would vomit. So, instead of listening to another "I love you" being spoken over every phone in the hotel room except mine, I decided to head to my old favorite park, Le Parc de la Tête d'Or, for a morning jog.

Le Parc de la Tête d'Or is in the sixth arrondissement of Lyon, an upscale neighborhood lined with fancy apartment buildings, clean streets, and corner *boulangeries*. I'd had the privilege of living in this quiet, peaceful area of Lyon with my host family, and I'd gone running in the park regularly by myself while studying abroad.

It was my first time back in more than five years, and as I walked underneath the massive green-and-gold-plated gate that protected the park, a sense of relief swept over me. I'd loved this place so much, and it felt so comforting to be back.

Two curly-haired little French girls romped with a floppy brown puppy as their mother lounged in the grassy field facing the lake, smiling to herself as the girls' laughter filled up the open space. Three lean male runners whizzed past me, their pale, thin legs stretching out in full strides as their tiny shorts just barely covered their butts.

I grinned as I broke into a jog behind them, and soon my jog morphed into a full-out sprint. All of the toxic emotions I'd been bottling up over the current state of my life seeped out of my pores as my feet pounded into the pavement.

As I rounded the first corner, something Katie had said to me the night of the wedding shot through my head.

What was it about Jeff that made you go so nuts?

Katie had a point. What was it about Jeff, about my attachment to him, that had made me even consider being with him again? After the online dating debacle, I should've had nothing left but disdain for that man.

But as a slight breeze whistled through the trees lining the running path, I finally had time to think. To recognize, for the first time all year, what was at the heart of all of this madness.

Clichéd though it was, I had dad issues.

Major dad issues.

Ever since I'd discovered my dad cheating on my mom at the age of thirteen, I'd gone stark-raving boy crazy. All through high school and college, I hadn't spent so much as a day without a boyfriend. And if there was even a small gap in between long-term relationships, I'd filled it with dates, hookups, one-night stands, you name it.

I couldn't be alone. And as I thought about all of those years after my dad's indiscretion, after the love had evaporated from our home, I realized that all I'd ever wanted was to have my family back.

And my never-ending quest for a man was just that—a search for family. For the kind of unconditional love my family had shared *before* my dad had cheated. I knew now that I saw his cheating as not only a betrayal of my mother, but also a betrayal of me.

If he had really loved me enough, wouldn't he have had the foresight to see what he was doing to me? That he was sweeping the stability right out from under his young daughter, taking away the comfort I'd grown to depend on as a child, and leaving me searching, frantically for someone who would bring that love back into my life?

My dad had broken up our family, and in Jeff, I'd seen an opportunity to get it back.

With this monumental realization, my pace slowed, my heart still pounding inside my chest. Jeff was seven years older than I, a grown man with a solid career. He was charismatic, unbelievably handsome, and an amazing lover. I'd fallen for him hard and fast, but now, looking back, I realized that I'd also fallen for the *idea* of him. Jeff's extreme physical passion for me in the early days of our relationship had led me to believe that he would *never* tire of me. That he would never stray as my dad had done. And when I thought back to the night he'd proposed at the Georgetown waterfront, I remembered clearly the feeling that had coursed through me at the sight of him down on one knee.

The love I felt for him was real, yes. But it wasn't only love I felt that night.

It was *relief*.

Relief that someone loved me enough to stay with me. To commit to me for a lifetime.

Because even though my parents had stayed together after

my dad's infidelity, I knew that, in his heart, my dad was somewhere else, and that in choosing another woman over my mom, he'd left our little family. Then, when every single boyfriend I'd dated continued on that same cheating streak, the message my dad had sent repeated relentlessly in my head.

You're not good enough. Every man you love will leave you for someone else.

With Jeff's proposal, I'd wholeheartedly believed that the streak was over. That I'd finally found the man who would love me forever. Who would make me feel whole again. Whom I could create a life, a home, a family with.

And when Jeff had betrayed that trust, I snapped. Hence, the man-hating blog. My unwillingness to commit to Luc or to let him in. My inability to support my friends in their happy relationships. And my choice to take Jeff into my hotel room that night.

Because that night, he'd chosen *me* over Brooke. And somewhere in the back of my messed-up head, his desire for me was the validation I needed to believe that I was worthy of a man's love.

About two-thirds of the way around the wide path that encircled the park, I slowed to a stop. I plopped down in the grass and lay on my back as I stared up at the fluffy white clouds floating overhead.

And as I listened to my heavy breath, in and out, my chest rising and falling, I knew what I had to do.

I had to let it all go.

My dad's betrayal. All of the broken hearts I'd suffered since.

Jeff's online dating profile and my streak of bad decisions this past year.

I couldn't change any of it. But I could let it go.

So, with each breath, I released a little more, and still more, until finally, the knot that had settled itself in my chest at the young age of thirteen released. My heart relaxed. I could breathe. I could finally breathe again.

I *was* worthy of a good man's love. I had won Luc's.

But even more important, I realized that I didn't need that love to validate me any longer.

I knew Luc might never come back to me. He might never even want to talk to me again. But I would be okay on my own. And if anything, he'd shown me that good men *do* exist. They're not all evil. They're not all cheaters.

I peeled myself up off the ground and thought about my blog and my article in *Bella Magazine*. Despite my man-hater attitude, and despite the fact that I'd encouraged Hannah to stray, inspired my mom to leave my dad, and alienated Katie, I still believed that I'd reached out to a lot of suffering women, and given them something to laugh at, and maybe even a bit of empowerment.

But I'd learned a lot this past year. And I needed to modify my message. I thought about how Lexi had let her past dictate her future, and to a lesser extreme, I had too.

And that was going to stop.

~

With a flutter of new, exciting ideas swirling through my head, I left the park and walked briskly down the quaint little *rue* where my host family had lived, wondering if they were still there. I had become really close to my host mom, a sweet yet strong-willed little schoolteacher who had done a hell of a job of raising four kids all on her own, keeping up a beautiful five-bedroom antique French apartment, all the while having a delicious homemade dinner on the table every night. She was a supermom if there ever was one. Her two youngest children, Aurélie and Mathieu, lived in the house with me while I was there. Aurélie was a few years older than I, and Mathieu a year younger. They'd become like a second family to me, which was one of the main reasons why I'd been so happy when I'd lived here, why I'd always looked back on my time in Lyon with such fondness. But, unfortunately, as time had passed and life had gotten in the way, we'd lost touch.

I reached the old stone building where their gorgeous apartment sat up on the third floor, and in my new resolve to take charge of my life, I decided to ring the bell.

After a minute or two, there was no answer. But just as I turned around to leave, a man's voice called my name.

"Charlotte? C'est toi?"

I blinked to make sure I was seeing him correctly. It was Mathieu. But a taller, buffer, more grown-up version of Mathieu. I smiled at him.

He rushed toward me, placed his hands on my shoulders and leaned in to kiss me on the cheeks. "I cannot believe it is you. What are you doing here in Lyon?"

"I'm studying in Paris this year, and I just came down with my friends for a visit. I'm sorry I haven't been in touch. I wasn't sure if you were still here."

"Yes, I am still living here, in the same home, and Aurélie lives just down the street. *Maman* has moved to Nice to take care of her parents, but she comes up frequently to visit."

"Wait a second, your English is perfect! What happened?" Mathieu hadn't been able to say much more than "yes," "no," and "hello" when I had lived with them.

"After you left, I studied in England for a time, so now I can speak English." He smiled his warm, familiar smile, making me feel better than I had in weeks.

"You must come for dinner tomorrow. I will call *Maman* to see if she can take the train up. She would love to see you."

"That would be wonderful."

"You can bring your friends too if you'd like."

"Thanks, Mathieu. I can't believe it's you. It's been five years, you know."

He placed his hand on my shoulder once more. "You were always our favorite exchange student. I am so glad you have walked into our lives again."

Wow, Mathieu had really grown up. What a sweetheart.

"Me too," I responded warmly.

"I hate to run, but I am just going home for lunch, and then I have to get back to work. So, does seven o'clock work for dinner tomorrow?"

"That's perfect."

Mathieu leaned down and kissed my cheeks.

"*À demain*," I called out as he headed toward his apartment.

"See you tomorrow," he replied with a wink.

I was on cloud nine after my fortunate run-in with Mathieu. What a man he'd grown up to be. I couldn't wait for dinner the next day.

I bounced south along the sparkly Rhone River, admiring the colorful architecture that lined the riverbanks. The buildings were painted in warm hues of yellow, orange, and light pink, their red rooftops reaching toward the feathery clouds overhead. Even the bridges boasted all different shades of blue, red, green, and bright white, making the gray buildings and bridges scattered throughout Paris seem dull in comparison. I crossed over my favorite pedestrian bridge, breathing in the scent of the water as I stood under its large stone archways, and then continued to stroll toward our hotel. As I tilted my head up toward the sunlight and felt the warm breeze brush against my cheeks, I smiled. I had forgotten just how much I'd fallen in love with Lyon. There was something magical about this place, something that didn't exist in all of the touristy sights in Paris, that made me feel at ease, like I was home.

When I arrived back at the hotel, the girls were all dressed and ready to go for the day. I filled them in on Mathieu's new, mature look and on our dinner plans for the next night. As I tossed my phone into my purse, it beeped.

I had a missed call.

Butterflies flittered through my stomach as I checked to see who it had been. *Please, please, please let it be Luc.*

But it wasn't Luc, it was Lexi:

Just met with a new counselor. Hottest man ever. Not sure if I can be a good patient when I'm staring at his pecs entire hour. Still making progress, though. Will try not to F up. Thanks for being there for me, Char. UR the best.

I wrote back:

Glad to hear you're still you. At least counseling sessions won't be boring. Don't have sex with him, though, k?

Lexi responded:

Honey, counseling sessions with me are never boring. Of course I'm not going to sleep with him...unless he initiates. How hot would that be?

I chuckled. Brad was right. Lexi was definitely coming back to life.

Later that morning, Katie, Fiona and I headed over to Vieux Lyon, the oldest and most charming part of the city, to feast on some delicious crêpes for lunch. I hadn't had much of an appetite during our first week there, but after my run and my release of all of that baggage I'd been carrying around for years, I felt ravenous. Not to mention as light as a feather. As we strolled down rue Saint-Jean, the main cobblestone street that ran through Vieux Lyon, we passed by an endless string of French restaurants, pubs, and sweet-smelling *patisseries*, their windows displaying row upon row of decadent French pastries. Fresh fruit, meat, and cheese markets spilled out into the winding road, the scent of the food making my stomach growl as we found my favorite crêperie, Le Banana's. After waiting for five minutes with no sign of the waiter, we decided to seat ourselves at one of the small wooden tables against the window.

When the waiter finally appeared, I ordered a *crêpe salée*—a warm, meal-size crêpe packed with Emmental cheese, ham, and tomatoes.

"Whoa, I'm impressed," Katie said as her eyes widened in response to my big order. "Are you getting a dessert crêpe too?" All I had been eating since we'd arrived were side salads and water.

"Hell yeah, I can't pass up a crêpe smothered in Nutella at my favorite place."

"Eating Nutella again—you're starting to come back to life," Katie said with a grin.

"How was your jog this morning?" Fiona asked.

"It was really good. It gave me some time to think about everything, and there's something I need to say to you girls."

Katie and Fiona shared a curious glance before focusing their gazes back on me. "What is it, Charlotte?" Fiona asked.

"First, I want to apologize. Properly and fully apologize for not being a good friend this past year. Fiona, when you and Andrew got back together, and Katie, when you started falling for Joe, I know I was less than supportive of both of you, but that was only because of the crap I was going through. It had nothing to do with either of you. You've both been such great friends to me, and the last thing I ever want to do is lose you from my life."

"Thanks, Char," Katie said softly. "You're not going to lose us. And there's something I've been wanting to say too. I'm sorry for the things I said the night of the wedding. I know your blog wasn't aimed at me or at my relationship. It just felt that way sometimes, but I shouldn't have taken it personally. You've been through a lot this year, between Jeff and your parents, and it totally makes sense that you would've wanted to renounce relationships. I wouldn't believe in them either if I were you. And I want you to know that I really did love your article in *Bella Magazine*. It was awesome, and after the wedding, I didn't want you to think I was lying about that just to be nice."

"Thanks, Katie."

"Ditto to that," Fiona said. "I loved that article. And I know you've had a rough year. I went through the same thing when Andrew and I were over. Your blog gave me a lot of inspiration, actually. It helped me stay strong when I felt like shit. You shouldn't be so hard on yourself, Charlotte. None of us is perfect."

"Thanks, guys. It's just that I've been carrying around so much baggage for a long time now, and for the first time, I feel like it's finally starting to lift. So I want you both to know that from here on out, you can count on me to support you through whatever is going on in your life. And on the topic of the blog, I've decided to keep it going, but to make some changes."

Katie took a sip of espresso out of her mini yellow coffee cup. "Ooh, this is exciting. What kinds of changes?"

"Well, for starters, I'll probably change the title from *Sleeping with Paris* to something a little less…slutty."

Our waiter appeared with our food right at that moment, and apparently he understood English, because he started laughing.

"*Bon appétit, Mesdemoiselles,*" he said with a sly grin.

After devouring a huge bite of hot, melted cheese layered with slices of juicy ham and ripe tomatoes, I continued. "Besides the title, I want to change the message. I want to start writing more about love, relationships, friendships, family. Issues that all women deal with."

"That sounds like fun," Fiona said. "But don't go and get all wholesome Suzy Homemaker on us. You're still going to be real and write about sex, right?"

I lifted an eyebrow. "If you're asking me to write a post about men's obsession with the *arse*, you can forget it."

Katie nearly choked on her food as all three of us burst out laughing.

"No, God. Please don't *ever* write about that," Fiona said, her face the shade of a cherry-red tomato. "You know what I mean. Your blog and your article were so successful because you were *real*. Don't give that up, okay?"

"I won't. I'm just going to take the focus off the man-hating. That's all."

"And it won't be focused on life in Paris anymore, since you'll be coming back to DC in a month once school is over, right?" Katie asked.

"I'm not sure. Truthfully, I haven't decided where I want to live since I lost my chance at that teaching job in Paris. I do realize now, though, that working with Madame Rousseau long-term was never a good idea. I could never have become wholesome enough for her to like me. Although, I could've tried a *little* bit harder."

"Don't worry about what that old cow thinks of you," Fiona said. "You don't need her to find a job. I mean, yes, maybe your chances of landing a post in one of those fancy private schools in Paris are over, but why haven't you thought about moving down to Lyon? You seem like a different person down here. It really suits you."

I glanced out the window and felt my gut tighten at the thought of leaving Paris. Or really, at the thought of leaving *Luc*. "Yeah, that's a possibility…"

Before I could go into the reasons why I did not want to leave Paris, the waiter arrived and cleared our plates. "*Voulez-vous un dessert?*" he asked, shooting flirtatious glances at all three of us.

"*Trois crêpes avec Nutella, s'il vous plaît,*" Katie ordered in her strong American accent.

"*Tout de suite, Mademoiselle,*" the waiter said with a wink.

"He's cute," Katie said, staring at his butt as he walked away. "You should ask him to come out with us tonight."

"Oh, right. All I need is to add one more guy into the drama," I said, rolling my eyes.

"Well, we're on vacation, and just because you're not dating like a man per se doesn't mean you can't have a little fun."

"Maybe, but I don't really think I'm up for all that right now. I need to focus on getting the rest of my life in order first."

A few minutes later, our chocolaty crêpes arrived in all their glory. Those shut us up for the rest of the meal.

"Mmm…this is better than sex," Katie said as she savored a huge bite of Nutella with a tiny bit of crêpe.

"Definitely," Fiona chimed in.

But as I thought of the last time Luc kissed me and held me in his arms, I wasn't so sure.

∽

On the morning of my twenty-sixth birthday, I headed back to the park for another run. Today's sprint felt even better than the day before's. As I jogged past a dedicated group of male rollerbladers weaving wildly in and out of a line of orange cones in their tight little shorts, I couldn't help but laugh. I thought about Fiona's suggestion that I consider moving to Lyon. There was no doubt in my mind that I would love living here again. The only thing stopping me was the thought of leaving Paris and never seeing Luc again. But with no word from him and a world of damage done to our relationship, I had to accept the real possibility that Luc and I were finished.

Even with all of the freeing realizations I'd made the day before, though, I knew I wasn't ready to give up hope. I missed Luc. And I still wanted to be with him more than anything. My feelings for Luc were different from what I'd felt for Jeff, or for any other man for that matter. They were not born solely from my need to feel love and acceptance from a man.

I genuinely cared for Luc. I loved him.

So as we spent my birthday doing our usual bout of open-air market shopping and city exploration, I secretly checked my phone every five seconds for a call from Luc. But when none came, I realized that no matter how strongly I felt for him, I couldn't force him to forgive me. Luckily, the girls kept me busy right up until seven o'clock, when we took the metro over to my host family's apartment for dinner.

My heart overflowed with excitement as we found ourselves in front of the enormous wooden doors that I had let myself into so many times. I buzzed the upstairs apartment.

"*Oui?*" a female voice called over the intercom.

I knew that voice right away—it was my host mom, Caroline. She had come home from Nice to see me!

"*C'est Charlotte,*" I called into the speaker.

"*Ah, Charlotte! Viens, viens!*" she responded eagerly.

We took the stairs up to the third floor, and there stood Caroline, Mathieu, and Aurélie, all waiting for us with huge, welcoming smiles on their faces.

Bisous were exchanged as they ushered us into the foyer and led us toward the living room to have an *aperitif* before dinner. That was another thing I loved about this family—and about the French in general. Tasty *liqueur* before dinner, wine during dinner, and drinks, dessert, chocolate, and coffee after dinner. What could be better than that?

As I entered the living room, I noticed that the older, more classic furniture pieces that Caroline had kept when I'd lived here had been replaced by a modern blue sofa paired with light-gray armchairs and a black-and-white rug. And sitting on the new sofa was a petite brunette holding a baby girl.

Mathieu placed his hand on the woman's shoulder. "Charlotte, this is my wife, Florence, and my daughter, Nathalie."

Mathieu was married? And he had a daughter? I'd had no idea. What was with these French guys and their hidden families?

Florence smiled at me and brought baby Nathalie over to meet me. "Mathieu is very happy to have you here," she said in a thick accent. "And we are so happy for you to meet our little girl."

"She's beautiful, Mathieu. She has your eyes."

He smiled. "Everyone says that." He leaned down and kissed his baby on the forehead. "I wanted to surprise you. I knew you would never believe that I was married and had a baby."

I laughed. "You're right. I wouldn't have. But I'm so happy for you. So the three of you are living here now?"

"Yes, after my mother moved to Nice, she let us have the apartment to raise Nathalie…"

Mathieu kept talking, but I couldn't focus on his words as I watched him put his arm around Florence and cuddle with his baby.

They seemed so happy together. So in love.

This was what I wanted. I didn't want to date like a man any longer. I wanted stability. A home. A family. And I wanted it with Luc.

"*À table!*" Caroline called from the kitchen, snapping me back to reality.

Having dinner with the family was just like old times. Constant laughter, messed-up translations, and ridiculously good food. Katie only knew some basic phrases in French, so my French family made an effort to speak English during the meal, which of course provided us all with endless entertainment.

Toward the end of dinner, we ended up discussing my future plans, and as soon as Fiona mentioned the idea of me moving to Lyon, the family jumped all over it.

"You can stay here with Mathieu and Florence in one of

the spare bedrooms," Aurélie offered as she downed the last sip of her red wine and poured herself another glass.

"Oh, I wouldn't want to impose," I said, hoping to God this was a real offer. I would *so* love to come back and stay with them for a while.

"You wouldn't be imposing," Mathieu chimed in as he looked over at Florence for approval.

"Of course it is not a problem," she agreed.

"Yes," Mathieu continued, "You can stay here while you search for an apartment."

I glanced over at Katie to see what she thought. "It sounds like a really good option," Katie said. "I mean, as much as I want you back in DC with me, you do love this city."

"It all sounds great, but I'd have to find a job, of course," I added, taking another sip of wine.

"I have a friend who teaches English at a language school nearby. If you want, I can put him in touch with you."

"Really? I'd love to talk to him. I've been teaching English to a French medical student up in Paris, and I've really enjoyed it." I started to feel hopeful until I saw Mathieu feeding baby Nathalie, which made me think of Luc and his daughter.

Could I really leave Paris and give up any chance of reconciling with Luc?

"I'll call him tonight, and I'll give you his number. Okay?" Mathieu said as he fed Nathalie another spoonful of mushy bananas.

"Sure, that sounds great," I said, knowing that despite my hesitation, I needed to take this seriously. Luc might not come back around, and moving to Lyon could be the path to getting my life back on track.

After we finished the main course, Caroline cleared the table and served us one of her magnificent pear tarts for my birthday dessert. Then she placed three bars of Lindt creamy milk chocolate on the table for us to savor with our tiny cups of espresso. Besides the fact that eating Lindt chocolate made me think of Luc feeding me chocolate in bed...*damn*...the rest of the dinner went off without a hitch. Fiona and Katie had a ball talking with the family, and I realized I felt more at home than I'd felt in my own skin in a long time.

Later that night, despite missing Luc, my spirits were up after the wonderful dinner we'd had with my host family, so I decided it was time to let loose and have some fun with my girlfriends.

I smiled over at Katie and Fiona as we walked through the cool night air toward the river.

"Girls, I think it's time for a trip to Ayer's Rock."

Katie grinned. "It's about time, lady. It's just over the bridge, right?"

I nodded as the three of us took off over the sparkling river and weaved past three college-aged girls who were hiking the bridge in short black skirts and three-inch heels. I glanced down at my more conservative dark jeans, my long-sleeved raspberry-colored top, and my black heels, and I smiled to myself. I felt relieved not to have to dress up in those skintight outfits anymore. Granted, these girls were probably headed to the same bar as we were, but with both Fiona and Katie in serious relationships and me on my new mission to *stop* using men, I had a feeling that our night would be very different from theirs.

After crossing the bridge, we turned the corner into the Place des Terreaux and zigzagged around the rows of miniature fountains that bubbled up in front of the Hôtel de Ville, which illuminated the deep-blue sky like a radiant palace.

We wound up a skinny alley and passed by a tiny corner market before finding ourselves at the entrance of Ayer's Rock—the bar where I had spent many a night dancing and having the time of my life back when I'd studied abroad. A rush of excitement flowed through me as we bounced into the crowded pub, a Prince song blaring over the speakers, the bartenders banging on the metal bells overhead, just like old times.

After we ordered a round of Sex on the Beach from a buff Swiss bartender, the three of us shoved our way onto the packed dance floor, took a few sips and got down to dancing.

Within minutes, a tall, blond guy with flirty green eyes approached Fiona.

"*Vous voulez danser?*" he asked her as he grinned and stretched out his hand.

Her cheeks flared up as she placed her hand in his and let him sweep her into the middle of the dance floor. I was surprised that Fiona would dance with anyone since she seemed so serious about Andrew, but as I watched her swing her skinny hips from side to side, I noticed that she kept about six inches between her body and his.

Then, as Gloria Gaynor's "I Will Survive" roared over the speakers, two guys with chestnut hair and dark brown eyes swirled in between me and Katie and took our hands to dance. Katie winked at me as she threw back another sip of her drink, then followed her guy farther onto the crowded, sweaty dance floor, where I noticed that she too was careful to keep her distance and ward off his wandering hands.

Without saying a word, my guy slid his arms around my waist and pulled me so close I could feel the heat emanating from his body. After I had danced with this nameless, professionless, handsome French man for about five minutes, he lowered his lips toward mine in an attempt to kiss me. And even though my uncommitted status made me free to take things as far as I wanted, I knew that I didn't want to kiss just another random guy. Sure, it might have taken my mind off missing Luc for the time being, but it wouldn't have erased the hurt.

I had made the mistake all year of thinking that by continuously hooking up with guys and by using them and treating them the way Jeff had treated me, I would somehow get revenge and triumph over Jeff and the whole situation. And what ended up happening was obviously as far from triumphant as I could've gotten. Revenge? Maybe. But triumphant? Definitely not.

And here was another handsome boy at my fingertips, begging for me to get started in this whole game again. But as attractive as he was, my heart wasn't there.

It was in Paris, with Luc.

I had to go to him. *Now.*

Just before the French man's lips were able to graze mine, I broke away from his grasp, grabbed the girls, and pulled them outside.

"What happened in there?" Katie asked as she wiped a bead of sweat off her brow. "That guy was *really* into you."

"I want to go back to Paris. Tonight."

"What? But we're not leaving until the morning."

"I have to see Luc. I have to tell him one more time that I love him. That I want to be with him. I'm so sorry to do this now, but I just have to. I hope you understand."

Fiona and Katie exchanged worried glances, but then Fiona smiled at me.

"I understand. Do you want us to come with you?"

"No, you two stay and finish the night. I think I should do this on my own. And I'll see you back in Paris tomorrow."

Katie grabbed my hand. "Are you sure?"

"Yes, I can't wait another day."

With that, I raced back to the hotel, packed my bags, cabbed it to the train station, and made it onto the last train to Paris.

TWENTY-FOUR

samedi, le 16 avril

*Second chances are like a sunny day after two weeks of rain in Paris
—unexpected and oh so welcome.*

A rush of adrenaline surged through me as the high-speed train barreled north toward Paris. I would tell Luc I loved him and only him. I would tell him about the life we could have together. I would tell him that I wanted to get to know his daughter. That I didn't need to go out and be with other men to feel fulfilled. That the only thing that made me happy was him.

When I reached my dorm, I took the old, rickety elevator up to my floor and ran down the hall to my room to drop off my suitcase. As I opened my door, I almost slipped on a white envelope on the floor.

"Charlotte" was written on the front...in Luc's handwriting.

My heart pounded as I stared at the letter for a few seconds, hoping I would find forgiveness inside. I sat down on the bed and, with trembling hands, I opened the envelope.

Dear Charlotte,

I'm writing to let you know that I'm leaving Paris this week. I finally got custody of my daughter, so I am moving away to live with her. This has nothing to do with what happened between us, but I didn't want to leave without telling you. I'm going to miss you, but maybe this is for the best.

Please don't forget me,
Luc

I dropped the letter on the floor and ran down the hallway to Luc's room. *Please, God, don't let him be gone already.* I pounded on the door, and when there was no answer, I tried the door knob. It was unlocked. I barged in to find…nothing.

He was gone.

He'd left without saying good-bye. Without even telling me where he was going.

A million unanswered questions raced through my head, but the one thing I did know was that I couldn't stand to be in his empty room for another second. I rushed back to my tiny dorm room all alone and collapsed on my bed, knowing that this was it.

I'd lost Luc for good.

∽

After taking Katie back to the airport that weekend and promising her I wouldn't hole up in my room again and disappear like I had the last time I'd been really upset over a guy, it was time to go back to school. Starting classes that Monday made me realize that I needed to get my ass in gear. No more time for whining, crying, or self-pity. I had a ton of papers to write and only two weeks to finish all of them. Yes, I had thrown away my chance at a private-school teaching job in Paris, but I was at least going to get credit for these courses. With all of my gallivanting around this past semester, I hadn't been the most diligent student, and now it was time to play catch-up so I wouldn't fail any of my classes.

Just as I'd experienced first semester, my professors had assigned nothing of significant value to complete during the semester, which made the chances of failure at the end of the semester that much higher. Since failure had never really been an option for me (in academics, anyway—my personal life was turning out to be a different story), I pushed all of the Luc drama out of my head for those two weeks, locked myself in my room, and got to work. I only left the building to run at the park every morning and to have dinner with Fiona or with Marc, who had thankfully chosen to ignore his mother's requests to have nothing to do with me ever again.

One night, after crumpling up an introduction to a paper I'd rewritten five times, I pulled out my phone, scrolled through the numbers, and stopped once I reached Luc's. I stared at it for a couple of minutes, as if just looking at his number somehow connected me to him. I knew it was idiotic, but since I was determined not to break down and call him, that was as good as it was going to get.

As I closed my phone and tossed it across the room onto my bed, I imagined what I would say to him if I did call. I knew that after what I'd done, I had no right to get mad at him about not telling me where he had moved and about not saying good-bye. He had clearly decided that he didn't want me to be a part of his life anymore, and I couldn't blame him.

The minute I'd discovered that Jeff was cheating on me, I'd had no problem denouncing him and moving to Paris by myself. How could I blame Luc for ridding his life of someone who had treated him so badly when I had essentially done the same thing to Jeff? Granted, I at least felt horrible about what I had done, whereas I was convinced that Jeff wasn't capable of feeling remorse or any other genuine emotion, except those that he experienced with his penis, of course.

Instead of calling Luc that night, I crossed the room, grabbed my phone, and hid it underneath my plastic mattress before rewriting that damn introduction for the sixth and final time.

The next night, though, with my head pounding and my eyes glazing over from one too many hours spent in front of the computer screen, I peeled my mattress off the cheap wooden frame and yanked my phone back out. I slid down onto the hard tile floor, flipped open the phone, and found Luc's number. As my thumb hovered over the Send button, I realized I needed to take action. I couldn't be so weak and desperate anymore.

So instead of hitting Send, I hit Delete.

I stared at the space in my contacts where Luc's number had been, realizing that this was it. I'd now eliminated all possibility of contact with him. We'd never exchanged e-mail addresses during the year since we'd lived across the hall from each other, and I'd already scoured the Internet only to discover that Luc had no social media presence whatsoever, so I really couldn't get in touch with him anymore.

I considered throwing my phone into the trash to seal the deal—that way I wouldn't have to go to bed one more night realizing that Luc hadn't called me and probably wasn't going to.

But just as I was about to pitch it, I remembered the low balance in my bank account and decided I'd at least saved an ounce of my own dignity in deleting his number. I didn't have to put myself in debt over it.

And now I had to move on. I had no other choice.

I tossed the phone back onto the bed and changed into a comfy T-shirt and a pair of shorts, determined to put in another few hours of paper writing and to *stop* thinking about Luc.

Five final papers later, I was finished with my school year in Paris. It felt extraordinary to turn in that last paper and to feel like I had (hopefully) passed all of my classes. I was paid up for two more weeks' worth of rent before I needed to decide what to do with the rest of my life, or at least with the rest of the summer. The idea of moving back to Lyon had been swimming around in my head ever since I'd found Luc's letter. If Lyon didn't work out, I figured I'd have to go back to DC. But my instincts—which I hadn't listened to for quite some time—told me it wasn't time to head back to the States. So I decided to shoot Mathieu an e-mail to follow up on that English-teaching job he had mentioned during dinner.

A few hours later, Mathieu wrote me back. He said he had contacted his friend Jean-Sébastien, who worked at a language school in Lyon, and that they had two full-time English-teaching positions open.

I made some last-minute revisions to my résumé and sent it along to Jean-Sébastien, who, to my delight, e-mailed me back that night right before bed and told me that they needed someone to start immediately. He asked if I could come down for an interview as soon as possible, and he even said that if the school really wanted me, they'd help me obtain a work visa, since I couldn't live in France with a student visa anymore.

I called Mathieu and Florence that night and asked them if I could stay in the spare bedroom for a day or two so that I could interview for the position. They were more than happy to offer up a bedroom to me, so no less than twelve hours later, I was on a train to Lyon.

The dark cloud that had hovered over me ever since Luc had left Paris lifted the minute I stepped off the train and found myself winding through the beautiful streets of Lyon. I loved this place. I could start fresh here. Leave the past and all of my mistakes behind. Now, I simply had to land this job.

Back at my host family's apartment, Florence greeted me warmly, then set me up in my old bedroom. My interview was in half an hour, so I hurried to change into my black interview pantsuit, touch up my makeup, and throw on some heels before trotting down the street to the language school. It was only six blocks from my host family's house. How convenient!

The school was small and bustling. Students of all nationalities buzzed in and out of classrooms. I approached the secretary at the front desk and told her in French that I was here for a job interview for the English-teaching position.

"You are Charlotte Summers?" she asked in a thick accent.

"Yes, I'm Char—" I began before she cut me off.

"I am so happy you are here," she said as she popped up out of her seat, revealing a no more than ninety-pound, five-foot-tall figure. "Jean-Sébastien is waiting. Follow me, we will get him."

I raced down the hallway after the teeny-tiny French woman and felt my nerves piling up in my stomach. I so, so hoped this interview would go well.

"Jean-Sébastien," the little French woman called as we rounded the hallway and entered a cluttered office.

"*Oui,*" a young, disheveled guy answered as he peeked over a massive pile of papers covering his desk. "Ahhh, you must be Charlotte!" A huge grin spread across his face as he stood up to shake my hand.

"*Merci, Colette,*" he said to the miniwoman as she bolted out of the room.

I'd never seen a person that little move so fast.

"Please, please, have a seat," he said with a solid American accent. "I am so sorry for the mess. The director is out of town, so I am taking his place for three weeks, and things have been a little…euh…well, never mind, you get the picture. Let's talk about you. Mathieu has told me a lot about you. He says you've taught French and English before. Is that right?"

"Yes, I taught French for three years at a high school in Washington, DC, and then I've been teaching English to a French medical student up in Paris this past year."

"Oh, great, so you've had large classes before…" He paused as he looked down at a copy of my résumé that was sitting on top of a mess of papers on his desk. "How long do you plan to live in Lyon?"

Hmm…tricky question. I knew in my gut that I wanted to move down here as soon as possible, and something else in my gut was telling me that it might not be a temporary move. So I went with my instincts, even if they were lying. I really wanted this job. "Probably at least two years, but maybe indefinitely."

His eyes lit up. "And when can you start? Would next week be possible?"

Yes, yes, yes!

"Yes, I could start Monday," I said, trying not to jump out of my chair.

"Perfect. Let me show you around the school and see what you think. If you like it, the job is yours."

I couldn't believe my ears. That was by far the shortest, not to mention easiest, job interview I'd ever experienced. Jean-Sébastien showed me around to all of the different classrooms and explained to me in French how everything worked. He told me that I'd work thirty-five hours a week (gotta love the French and their abbreviated workweek), that I'd have the entire month of August off (love the French vacation system), and that I'd get my first paycheck after two weeks. The salary was low, but anyone who wants to be a teacher has to accept the fact that they're not going to make millions, and since I'd already consented to that fate a few years ago, I knew I could make ends meet. Plus, if it got me to Lyon, what was there to question?

"So, what do you think?" he asked after we'd toured the whole school.

"I'll take it," I said, smiling one of the biggest smiles I'd had in a long time.

And that was that. I signed a contract and had three days to get back to Paris, pack up my things, and move to Lyon. Mathieu and Florence were thrilled and said I could stay with them while I searched for an apartment. Things couldn't have fallen together more perfectly.

The only unwelcome thought that still lingered in the back of my mind was that once I left Paris, Luc would have no way to find me.

∼

Fiona and Marc came over that weekend to help me pack up my room and get ready for my move to Lyon. It was much sadder than I'd imagined it would be. Even though I'd spent the entire year using men to escape my problems, it was still a damn good time. My room felt like home now, I loved my neighborhood and my park, and Fiona and Marc had become two very dear friends. The sadness that came with leaving made me feel good, though, because it showed me that even though I hadn't handled things perfectly this year, my time in Paris was anything but a waste.

"I can't believe you're staying in France," Fiona said as she tried to catch her breath after heaving a huge box of my clothes up onto the bed. "I guess I never really considered staying after this year, but if I didn't have Andrew, I might've ended up doing the same thing."

"I know, it all happened so fast too. I mean, I just got the job like a day ago…I can't believe I'm already moving down there," I said, wiping the sweat off my forehead. My dorm room didn't have air-conditioning, and judging by the rise in temperature, it was clear the summer months were almost here.

"You're going to see me a lot, since my dad lives down there. We'll have you for dinner next time I come down," Marc said as he passed me another box.

"I can't wait to meet the rest of your family." As long as they were nothing like his mother. Ugh. "It is kind of sad to be leaving Paris, though."

"I know…I don't want you to go. I still have another two weeks here, and it's going to be so lonely without you," Fiona said, looking a little teary.

"I wish I could stay a few more weeks too," I said as I taped up the last of the boxes. "But, you'll just have to come back to Lyon to visit."

"Definitely. Probably not for a little while, though…I have to work on getting a job at home first so I can pay for the ticket!"

"Tell Andrew to pay for it…Shouldn't he owe you some kind of monetary reward since you were kind enough to take him back after everything?"

"Yeah, in theory, that would be nice. But…I don't think that's going to happen." Fiona laughed as she taped up the box she was working on.

"We should have lunch this week after Charlotte leaves if you don't have anything to do," Marc said to Fiona, a cute grin spreading across his lips.

"Yeah, that'd be great," Fiona said as her cheeks flushed bright red. "Do you still have my number?"

"Of course I still have your number," Marc said.

Fiona held his gaze for a few extra seconds, then her eyes darted to the floor.

I couldn't help but let out a little giggle.

"What?" They both asked in unison.

"Nothing…" I trailed off as I smiled at them.

Marc and Fiona helped me take a hefty load of boxes over to the post office to ship to Lyon, and then they helped me clean up my room and get everything completely packed up so I'd be ready to go first thing the next morning. I couldn't have asked for better friends.

"All right, guys, I'm taking you both out to dinner," I announced when we had finally finished.

"You don't have to do that," Fiona responded.

"I don't want to hear it. You've both been so wonderful to me this year...through everything, and, well, it's the least I can do. Plus, it's my last night in Paris, so we have to go out." I looked over at Fiona and saw the tears welling up. "Don't start, or you'll make me start," I said as I leaned over and gave her a hug.

The three of us took the warm, smelly RER train together up to the Luxembourg stop. We wound our way through the cobblestone streets near the Panthéon and found a beautiful French café where we sat outside under the moonlight and enjoyed way too many glasses of wine. Sitting there at that adorable restaurant with my friends made me so happy I'd decided to stay in France. I knew I'd made the right choice.

I watched as Marc continued to flirt with Fiona throughout dinner, and with each sip of wine, Fiona's eyelashes batted a little harder and the rosiness in her cheeks reached the color of a chili pepper.

Stuffed and giddy, the three of us walked over to Rhubarb after dinner to conclude my last night in Paris with another drink. Marc slipped his arm around Fiona's waist as we stumbled over the cobblestones to the bar, and by the way she laid her head on his shoulder and gazed up into his eyes, I could tell she'd forgotten all about Andrew.

"What can I get you ladies to drink?" Marc asked as we arrived at the bar.

"I'm actually just going to run to the restroom real quick," I told them.

On my way back up to the bar, I had to squeeze past three different sets of dying couples, their bodies intertwined on the dance floor, their noses pressed together, their lips brushing against each other's skin.

And then I remembered that the last time I'd been to this bar had been with Luc. We'd looked just like those couples, unable to take our eyes, or our hands, off each other.

And there it was again. That feeling I *thought* I was getting rid of. That nauseating anxiety that crept up from the pit of my stomach.

I was in love with someone who didn't love me back. Or if he did, I had ruined it.

I told myself I would be okay. I was moving to Lyon. Starting a new life. Even still, I wasn't really in the mood to be in that bar anymore. Just as I made my way back toward the bar, I was jolted backward as I spotted Marc and Fiona locked in a long, passionate kiss. And from the looks of it, their kiss wasn't ending anytime soon.

I waited off to the side until they came up for air, and then approached the newly formed dying couple. Fiona's face flushed when she realized that I had witnessed the whole thing. She was, in fact, still officially with Andrew, and she was not the cheating kind. I knew she'd be reeling about this one once she woke up in the morning, but I was secretly happy she'd done it. Marc was perfect for her. And with Andrew's bizarre *arse* obsession, something had to give.

"I think I'm going to head out," I told them. "I'm really tired, and I have to be up early tomorrow to catch my train. But thank you both so much for everything—for all of your help today, and for being such great friends. I'm going to miss you both so much." I leaned in and gave Fiona a squeeze.

"I'm going to miss you too. But we'll visit each other, promise?" Fiona looked me in the eye as she struggled to stay standing. She'd exceeded her normal limit of two drinks by about five.

"Promise," I answered back. "And I'm going to see you a lot, right?" I asked Marc as I hugged him.

"Yes, of course. You've been the best English teacher."

"Thanks, Marc," I said as I smiled at the two of them. "All right, I'll talk to you both soon." I turned and left them there to continue their night of passion. Fiona deserved to have some fun; she was always so well behaved. And maybe this would open her eyes to what a great guy Marc was and, at the very least, show her that there were other guys out there besides Andrew.

I hailed a cab back to my dorm so I could have one last look at Paris at night before heading down to Lyon in the morning. Smiling at the sparkly white lights of La Tour Eiffel twinkling off in the distance, I realized that while I was sad to be leaving this magical city, Paris would only be a train ride away. I was ready for a new start, and in just a few short hours, it would all begin.

TWENTY-FIVE

dimanche, le 8 mai

And just when you thought you'd never enjoy chocolate again...

"You are sure you are comfortable watching the baby while we're out?" Mathieu asked as he held the door for Florence.

I bounced baby Nathalie in my arms and smiled at them. "I'm sure. You two go out and have a good time."

"Call us if you have any questions at all, okay?" Florence said nervously as she took one last glimpse of her daughter.

"I promise. Now please, have fun and don't worry about us."

I closed the door behind them and carried baby Nathalie into the living room where I sat down on the couch with her. It was my second week at Mathieu and Florence's apartment, and I'd volunteered to watch Nathalie for the night so the two of them could go out to eat. I was a bit nervous as I hadn't spent much time taking care of babies, but it was the least I could do, considering they'd offered to put me up until I had enough money to rent my own place.

I bounced Nathalie on my knee and watched as her cute brown curls bobbed up and down and she let out an adorable giggle.

This wasn't so bad.

Just as I smiled back at her, though, her little pink lips formed into an oval, and out came the loudest, most piercing cry I'd ever heard.

What happened?

I continued bouncing her on my knee, but her cries only intensified. I stood up and swayed from side to side as I patted her lightly on the back, but nothing seemed to be working.

I paced up and down the hallway with the little bundle screaming in my arms, her cries drowning out the sound of the creaky wooden floors, and wondered what I should do next. Florence had just fed her and changed her diaper, so maybe she was tired?

But, after an hour of bouncing, rocking, singing, swaying, trying to give her another bottle, and even performing a dancing puppet show, I was losing my calm. I laid her down in her crib, hoping she would fall asleep, but no such luck.

I didn't want to worry Mathieu and Florence, but I decided I needed to do something, so I called Fiona in London, where she was now living with Andrew.

"Hey, Charlotte!" she answered.

"I need help," I told her.

"What is that noise?" she asked. "Are you in a fire station or something?"

"No, it's Mathieu's baby, Nathalie. She's been crying for almost an hour. I've tried everything and she won't stop. Do you have any ideas?"

"Is she hungry?"

"No, she's not hungry, she doesn't need a diaper change, and she won't sleep. Don't babies just eat, poop, and sleep? What other problem could I be missing here?"

"Have you tried a movie?"

"Mathieu and Florence aren't big on letting her watch television."

"Well, they're not the ones that have been listening to her cry for the past hour, now, are they?"

"True." I flipped on the TV and scrolled through the channels until I landed on *Finding Nemo* in French. I popped Nathalie into her bouncy seat in front of the television and held my breath, hoping this would work.

Lo and behold, as her eyes fixed on the colorful fish swimming around the screen, her cries died down, and a tiny smile crossed her lips.

I breathed out a long sigh. "That was really intense."

Fiona laughed. "How much longer are you going to be staying with them?"

I sank down on the couch and felt myself relax as baby Nathalie became more engrossed in the movie.

"I won't get my first paycheck from the language school until next week, and even then, I don't know if I'll have enough money for a deposit on an apartment just yet. I hope it's not long, though, because I feel like I'm imposing on their time as a family. Plus, Nathalie wakes up wailing every single night. I bought some earplugs, and even those don't keep the sound out. But it's a free place to stay, and you saw their apartment—it's gorgeous. So I really shouldn't complain. Enough about me, though. How's life in London? How are things with Andrew?"

Fiona had never mentioned her make-out session with Marc, so I'd never brought it up either. I wondered if she even remembered that it had happened—she *had* exceeded her two-drink limit that night.

"Um…well, you know. *Interesting*."

"Interesting? In a good way or a bad way?"

"It's just that I got used to living on my own in Paris, so it's been quite a transition to have him around *all* the time."

"At least he doesn't wake up crying in the middle of the night," I said with a laugh.

"Very true. It's fine, though. Things are going…fine."

I could hear the undertones of something else brewing, but I didn't want to push.

"Oh, I wanted to tell you something," Fiona continued. "I spoke with Lexi, and she told me the reason she's in New York. About her suicide attempt? You've known about this the whole time?"

"Yeah, she asked me to keep it private. I hope you're not mad."

"No, of course I understand. That's not information she probably wants spreading around. But, God, that's awful. I can't believe she's been so depressed all year…to the point of wanting to take her own life. I wish I had known. I would've been there for her more. I just got so angry with her after that night with Marc. She seemed so careless and slutty to me. But now it all makes a little more sense."

"Did she tell you that she didn't sleep with Marc after all?"

"She didn't?" Fiona asked.

"No, I spoke with Marc about it too. He only took her back to his place because he was worried about letting her go home alone. He's not interested in her, Fiona. He never was."

Fiona didn't say anything, but I swore I could hear her mind spinning over the line.

"He asked about you on the phone the other day," I continued.

"Really?"

"Mm-hmm. I think he misses you."

"Oh, I don't know about that." Fiona hesitated for a moment. "He has been e-mailing me recently. We're just friends, though, of course. I'm happy here with Andrew."

"Of course. Nothing wrong with staying in touch, though."

"No, not at all," she agreed.

I hoped that if Andrew wasn't the right person for Fiona, she would realize it before it was too late. But, seeing as how Fiona wasn't exactly a risk taker, I doubted her relationship with Marc would go beyond an e-mail flirtation.

∼

The next morning, while Nathalie was in the middle of one of her hour-long cry sessions, I was searching for a pair of earrings I thought I had lost when I came across something else I hadn't thought about in months.

My engagement ring.

I hadn't taken it back out of my jewelry box since the night my mom had told me about the divorce. I couldn't believe I had totally forgotten about it all this time. I guess I *had* done a nice job of keeping myself busy in Paris.

I ran my finger around the platinum band and stared at the two-and-a-half-carat diamond, expecting to be hit with pangs of sorrow, expecting the tears to begin welling up at any moment. But, to my surprise, I felt nothing. It wasn't a symbol of lost love or love gone bad, or whatever you'd want to call it. It was just a piece of jewelry. A really expensive, beautiful piece of jewelry. That's right, an *expensive, beautiful* piece of jewelry.

Suddenly I knew exactly what I needed to do with that ring.

After getting the skinny on the best jewelry stores in town from Florence and putting on the classiest outfit in my closet, I was on my way downtown. I had no idea what Jeff had paid for the ring, but I knew that for all of Jeff's shortcomings, there was one thing he was not. And that was cheap. The man was loaded, and he wasn't afraid to throw large sums of money around. Luckily for me, I happened to be in possession of one of his larger purchases.

I strolled into the expensive jewelry store Florence had insisted I visit and marveled at the vast collection of diamonds and jewels lighting up the glass cabinets.

A woman in a slim black business suit approached me. *"Je peux vous aider, Mademoiselle?"*

I reached into my purse and whipped out the diamond engagement ring that I was hoping would give me a little extra boost in my quest to secure my own apartment.

After I let her know of my intent to sell the ring, the woman's dark-brown eyes widened just the slightest bit as she took the blue ring box from my hands and inspected the diamond.

She walked over to a man in a dark-gray suit, who I assumed to be the store manager, and within seconds, three more salespeople were called to the scene. As they carried out a series of inspections, all the while talking so low I couldn't hear a single word, the woman in the black suit appeared with a glass of sparkling water.

"Merci," I said with a smile as I followed her over to a comfortable seat in the corner of the store. She sat with me and buttered me up for about fifteen minutes before the manager nodded in her direction and she left me there to finish my bubbly water.

A few minutes later, they called me over to the counter. The manager informed me in French that they had valued my ring at more than $25,000.

As I felt the smile on my face widen, I had to resist the urge to jump up and down like an excited little girl.

I knew the ring had cost Jeff a lot, but I'd believed it was worth maybe half that. Plus, with the less-than-desirable exchange rate going on right now, I'd hoped to make a couple thousand euros at best. But some higher power must've thought I deserved much more than that after everything I'd been through with Jeff because I walked out of that blessed jewelry store with a check for 18,000 euros.

I remained as calm, cool, and collected as possible as I left the store with that fat check in my purse, but as soon as I was a few blocks away on a deserted side street, I literally started skipping. And then I burst out laughing. I doubled over and laughed so hard my sides ached. I felt *so good*. It wasn't just the money that was making me giddy—well, okay, that was a huge part of it—but it was the freedom I felt. I was in Lyon, and I loved it here! I had come here of my own free will, and my move had nothing to do with a man. I wasn't chasing a man, I wasn't running from a man—I was just here because I wanted to be. And since my teaching paychecks were small starting out, this extra money would help me secure a nice apartment and move out on my own. Hell, I could even furnish the apartment! And the first significant purchase I would make once I found a nice place was definitely going to be a bed—a huge, comfortable, cushy, expensive bed.

The next week, Aurélie and I were out apartment hunting when we found my new home. It was just south of Bellecour and was within walking distance of the Perrache train station. It was a large studio—well, as large as a studio can get—and with its shiny hardwood floors and newly painted sea-blue walls, it was beautiful inside. Not at all like the slew of dingy studios I'd been looking at prior to the monumental ring selling. I knew this place would go fast, so I decided to go for it. Because of the nice sum of cash I'd recently collected—*thank you very much, Jeff*—I was able to write the landlord a check for the deposit and for the first month's rent right then and there. And just like that, it was mine. Well, mine to rent, that is. Ring money or not, I certainly wouldn't be buying any real estate on my meager teacher's salary.

Mathieu and a few of his friends helped me move all of my boxes and suitcases into my new studio, and I had that place unpacked and fixed up in less than a week. I even went out the day after I moved in and purchased my very own double bed. No more pathetic plastic cots for me. I would be sleeping in style...and not waking up with back pains in the mornings!

One evening, as I curled up in my cozy bed and wrapped my crisp new sheets around my legs, a flash of Luc's warm smile invaded my head. I squeezed my eyes closed and buried my face in the pillow, hoping I could erase the picture of his laughing chestnut eyes and his sexy five o'clock shadow from my mind, but I couldn't.

I realized then, as I lay there alone in my new home, that even though I'd done the best I could to move on with my life, that gut-wrenching feeling that I'd lost the one guy who I could've really been with *still* hadn't escaped the pit of my stomach. I was becoming quite skilled at ignoring it, but here it was again, waiting for me in the quiet night inside my apartment and sure to be gnawing at me first thing in the morning when I woke.

I thought about a night I'd gone out with Mathieu and Aurélie just the week before, and how I'd politely but firmly declined when one of their friends had tried to put the moves on me. There hadn't been anything wrong with him...but he wasn't Luc.

I flipped over on my back and stared up at the ceiling. I knew I couldn't wait forever, but I just wasn't ready yet for any kind of relationship, whether it was a one-night stand or a couple of friendly dates. And as much as I missed having sex—sometimes I felt like I was going out of my mind—I couldn't bring myself to do it with someone new, someone I didn't care about. Katie and Fiona had been encouraging me to get out there and date other people, since they didn't have much hope that I'd ever hear from Luc again. But something in me was holding out.

After tossing and turning for a solid half hour, my thoughts consuming me and keeping me wide awake, I finally threw in the towel and climbed out of bed. I sat down at my computer and pulled up my blog. I hadn't posted anything new since I'd found out about Luc's daughter. I scrolled through all the entries and read through the comments. Then I pulled out my magazine article and read it again. Wow, I really had portrayed myself as a serious man-hater. Amid all of my bashing, I did have some good points, but I felt like a different person now. And I wanted to make up for what I'd done.

I still planned on giving the blog a major transformation, like I'd told Katie and Fiona, but first I picked up the phone and dialed Beth, the editor at *Bella Magazine*.

"Beth Harding," she answered.

"Beth, hi. It's Charlotte Summers."

"Charlotte! How are you? We've had such an incredible reaction to your article. Everyone loved it. Are you still blogging?"

"I'm actually reworking the theme of my blog a bit, so hopefully you'll like the new look. But that's not why I called. I have an idea for another article that I want to run by you if you have a minute."

"Of course. Shoot."

After I explained my idea, Beth responded, "I love it. How soon can you get me the first draft? I'd love to squeeze it into our August issue."

"Is tomorrow soon enough?"

"Perfect."

And with that, I spent the entire evening at my computer, composing a new article that reflected the new me.

∼

The first week in August marked the beginning of my four-week vacation from work. God, I loved France. I considered going home to visit my family, but my parents were still separated, and I didn't want to upset the inner calm that I had found in Lyon. The thought of going home to visit my mom, who was still living with my crazy aunt Liza in Florida, or to see my dad and his girlfriend in Ohio, wasn't at all appealing. So, instead I chose to stay and have a relaxing month all to myself in Lyon.

Most of the friends I had made through Mathieu and Aurélie were off traveling for the month, so I had a lot of time to sleep in, read French novels, and my new favorite—go out to eat. Lyon is known as the gastronomical capital of France, and deservedly so. The food is phenomenal. Since I had decided not to travel, I chose instead to treat myself to a new restaurant every week and to spend my afternoons sitting outside at cafés reading books and drinking wine. I couldn't imagine a better way to spend the month.

By the first week of August, *Bella Magazine*'s latest issue had already hit newsstands in the US. I had been waiting for Katie to mail me a copy, so one lazy morning, as I checked my mailbox and saw a giant envelope stuffed inside, I knew it had arrived. I tore it open and flipped through the pages until I found my piece.

How Not to Fall in Love in Paris
by Charlotte Summers

For the past year, I've been running around Paris and dating like a man—which basically means that I've been using men for fun and sex to protect my heart from getting hurt again.

Each week, as I logged dating lessons and tips into my "Sleeping with Paris—A Girl's Guide to Dating Like a Man in the City of Love" blog, I received countless notes of encouragement from women just like me who'd been thrown to the curb by their cheating exes. So, I thought I was on the right track. I was helping women everywhere to get over their past and move on to a happier, brighter future. One that didn't involve heartbreak and sadness.

To demonstrate my points, I exploited the lives of the men I was seeing. Namely, one infamous man, who you'd probably recognize from my blog as Half-Naked French Hottie. To show a little more respect this time, we'll call him by his first name—Luc.

As I reminded women everywhere just how sketchy guys can be, citing examples of how Luc was answering mysterious phone calls, telling another woman he loved her over the phone, and disappearing for weeks at a time, Luc was actually doing something noble. He was fighting for someone he loves—his three-year-old daughter. Getting custody of his little girl was the reason behind all of his late-night calls, and as soon as I gave him the chance to tell me about her, I knew I had made a huge mistake.

All year, I had wrongly grouped Luc in with the rest of the bunch—sleazy men, that is. Yes, men can be creepy. Men have broken our hearts. Men have cheated on us. You name it, they've done it. But, what I found out is that by dating like a man and guarding my heart like it was a national treasure, I had become my own worst enemy—a person who carelessly stomps on the hearts of others to advance her own agenda.

Even though I'd never verbally committed to be in a relationship with Luc, I had done to him exactly what other men had done to me. I had used him all year to get over my ex. I had abused his feelings for me so that I wouldn't appear desperate and alone at a wedding in front of my ex and his girlfriend. Then I carelessly disregarded his feelings and jumped at the first chance to be with my ex, only to realize it wasn't him that I wanted anymore.

It was Luc.

Somewhere in between all of the nights we had shared together—the laughs, the talks, the sex, and the chocolate—I had fallen for Luc. I loved hanging out with him. I loved his accent, his sense of humor, and the way he wanted me anytime, anywhere. I had fallen for him without even realizing it. But, of course, since I was unwilling to admit that I was staring love in the face, I went and messed it all up before this monumental realization occurred.

In my defense, you may say that Luc was taking those weird phone calls, he was *disappearing and telling another woman he loved her over the phone. How was I supposed to know he was fighting for custody of his daughter? Well, that's just it. In my quest to date like a man, I'd made a rule that women should avoid all serious talks with men. We were just having fun, remember? Luc had tried to tell me about his daughter. Several times. But I cut him off. I wasn't having it.*

In the end, I lost Luc. I lost a good man because I was too afraid to put my heart back out there and accept that I'd finally found someone who would love me for me and who would never hurt me the way I'd been hurt in the past. Dating like a man can be fun, but eventually, you may meet a man who's different. Who isn't like the rest. And if you're smart, you'll stop the games, you'll listen to him when he's pouring his heart out to you, and you'll tell him you love him.

Luc, if you're out there, I still love you. And I always will.

As I felt a tear roll down my cheek, I knew I'd come a long way. Whether I ever heard from Luc again or not, I had publicly admitted my wrongs, and I'd put my heart on the line. I could only hope that the next time I met a guy as wonderful as Luc, if I *did* ever meet a guy as wonderful as Luc, that I would be brave enough to love again. As I stared at my own words in print, I felt confident that I would.

∽

On a beautiful Sunday afternoon, one week after my article had come out, I was sitting outside at a sidewalk café in Vieux Lyon enjoying a glass of Chardonnay and reading a French novel I had just picked up at the bookstore. I was totally immersed in my book when I heard my phone ringing from inside my purse. It was a long number, so I assumed it was someone from home.

"Hello?" I answered.

"Charlotte! Hey, it's Fiona."

"Hey, Fiona, what's going on?"

"Well, I have some news," she said, sounding much more excited than she had during our last few conversations.

"Ooh, do tell." I really hoped she wasn't engaged or pregnant, or both.

"I'm coming to France!" she yelled into the phone.

Whew, thank God. "You are? When?"

"Next week!"

"What? Why? I mean, I'm so excited you're coming, but what prompted the last-minute visit?" I had just talked to Fiona a week before, and she hadn't mentioned anything about flying over here, so I wasn't sure what she had up her sleeve.

"You're not going to believe this, but I broke up with Andrew, and Marc bought me a plane ticket to France."

"Whoa, back it up! You broke up with Andrew? And you're with Marc now? And I'm going to get to see you? How did all of this happen? Why did you break up with Andrew?" I was filled with questions but *so* excited that she had taken charge of her life. I'd never thought it would really happen, though. She was always so passive that I never thought she'd stand up for herself and get over him.

"Remember your last night in Paris, how Marc and I kind of..." she trailed off.

"Yeah, I remember. How you were kind of making out in the bar?"

She giggled. "Yeah, that. Well, we also kind of spent the night together."

"Oh, my gosh, you didn't!" I shrieked.

"We did."

"And?" I urged her, not believing my ears. Since Fiona had never mentioned it again, I had just assumed that she had gone home alone that night. I really didn't think she would've taken things all the way, since she was still with Andrew.

"Charlotte, it was amazing. He's just so sweet and so handsome. After that night, we spent practically every day together before I left. But I was still with Andrew, and I didn't know what to do. You know I never do anything like that."

Ain't that the truth. "I know. So then what happened?"

"I went home and tried to make things work with Andrew. But after being with Marc, I really started to see through Andrew, and I *finally* realized what a selfish jerk he is. You were right about him all along. Marc and I were e-mailing every day, and I was leaving the flat as much as I could to sneak in phone calls to him. After a little while, I started to feel kind of scummy about the whole thing, but I knew that I wasn't in love with Andrew anymore. So a couple days ago, I broke it off, moved back in with my parents, and Marc and I are officially together now." I could hear her beaming over the phone.

"Oh, my gosh, congratulations! You have no idea how happy I am that you're with Marc and you're done with Andrew."

"Yeah, I didn't get the impression that you cared for him too much. But now I see why."

"So how long are you staying in France?"

"I have a one-way ticket, and I'm already looking for jobs!"

"Seriously? Oh, my gosh, that's so exciting. I'm so glad I stayed now. And Marc's dad is in Lyon, so you guys will be coming down here a lot, right?"

"That's the other part of my news. Marc just finished medical school, you know, and he found out that he's going to be working in Lyon."

"So you're both moving here?" I asked, ready to jump out of my chair.

"Mm-hmm…I'll be in Lyon in less than a week, and hopefully, if it all works out, I'll be there to stay!"

"Fiona…I can't even believe this. This is seriously the best news I've had all year." I smiled to myself and took a huge sip of wine in celebration. "I don't know if you've heard from

Lexi recently, but she's doing a lot better and moving back to Paris this month too. And she's bringing Dylan with her, the guy she's been in love with for years."

"That's fabulous. We're all going to be back together again. You have no idea how excited I am. I can't even stand to wait another week. I'm just dying to be with Marc again." Fiona then lowered her voice and said, "Charlotte, I think I'm in love with him."

"Whoa...using the *L* word already." I chuckled. "I'm so happy for you, Fiona. Marc is such a sweet guy, and you two make a perfect couple." The thought did cross my mind that if she and Marc were to get married, Madame Rousseau would be her *mother-in-law*. The thought was too awful to think about. Plus, I didn't want to rain on her parade.

"There's actually more good news," she sang into the phone.

"Seriously? Did he propose or something?" Did Madame Rousseau get hit by a bus? God, I was awful.

"No, this is about you."

"Me?"

"Oh shoot, my phone is dying. Charlotte, are you..."

"Fiona? Fiona, are you there?" Just then, I lost the call. But what was she going to tell me? I had to call her back. I was about to dial her number when my phone rang again. I answered it without even checking the number because I just assumed it was her.

"Hey," I answered. "So, what's this good news you were about to tell me?"

"Charlotte?" a man's deep voice said on the other line.

I almost dropped my wineglass—it was Luc.

"Luc?"

"Bonjour, Charlotte, how are you?" he asked, sounding way more excited to talk to me than I ever thought he'd be.

I didn't know what to do. How to react. I'd imagined this scenario hundreds and hundreds of times since we last spoke, but I never actually thought I'd get the chance to talk to him again. I couldn't believe he was calling me after all this time. My heart almost jumped out of my chest. *Calm it down, girl,* I told myself. *Try to act normal.*

"I'm doing great, how are you?" I wanted to ask a thousand more questions, like *Where in the hell are you?* for starters, but I decided to keep it simple for now. No need to scare him away—it had taken him more than four months to make this call.

"I'm all right, but..." He paused for a second. I could hear a lot of background chatter wherever he was, but amid the chatter, he said softly, "I miss you."

I had a hard time realizing this was actually happening. That Luc was really on the other end of the phone telling me that he missed me. That horrible feeling that had eaten away at me for so long finally lifted, and now to replace it was pure excitement.

"I miss you too, Luc, so much."

"You look beautiful," he said, sounding out of breath.

"What?" I perked up in my chair, totally caught off guard. "Where are you? How do you—"

He cut me off. "*À droite,*" he said. *To your right.*

This couldn't be happening. I jerked my head around so fast I practically gave myself whiplash. I combed the old cobblestone street frantically. Was he here? Where was he? There were so many tourists walking up and down the street, I wanted to yell to everyone, *Stop moving! The love of my life is here, and I can't find him!*

Suddenly, the crowd parted, and there he was. He stood there showing off his nice tan in a white T-shirt, jeans, and sneakers, with his light-brown hair tousled and just a little bit of scruff on his chin and cheeks, just like the day I'd met him. We locked eyes for a second before we both broke into huge smiles.

"Hello," he said into the phone as he picked up his pace, grinning the whole way.

"Hello," I answered back, unable to take my eyes off him. I couldn't believe he was here. He was really here!

The world moved in slow motion as he walked up to my table, kissed me on the cheeks like he always had, and sat down next to me. I was speechless.

"Are you okay?" he asked.

"Yeah, sorry, it's just that I—I can't believe you're here."

"Me? I live here," he responded matter-of-factly.

Oh, my gosh. I couldn't believe my ears. *This* is where he had moved to be with his daughter? I'd been living in the same city as Luc all summer and hadn't even realized it? Then I remembered that he had told me he had family in Lyon. But it had never even crossed my mind that he might be here. When he left me that letter, it felt more like he had disappeared off the face of the earth, not moved two hours away from Paris to the exact same city that I had decided to move to.

"I live here too," I responded, unable to wipe the dumbfounded look off my face.

"I know, Lexi wrote to me and told me."

"Lexi got in touch with you?"

He nodded. "She got my address from Benoît. She sent me your article, Charlotte. The second one."

"She did?" I couldn't believe Lexi had done that for me. Turned out she was a romantic, after all.

Luc smiled gently. "Yes, after I read it, I had to find you. So I contacted Fiona, and she told me you were here and that you hang out in Old Lyon. As soon as I received her e-mail, I ran over here as fast as I could." Luc paused as he gazed into my eyes. "And here you are, looking as beautiful as always."

He reached across the table and covered my hand with his. I thought my heart was going to melt into a puddle right there on the cobblestones.

"Charlotte, I haven't stopped thinking about you. I thought you had probably moved on and were with another man now."

"No, I haven't wanted to be with anyone since you. I haven't stopped thinking of you either. I'm so sorry for—"

Luc placed his finger over my lips. "Shhh. I know. I am sorry too. I am sorry for not telling you where I was going. And for not telling you about my daughter sooner. It wasn't all your fault, you know. Just like you, I wasn't ready for a relationship when we first met. I had a lot of processing to do after my divorce. But things are different now."

"Things are different for me now too, Luc. And I'm just so happy your daughter is back. So, she's here with you in Lyon?"

Luc beamed from ear to ear. "Yes, Adeline is here. I want you to meet her. You will love her."

"I can't wait," I said, squeezing his hand, still not believing this was real.

My cheeks blushed as Luc's eyes flirted with mine from across the table.

"Would you like a glass of wine? Do you have to be anywhere?" I asked, hoping we could make this moment last forever.

"No, not for a couple hours. Adeline is at nursery. I'd love some wine." He motioned for the waiter to bring over another wineglass while I admired his incredibly sexy physique and tried to wrap my head around all of this.

"So, why did you choose Lyon?" he asked as the waiter poured him a glass.

I told him the whole story, from my trip to Lyon with the girls to visiting my host family and meeting Jean-Sébastien, to moving into my apartment and now reading at cafés by myself and drinking wine every afternoon. He told me all about his new job and about his summer here with Adeline.

As the alcohol went straight to my head, my four-month

sex drought started to catch up with me, and suddenly, I wanted him—badly. Not just physically—although I'd be lying if I said I wasn't fantasizing about ripping his clothes off and having my way with him—but in every way possible. I wanted to be with him and only him. I wanted the chance to love him again.

"I want to take you somewhere," he said as he leaned across the table and tucked a strand of hair behind my ear.

"Where?" I asked, knowing that I didn't care where he was taking me. I would go anywhere with this man.

"You'll see." He insisted on paying the bill, then took my hand as he led me through the winding cobblestone streets of Old Lyon. We arrived at the river, where the sun was just beginning to set. Luc stood behind me, and as the fiery orange sun disappeared behind the deep violet waters, he wrapped his arms around my waist and whispered in my ear, *"Je t'aime, Charlotte."*

I turned around, took his face in my hands and gazed into his warm chestnut eyes. "I love you too."

He gave me a flirty grin as he leaned down and gently placed his soft lips on mine. Then he whispered something else in my ear as his hands roamed over my body.

"J'ai envie de toi." I want you.

It was as if he had just let a lion out of her cage. I was ravenous for his body. In true dying-couple fashion, we couldn't keep our hands off each other as we strolled back to his apartment a few blocks away and kissed each other on the couch as we waited for Adeline to come home.

Not long after, we heard a teeny knock on the door.

Luc ran to the door, swung it open, and there stood his little girl, with her auburn hair pulled back into a ponytail and her big green eyes looking up at her father like there was no one she loved more in the whole world. Luc thanked the other parent who'd dropped her off, then picked Adeline up and swung her around in his arms.

"*Papa,*" she cried. "*Tu m'as manqué.*"

"I missed you too," he said as he set her down and led her over to me.

"Adeline, this is Charlotte, the woman I've been telling you about."

As she batted her long eyelashes and swung her little pink purse from side to side, I knew that Luc wasn't the only person I was falling in love with. I knelt down to greet her, feeling my heart bubble over with warmth as she leaned in and gave me two mini*bisous*.

"*Bonjour, Charlotte,*" she squeaked in the most adorable French accent I'd ever heard.

"*Bonjour, Adeline.* You speak English?"

"Yes, my daddy is teaching me."

I glanced up to find a big grin on Luc's face. "I thought we might see you again, so I've been giving her a lesson every day."

I stood in the doorway of Adeline's bedroom as I watched Luc read her a story, tuck her in, kiss her good night, and then stroke her hair until she fell asleep. My heart was bursting with love for him. This is what he had been so intent on getting back, and it all made sense now.

As Luc closed her door, he whispered, "You like my little girl?"

"She's just like her dad—adorable and impossible not to love."

With that, Luc picked me up and carried me into his bedroom, where, for the first time, we truly made love.

Afterward, he fed me square after square of delectable, creamy milk chocolate in bed.

And so, in lovemaking-and-chocolate-induced comas, we fell asleep in each other's arms. As I was drifting off, I felt something that I had never truly felt in my life. Something that was way better than all of the sex and chocolate a girl could have.

I was in love.

The kind of love that consumed every cell in my body, every ounce of my soul.

And the best part of all was that I knew in my heart that he loved me back.

A Note from Juliette

Thank you so much for reading the new, updated edition of the first book in my *City of Love* series, *Sleeping with Paris*. I hope you enjoyed Charlotte's journey through Paris, and I am excited to tell you there will be much more to come!

If you would like to leave an honest review for *Sleeping with Paris* on the site where you purchased the book, I would appreciate it so much. Reviews are so incredibly helpful for authors, and I have been touched by the lovely reviews many of you have left for my books over the years.

Much like Charlotte, I fell in love with Paris the minute I stepped foot onto its lively cobblestone streets, and I have been writing books based in this beautiful city ever since. Read on for descriptions of all of my novels and to find out how you can receive three of my bestselling books for *free*!

Juliette Sobanet's Free Starter Library

One of my favorite parts about being a writer is building a relationship with my amazing readers! I love hearing from you, and I also love letting you know what's going on in my world. Occasionally I send out brief newsletters with details on my new releases, special offers just for you, and other exciting book news.

If you'd like to be the first to find out about my new releases and receive your *free* Juliette Sobanet Starter Library, I'll send you:

1. A free copy of the award-winning first novel in my *City of Love* series: *Sleeping with Paris*.
2. A free copy of the bestselling novella in my *City of Light* series: *One Night in Paris*.
3. A free copy of the first spicy novella in my *City Girls* series: *Confessions of a City Girl: Los Angeles*.

To receive your free ebooks, simply head over to my website at *www.juliettesobanet.com* and sign up for my newsletter. I'll be thrilled to send them to you!

Also by Juliette Sobanet

City of Love Series

SLEEPING WITH PARIS
CITY OF LOVE BOOK 1

∼

Charlotte Summers is a sassy, young French teacher two days away from moving to Paris. Love of her life by her side, for those romantic kisses walking along the Seine? Check. Dream of studying at the prestigious Sorbonne University? Admission granted. But when she discovers her fiancé's online dating profile and has a little chat with the busty red-head he's been sleeping with on the side, she gives up on committed relationships and decides to navigate Paris on her own. Flings with no strings in the City of Light—*mais oui!*

Determined to stop other women from finding themselves in her shoes, Charlotte creates an anonymous blog on how to date like a man in the City of Love—that is, how to jump from bed to bed without ever falling in love. But, with a slew of Parisian men beating down her door, a hot new neighbor who feeds her chocolate in bed, and an appearance by her ex-fiancé, she isn't so sure she can keep her promise to remain commitment-free. When Charlotte agrees to write an article for a popular women's magazine about her Parisian dating adventures—or disasters, rather—will she risk losing the one man who's swept her off her feet and her dream job in one fell swoop?

Kissed in Paris
City of Love Book 2

~

When event planner Chloe Turner wakes up penniless and without a passport in the Plaza Athénée Hotel in Paris, she only has a few fleeting memories of Claude, the suave French man who convinced her to have that extra glass of wine... before taking all of her possessions and slipping out the door. As the overly organized, go-to gal for her drama queen younger sisters, her anxiety-ridden father, and her needy clients, Chloe is normally prepared for every disaster that comes her way. But with her wedding to her straitlaced, lawyer fiancé back in DC only days away and a French con-man on the loose with her engagement ring, this is one catastrophe she never could have planned for.

As Chloe tries to figure out a way home, she runs into an even bigger problem: the police are after her due to suspicious activity now tied to her bank account. Chloe's only hope at retrieving her passport and clearing her name lies in the hands of Julien, a rugged, undercover agent who has secrets of his own.

As Chloe follows this mysterious, and—although she doesn't want to admit it—sexy French man on a wild chase through the sun-kissed countryside of France, she discovers a magical world she never knew existed. And she can't help but wonder if the perfectly ordered life she's built for herself back home really what she wants after all...

Honeymoon in Paris
City of Love Book 3

∼

The sassy heroine of Sleeping with Paris is back! And this time, chocolate-covered French wedding bells are in the air...

It's only been a month since Charlotte Summers reunited with her sexy French boyfriend, Luc Olivier, and he has already made her the proposal of a lifetime: a mad dash to the altar in the fairytale town of Annecy. Without hesitation, Charlotte says *au revoir* to single life and *oui* to a lifetime of chocolate in bed with Luc. She's madly in love, and Luc is clearly *the one*, so what could possibly go wrong?

As it turns out, quite a lot...

On the heels of their drama-filled nuptials in the French Alps, Luc whisks Charlotte away to Paris for a luxurious honeymoon. But just as they are settling into a sheet-ripping, chocolate-induced haze, a surprise appearance by Luc's drop-dead gorgeous ex-wife brings the festivities to a halt. Luc never told Charlotte that his ex was a famous French actress, *or* that she was still in love with him. Add to that Charlotte's new role as step-mom to Luc's tantrum-throwing daughter, a humiliating debacle in the French tabloids, and the threat of losing her coveted position at the language school—and Charlotte fears she may have tied the French knot a little too quickly.

Determined to keep her independence and her sanity, Charlotte seeks out a position at *Bella* magazine's new France office while working on a sassy guidebook to French marriage. But when Luc's secret past threatens Charlotte's career *and* their future together, Charlotte must take matters into her own hands. Armed with chocolate, French wine, and a few fabulous girlfriends by her side, Charlotte navigates the tricky waters of marriage, secrets, ex-wives, and a demanding career all in a foreign country where she quickly realizes, she never *truly* learned the rules.

A Paris Dream
City of Love Book 4
A Novella

∽

After the loss of her beloved sister and both of her parents, overworked talk show assistant Olivia Banks sets off on a Paris adventure to fulfill the dreams she and her sister once had as little girls. Olivia only has one day to devote to the City of Light before she must return to her demanding job back in Manhattan. But when she steps out of the cab onto the cobblestoned streets of Montmartre and meets a sexy *boulanger* who wants to help her make all of those dreams come true, Olivia realizes that Paris may have more in store for her than she ever could have imagined.

City of Light Series

~

One Night in Paris
City of Light Book 1
A Novella

~

When Manhattan attorney Ella Carlyle gets a call that her beloved grandmother is dying, she rushes to Paris to be by her side, against the wishes of her overbearing boyfriend. Ella would do anything for her grandmother and jumps at the chance to fulfill her dying wish.

But things take a mystical turn when Ella is transported to a swinging Parisian jazz club full of alluring strangers…in the year 1927! As the clock runs out on her one night in the City of Light, Ella will attempt to rewrite the past—and perhaps her own destiny as well.

~

Dancing with Paris
City of Light Book 2

∼

In Paris, a past life promises a second chance at love.

Straitlaced marriage therapist Claudia Davis had a plan—and it definitely did not involve getting pregnant from a one-night stand or falling for a gorgeous French actor. She thinks her life can't possibly get more complicated. But when Claudia takes a tumble in her grandmother's San Diego dance studio, she awakens in 1950s Paris in the body of Ruby Kerrigan, the glamorous star of a risqué cabaret—and the number-one suspect in the gruesome murder of a fellow dancer. As past lives go, it's a doozy...especially when an encounter with a handsome and mysterious French doctor ignites a fire in Claudia's sinfully beautiful new body.

But time, for all its twists and turns, is not on her side: Claudia has just five days to unmask the true killer, clear Ruby's name, and return to the twenty-first century. To do so, she must make an impossible choice, one that will change the course of *both* of her lives forever.

∼

Midnight Train to Paris
City of Light Book 3

∼

When hard-hitting DC reporter Jillian Chambord learns that her twin sister, Isla, has been abducted from a luxury train traveling through the Alps, not even the threat of losing her coveted position at *The Washington Daily* can stop her from hopping on the next flight to France. Never mind the fact that Samuel Kelly—the sexy former CIA agent who Jillian has sworn off forever—has been assigned as the lead investigator in the case.

When Jillian and Samuel arrive in the Alps, they soon learn that their midnight train isn't leading them to Isla, but has taken them back in time to 1937, to a night when another young woman was abducted from the same Orient Express train. Given a chance to save both women, Jillian and Samuel are unprepared for what they discover on the train that night, for the sparks that fly between them . . . and for what they'll have to do to keep each other alive.

Midnight Train to Paris is a magical and suspenseful exploration of just how far we will go to save the ones we love.

City of Darkness Series

~

All the Beautiful Bodies
City of Darkness Book 1

~

Take a trip to the dark side of Paris...

After surviving a brutal childhood, Paris-based writer Eve Winters has lived her entire adult life totally under the radar. That all changes one warm spring day when she releases an explicit memoir detailing her dangerous foray into the world of high-end prostitution, and her scandalous affair with a prominent married businessman. The morning of the release, Eve is set to land in New York for her glamorous book launch party...but there's just one problem—she never boarded the plane.

Across the Atlantic, in a Park Avenue penthouse fit for a queen and her millionaire husband...

Acclaimed New York author, writing professor, and socialite Sophia Grayson is all set to attend the book release party of her former student, Eve Winters. *Except...*Eve never shows. When the news travels from Paris that the author has gone missing, Sophia spends the evening reading Eve's shocking memoir. What she discovers in its pages turns her perfect Park Avenue façade upside down and sends her searching for the truth in the one city she'd sworn off forever, the city where she'd locked away her own sordid past and thrown away the key...*Paris*.

True Stories in the City of Love

Meet Me in Paris
A Memoir

∼

What does a romance novelist do when she loses her own happily ever after? Take a lover and travel to Paris, obviously. Or at least this is what Juliette Sobanet did upon making the bold, heart-wrenching decision to divorce the man she had loved since she was a teenager. This is the story of the passionate love affair that ensued during the most devastating year of Sobanet's life and how her star-crossed romance in the City of Light led to her undoing.

Meet Me in Paris is a raw, powerful take on divorce and the daring choices that followed such a monumental loss from the pen of a writer who'd always believed in happy endings…and who ultimately found the courage to write her own.

∼

I LOVED YOU IN PARIS
A MEMOIR IN POETRY

~

In this companion poetry book to her sizzling memoir, *Meet Me in Paris*, Juliette Sobanet gives readers a heartbreaking look into the raw emotions of a romance novelist as she loses her own happily ever after. From the impossible pull of forbidden love to the devastating loss of her marriage, and finally, to rebuilding life anew, Sobanet's courageous poems expose the truth behind infidelity and divorce and take readers on a passionate journey of love, loss, and ultimately, hope.

City Girls Novella Series

Confessions of a City Girl: Los Angeles
City Girls Book 1

~

When talented DC photographer Natasha Taylor meets alluring investor Nicholas Reyes at her first exhibit, a harmless invitation to join him for a weekend in Los Angeles turns into a passionate love affair that awakens Natasha in ways she never could have imagined.

~

Confessions of a City Girl: San Diego
City Girls Book 2

~

When overworked CIA agent Liz Valentine sets off for a yoga retreat on the gorgeous beaches of San Diego, the last thing she expects to find is love. But when one oh-so-enlightened yoga instructor catches her eye—and her heart—Liz must decide if the loveless life of a secret agent is truly what she wants after all.

∽

Confessions of a City Girl: Washington D.C.
City Girls Book 3

∽

When recent divorcée and famous romance novelist Violet Bell loses her once lustrous career writing happily-ever-afters, a whirlwind weekend in the Nation's Capital with her closest college friend—a sexy British speechwriter named Aaron Wright—could have her wondering if *Mr. Wright* hasn't been right underneath her nose all along…

∽

Confessions of a City Girl Boxed Set

∽

Read all three *City Girls Novellas* in one sizzling boxed set!

Acknowledgments

Huge thanks to my wonderful agent, Kevan Lyon, for taking a chance on me and for helping me to become a better writer. Your guidance and editing expertise helped make this book shine. I would also like to thank my fabulous foreign rights agent, Taryn Fagerness, for bringing Charlotte's story to new landscapes.

Thanks to my incredible critique partners, Karen, Sharon, and Mary for reading several drafts of this novel and for being such wonderful friends and writing teachers. Special thanks to Sophie for being my writing partner in crime, my France buddy, and a fantastic friend, and to Angie, Kara, and Kelly for being amazing friends and beta readers.

To my France friends for making those times some of the happiest in my life, especially Deirdre, Sarah, Ed, Molly, Annie, Mark, and my amazing host family. Thanks to Jessica for being my loyal friend through it all, and to Amanda for being like a sister to me.

Thanks to each and every one of my fabulous girlfriends who, whether you meant to or not, served as an inspiration for this novel. A most loving thanks goes to my mom and dad for always encouraging my creative side, even when it wasn't practical.

And finally, thank you to my loyal, amazing readers. I appreciate your book love and your support more than I can express.

About the Author

Juliette Sobanet is the award-winning author of five Paris-based romance and mystery novels, five short stories, a book of poetry, a bestselling memoir, and the screenplay adaptation of her first novel, *Sleeping with Paris*. Under her real name of *Danielle Porter*, she is the author of a new thriller titled, *All the Beautiful Bodies*. Her books have reached over 500,000 readers worldwide, hitting the Top 100 Bestseller Lists on Amazon US, UK, France, and Germany, becoming bestsellers in Turkey and Italy as well. A French professor and writing coach, Juliette holds a B.A. from Georgetown University and an M.A. from New York University in Paris. Juliette lives between France and the U.S. and is currently at work on her next novel. To receive three of Juliette's books for free, visit her website at *www.juliettesobanet.com*. She loves to hear from her readers!

Made in United States
North Haven, CT
25 August 2023